TARGET OF OPPORTUNITY

BY LIZA LEE

TARGET OF OPPORTUNITY

LIZA LEE

Developmental & Copy Edit by - Kenneth Zink
Proofreading by - Alexandra McLaughlin
Cover Design by - Samantha Sanderson-Marshall
Interior Design by - Sabrina Milazzo, www.sabrinamilazzo.net

For Della

1 INÁCIO

Don't worry, old man, *I am not one of them.*

I am coming for them.

The assassin was not yet worried about his witness, even with the shotgun in his hands. The Colombian farmer eyed him from his back porch, spotlighted beneath a bare lightbulb. His gangly arms didn't look strong enough to hold a water bucket, but he wielded his twelve gauge like a young man. The trespasser knew he was nothing but a two-legged menace to the farmer, nothing better than any other predator who thrived in twilight's eight-hour shadow. To those in the business, he was known only as Inácio. He kneeled beside an old barn where he double-checked his equipment.

Inácio's spine shivered when he heard the pump of the shotgun's forestock.

"*¡Dale! ¡Te volaré!*" the elder belted out.

Inácio snapped his head around and drilled him with aggressive eyes but did not advance.

"Stay away!" The old man staggered, his Spanish stumbling from his mouth.

Inácio pulled out his pistol from under his jacket to rack back a round in the chamber.

"I don't want any part in this! Leave me in peace!" A screen door slammed, and his witness was out of sight.

As Inácio rose from the grass, his knee popped. Muscle soreness was his daily reminder of the toll from a decade-long career. There were times he felt much older than thirty-four. He took one more cautionary glance for his armed watcher. He and his weapon were gone. The farmhouse sat skewed at the edge of nature's wooden city. The jungle was as alive beneath the night sky as it was under the sun, except the darkness brought another level of danger.

I have to hurry if I'm going to reach the compound by dawn.

A mile was different when navigating through a jungle under the threat of big cats. The chilly February temps were refreshing to him, albeit rare. He fixed his night-vision goggles to his face and skulked closer. The forest morphed from a murky nightmare to glowing ovals of eyes. He took off at a run and paid close attention to the noise expelled with each step. Thick underbrush snagged at his clothing with sporadic threats to undermine his balance.

When he met the edge of the valley, he saw his intel was almost accurate. Their bulwark was a homemade barricade of metal strung with coils of razor wire. That detail checked out. The inclusion of watchtowers and a trench were something his briefing had left out. He felt solely responsible for the heightened security. Inácio was his employer's premier choice to fulfill the string of contracts targeting key leaders in the cartel.

There he was again, ready to wreak havoc on their ranks. Inácio massaged his blocky bicep, still sore from training. He stayed ahead of his adversaries by building up his body and abilities. Fortune could never ensure success the way discipline and preparation could. Tonight, he was as ready as he ever could be. It was an ambiguous process of checks and balances.

Each breath became intentional as he held on to his composure. Anxiety was not his concern; he had been hunting men for too long to be plagued with fear. Complacency through overconfidence was the real enemy. Ten years was a long time to commit to a singular purpose. Like anyone working the same job for years, it was easy to get comfortable. He took in the minute details of the environment while he prepared his mind. Inácio reminded himself to never underestimate anyone.

He moved at an uncanny low volume through the brush, using nature's organic beauty for concealment. Enormous fern leaves brushed across his face and spidering vines created thick walls between every tree and plant. He pressed a shoulder against a wide oak and withdrew a cylinder from his jacket pocket. Through the object's lens he squinted, and on the other side he saw a completely different landscape. The thermal vision highlighted new layers of information.

Warm bodies were everywhere.

A red heat signature slouched against a tower's railing. The person looked busy picking something off their shoe. The second tower sat diagonally to watch over the rough road connecting to the north. The monocular couldn't show everything, but it was enough. He lurked toward the outpost. Murmurs among the guards shifted from normal speech to yawns. A spent cigarette was flicked into the air and sailed into the grass while a congested cough rattled out here and there. Noises were very distinct at three in the morning.

The guards gravitated toward one another to cure the boredom. Their selfishness left behind vulnerable gaps and Inácio noticed them. In the past, he experienced their exhaustion on night watch as a soldier. The dull hours made it hard to imagine any mishaps could happen. They carried their rifles like awkward weights rather than lethal weapons. Some were loaded down with a ridiculous amount of equipment. Belts of ammo and specialized radios were draped over them like garlands. Most of them were no more than kids to Inácio. The structure they protected could not have been more than a couple of acres long as it was wide.

When he closed in, Inácio put away his thermal monocular. All his natural senses tuned in around him. The danger was a song to his bold character. His first step was to choose a point of entry. The ground which shifted under his boot acted as a cautionary signal to watch his step. His toe mashed onto the eroding edge of the trench. He hopped down and sunk the wood planks into the slimy mud. He made wide strides as he slinked through the gap.

Eventually, the trench opened like a ramp to level ground. The other side revealed its hidden barracks and stores of illegal merchandise. They appeared to be busy building fortifications during the day. Inácio stepped over piles of lumber and around buckets of tools. He zigzagged across their wooden walkways that covered every worn path.

Without warning, a shaded figure of a man made Inácio pause.

The militant sprung from the ground like a prairie dog and drifted toward a group forming at the west gate. Inácio froze. He covered his eye with the thermal monocular again. A content growl rumbled in his throat after he found so many corners void of life. Darkness was his friend. He ducked into tall weeds before he determined it was safe to enter the next open area. With an upright walk and purpose, he gave off the impression he belonged here.

Moving from orange campfire lights to pitch-darkness, he crept past collections of tarp shelters which covered the snoring sleepers. Inácio paused at the next building to assess his surroundings. It was a game of confidence and caution. He took in a breath and let it out as slowly as he could. Arrogance had no business here. His fingers twitched, ready to grab his pistol or knife. He ran his shoulder across the metal wall.

Inácio pawed around the corner then pivoted toward the closed door. The only sounds came from hushed chatter outside. His eyes and ears were open for any clues as to the precise location of his target. None of the voices heard so far matched the pitch he listened for. Inácio pressed his arm against a door and cracked it open with ease. His eyelids narrowed and he stared into the black for any detail. Feet shuffled from the other side before the door flung open.

Inácio withdrew his arm and shifted back around the building. Several footsteps splashed into the mud from inside. His pistol was in his hand like it had been there the whole time. He peeked around the corner when the tramping faded. A handful of men threw their jackets on and adjusted their rifles over their torsos. One man paused to pick up the slack of his ammunition belt, his wet boots squishing as he jogged to catch up. Where they were headed in such a rush drew his curiosity.

A lead worth following?

Placing his hands in his pockets, he lowered his head and stalked the group at a distance. Inácio was too far away to make out their low grumbling. He tailed them until he found a solid place to hide himself. The men halted at a gate forty feet away. They cracked their knuckles and faced down the dark road with crossed arms. Tucked behind a wall of sandbags, Inácio kneeled and waited.

Headlights rose like the sun over the distant ridge. Breaking over the horizon, their beams spread across the dirt road and onto the line of men who waited at the entrance. Three battered trucks approached, engines rumbling to an idle. Dents, holes, and cracked windshields were no doubt war wounds of their own. The men on foot paced toward the vehicles together and threw the back doors open.

Their arms reached inside and pulled several people out. Each passenger was bound by the wrists. Dark hoods over their heads blocked their vision. Inácio listened to their gagged, choked screams. The passengers were slammed onto their knees at the gate's threshold. The drivers and the men from the outpost paced and kicked the dirt, like they were waiting for someone. Inácio looked behind him and noticed an hourglass figure emerge from the opposite side of camp. He smelled money.

"Remove their hoods!" Her hiss commanded instant obedience. For the men, it was as if the completion of the task was a race. "You think you can fuck me over?"

Several pairs of eyes, young and old, squinted at their surroundings. The captives were a complete family. The father kneeled beside his wife, who leaned against his shoulder for comfort. Those who could only be their three children to their left, wailed. The cries from the kids made them sound a lot younger than they looked. The father's begging came out in an incoherent ramble.

The source of the sinister voice emerged from the shadows, the light shedding across the target's dark eyes. Proof of her evil deeds tattooed every inch of her face and neck in an array of skewed symbols and numbers. A chill tickled its way up Inácio's spine. *She's killed more than I have.* She strutted by his hiding place and walked further into the light. The curls of her short hair snaked out in a crazed mess.

She halted before the family fifteen yards away. Her arms were crossed tight over her chest, her sleeveless shirt showing off the strength in her arms. Each hostage tossed their gaze away as she scorched them with her own.

"Do you know who I am?" she seethed. The father tripped over every syllable before he managed to squeeze out the word.

"M-Medusa."

"If you know, you shouldn't have tried to double-cross me."

He jumbled an apology in return.

"You are forty grand short." Her voice was close to a shriek. "That is twenty more than last month." She turned toward one of the drivers. "Where did you find them?"

"Walking between farms to avoid the checkpoint. Bags packed and everything." Her back slithered straight, and she made an agreeable hum like she expected nothing less.

"Now you force me to punish your family for your failures." She held out her hand. A handgun was dropped into her palm. A bright flash and a pop threw his wife into the puddle behind her. The trajectory of the bullet splattered red across the husband's face. His bottom row of teeth protruded across a gaped jaw. His eyes were glued ahead, stuck in an empty stare. The stunned children bellowed out their anguish.

"You owe me sixty plus interest, or your kids are next." With a casual nod, she ordered her men to drag the family back into their battle-worn trucks. The children were carried away kicking and shouting while their widowed father fell limp. The men shut the family inside with their dead mother, then turned back down the road at a prompt pace. Injustice, nothing new. He saw it all the time, whether it was from his hand or another's. When evil turned redundant, so did a man's resilience.

It was obvious how much she enjoyed going about as the *Medusa*, her wrath going unchecked. Inácio knew her real name to be Paula Sánchez. She was no product of her environment. His target had an ungodly privileged upbringing. Paula was evil for its own sake. With a cold face, she returned further into the outpost by herself. He waited until Paula widened the breadth between herself and his hiding place, then followed her route.

Inácio's steps consumed his target's petite impressions in the tacky mud. He picked up two ammunition canisters from his hiding place to demonstrate his belonging for any man watching. Paula entered a small building tucked into the northwest corner. Inácio stood at the door for a moment before he encircled the structure in search of other entry points. He abandoned the ammo cans and unholstered his gun from inside his coat. The grip of his favored pistol was smooth and comfortable in his hand. He held it flat against his chest and pointed its muzzle down.

His steps were careful as he rounded the last corner of the building. There was no secondary door or window slit he could slide his suppressor through. That approach was one of his favorites. Inácio leaned his back beside the door and took in one more quick study of the surroundings. No one, at least awake, was in immediate view. His knuckles made a solid knock on her plywood door.

Her voice snapped. "*Qué quiere?*"

"*¿Oye, Paula?*" His voice was dull and unimposing.

"*¡Oh! ¿Eres tú, Rojas?*" Her tone changed from dismissive to playfully interested. She moved to the door.

Inácio raised his pistol.

She continued with her impish voice as the handle angled down from her pressure. The door broke its alignment, spreading the soft light of a lantern across the ground outside. In one fluid motion, he stepped into the narrow space and took the woman by the throat. He forced her back inside and hid her from view. Her eyes bulged, lighting up like a vermin trapped in snare. Gargled scorn was stuck in her constricted throat. Through her bared teeth, Inácio noticed some of them were filed to sharp points.

She cursed him with her stare, then looked up at the dark barrel of death placed inches from her forehead. With as little mercy as she'd shown to her recent murder, Inácio pressed the trigger and allowed her dead weight to drop from his harsh grip. Her body fell to the ground like that of any other inanimate object. Her wild hair spread across the grassy floor in a ray of deep brown threads. Streams of blood flowed from her mortal wound, nose, and ear. Inácio cracked his knuckles before he snapped a picture with his phone. It captured her oozing face frozen in malice.

He hit send, then took a second to look around the tiny room. An expensive ring on the card table caught his eye, prompting him to steal it. He took her jacket hung over a chair, and threw it over the lantern to block the light source. He wasted no time and strutted back the way he came. The idea of a hot shower and a bed called to every tired muscle. With his pistol returned to its holster, he wormed his way around the encampment toward his exit.

At the edge of the trench, he scanned for any last-minute threats. All was quiet above and below. *Why walk into that crap again when I can just jump across?* A small leap was no challenge for him. When his boot connected to the other side, he lost all traction across the shifty grass. Inácio fell into the trench and landed flat on his back.

"Fuck!" The wooden boards made sure not to miss a single vertebra in his spine.

The deep trough came alive with laughter.

Inácio squirmed and leaped to his feet.

Directly to his right, a camouflaged trench dweller squatted on a little stump. His cheeks rose in amusement like two large red hills beneath his eyes. Inácio had missed him by inches. Now he wished he knocked the guy out cold with his ass.

"*¡Estúpido cabrón!*" He sneered with his dirty face and chuckled a few more times. When his eyes stopped squinting, alarm replaced delight. "Shit—"

The man's finger moved over his radio and Inácio lunged to stop him. He knocked the heavy-set man from his little stool, leaving them to wrestle for the rifle between them. Inácio's palm smashed over his mouth and nose with immense pressure to prevent any call for help. His other palm jammed itself down, blocking access to the trigger. His enemy snorted under a flattened face and fought for every breath. He threw fists, landing only a few across Inácio's cheek.

Inácio's eyes seethed with a violent determination to kill. It was a primal act of survival from an unspoken truth that this was a struggle to the death. Desperate hands clawed at Inácio's face, ripping his mask off in the process. Inácio used everything within himself to keep the rifle from firing while trying to crush the man's nose with the other. He lowered his body further and felt the man's right arm give way. Stress put a heavy strain in his breath. Animalistic groans emitted from the depths of his chest.

Death needed to move fast before Inácio's own body gave out. In his critical effort to keep the man quiet, he broke the silence himself and released his stress through a hoarse war cry, his face ablaze with strain. The older man reached for Inácio's knife at his belt. Inácio tried to shimmy his hips away, but it was too late. His opponent held it by the handle and pointed the edge at his sternum.

Inácio hooked his knee over the man's wrist. It was all the leverage the man under him needed to launch him over his head. Inácio front-flipped and landed with a splash into the mud, the rifle landing beside him. The large knife stayed behind in his hand. The militant gasped for air beneath a broken nose, swiping at the air between them. Leaping up in a blurry frenzy, Inácio smashed his head against the opposing man's forehead and forced him flat on his back.

The hard knuckle protectors on his gloves shattered what was left of the man's nasal cavity, caving it in further. Inácio turned him onto his stomach. The man tossed and fought with waning strength. A deep frown burrowed into Inácio's brow while he forced his enemy's face into a shallow puddle. Long seconds later, the man's spasms faded into the desired stillness. Tremors rocked Inácio's body as he stumbled to his feet.

He blinked through a spinning blur of darkness, searching for other threats. He uncoiled dead fingers from his blade and crossed it over his body. Inácio rocked on two feet as he missed the knife sheath before wrangling it back in place like a drunk man. His head tilted back and gasped toward the sky for the crisp cool air. His arms scrabbled for a grip over the soft wall and inched onto the grass. He rolled across the ground and crawled upright.

A glint from the dim trees caught his eye.

That better not be what I think it is.

His feet found balance again and the trees calmed their rotation. From the side of his eye, he took a glimpse at the mysterious shimmer floating in the dark. Inácio swallowed hard. A trail camera. Perfect. Like it wasn't too late, he fumbled with his balaclava and twisted it back.

The cartel had his face.

2

DELILAH

"This is it, people, our last great adventure as a group!" Carson's announcement startled Delilah out of her daydream. For the past two months, she'd watched her boyfriend's anticipation brew to a raging boil. "Guys, I cannot wait for you to see this hotel, it's awesome."

"And that doesn't make you sad?" Sara asked from her seat. Delilah hadn't seen her smile once since they got to the airport.

"How does one become sad with a five-star hotel in Rio de Janeiro?" Carson said with a smirk.

"Not the hotel, rich boy. I mean our last spring break, or whatever the hell this is." Sara adjusted her glasses.

"I agree with Carson." Dorothy's voice was upbeat. "I can't wait to see the hotel." Across the aisle, she peeked at him over her laptop screen. Delilah sat up straight. Dorothy had a way with her words that brought every nasty insecurity out of Delilah. It was a challenge to date someone like Carson. His golden hair swept tastefully to the side with a clean-cut style to match. He was the cute frat boy in every college movie.

"I can't wait until we can board." Josh, Carson's best friend, racked his neck back and sat slouched down in his seat. The position elongated his legs to stilts.

"I've waited months for this. A few more minutes won't hurt." Carson shrugged. "I say we hit up some bars after we land. I know some good ones."

"Sounds like one giant headache," Sara mumbled. She switched from staring at her laptop to staring at her phone. "Don't forget, some of us have homework. It wasn't my idea to take this trip only weeks before mid-term exams."

"There needs to be someone sober to lead us back to our room," Carson teased.

"Don't put words in my mouth. I said nothing about being sober. I just know what 'hitting up a few bars' leads to."

Carson turned toward Delilah. It was his silent way of telling her she needed to be the responsible one on the trip while everyone else was free to have fun. Delilah clenched her jaw out of habit. She was bound to do whatever he wanted because the early spring break was so important to him and the rest of his friends. Pictures from his study-abroad trip last year didn't do it justice, he insisted. He'd hyped up the city until it took the shape of heaven in her imagination. Delilah relaxed her jaw and summoned a smile.

"You know me, the responsible one."

Josh fixed his slumped position. "Can we board already? This shit's making me tired."

"Couldn't make us get here any earlier, could you, Carson?" Sara went on. Tommy, her boyfriend, nudged her in the arm. Carson didn't respond. Delilah found her personality as draining as that of her boyfriend but excluding her wasn't an option. She and Tommy were one package. Josh yawned aloud until his eyes watered.

"Shh! They're trying to finish their papers!" Sara scolded. Dorothy and Quincy typed away with lightning speed. Quincy's big curly hair formed natural dark blinders to anything outside her periphery.

"You'll have enough time to do that on the plane. C'mon guys," Carson said.

"Nope! The airline has all three seasons of *Dr. Lindsay* and me and Dorothy are watching the whole thing!" Quincy said, like it was non-negotiable.

"How do you find that out?" Devan popped up from behind the girls on the opposite row of chairs. Quincy shook her head.

"Ever heard of Google?"

"Have a good nap, Devan?" Tommy asked as he straightened his hipster suspenders.

"Uh-huh. I can sleep anywhere."

"Short people privilege," grumbled Sara.

Delilah fiddled in her seat next to Carson, her fingers applying pressure to her scalp. Another pulsating headache was in its early stages. She hoped to receive comfort from Carson, but instead he shot her a frown. His disapproval made her sweat. Delilah dug through her purse.

"I'll take care of it, I think," she argued.

"Don't tell me you forgot your prescription," he said.

"I think I left it on my dresser. I meant to grab it on the way out, I swear."

"That's smart, considering we're leaving the country."

"It's okay. It might go away."

"Common sense would dictate that you at least buy some pain-killers before we take off, yeah?"

"Thank you for the input." Delilah left her chair and stood before the busy terminal hall.

Passengers buzzed back and forth like busy highway traffic. She looked back to see Carson pull out his *Making Billions* book. There was no one she knew who was more driven.

Make him happy.

Before she risked being trampled by a businessman running late to his flight, her phone dinged, and then dinged a few more times. A barrage of essays in text form lit up her phone, all from her mom. The messages were packed full of precautions and I love yous. There wasn't a single one from her dad. *That's okay, Mom worries enough for the both of you.* The thought of typing replies to all of them made her head spin even more. She needed aspirin, badly.

Delilah made for the little shop across the hall. It was her first time at an airport, and the environment reminded her of her own brain, stress and anxiety everywhere. Unsure how to navigate it, she ducked and bumped into strangers who had no time nor the care to use their manners. Delilah clawed at the side of her skull. The stress-induced headache formed perfectly along the scar beneath her hair. Her mom and Carson's emotions were all too much at once. She soothed the fears on one end and walked on eggshells on the other. That was her next ten days, and the knowledge didn't help her pain.

"Welcome," a friendly voice greeted her from behind the counter.

She dropped her hand from her head to pretend she wasn't in impending agony. Every theme revolved around Ohio from T-shirts to hats to keychains, the state she'd never left once in her twenty-four years of age. The quick-release soft gels were conveniently placed beside the XL-size chocolate bars. They knew their customer base. She paused to think about Carson. If she came back without buying him something, she'd never hear the end of his passive aggressive moans and groans.

Delilah browsed the book rack. Her eyes locked onto a title that promised anyone could turn a dollar into a million dollars, or something along those lines. Her pain killed her patience to look any further. *He'll love it.* Delilah walked toward the counter with her purchases. Nearby, bottled water was *only* $2.50 each so she looked forward to seeing the total of her order.

"Is that color called lavender?" The cashier studied her hair.

"Lilac, actually. Same thing, pretty much." Delilah threw in an extra bag of candy.

"Are you a natural blonde?"

"I am."

"You're so lucky! I'd have to bleach my head three times over to get a soft shade close to that. $44.07, please."

"Yippee." Delilah reluctantly pulled out her cash. "This is going to be an expensive trip."

"Yeah, sorry. They take advantage of the desperation. You must be going someplace warm dressed like that in February. $5.93 is your change."

"I'm headed to this thing called Carnival out in Brazil."

"Whoa, well don't let me keep you. Thank you for coming in. Lilac really does suit you."

"Tell my boyfriend that."

Delilah took her items and returned to the frenzy. It was an enormous change to her usual homebody lifestyle. The crowd made her shiver with fluey waves. Every instinct demanded she stick to what she knew and never leave. It was a personal rule she wished she'd followed instead of agreeing to Brazil. She was taking her first step into the pedestrian highway when her breath was stolen from her lungs. It felt like she'd whacked straight into a brick wall, but it wasn't just any wall.

The man Delilah bounced off of looked down at her with a lingering eye. He was a young, attractive US Marine all fixed up in his dress blues. His presentation was professional, crisp, and clean; a man who followed a higher standard. It would have been easy to look past her. Everyone else did.

Without a glint of shyness, his eyes followed a deliberate pattern from her head to her bare legs. Delilah's face blushed bright red. He looked strong and capable, attributes she'd just discovered she liked. The Marine continued his composed walk and took one more look at her before he was sucked into the crowd. Delilah double-checked who was around her. There was no tall, hot model nearby or a busty woman rocking mile-high stilettos.

He wanted to look at me? A short, slightly emo girl who avoids the sun like some kind of nightcrawler?

If she was able to attract that caliber of attention, she needed to get out more. Leaving her boyfriend for him wasn't an option, but the attention brought her the first real happiness of the day. The endorphins alone subsided her headache. All she'd needed was a little distraction. She guzzled down a few capsules anyway when she returned to her seat.

"Did you forget how to walk?" bellowed Carson. Delilah involuntarily squeezed her bottle and sent water pouring down her chin.

"Sorry, what?" She wiped her face.

"I watched you run into that guy. I'm hoping you just forgot how to walk."

"It was an accident."

"I could see you were enjoying the attention. That was no accident." Carson shifted his weight and leaned away. Delilah experienced the familiar urge to explain her actions. Her throat tightened and her voice diminished. She always told herself that next time would be different and promised herself she would speak up. This was next time, and the time after too. There was not an eloquent thing she could say to warm his cold shoulder.

His gift!

"Hey, I got you something." Delilah handed over the plastic sack. Carson's eyebrow lifted. He dug into it like a child on his birthday.

"My favorite candy and a book?"

"Flip it over. Look at what kind of book."

"Ohhh..." His voice dropped at the end as he spun the book around in his hands like it was an extraterrestrial object.

"Do you like it?"

"Getting to a million really isn't my problem babe, but thank you. Who's Dimitri Collins?"

"I dunno, I guess a millionaire."

"I'll take a look at it sometime later. Seems very... interesting." Carson stuffed the book in what little space he had left in his carry-on. "Good job on the candy though." He ripped the package open and threw several pieces into his mouth. His shoulders lowered as he re-opened his book on billions again. This was the relaxation in him she wanted. Delilah grinned with victory. There was a giggle from across the aisle.

"You guys are cute," Dorothy said, her lips puckering over the word 'cute.' Delilah wondered what her secret was. Dorothy never had a problem getting Carson to laugh, none of them did. Maybe if her dad didn't demonize dating her whole life, she'd know what to do before diving into a long-term relationship. Another cackle beside Delilah drew her attention. Carson laid his phone at the center of his open book.

"Your dad is texting me."

"Really?" Delilah sat up straight and looked at her own phone. *Does that mean he texted me?*

"He's telling us to have a good trip."

"That's nice of him, I guess." Delilah unlocked her phone. No message from her dad. She swallowed down the negative thought that threatened to nip her with its twinge. At least her mom cared, even if it was too much.

"Apparently we have to stick together." Carson typed a quick reply. "I don't think your dad has any clue how much I know this city. I mean, what does he think is going to— Holy crap! Are those all from your mom?" He pointed to her screen that was filled with notifications.

"Yes." Delilah blushed.

"I hope this isn't going to last the whole trip. I can't take it. We're adults, you especially," he said, reminding her that she was old for an undergrad senior.

"It's annoying, I know. It's just, after everything that happened, she's still on edge."

"It's been years. All you do is take care of her for something that happened to *you*. It's bizarre." He shook his head.

"Carson, there's more going on with her mentally than the trauma from my car accident."

"I don't need another play by play, please." Carson held up his hand in a blocking gesture. "Let me enjoy our last trip." His shoulders tensed again.

He'll calm down. Wait. What did he mean by our? Our. As in, just us or the whole group?

In the fall semester, she researched maladaptive perfectionism, a study that may or may not have been inspired by her boyfriend. If there was a single takeaway from the condition, it was that perfectionism could turn people into monsters. As a future psychologist, it was her job to understand and sympathize with others, Carson's quirks included.

"Guys," Devan said, "any of you watch those viral videos where the people are stuck on a plane with a non-stop screaming kid? What if that's us?" His already buggy eyes pouted under his curly reddish hair.

"Don't worry, your mom gave us your bottle-feeding schedule so that doesn't happen," Josh reassured. Devan laughed along at his expense.

Soon, Carson was at the edge of his seat as he compared the time on his watch to the time above the airline desk. Delilah flipped her short waves from her eyes and watched one of the attendants open the door to a long tunnel.

"Finally, shit." Carson's shoulders settled.

"I haven't flown first class in forever, so this will be nice," Quincy reflected, her zillion dark spirals hopping with every word. Delilah got the sense she was ignorant of her entitlement.

"A bunch of white Midwest kids headed to a sunny beach along the equator. Nothing can go wrong there," Sara said.

"The equator isn't that close, is it?" asked Tommy.

"I'm from Philly so you guys can dry up on the beach. I'll be at the bars!" Josh corrected. He was the first one to stand up and the most prepared of them all with nothing other than a wallet and phone in his pocket.

"You're not from Philly, you're from suburbia, loser!" Carson huffed.

"Then why do I talk like this, Carson?" Josh enunciated each Philadelphian syllable. Tommy scowled from his seat and gestured toward Josh's towering frame.

"You literally just started talking like that! You're a spoiled prep school kid like Carson."

"That's why they get along so well," Dorothy said, throwing her plaid bag over her shoulder.

"I'm from the inner city, fool!" A small spray of spit dissipated through the air. His accent started to resemble more Boston than Philly.

"Shush!" Sara's finger was smashed over her lips like she was an angry librarian. "Everyone's staring at us."

"Oh my god, sit down, please." Quincy grabbed hold of Josh's wrist.

"Why? I thought we were boarding."

"You look like an idiot, I hope you know that," Carson told his friend with a grin.

"Says the guy with little flowers printed on his shorts," mocked Josh.

"They're anchors," Carson defended. "Anchors!"

"Whatever, I'm boarding." Josh turned toward the roped off entrance, brushing past a few passengers in wheelchairs who inched closer to the gate.

"How much has he had to drink, Devan?" Sara asked.

"None."

"Correction," Tommy interrupted. His fedora bordered the back of his head like a religious halo. "It's not how much he had to drink, but what. His body is made of at least twenty percent alcohol when sober. You didn't happen to be around any Mexican restaurants earlier, did you?"

"Mmm, I did lose sight of him for like ten minutes earlier." Devan peered at the ceiling in reflection.

"Ten minutes is all he needs." Tommy's hands fell to his lap.

"Sara, guys, just relax. He's not drunk, okay? This is who he is, a man child," Carson explained. "We can't take this kid anywhere, remember?" In Delilah's unspoken opinion, none of the guys knew how to act decently in public. She hardly saw them anywhere but a bar when they were off campus.

"Excuse me sir, we are only opening the gate for priority passengers at this time." The desk attendant stepped in front of Josh, unbothered by his stature.

"Oh, I'm priority," Josh replied, pointing to his chest with a thumb.

"Are you active-duty military personnel or possess a physical disability that requires assistance to board?"

"Yes, I'm business class." Everyone associated with him made unanimous facepalms. Carson groaned then chuckled to himself. Josh returned to his friends with a flushed smile.

"Business class is not a priority to this airline, guys." It took only a second after his return for the front desk attendant to make her next announcement.

"Now boarding for all business class passengers."

"Oh, wow!" Josh tossed his arms in the air.

"Patience is a virtue." Sara patted him on the back.

Delilah watched Carson turn almost giddy. His teeth sparkled through a giant grin and he subtly danced in place. Delilah perked up, then hooked her arm through his. Carson swung his head around and glared at their interlocked elbows.

"Hey, do you mind? I can't get my passport if your arm is there," he said. Delilah vacated from his side and pretended like she was never there. After three years on and off again, Delilah was still lost on how to make him happy.

3 DELILAH

When the group settled into their puffy leather seats, they discussed what they would order off the laminated menu. It was hard for Delilah to believe planes could be so big and still defy gravity.

"Hey, hey you guys, guess what?" Josh asked in sort of a whisper. Carson and Delilah eyed him from across the aisle. "In a plane crash we're the most likely to live 'cuz we're in the very front of the plane. Fun fact."

"Pilot favors his side," Carson said.

"Group D is fucked!" Devan said too loud, seated next to Josh. His hyena laugh drew in annoyed stares from serious older men assigned to the row behind them.

Shut the fuck up, Carson mouthed over at him.

"We are so getting kicked off," muttered Sara nearby. A voice between Delilah and Carson's seats called out ahead.

"Want to watch *Dr. Lindsay* with us?" Dorothy asked.

"Probably not." Carson touched the screen, beginning to browse its features.

"What are we supposed to do with all these pillows?" Delilah heard Devan ask from across the cabin.

"It's not a soap, I swear! We could all watch it together!" Dorothy suggested.

"No one wants to watch *The Wizard of Oz* again with you, Dorothy," Josh jabbed, cranking his head around.

"That is not what I was referring to and I don't even like that movie, by the way."

"That's a classic!" Quincy gasped, seated beside her.

As the preflight excitement filled the business-class cabin, Delilah tuned out the chatter. As a small-town girl, she felt out of place, but luxuries were part of the perks while dating Carson. At twenty-two, he'd already made leaps as an entrepreneur/investor and was expected to surpass even his mother in the world of business. He was also a one-man-show business reporter and economist. His correct advice earned the trust of some of the most successful people in the world. The article *Forbes* wrote on him was framed in his dorm. Carson gave real economists a literal run for their money.

Business and the global market dominated every spoken thought. Both his parents were corporate go-getters who'd met, married, and split in Rio de Janeiro. Their investment ventures still ran deep there, and it was what had led Carson to adore Brazil so much. For Delilah's boyfriend, the capital city stood for nothing else but a brilliant future of possibilities. A fancy airline seat and a large hotel to look forward to weren't the only generous expenses the rising star had bought. Gift-giving was what he was best at in their relationship.

He added a few nicer possessions to her jewelry box in exchange for her commitment, like the expensive gold bracelet that graced her wrist. It had come to her tucked nicely in a hinged velvety case. She couldn't forget the sparkly earrings that dangled from her ears either. Those had also come in an expensive box that felt wrong to throw away. To admire them acted as a reset to Delilah's brain, a shift from dejection to gratitude. His gifts reminded her that Carson appreciated her, even if it was in his own way.

Delilah spun a strand of her hair around her finger at the idea of leaving solid ground. Lower-tier passengers scooted through and filed in behind them. She noticed the flight attendants exchange vexed glances like they expected her group to be a handful. Carson groaned next to her.

"I forgot my earbuds in my bag," he said.

"What about the plane's headphones?" Delilah picked them up from his seat. His bag was already stored in the overhead compartment.

"Eh, I'd rather use mine. That kind of grosses me out." Delilah was surprised considering they were the special first-class kind. "In other words, if you put your legs down, I can get to my bag."

"Nope, I'll get it." She dropped her crossed knee and sprang into action.

"Sounds good—I mean, if you're sure." He held up his hand and touched her wrist, decorated with his gold.

"It's no problem! I'm in the aisle seat, so it should be me." She lifted the compartment lid and scanned the stacked bags. Quincy's leopard-print suitcase and her own had wedged his stowaway in the far back. Delilah propped herself on her toes and tried to reach the zipper.

"Let me help you, ma'am." Strong arms cut into view and pulled Carson's bag free. The scent of lavender aftershave tickled her nostrils. Delilah turned to see an attractive pilot with a full golden-brown beard. He smiled politely with flawless straight teeth.

"Here you go," the man said. Carson's bag rested at her feet.

"Thank you, sir." She sensed her cheeks flush. Delilah dug around the small pockets.

"The front left one," Carson said, his voice monotone. Her eyes flicked ahead, and she saw the pilot's black trousers still in front of her. No pressure or anything.

"Here they are." She offered them to Carson, who scooped them up without a word.

"Would you like me to put it back for you?" the pilot asked. Delilah glanced over at Carson, who shot darts from his eyes. *Don't start ruining things now.*

"No, it's okay, I got it."

"It's no problem."

The pilot grabbed the bag from her hands and pushed it in with a shove. He was tall, tan, and looked dashing in his dark uniform. There was a man who had experienced the world. The gold wings pinned to his jacket glimmered with success and years of hard work. Slipping behind her, he headed in the direction of the cockpit. He stood outside its door and made small talk with the staff. Her life was in his hands and in a way, his job was to take care of her for the next ten hours. A chill spread over her thighs.

Delilah sat down and leaned over the arm of her seat for a better view of the pilot. She let go of her hair when she realized how tight she'd wound it around her finger. Delilah threw herself back into the seat when the pilot took a look at seat 1B and caught her starry-eyed stare. After a second, she peeked from behind the blue curtain again. His dark brown eyes ran up and down her legs and gave her a crooked, "I see you over there" grin. Delilah reset herself in her seat and fanned her hot face.

The point of Carson's elbow struck her arm.

"Ow!"

"He's not looking at you, if that's who you're gawking at."

"Who?" She rubbed her arm and pretended she didn't understand.

"Do I really need to spell it out?"

"I guess you do." She scratched at her leather chair.

"First it's staring at guys in the terminal and then you flirt with the pilot right in front of me?" Carson tilted closer and whispered in her ear. "Do you really think Mr. Baywatch pilot is looking at *you*? He's probably staring at Quincy. She won Miss Ohio last year. She's probably going to be on the cover of *Vogue* one day. She's got natural beauty, and she didn't have to dye her hair to get it." Carson's glare lingered for a moment.

Don't cry, don't cry, don't cry.

Delilah mentally shoved the emotion into a locked chest. All the pain, stuffed to the very bottom, under a bunch of other crap. After almost four years of psychology education, she still didn't understand why those who loved her could be so hurtful. Delilah tightened up her whole body and returned her focus to the pilot, swishing her hair in Carson's face in the process.

"Hey Cap," Devan called out to the pilot. "Is the front of the plane safer than the middle and back of it?"

"It doesn't matter where you're sitting. I keep all my passengers safe." The direct tone in his words was unrattled by any doubt. Of course. She knew she couldn't be the only one to notice his rare looks. The pilot glowed with command and authority.

"But let's say an engine blows. You'd probably need a few extra hands on deck, right?" Devan always tried to find some kind of in with someone important. What benefits he expected from it were anyone's guess.

"Why? Are you a pilot?" the man inquired, popping a mint into his mouth. Even with all the curious eyes focused on him, he was completely comfortable being the center of attention.

"Yeah, I got my license, and I fly—"

"No, you don't," Josh interrupted. Devan grinned, caught in his white lie.

"Well, I almost have all my hours for my license, so if you need some backup, I'm here."

The captain's chest jumped with a slight chuckle.

"Alright, if we got to bring this bird down, I know where to find you..."

"Devan, seat 1E."

"Devan in 1E, got it." He pointed his finger like a gun. Cocking his head to the side, he shot another glance at Delilah's legs, then turned toward the cockpit. Her stomach leaped at the thrill. It resembled the way Carson *used* to look at her. It made her think back to the first time she saw her boyfriend. He was a volunteer in her first experiment that explored the neurological connection between symmetry and attraction. Instead of paying attention to the cards, he could only comment on how symmetrical Delilah's face was.

"Quincy, the pilot was staring at you," Carson belted out.

"Oh my god, he is so hot!" Dorothy yelped.

"Hate to break it to you, but it wasn't me he was looking at." Quincy tapped Delilah on the shoulder. She couldn't control the joy stretching her cheeks wide. At least one of his friends had enough insight to read through his antics.

"Whatever," he growled. He shifted toward the window like a child pouting in time out.

****

Delilah watched her Ohio safe haven shrink until all she saw was sky-blue. After a while, the excitable energy in business class slowly quieted into steady white noise. Carson and his friends retreated into their own worlds with headphones and airline blankets. Delilah looked over to see Josh stretched out, sound asleep to the explosions of the action-packed movie channeling through the wire of his headset. To her left, Carson's eyes sagged at the images flashing across the screen. She took a final sip of her orange juice and checked the time on her phone.

Thirty minutes past midnight.

A text from her mom sat unopened. To know it was impossible to respond gave her a sense of unexpected peace. Carson's head bobbed forward as his eyes closed with every accidental nod. They hadn't said a word to each other since their little spat. Sitting in silence on the way to a vacation didn't sit right with her. She felt some responsibility for bruising his fragile ego.

Delilah unzipped her purse and separated the pronged metal one tooth at a time. Her hand sunk to the bottom and took out her tiny bottle of scented lotion. Carson's chin finally rested on his chest, and a faint snore gurgled from his throat. He didn't feel a thing when her hand snuck under his blanket and unbuttoned his shorts. He threw his head up when she touched him with the cold lotion.

"What the—"

"Shh! Just relax," Delilah whispered. Carson glanced around before he slapped on a skewed smile. She knew this was the kind of physical touch he wouldn't mind. Delilah stretched both blankets over their divider, just in case.

"What did I do to deserve this?" he asked.

"Nothing," she said honestly. "I don't want you mad at me."

"Keep going and you'll get me there," he said as he stiffened. He closed his eyes and pushed back against the headrest. His lips curled up at the ends. Delilah watched all the tension between them melt away in her grip.

"I love you," her voice almost sang.

Delilah waited with eagerness for a response that never came. She'd heard him say it once on his own, so it had to be true. Her hand pumped faster as if it could squeeze the words out of him. Delilah blew out a sigh and let her eyes wander, staring into the space where the handsome captain once stood. Through her imagination, she found escape. She quieted her loneliness, her worries, and zeroed in on another dimension.

In her ideal world, she was a man's treasure. There was no chase for his attention because he paved the path ahead with his love. She wasn't left to beg for his touch when she needed him the most. Broken promises weren't mended with gold or gems. If she concentrated hard enough, she lost herself in her imagination. Delilah saw herself held by the broad arms of love and devotion. Teeth scraped over her bottom lip. She could picture it, but she had no idea what it felt like.

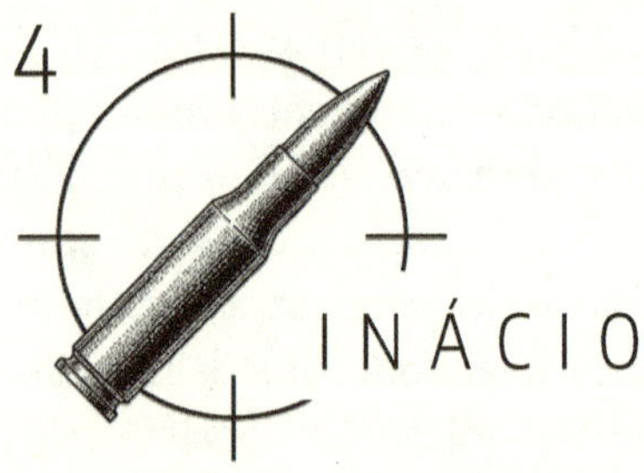

4 INÁCIO

The motorcycle struck pavement as Inácio created a comfortable distance between himself and the cartel compound. Clumps of mud and grass trailed behind him. When the trail dropped off, he made a U-turn and headed in the opposite direction. Another success under his belt he could be grateful for. His body, though, didn't feel like a winner. With every dip and lump in the road, the soreness down his back panged. The easy times didn't last long without the job reminding him that beneath it all, he was just a man.

He twisted and stretched his torso in his seat, but nothing alleviated his discomfort. Leaning into the curves, he accelerated toward his next address. The sun broke over the horizon and failed in its job to rejuvenate his thirty-two hour sleep-deprived state. Concern over the camera capture of his face did more to wake him up. Daylight hit the green landscape before a blue sky, inviting nostalgia. The view was a snapshot into his childhood. What he wouldn't give to go back twenty-five years and stay with his mother in the Brazilian favelas.

His small-town destination was wide awake by the time Inácio kicked the bike's stand into place. Its engine hissed with heat. Across the street, a pepper-haired supermarket owner opened his doors for the business day. A middle-aged woman who looked to be his wife stood in the entrance and watched Inácio's every move. A frayed broom was in the shop owner's hand as he vigorously returned the dirt to the street. He broke his task when the woman tapped him on the shoulder. He carried the broom like a walking stick and stood behind her. She nodded toward Inácio and said something over her shoulder. Inácio wondered how the middling couple had become involved in the criminal business in the first place.

Probably money.

Money was the sole motivator for all, including himself. Inácio's wide backpack felt twice as heavy as normal. He propped the full-face helmet under his arm and limped across the street toward the store. Mocha-shaded dirt flaked off his gloves, arms, pant legs, and torso. Specks sprinkled from his messy black hair that hung lopsided over his forehead. His knee flared with inflammation, but he was too tired to allow pride to let him pretend he was fine on the outside.

He wasn't fine. He was ready to drop. After a full night's sleep, he hoped his body could work out its kinks. His droopy eyes took a half-assed glance at the environment around him. Danger didn't die with the contract. Inácio scraped his boot treads at the sidewalk's edge before he shuffled to a stop inside the market. The man and the woman leered and stood silent until he gave the code. *I must look terrible.* It took his brain a minute to catch up.

"*Buenos días.* Do you have a room for one?"

"Yes, sir. Follow me." The husband made a miniature bow. He led Inácio through the back of the small store and up a narrow staircase. Inácio couldn't pretend to like the setup. Any safehouse owned by civilians wasn't truly safe. Then again, everywhere he went fell short of his standards. They passed a door decorated with handmade crafts and stopped in front of the second apartment in the skinny, pale hallway.

He loosed a whine under his breath when he realized his assigned safe house was on the other side of the wall of the owner's home.

The host fiddled with his key ring with shaky hands. The deadbolt released and the cheap door opened with a loud squeak. Inácio slid past him, trying not to brush him with his dirt. His security-centered mind balked. *Who would put a deadbolt on a door that's thin enough to be called cardboard?*

"If you leave your clothes in the hall, my wife will wash them for you, sir." His words were quick and tight before he rushed down the stairs. Inácio turned back toward his reality.

Bare bones.

The linoleum peeled at the corners and the floor creaked under his weight as loud as the door. On the bright side, no one could creep up on him, even in their socks. The emptiness made him *almost* disappointed Talia wasn't there. She was the best assassin he knew, and so resourceful it was scary. She often beat him to his own refuge and waited for him to walk through the door. He remembered her flawless figure the last time she greeted his arrival. Her curves had swayed like an ocean wave against the doorway, half-naked, while she pinched a joint between her lips. Colorful flowers tattooed their way up one of her thighs and over her hip.

The shades were so vivid, he'd almost felt the flowers' leafy texture under his fingers. He loved to run his hands up the blossoming vine and taste her bronze skin as he did. Her seductive brown eyes had raptured him and within seconds he was on top of her, drinking her up. She was a Tabasco-spiced tequila shot and she burned all the way down. Those were his final good memories of her before she'd shut down and looked at him like he was a stranger. One would have thought he'd grown another head before her eyes. Inácio blinked the images away before the recollection went too far.

He peeled off the sweat-soaked layers and dropped them outside his door. Inside the bathroom, the mirror reflected a caramel body bruised black and blue. He poked at the blue shiner left on the soft tissue beneath his eye. Its sting was minimal compared to how the rest of him felt. Behind his pain was the passion which reigned over his soul. All of it artistically covered his entire torso and arms. Like a picture book into his past, the tattoos were the only tangible thing he had left of his true identity.

Cold water soon descended from the showerhead with inconsistent pressure. Sometime between the clanky plumbing and the knock on the door, he startled awake. His hand was gripped around something glassy. Like he'd lost time, he couldn't remember when he got out of the shower and obtained a beer. At some point, he'd passed out on the springy mattress. His drink was lukewarm, and he set it on the old table beside him. He rested himself back onto his elbows and listened.

The person knocked again. By the kind of sound it made, Inácio assessed the knuckles were small, like a woman's. The sound persisted in its gentle manner. Taking himself to the door, he opened it with a little aggression. The shop owner's wife was halfway down the hall. She turned back around and revealed a plate of hot food in her hand. The grip on his pistol relaxed. He hid it behind his back before she saw it.

"*Buenos días, señora,*" Inácio greeted in a hoarse voice. He was puzzled as to why she was there.

"*Buenas noches,*" she replied, correcting his time of day. His jumbled mind discerned the darkness at the bottom of the stairs. She asked him if he was hungry and lifted a dinner plate, full of home-cooked food. Inácio gave her a side-eye. *And why would you be doing this for me?* She looked innocent enough, but so did a lot of people before they turned sour.

"You first," he challenged. Restrained outrage wrinkled her face before she proved it was not poisoned. Once she swallowed her bite, he accepted the plate with a content smile.

"*Gracias.*"

"*De nada,*" she snapped. Her husband joined her and laid a sack down by the door.

"Your clothes, *señor.*" He took his wife by the arm and led her to their home down the hall.

Inácio returned inside and kicked the door closed behind him. He sat at the tiny kitchen table and satisfied his growling stomach.

His plate was filled with double portions. *Probably some kind of bribe to keep themselves on my good side.* Whatever the motivation, the food was excellent. Unwrapping the fresh tamales, he inhaled the meaty insides. He scooped the entire avocado out onto his bread and shoveled down the rice and chickpeas. Every bite slowly revived his strength.

A vibrating pulse in his pocket shook him from bliss.

"*Aló,*" he opened in Brazilian Portuguese.

"State your ID number, my friend," requested the familiar voice.

"It's 431084, shithead." Inácio took in another large bite of food.

The man on the other end laughed. "Hey buddy, how you doin'?"

"Alive."

"I hear that! Your pic was received and accepted." The man known only as "Schafer" relaxed his voice into his natural North Carolina accent. Inácio got along so well with his handler, he often forgot they had nothing in common other than their work.

"I expected nothing less," Inácio replied.

"We laughed a little," Schafer added. "It's always nice when the person deserves it."

"I knew you would find it funny."

"You get out clean?" Schafer asked.

"Of course." Without Schafer being there face-to-face, Inácio allowed his eyes to flicker deceitfully around the room.

"Damn, well the kill was sure clean. I'll have your *dinero* off to ya soon. No loose ends as usual then, huh?" Schafer felt more like a friend than an authority figure most days. It was only when he tried to hold Inácio accountable that Inácio was reminded he was beneath Schafer in the hierarchy.

"Nope, no fallout to worry about." The lie came easy. Honesty was punished rather than rewarded in their profession.

"Fantastic. Don't make me ever have to tell management anything but positive things. That's my only rule."

"What they don't know won't hurt 'em," he said, testing Schafer's boundaries.

"Yeeeeah, well, you know. I still need to do my duty."

"I understand. Something is bound to get me sooner or later whether it's the boss or the job."

"Same, friend, same."

"What do you have for me?"

"I got a guy comin' to you now. Should be there after midnight. I'm still stuck in freakin' Bogotá for the uh, whatchamacallit," Schafer huffed. He had been worked down to the bone for a long time. "Whatever. I don't even care anymore, to be honest," he added.

"Wow, this Colombian frenzy doesn't end, does it?"

"No, it don't. It really don't. I've got guys stretched between multiple jobs, and it's a nightmare to keep everything from imploding on itself. That's my problem though, not yours."

"You can make it mine," Inácio offered. "You know I have your back."

"Nah, I need you for more important jobs, but thanks. You'd hate it anyway. Too much of getting the timin' just right so the other guy isn't screwed. Besides, I avoid sticking my best in those situations until it's the only choice I got left, or until somebody dies—one of the two."

"Where am I headed now?"

"Oh, your fortune is changin' Inácio. No more dwelling in huts and hootches. Guess where you're headed?"

"The town over?" It was pure pessimism.

"Nope! Get your stuff ready, you're headed to your old stompin' grounds in Rio de Janeiro. Congrats!" Inácio paused between bites to beam.

"When do I leave?" he asked like it was any other day. A revitalized tickle leaped in his chest.

"I think right away. My new guy will clue you in on the details when he gets there."

"The rest of my things are still up in Bogotá."

"Ah, crap. I'll uh, get it sent down to ya."

"Don't worry about it, I'll figure it out."

"No, I'll take care of it. Brazil isn't bringing in too much business right now so I'm *hoping* you'll get some cool-down time once it's finished."

"Who's this new guy?"

"He's my new assistant. Real smart, but it's all the book kind, ya know? We call him Woody. You'll see why. It's his first time makin' a meet alone with a guy like you so take it easy on him."

"I think you forgot who you're talking to."

"Nah, I'm just playin'. Scare the shit out of him. He needs it or the boss will flush him like the last. I kinda like this kid. I don't want to see him eat the dust so soon." The wind picked up on Schafer's end, a sign he was on the move. Inácio could only think about his attention being spread across too thinly, placing him at risk.

"Where do they find these people, Schafer?"

"Lord only knows. It's the new generation."

****

Inácio stared at the floor as his nose dipped into the diamond he'd shaped with his hands. The exercise began to fuel his energy and numb the soreness. Sometime between his third set of push-ups, several footsteps thumped up the stairs. Schafer's entourage had arrived. Inácio rose and caught his breath. The time on his cell was 0200 on the dot. He was sure his hosts didn't appreciate the late visit, but it wasn't in their power to complain.

The men who filed into the apartment packed the tiny kitchen in seconds with their enormous statures. Like trained dogs, the bodyguards fixed their eyes on Inácio, who sat at the table in a squeaky metal chair. He channeled his annoyance through finger taps across the table. His chest heaved from his workout and the veins across his swollen muscles popped. Inácio's brown eyes looked over the three men who towered in front of him, developing a mental plan to kill all of them and no doubt they were doing the same.

A four-eyed college-aged boy with brown hair appeared from behind the guards. His little suit fit him well for his lanky size and it was obvious where the nickname "Woody" came from. With a rectangular head and high cheekbones, he was a real-life copy of the animated cowboy. Inácio wondered if Woody felt safe surrounded by mercenaries. One of the rigid men moved toward him. The floor creaked behind the chair.

"You know the drill. Stand up." The man's directive was stern and impatient. Inácio refused to obey any stupid order without some level of defiance.

One, two, three, four, five, six, seven… eight, nine, aaannnd ten. When he reached ten, he rose at a lazy speed.

The guard's knuckles cracked, like he was ready for him to resist. The others fixated on him from across the table. The hunger for a fight shined from glossy eyes. They were trained to drop disobedient assassins and protect the handler as if Inácio's bloodlust was so strong, he could kill at any second. He found it an insult to his intelligence. At each meeting, he was tempted to take them up on the challenge, but he refused to allow them the satisfaction; he wanted Brazil too much for that.

Inácio stood, turned around, and placed his hands on his head. The mercenary provoked him with every harsh grab of the pat-down. He manipulated his balance by sandwiching Inácio's interlocked fingers under a flat palm. The guard kicked Inácio's ankle and forced his feet to spread farther. So tempting. Inácio ground his teeth until he heard the friction of enamel. Inácio's gun was stolen from his waistband, and so was his backup, and they were both handed off to another guard.

"You're done." The guard released him with a shove. Inácio sat down in front of Woody, who fidgeted around with a shiny blue pen. His Adam's apple bobbed with a deep swallow.

"Evening, Ignacio, sir."

"I-nácio," he enunciated.

"Right, sorry." His head shook and he avoided direct eye contact. "Inácio."

This kid isn't ready for this.

The young man dug into his leather briefcase in his lap and pulled out a tablet. With his smooth skin, adolescent frame, and trembling hands, Woody looked far out of his element. Inácio flopped his inked arm down onto the tabletop and caused it to quake. Woody bounced in his seat at the sudden rattle. The guards on the other hand, didn't flinch. It was obvious they were no less intimidated by Inácio than he was of them.

"How long will this take, Woody?" Inácio knocked on the table.

"Not long sir, j-just one moment." He cleared his throat.

What do the executives see in this boy? After a lengthy perusal through its files, Woody spun the tablet around, careful to only show Inácio the photos. His bony finger swiped at the screen to one side.

"Sorry, no printouts allowed for this one."

Inácio tilted forward and memorized every detail of the middle-aged balding target. The various angles and settings allowed Inácio a full glimpse of his clothing trends and physical appearance. A little short, a shiny head, and not too overweight. He wore a similar dark suit in every photo, but the same red pin on his left lapel. The target's full name lit across the screen on the final slide. *Benjamin Curtis Geerman.* Beside it was a location, time, and method. Inácio nodded his head and sat up to show he was done.

Woody closed the application and returned it to his briefcase.

"Is that all?" Inácio shifted in his creaky chair.

"Your target should be landing in his private jet in Rio de Janeiro right about now." Woody took a look at his watch. "He is attending an invite-only annual global summit for financial executives that will be underway this week. Their home base will be at the address you saw on the last slide. I found a few peculiar geographical points of interest in the area—"

"I will look into that myself."

"Right, uh, good. I'm sure you know all about that. I didn't mean any offense." Woody sunk into his seat.

"You think I can't do my job?" Inácio asked with a blank stare. He wasn't completely serious, but Schafer would be disappointed if he didn't try to give Woody a hard time.

"No, I mean, sir—"

"I don't need a skinny *caralho* like you telling me how to do my job, do you understand?"

"*Caralho?*"

"Dick. You don't speak Portuguese?"

"I-I'm still learning. I know Spanish, though." Woody's noodle torso wiggled.

"Better add that to your vocab flashcards."

"Mm, yep," he replied, tight-lipped.

"Do you feel safe traveling alone with your babysitters?" He watched Woody look up and behind him as if he was going to find emotional support from security. A small gasp escaped his mouth.

Presenting the new generation of assassin handlers. Inácio was so matter-of-fact with his words, even he would have believed them. As long as Inácio kept his hands to himself, the security detail was bound to keep their fingers off the triggers.

"They're just men, you know. They bleed like everyone else. What's your plan when they go down?"

Woody adjusted his round glasses with a shaky hand, unable to produce a strategy. "Uhm, I don't know. There are a lot of missing factors in your question. If you don't mind me saying."

"I mind."

"I can't do anything, I don't think. I just graduated from college."

"You're at peace with being captured and tortured for your secrets?"

"No, of course not. I don't know what I could possibly do *if* that ever transpired."

"Transpired." Inácio scoffed at his word choice. *Is he writing a school paper?* "If you want to survive in this world, you need to throw away that higher education. Words won't save you here. You should ask Schafer to teach you a few things." Inácio sat back.

He didn't expect Woody to understand the purpose behind his harmless hazing. The boy was in training to become a supervisor. If he made it through training, he was going to be responsible for human life. Could Inácio put his life in Woody's hands? Not while he quivered like a leaf in an assassin's presence.

"I understand."

"Not yet you don't. If you're lucky, you could live as long as Schafer. He's a whopping forty-five." He exaggerated the words for dramatic effect, yet there was truth at their core. Inácio stood as he skidded the chair away, and Woody took his cue to leave. Inácio swung his heavy backpack over his shoulders and adjusted the straps clamped over his T-shirt. He held out his hand for the return of his weapons and made an involuntary sarcastic smile. The mercenary didn't reciprocate.

"Director's assistant leaves first, then us, then you," said another guard in a very American voice. He possessed the bearing of a proud American veteran. Inácio spotted the tattoo on his hand, recognizing the Latin as the Green Beret motto. The guard had no clue the man he saw as a threat once shared the same title. Would it even matter to him if he knew?

"Fine." Inácio shrugged. He took a step back and Woody spun around to leave. The novice handler marched out the door and escaped down the stairs. His followers headed toward the exit behind him, dumping his pistols in the trash can on the way out.

"*Caralhos,*" Inácio muttered.

5

DELILAH

Rio de Janeiro was like landing on another planet, at least for a girl who'd never left Ohio before. The small connecting flight from São Paulo had seated its passengers in egalitarian rows. Delilah was buckled in beside a window and daydreamed into the early morning view. The sun showed off the brilliance of little green mountains bulging out of the developed city in random order. Their beauty spilled from the land into the shallows of the sea, bright turquoise lining its beaches until it faded into deep, endless blue. Through low altitude, the forest appeared just as infinite. It reminded her of the stunning background she only saw in movies. In person, the experience was downright celestial.

"It's like *Jurassic Park*," Devan said. The commotion in the cabin buzzed. A nervous tickle of anticipation riled their sleepy mood again after their long hours of travel. An embarrassing small tear reached the bottom edge of one of Delilah's bottom eyelids. She breathed in her new world like it had replaced the oxygen with something mystical.

Look at what's possible when you step out of your comfort zone, Del. It was hard not to be disappointed with how antisocial she'd been since her accident. Depression was like a crutch, her warped safety bubble. She'd suffocated in its tainted air for six long years. The gorgeous world outside the window made her wonder how deep her regrets could go. The learned caution within her tempered the eagerness. *Just wait and see.*

Before she had time to psych herself out, they landed, and she was riding in a taxi in no time. Wind invaded the crack across the rattling rear window. The foreign landmarks inspired so many questions in Delilah, but each time she whirled around, Carson had his cell to his ear. All he needed was a suit, a limo, and an assistant to fulfill his all-business attitude.

"Hi Claire, we're on our way over," he began. Claire was his mother. It was more correct to compare their relationship to investment partners than one with any biological connection. According to her boyfriend, his mother traveled around the world, made money, and broke away to see him a couple times a year at best. He never expressed any hints of neglect, but Delilah didn't like it. In her opinion, he'd never had the proper bonding experience a child should have with their mother. Still, he wanted to be just like Claire.

"Absolutely." He had the rigid tone of someone in a job interview. Delilah rolled her eyes. "We are two minutes out… You will be in a meeting… That is perfect, actually… We will catch up later, yes… Goodbye." Carson stuffed the phone in his pocket. After a few seconds of silence, he shifted in his seat and crossed his arms.

"So, your mom isn't meeting us?" She asked her question with a soothing tempo. Delilah had never met the woman before.

"No. She's extremely busy getting prepared for the summit. We'll see her later." His whole body pivoted toward his smudged window.

"Oh, I'm sorry."

"Pff!" Carson fanned his hand toward her. "It's business."

"Okay, I get it." Delilah wanted to leave it at that. *Please, not another fight.* She held her breath.

"Hardly," he huffed. "I don't even expect you to understand, not with your upbringing. Our families are completely different with their expectations."

Delilah bit her tongue.

"Success takes sacrifice. Plain and simple."

Stop trying to console someone who doesn't want to be consoled! She knew better than to offer Carson sympathy. When he caught wind of anyone feeling sorry for him, they found themselves on the receiving end of a debasing lecture. Delilah copied his crossed-arm posture. *Haven't I earned his trust by now?*

****

The grandeur of their hotel placed all their problems on the back-burner with its elegance. The building was enormous, luxurious, and very white. The taxi had hardly stopped before her door was opened by a stately-dressed bellman. He grinned at her from his silver-lined uniform. In a graceful gesture, he offered her a hand.

"Why, thank you." Delilah put a palm over her chest like he didn't do this for just any guest.

"Welcome to the White Shores, madam." He bowed at the waist. She blushed.

"I will take your luggage, sir," another bellman told Carson, who stood by the popped trunk of the taxi. Other matching uniforms spilled from the hotel to meet the following two taxi cabs that pulled up behind theirs. Their friends rushed from the back seats and looked around with stars in their eyes.

"Wow!" Dorothy drew her sunglasses to the end of her nose. "This is pretty impressive, Carson. Good job."

"You haven't seen anything yet," he said.

"You've been here before, right?" Delilah asked him.

"Oh yeah. My mom is an investor. I can't wait until you meet her."

Delilah's mood lifted. *He really wants me to meet her.*

The lobby's theme brought guests into a lavish space without sacrificing a tropical beachy vibe. Its corners were angular and modern with the front desk sitting at the base of a double stair-case. Carson swaggered through the doors like his name was on the building. He was a natural in the high-end environment, even bringing Quincy and her expensive taste in diamonds to shame. Delilah loathed her own casual jean shorts, and her toes writhed in her worn-out shoes. She wondered if anyone else in the group shared the same moment of peasanthood.

Two women, each with a high-set ponytail, greeted them from behind the counter. If it had not been for their different hair colors, they would have looked like identical twins in their matching dresses. They smiled at everyone but only spoke to Carson.

"*Bem vinda, senhor,*" they said at the same time. Carson replied with near fluent Brazilian Portuguese. He leaned an elbow on the counter as if to say, *Yeah I pretty much own the place and all these people.* One of the twins clicked her nails over her keyboard. Once Carson confirmed the reservation, the staff changed from professionally accommodating to servile.

"He's so cool," Josh squealed. It was smothered in sarcasm.

"If only I had flowers on my shorts," Devan added. The rest followed their jokes with muted chuckles, except for Sara.

"Yeah, no one takes any man seriously in salmon pink," Tommy said with a pointed finger of shame.

Delilah's singular language skill bore her quickly away from Carson's exotic conversation. She turned and peered up at the railing which lined the second floor between staircases. Guests mused in the space above and spoke amongst themselves or on their Bluetooths. She didn't allow her eyes to trick her into believing they were as average as she was. Even dressed down, their choice in lodging gave them away.

Across the lobby from where they stood, a powerful woman marched to the elevators. Two brawny men followed, and all three disappeared behind its golden doors. *She must be the real kind of important, like Carson wants to be.* At the sitting area were Josh and Tommy, who were busy digging in a decorative vase at the center of a glass table. Their rough handling misshaped the perfect arrangement and sent some petals snapping off their stems.

"Stop it!" Sara stormed over and slapped her boyfriend's hand. Tommy was impervious to her abuse. He pulled a blue daisy-looking flower out and presented it to Josh. Josh snatched it from his hand and carried it to Devan, who was at the front desk. The blossom weighed down his tiny T-shirt pocket. Josh and Tommy bent down to meet his shorter stature, laughing until the flower was sitting like a perfect boutonnière.

"There, now people will know you're important, like Carson," Josh said.

Tommy took Devan by the shoulders and shook him slightly. "You are beautiful. Never forget that."

Devan nodded with his usual cheeky grin. He touched his new flower as if it were a legitimate gift.

"Would you guys stop? You're so embarrassing!" Sara's face glowed.

"Dude, I told you not to bring your mom along," Josh told Tommy. Sara punched his arm in return.

"Ow! You're so freaking abusive."

"If you could act like an adult for an entire second, I wouldn't have to be."

Josh mocked her sassy body language with a snap of his finger in her face. "Bitch, please," he said.

Delilah's attention drifted away from their antics. In the far corner of the lobby, a rugged man stood by with his hands overlapping in front of him. His mean mug swiveled in every direction. An older gentleman with long white hair stood nearby. He was busy typing away on his phone. When he moved, the big guy did too.

"What in the world are you looking at, Delilah?" asked Dorothy.

"That bouncer-looking guy over there. Don't you guys notice him?"

"That guy?" Josh asked, pointing with his distinct long arm. Dorothy gasped and reached up to pull his arm down.

"Yeah, what do you think he's doing?" she asked.

"Hell, if I know." Josh shrugged.

"Guys, I'm pretty sure he's like a bodyguard," Quincy said.

"Really?" asked Tommy, squinting closer. He tucked his thumbs behind his suspenders.

"Definitely," Quincy insisted. "So, let's not be so obv—" The suspected bodyguard swiveled his head toward the group like a statue coming to life. Everyone swirled around as fluid as a school of fish.

"Quick! Make like normal people!" Tommy ordered.

"What's normal?" asked Josh.

"Around here, I think it's snobby," Delilah whispered.

"Whoa!" Devan's jaw fell.

"She speaks!" announced Tommy. Josh nodded his head in approval and held out his hand to give Delilah a high-five.

"Okay, okay, I hear ya Delilah."

"It's always the quiet ones," said Sara.

I have a voice? Where did that come from?

"What are you weirdos doing?" asked Carson. A stack of keycards was in his hand.

"Entertaining ourselves," Devan replied.

"Dude, your girlfriend said a joke! Like she talked out loud and everything!" Josh said, pointing at her. Carson barely flicked an eye in her direction.

"They wrote everyone's names down on the keycards, so take yours." He held them out for everyone. "Surprise, our rooms are at the top, so follow me." They obeyed their fearless leader and trailed him to the elevators.

"Hey Carson, did you see all those limos and Cadillacs outside?" Josh jogged a step to catch up to him. "We all rolled up in taxis!"

"Your mom should have had fancy Town Cars waiting for us," Devan added.

"Yeah!" Josh agreed with a fist bump. "You should have seen the way the driver looked at us. We had to give him a big tip just to leave."

"They kinda have a point. Your mom does own the hotel, right?" Quincy asked.

"She's an investor." Carson's voice was terse. "She's really busy, guys. Just be grateful you don't have to pay a dime to stay at a place like this."

"We're just joking, Carson," Quincy reassured with a pat.

"I need a nap." Dorothy yawned. "Can we have a couple hours to relax?"

"I wanted to hit the beach as soon as possible. I miss it," Carson said.

Two more bodyguard types trekked in from the front entrance and stopped next to Delilah's group at the next elevator. With gruff voices, they spoke to one another between gulps of their to-go coffees.

"Hey, Carson," Josh elbowed. "What's with the fuzz?"

"They're security for the summit, dude," Carson whispered.

"Oh, so Quincy was right, they are bodyguards."

"Yeah, my mom's got like two," he said with a shrug, like it was typical for anyone.

"Damn, that's sick!" Devan said too loud. "I figured that or hit men."

"But, why?" asked Tommy. "I thought they were just business people, entrepreneurs, crap like that."

"They are, but every country has its own threats." Carson looked around as if he were about to reveal some classified information. Everyone closed in. "As awesome as it is here, there's like some serious shit going on. Organized crime, large scale war between gangs and the police..." Carson's voice faded as Delilah's hazel eyes were pulled to the guards beside them. She wasn't sure what was stronger, her attraction toward the masculine men or her aggravation toward Carson drooling over himself.

"Yeah, no kidding. This is my twelfth destination in a month," said the closest bodyguard. Like the handsome pilot from the previous day, she picked up on his confidence even as he stood there coolly with a few extra buttons popped open on his dress shirt. His beard thickened a wide jaw and his bald head bore a perfect polish. He smelled like orange-citrus and caffeine. A clear spiral earpiece disappeared into his crisp collar. Her dad used to wear one just like it for work.

While they spoke about the quirks of their job, the guard she studied caught her shape out of the side of his eye. His attention was a defibrillator for her heart that she hadn't realized was so sick. In a nonchalant motion, the guard moved his wrist over the end of his linen jacket and hooked it under his arm. The rush captured her breath when she feasted her eyes on his semi-automatic pistol.

The leather holster on his belt showed off the distinct outline of the barrel, securing it tight within its folds.

The bell to his elevator dinged. Before the bodyguard entered, he twisted his head around and gave her an unabashed wink. Delilah finally lost her nerve and darted her gaze away. She raised her eyes in time to watch him vanish behind the doors. Masculine prowess. He stood for a different kind of power than the type Carson craved.

6

DELILAH

The elevator doors opened to a chic and trendy hallway. The blue walls and white trim created an oceanside realm all the way to their rooms. Tommy and Sara joined Carson and Delilah in room 905 while the rest continued to the end of the hall. Inside was everything Carson had described and then some. Their luggage met them at the center of the foyer, each piece joined in a neat pile. Luxury surrounded her from the velvety furniture to the intricate molding. Paintings hung beneath narrow lights like displays at an art gallery. Roman columns towered on each side of the living area.

Delilah's fingers slid across their ribbed design. She stepped up from the single marble stair to a hardwood floor warmed with fringed rugs and furry throw blankets. The living room separated two bedrooms split between the couples with enough space for a grand piano near the veranda. On the opposite side of the foyer was a complete kitchen connected to a dining area. The shine of the chandelier hovering over the large table reached across the entire space. A small family could live comfortably here.

"Feel like a bath later?" Carson called from their private bathroom. Delilah entered to see him sitting on the corner of a spa tub with enough room for two.

"For sure." A chance to grow closer. "That sounds amazing."

"Did you see the plate of chocolate in the entryway?"

"No, I don't think so." She enclosed her fist around the shiny wrapped sugar.

"It's made from cocoa grown right here in Brazil. That's what Claire said."

"Wow, that's super—"

"But don't overdo it. Our habits make us who we are, ya know." Carson wandered by her and into the bedroom.

"Never." Delilah crept toward the trashcan and tossed the candy in. She didn't want Claire's chocolate anyway. Carson flopped his suitcase on the bed and began unpacking. He organized his clothes into the mahogany drawers like this was his own bedroom. Casual T-shirts in one and going-out shirts in another. Her shoulders sunk as he appointed a drawer only for socks. His wardrobe reminded Delilah of guys who spent all day on the golf course or drank tea on yachts.

"Aren't you planning to unpack?" He danced between his suitcase and the dresser.

"I was just waiting to see how much room was left for my things when you were done."

"There's still a bottom drawer. You can have that." When he finished, he turned toward her before leaving the room. "By the way, I noticed since we got here, you haven't looked at your phone once. I kinda appreciate that."

"Well, you know, I want to live in the moment." The second he left, Delilah scrambled for her phone, still in airplane mode. When the connection returned, a flood of messages from her mom filled her inbox. *Oops, she had a busy night. Sorry, Mom.* Delilah sent her a quick text to at least let her know she could stop worrying—if that was possible. She did Carson a favor and silenced her notifications.

The guilt of it stung sharply. Delilah turned toward her suitcase and flipped open the lid.

****

When Delilah opened the bedroom door again, she was dressed for the beach. She yanked the blue beach dress further down her porcelain thighs. When she did the math, the last time she wore a bikini was back in high school. Sara opened the door for Dorothy and Quincy, who stood around in the foyer to chat. Tommy, Josh, and Devan were stretched out over the sofas, lost in the infinite scroll of social media. On the other side of the grand piano, Carson leaned against the veranda railing, smiling and talking on his phone. The warm air blew gently over his hair while the sun worked to tan his smooth complexion.

Delilah paced closer to the open doors. The sheer curtains bounced and swooped from the fresh air, making Carson look like a new man with the city backdrop. It was the perfect promotional snapshot for a company like Abercrombie & Fitch. Delilah didn't understand the Portuguese he spoke, but she did recognize a familiar tone. It was charming, smooth, and a little whiny. It was similar to the way he'd first won her over with his flirtatious appeal. Carson raised his eyes toward her then turned away to face the view. It took another five minutes for him to drop his cell in his pocket.

"Alright, sorry guys, I'm ready." Carson took the last swig of his drink and abandoned it on the piano.

"Who was that?" Delilah asked.

"A friend." Carson turned to Devan and slapped him on the back. "Wake up, buttercup!" Devan opened his eyes and wiped the drool from his mouth.

"About time." A giant yawn escaped him. Delilah followed the group into the hall where everyone's bored energy slowly recovered.

****

The vibrance of the city's coast was breathtaking, or so Delilah assumed. She didn't quite reach a sufficient height that allowed her to see the ocean in its full glory. They were surrounded by masses of beautiful bronze bodies. Locals and tourists blended on the sand and the wide walkway. It was nothing like little Charm, Ohio. Delilah felt her skin tingle under the constant flow of UV rays.

Quincy spun around in all directions with her selfie stick, smiling wide, capturing herself in every scene. Mixed in with all the people were police who were posted intermittently, in wait for emergencies. The beach was a smorgasbord of beautiful women in string bikinis. Delilah's ears were overwhelmed at the abundant mix of foreign speech patterns passing by. The beach bar Carson led them to had become one with an impromptu dance party in the sand. A mob bounced and jived to the music that played loudly over Bluetooth speakers. The hyped energy radiated to the sidewalk above and spread to all those who were looking to jump-start their Carnival week. Carnival was one giant city-wide celebration, Carson had told her.

The bar was small and packed in every corner. She foresaw Carson arriving and never leaving, especially with Josh around. To stand around and drink for hours was not her idea of a good time… not anymore. Today, she wanted to feel the real ocean on her feet.

"Hey, do you mind if I catch up later?" Delilah projected over the music and chatter.

"What?" Carson whipped around. "You want to wander off on your own? What gives?"

"I want to see the ocean."

He looked around with narrow eyes. "I don't want your dad mad at me. He told me to keep you close." Carson rubbed his chin.

"I won't go far. The beach is right there. Don't worry about my dad, he's not here. Unless of course, you want to come with me."

"Well, I did just get here. Sure, I'll call you when we leave."

"If we leave!" Josh blurted from over Carson's shoulder, a bottle already in hand.

Delilah hooked her sandals between her fingers and chased the blue tide. It had been forever since she ran, especially out of pure joy. She couldn't help but smile while she separated herself from her people. Her toes sunk into the deep sand, making her run in slow motion. No one else on the beach paid her any mind. She could do whatever she wanted. The white foam reached out to her and covered her feet to her ankles.

Delilah looked back at the bar and felt a thrill at being separated from her only tie to home. The women around her mingled with certainty. They were there to party and knew what they wanted. Their hips swayed to the Latin music, in touch with their beauty. Their tiny triangular bikini bottoms showed off their skin and curvy shapes. She stripped off her dress and exposed her body like the rest. Delilah turned back one final time until she strolled too far away for any of her classmates to see.

Her antisocial habits had not been kind to her skin. The dim light of her dorm room had turned her into a real-life china doll. Her stomach and thighs were bright reflectors of the sunlight. The bikini string was tied over her hips softly, the top snug around the back of her neck, lifting up her small bust. Looking down at herself under the light, it was as if she were seeing herself for the very first time.

The breeze rustled her short waves and tickled her hidden scar. She felt wrapped in some hidden force that promised safety. Delilah relaxed her arms from her waist and let herself be seen by all. The tide smacked into her ankles and pulled away the regret of the lost time. Closing her eyes, she wanted to blend in and disappear into the crowd.

"Hey, excuse me, hi," said a guy's voice behind her. Delilah turned around to a blue-eyed macho man.

"Sorry, I'm not in your way, am I?"

"No? Uh, American, right?"

"Yes… how'd you know?"

"You look like a California girl."

"Oh, I'm a little too pale for that." California? Yeah, right.

"Hang around here long enough and you won't be. My name is Carlos." His body was exactly what a foreign girl could expect to find on a tropical beach: trim, cut, and rock-solid. He had a fresh taper-fade haircut and a pair of gold-rimmed sunglasses. His skin was a deep shade of copper, so much more adjusted to the outdoors than she could ever dream of her skin becoming.

"It's... Sarah."

"Nice to meet you, Sarah. You here alone?"

"My boyfriend is right over there." She pointed nowhere specific. Carlos scanned the thick crowd.

"Where?"

"Really close by. He's with his friends drinking the day away. I didn't really want to do that. Can't really get his proper attention when he's like that."

"So, you probably don't want to come party then?" He opened his hand toward a cluster of umbrellas not far from the water. There were both young men and young women sitting around with drinks and listening to the large speaker between them.

"I'd have to ask..." In Ohio, her answer would have been a definite no. But in Rio, she wasn't surrounded by people who knew her and whom she was dating.

"It's okay, you don't have to. You looked all by yourself, so I thought maybe..."

"Well..." *You shouldn't.*

"Never mind. It's okay. It was nice meeting you." Carlos walked away. His short tight swim trunks stretched snuggly over his muscular butt and thighs. *Who else is going to give you this time of day? Carson?*

"Wait! I'm down to party." She winced, feeling like a parent trying to be cool. Delilah followed her new friend to a makeshift sand mound surrounding his group. The moment she stepped over it, their music bumped through her body.

"Sit down, Cali girl." His bulging arm pulled over an empty folding chair and he sat down on a towel. The group looked at her through colorfully tinted sunglasses. None of them seemed fazed about Carlos adding a strange girl to the mix. "This is…" He pointed to each person, naming off everyone present, all the names pretty and exotic. All were obvious veterans of beach life. Carlos opened the cooler. "Beer?"

"I don't drink beer, really."

"Wait, I know." He dumped his hand into the ice and pulled out a bright Blue Lagoon bottle. "Better?" *Don't accept drinks from strange men.* Her dad's voice was incoming at full force.

"What the hell." Delilah grabbed it and took a sip, enjoying its fruity pineapple flavor.

"You like?"

"I forgot how good that could taste."

"I was a little worried about you out there. You got no base."

"Base?" She leaned in to hear him better. The loud music pulsed into her eardrums.

"Your skin. It's so white!" he hollered.

"Told you I'm not from California."

"You want a song?"

"I don't think you'd like what I'd pick." She wasn't confident her punk rock bands matched the energy.

"Let me show you how we do it down here."

Carlos cranked up a new track and sent the tropical house beat, creating an instantaneous effect on the surrounding people. Women teetered on their toes to warm up for their big twerking shows. Carlos stood up and joined the shaking crowd. The woman sitting next to Delilah took her arm and brought her to her feet. Delilah's ego told her to sit down before she embarrassed herself. It argued she'd only look like a fool, but it didn't account for her environment.

No one was there to judge anyone else. They were there to have a good time and Delilah would be the odd one out if she didn't join in. Delilah mimicked the woman's moves, bending at her knees and shifting side to side. Her new acquaintances nodded in approval. Carlos made his rounds with uncanny charisma. He brought together their fraction of the beach into one partying mass. Delilah couldn't help but grin and get lost in the moment. *Welcome to freedom.* Rio de Janeiro had always been Carson's thing, but maybe there was room for her too.

****

Time at Leblon Beach passed without thought or consequence. She lost herself in the sea of activity. Her adoptive group danced, chatted cheerfully, and danced again. Delilah couldn't understand a word unless Carlos was there to make a rough translation. After a while, it didn't matter to her. She relished knowing she was lost in another world, and no one knew where to find her. The separation from her phone was marvelous.

"Sarah," Carlos said. "We are leaving to go eat." Delilah sprung up as if the concept of time management had just poofed into existence.

"I could eat!" She brushed the sand off her phone to check the time. Frustration gurgled in her throat. "It's three PM already?"

"Yeah, you've been hanging with us for hours." Delilah saw several missed calls not from her mom, but from Carson. They were accompanied by confused and angry text messages.

"Oh my god! I gotta go!" In a flash, she pulled on her dress.

"Are you sure you don't want to come?" Delilah took a sharp breath through her teeth. Brazilian friends of her own? Carson would be so jealous.

"I can't, I'm sorry. My boyfriend isn't happy with me."

"Hey, it was cool to party with you. Until we meet again!"

Trekking through the thick sand, she used the shade of her hand to read her dark screen. The light made it hard to know if the alert said there were six or eight missed calls from Carson. *So, I have to disappear to get his attention. Got it.* Carson's notifications were listed beside the friendly messages from her mom, asking if she was having fun at the beach. Delilah had forgotten about the pesky family tracking app.

No real privacy, even across the world. She called Carson back to hear endless ringing. The laughter from the beach caught her attention again. It tempted her back with promises of escape. Something inside commanded her to stay. *Don't go back to the room*, it begged, but she didn't know what other choice she had.

****

The lobby encased her face with its frigid air. The rapid temperature change brought her tender sunburns to life. The halls were much busier than when she'd left. Guests in fashionable suits were around every corner. She hustled her way into room 905, still barefoot. Like she was in deep trouble, she accessed the room with her keycard and made sure there was no sound from the latch. Her ears perked up, expecting to hear Carson cursing her name. Instead, another type of noise floated from the living area.

The piano keys played to a fine line, from clumsy to melodic. Delilah tiptoed forward and peeked from behind a column. Two heads were obscured behind its open lid. A man's bare chest filled in the gap between the piano and its lid. It looked like Carson's chest. Creamy smooth skin with slight muscular definition. Whoever it was turned toward the person beside him. Long dark hair hung as the girl popped her head around.

Who is that?

Delilah's eyes were glued to the white bra strap hanging down over her shoulder. The girl also lacked a shirt. Delilah became aware of the clothes lying on the floor beside them. A choke of dread gripped her throat.

7 DELILAH

"Carson? Is that you?" As if on cue, the dark-haired girl behind the piano snatched her shirt from the floor and scurried past Delilah, her eyes to the floor. The front door slammed shut and Delilah waited for the guy on the bench to show himself. "Carson?!"

"Yours truly." Carson's blank face ducked behind the lid and made her stumble back on her heels. A twist in Delilah's gut seized her. After about a slow minute, her boyfriend stood up from the keys and broke the painful silence.

"So, did you have fun?"

"Fun? Who was that girl?"

"Her name is Alessandra. We dated a little, before you and I got serious." His classic, "it's no big deal" shrug followed.

"We've been serious for three years, Carson."

"Oh c'mon. So, who was the guy?"

"The guy? What is going on?"

"No, no, Delilah, do us both a favor and don't play dumb."

"Are you mad about the beach?"

"Am I mad? Am I mad you ignored my dozen calls because you were too busy dancing on some dude? I dunno, what do you think?" The crater his frown formed above his nose held no mercy. The edges of his palms turned white as he leaned against the piano.

"I wasn't dancing on anyone! I was just... dancing!" Delilah bent at the knees, her words bubbling up like boiling water.

"Whatever. If you wanna lie about it, that's fine." His arms made a tight knot across his chest. Desperation erupted in her throat as she sensed Carson building a stony wall between them.

"When you went to the bar, I thought you'd be there for hours!"

"You know what they say about making assumptions. I *actually* came to look for you. I was gonna give you all that attention you crave so much, buuut of course, I found you rubbing up on some guy." His eyes rolled back toward the ceiling like he was recalling the trauma. "To think, I was so worried about you."

"Ugh! Carson, that's not what was happening. I was just hanging out! I would have heard you call, but I've been keeping my phone on silent since it bothers you so bad. Why are you being like this?" She put her hands up like she could crunch him up into a ball. "Wait, don't turn this around on me! I just found you shirtless in our hotel room with some girl! Care to explain that?"

"Sure, I will. Alessandra called earlier and wanted to hang. I wasn't going to since I got my girlfriend here and everything. Pretty inappropriate, you know. Changed my mind when I saw you pulling that shit."

"So, instead of talking to me about this imaginary thing you saw, you cheated on me?" Tears ran trails down her cheeks and her nose grew stuffy with betrayal.

"Not yet. I was on that road till you walked in." His tone sounded like she'd ruined his Christmas.

"Fuck you!" His actions were the worst incident of retaliation in a long history of payback.

"Mmm no, fuck you, actually," he said, with a jabbing finger. Delilah flopped into the couch, blindsided. *You asked for this. Why are you even surprised?* She felt like the stupidest person alive. Her scar throbbed from the sudden stress.

"I-I'm sorry I just wandered off. I should have called. I just don't understand what I did to deserve this. What do we do now? How do we get past this? We're all the way in Brazil!" The more Delilah begged for his mercy, the lower she sank into a deplorable rut. The satisfaction was all over his face. He enjoyed it. Her butt dropped to the floor and she squeezed her knees for dear life.

"I think you should leave," he said.

"Leave where? I'm away from home, halfway across the world!"

"I don't know. You can find a hostel or a flight back home."

"Did you plan this?" It seemed too vicious to be spur of the moment.

"No, I paid for your ticket. You know I don't throw away money."

"Then why are you doing this now?"

"Break-ups happen when they happen. I saw you doing something that is not okay with me, and it's over. This trip is everything to me and my friends. It's not fair to them or to me if we're not getting along. This is *my* trip."

"You're being so irrational!" she screamed into her lap. Through her tears and pain, the enchanting architecture and decor of their room melted into an ugly pile of sludge, just as she'd been beginning to see a little bit of color before his heavy blow. Carson sighed and dug into his wallet, dropping a stack of green bills on the floor beside her.

"That should offset the cost of anything you have to pay for."

Delilah tried to speak through uncontrollable gasps of air.

"Just stop." He gagged with disgust. "It's been a long time coming and you know it." His lips were tight with tension, but he wasn't close to dropping any tears.

A loud knock made Carson's icy expression break. He strolled to the door and opened it to a hallway loud with the wild college students. Her face turned hot with embarrassment.

"Hold on, I'll be right back," he said. Carson left whoever was at the door and breezed past Delilah, broken on the floor. She peeked her head above her elbow to see Josh towering in the foyer. His eyes opened wide as he drank from a coconut. A sales tag swung from his new lime-green sunglasses.

"This is awkward." Josh took a big gulp through the straw. "Are you okay?" To her horror, Devan, Tommy, and the girls filed in behind. Quincy recoiled and pushed everyone except for Josh back into the hall. Josh wasn't so apathetic. "Dude, what did you do?"

"I didn't do anything." The edge returned to Carson's voice. He never enjoyed being challenged, especially by people he thought should always be on his side. Her boyfriend—her ex-boyfriend—paced around the hotel suite and scrambled through his belongings.

"Then why's she on the floor crying?"

"We just broke up Josh, okay?"

"Who breaks up on vacation?"

"She decided to run off with some guy today. Shit happens."

"Delilah ran off with a guy?" Josh wrinkled his nose. "That doesn't sound right."

Her fingers dug in around her shins.

"That wasn't even the main reason, just the last straw. It's hard to feel appreciated when your partner is still hung up on her shitty past. I can't do it anymore!" Shitty past?

A courageous surge brought her to her feet. "You don't know anything!"

Carson stormed closer. "Believe me, I don't want to know any of it anymore! We'll be back late tonight. Should be enough time for you to figure something out, right?" He turned to Josh. "Let's get out of here."

"You can do better," Josh whispered to her as he followed Carson through the foyer.

Thanks, she mouthed. Josh waved his big hand before disappearing out the door. Delilah fell back onto the couch and let it all out, revisiting those past regrets that divided her family. Was there anyone else to blame but herself? Guilt and shame revisited her in her vulnerability. The night when she ruined everything conquered her thoughts.

She'd had a bottle of whisky in one hand and a blunt to her lips when she lost control of her dad's truck. Carson was wrong, she wasn't hung up, just mourning in a way. Delilah missed the father-daughter bond she'd thrown away like trash. Her dad used to look at her with pride. Most of all, she missed her mom's good mental health. Delilah's poor choices had caused her depression to spiral. Delilah shut her eyes and let herself careen back into the familiar black hole.

Just for a little while.

It was familiar and in a warped way, safe. She lay back and rested her head on a couch cushion. Tears leaked through while old memories played over and over again. She remembered the day her mom had told her she'd missed her own high school graduation. It hadn't even occurred to Delilah until right then. Her grandparents, feeble in their old age, had attended the small function. They had no idea what she had become. That was the day she officially became a loser.

Alcohol and drugs were really all she could remember from age sixteen to eighteen. Images of her mom literally picking up the havoc Delilah left behind flashed before her. Broken dishes, a broken phone, the antique cupboard her mom cherished. Everything was at risk when Delilah was impaired. Her dad's preachy lectures only made things worse. Those were the days when Delilah was void of shame for what it did to her parents, every day wearing them down little by little.

8 INÁCIO

The final hit confirmation pinged over his smartphone. The text prompted the countdown of death for one unfortunate Richard Geerman. Inácio was almost disappointed that the contract turnover was so quick. He wanted more time to take in his roots. Every vibrant color of nature and each whiff of Rio's bold spices along the street settled his mind into a lost past. One taste of the samba rhythm and the energetic drum beat in his imagination long after the music ended.

Weakness breathed on him when he caught a glimpse of his old neighborhood. The city was his until he got too close. His mother's memory was written on every wall and walkway. Inácio hadn't stepped foot within it since he'd left it for America twenty years ago. It wasn't because he was scared; he wasn't scared of anything. It just wasn't necessary to get any closer…

There was at least some solace while he waited among the scaffolding at the center of an empty construction zone. His sniper's eye was sharp as an eagle peering down from his high perch. Below him, the White Shores hotel sheltered his next object of prey. Inácio filled his lungs with Brazilian air, thumbing the message across his screen. The text auto-erased, and all he could do was hope for the cooldown time Schafer had promised after.

The client requested one condition for what was to be a simple execution: *elaborate and worthy of international headlines.* Inácio was prepared to give the world a show for the doubled paycheck it meant thereafter. The unfinished condominium was at the perfect height and distance for an easy thousand-yard shot. To make a one-square-foot shot into a collateral-riddled area was not so easy. He cracked his knuckles and chose to place full trust in his calculations.

Like a sacred ritual, the sleek weapon was set up in the ideal position near the edge of the bare concrete floor. The sniper rifle was everything a man aspired for himself. Long and heavy, it was as powerful as it looked. Twisted at the end of its barrel was a thick head to help suppress its mighty expulsion. The hefty length was supported by its retractable rods. The black rifle gave its user divine authority over anything seen through the scope. In Inácio's hands, the weapon was an enhanced extension of his dangerous skill.

He cupped the full magazine in his palm and lifted it into the rifle until he heard a click. Inácio lowered his hips to the hard ground, flattening his lower half. His torso curved to meet the butt where his cheek rested. A forefinger and thumb traced their way forward, pulling back the loading mechanism. With a firm hold on the grip, his trigger finger lightly stroked the rifle's cold nickel-coated surface. It begged for the heat of engagement.

The small mirror on the ground beside him was angled to catch potential threats that could emerge from behind. Plastic sheeting surrounded him, hanging from the scaffolding and moving with the breeze. The arrival of Carnival pulled the workers from their stations for the day, opening the entire premises to his disposal. Inácio pulled up his black sleeves, his forearm hairs tickling his skin as the breeze shifted. The wind meant more to him than keeping himself cool. It was a factor that changed his approach to the smallest detail.

The shifting environment was part of one large formula. The elevation and cross-wind had been accommodated for, and he waited for the glass doors of White Shores to open to the target. Geerman's driver waited at the peak of the horseshoe drive with the town car. Germany's colors waved from the antennas. According to Inácio's watch, Geerman's time was up. Inácio's breath was steady and calm. The heightened sense of anticipation dulled into serenity. When his heart steadied to an even pace, he was past anything ruffling his feathers. Nothing could ever come between himself and his target.

Any minute now.

Sixty seconds late... Not unusual.

120 seconds late... What time did that kid say this summit started?

Hrm, five minutes late. I only have time.

Fifteen minutes passed and nothing. He released a deep breath, reminding himself to stay patient. Rio and his past would still be there when he was done. In the best-case scenario, Geerman was held up and in the worst case, he'd been tipped off. The cell in Inácio's pocket buzzed.

"Inácio." He recognized that husky voice anywhere.

"Why are you calling me, Talia?"

"Are you in Rio?"

"I thought you always knew where I was."

"I do. This is me being polite. I want to see you."

Inácio bit his bottom lip.

"Is it as hard for you as it is for me to stay away from each other this long?" Her volume was soft, but she was anything but gentle.

"I don't want to see you." Inácio ended the call. Talia's serpent heart needed to stay away from his own. Flicking his phone to the side, he readjusted his posture.

During the period of delay, dozens of hotel guests came and went. The summit had completely taken over the building. Every guest who departed hotel grounds was uniform in their dark business attire. Tall women in stilettos rushed from the front doors, their hair done up snugly. They blended together with uptight career-driven staleness. It wasn't Inácio's cup of tea. On the other side of his crosshairs, a colorful blip interrupted the boring blur of people. She was a pop of color and youth among the muted suits. Trailing her heels was a sparkling purple suitcase on its wheels.

"Mmmm," Inácio hummed out loud.

The enormous suitcase dwarfed her stature. Her hair was barely long enough to tickle her shoulders. Inácio never thought he'd see the day where he was attracted to a woman with purple hair. It was obvious from her sunburnt skin that she wasn't from around here. The V of her collar concealed most of her cleavage, leaving plenty to the imagination. The breeze teased his appetite by shifting around her skirt. Wind had other practical uses too.

Inácio wished for a sudden gust to sweep the dress into the air in classic Marilyn Monroe fashion. Behind the scope, one curious eyebrow rose in intrigue. The woman stood out among the hotel's usual guests like a shiny diamond in the rough. She paced around, looking both beautiful and sad. No matter how much he enjoyed his entertainment, his jaw clenched.

She stood in the pathway in which his target was expected to be at any second. Inácio wanted to avoid sending the .308-caliber round barreling in her direction if he could help it. Inácio could only imagine how the powerful shot would obliterate someone her size. The girl held her phone to her ear as she wiped away tears with her fingers.

Out of the way.

As if she'd heard him, the phone dropped from her ear, and she moved to the safety of the parking lot.

Inácio could breathe again.

He switched to his spotting scope and tracked her movements between the hundreds of vehicles, then turned to his rifle scope again. Geerman's Town Car continued to idle at the apex of the horseshoe. *Where is this guy?* Inácio's wandering eye brought him back to the woman who strolled deeper into the sea of cars. It didn't take him long to hone in on a new threat. Inácio read bad men like a book. If he had one wish, it'd be to have her number so he could tell her to pay attention. As always, he watched the scene play out at a safe distance.

A beefy man with a pistol anchored to his hip walked with a chilling certainty toward the woman. A second man followed with a more casual posture, his hands resting in his pockets. This wasn't their first time. The large one moved fast. His bear paws grabbed her and lifted her feet from the ground. She was nothing to him in size or meaning. It was hopeless. The vehicles boxed them in perfectly.

Per Inácio's personal protocol, intervention was not an option.

Intervention is not an option.

Inácio returned his sight to the front doors. Geerman's driver paced at the back passenger door.

Keep focused.

The power that rested within him roared in opposition.

One more look. Nothing I haven't seen before.

Inácio aimed the spotting scope just in time to see the woman flipped on her back. The corner of his eye twitched as he watched her head knock against the blacktop. The armed man pinned her legs with a straddle and secured his control through savage backhands to her small face. Her flailing arms fell limp at her sides.

She's not your fight.

Inácio abandoned his extra scope to the side and nestled back behind his gun. He relaxed his shoulders and put her out of his mind. Every so often, he was given the chance to shift the fate of many innocent people in his path, but never did. What was so special about her that he would risk missing his target? *Nothing.* Inácio could ignore her torture and still get a full night's sleep. An annoying thought poked its nasty finger in the back of his skull. It was the kind that if ignored, he might actually lose sleep over it.

She's pretty enough to look at, but not worthy enough to save?

Fuck.

Inácio scooted his torso across the rigid concrete floor to give him a better advantage. As if on cue, the breeze picked up and shifted direction again. He deserted his objective and locked his crosshairs onto the woman and her attackers, gulping down the impending dread. It was difficult to judge their elevation in comparison to the hotel's front doors. There was no time to measure the rest of the factors like the curvature of the earth, the wind direction, or its speed.

The man above her tugged on his belt. If Inácio shot at the scum on top of her, there was the very real possibility he could miss and kill her instead. She had seconds before her life was changed forever. Inácio had even less. He switched his aim toward Geerman's ride and saw the target himself waddling to the open door.

Foda-se essa merda!

Inácio only had time for a single clean shot.

9

DELILAH

Moments Prior

When her eyes opened, it was a different time of day. The light hit differently through the windows in less direct orange streaks. The hotel room was still quiet for the time being, and her body was still stuck in its weird haze. Delilah leaped awake with a sense of urgency and ran to the bedroom to pack and change.

Ah! What am I going to do?

She scorned the thought of her house. All alone with her parents after being dumped sounded mortifying. All she would do was disappoint them, her dad in particular. If Delilah stayed, the beach could be her world. Maybe she would even run into Carlos again. On the other hand, the idea of living in a foreign city alone was intimidating. Plus, it would mean she had to sit next to Carson on the return flight.

Yikes, what's worse? Carson. Always.

Delilah jogged into the bathroom and caught her reflection in the tall mirror. Her cheeks were red around the edges and her mascara streaked across her features. Delilah splashed buckets of cold water onto her face to help erase any signs of her break-up.

With a sloppily packed suitcase, she rolled through the lobby, her eyes glued to the floor. She adjusted the circle dress around her waist and ran her thumb over her neckline, shifting it over. The new outfit was meant to make her attractive to Carson. *Now no one will admire it.* She marched out as fast as any of the other businesswomen during her final exit, throwing her purse over her shoulders. Her eyes weren't finished leaking tears across her cheeks as her thumb swiped over her dad's contact info. Unfortunately for her, he was much more reliable in emergencies than her mom.

"What happened now?" Immediate aggravation was present in his voice.

"Sorry, Dad." Delilah paced beside an idling car and the front entrance.

"You should be calling your mom, not me. She's outside tending to the flowers if you want to say hi."

"Aw, she is? Wait, no! I will call her after I talk to you first. It'll be real quick."

"Go on, just say it. What do you need?"

"It's Carson, Dad." Her embarrassment fed the shakiness in her voice.

"Del," he sighed. "Why can't you take it easy on the guy for once? He bought you a ticket and a hotel. Show some gratitude. Do us a favor and don't tell your mom or she'll think about nothing else the entire time you're gone."

"It's over, Dad."

"Over? Like for the day?" He munched on something crunchy, his food mashing in her ear.

"No, forever!" Aching for comfort and understanding, her tears hit their second wind.

"Mhm." *Crunnnch.*

"I'm serious! He kicked me out of the hotel and I have nowhere to go."

"Oh my god, what did you do?"

"Seriously? What did *I* do?"

"Carson is an upstanding young man. He wouldn't kick you to the curb in a foreign country for no good reason."

"Hate to break it to you, but it was for no good reason. Dad, please help me."

"You can't stay with another one of your friends?"

"They're not my friends, they're *his* friends, and no. He wants me gone."

"So, you need me to get you home then."

"That or I stay here until my flight and—"

"No, no. I can't let you stay in Brazil by yourself." He groaned in obligation. "You don't even speak Spanish, do you?"

"It's Brazilian Portuguese."

"What?"

"Never mind."

"Get a taxi or whatever you kids use these days and get to the airport. I'll have to scavenge up some money for a flight."

"I have cash."

"Nope, you better hang on to it, just in case. You can pay me back when you land," he said, his voice turning dry.

Delilah's face sunk into her free hand.

"If you guys make up, tell me at once. A plane ticket isn't cheap."

"I'm never going back."

"Mm-hmm, sure."

Delilah stomped her sneaker onto the blacktop and bit her tongue.

"I hope you won't have to wait at the airport for long, but it's better than being out on the streets. I'll call you when it's done. Love you."

"Thanks, bye." *I hate that I still need him.*

Delilah questioned her decision, but the truth was, she was more comfortable under parental guidance than out on her own. That truth made it worse to turn to her parents for help. Her dad knew how to put the fear of God into any ideas of travel. *He still doesn't trust me.* Fancy tinted cars entered and exited the hotel lot as she sought the road on the other side. Delilah's ride request application on her phone force-closed several times.

"You would pull this crap right now!" The glitched screen demanded her full attention. She glanced up just enough to avoid walking into a parked car or getting run down by hustling valets. Delilah blew out relief when the app finally loaded and brought up the map of available cars.

"Hey, you." Before she processed who'd spoken, her cell phone was sent spinning away like a Frisbee. It shattered against the pavement, and an unbearable constriction squeezed around her entire neck. Not one inch of her throat was spared. The man's skin caked under her nails with every scratch. A hand reached up her dress to grope all the places it shouldn't. She kicked, she squirmed, and it did nothing.

Why is this happening?! What's going on?!

Before he cut off all blood flow, she clung to the last of her senses and took a good look at her attacker. The man from the elevator. What breath she was able to take in was filled with the smell of musty citrus. Everything outside of his hungry face blurred into the background. He tossed her around like a rag doll. As she caught air, a hard smack met the back of her head.

Who hit me?

She stared up at the sky. Colorful stars blinded her vision. An unbearable weight smashed her into the ground. Delilah knew she was hurt, but she couldn't feel anything above her fear. Stunned and confused, she thought she was going to die. After the pressure relaxed from her throat, she was able to cough out a pathetic plea for help.

What was meant to be a scream came out more like a whine. A blunt blow struck the side of her face and then again on the other side. Her ability to think straight was tugged further from reach. Blackness strobed at the edges of her vision. The man spoke to someone.

"Keep watch."

"You're the bodyguard, I thought that was your job."

"Do what I say, will you? You'll have your turn."

"Put her in the van. It's too risky out here."

"No one can see us. Packed car parks make the best concealment."

"Dammit, Michael!"

"Shut up, I'll be quick." He jerked her panties down and undid his belt. There was nothing in all her power to stop what was about to happen. Delilah blinked her eyes at the man hovering above. His shape curved and twisted over a twirling backdrop.

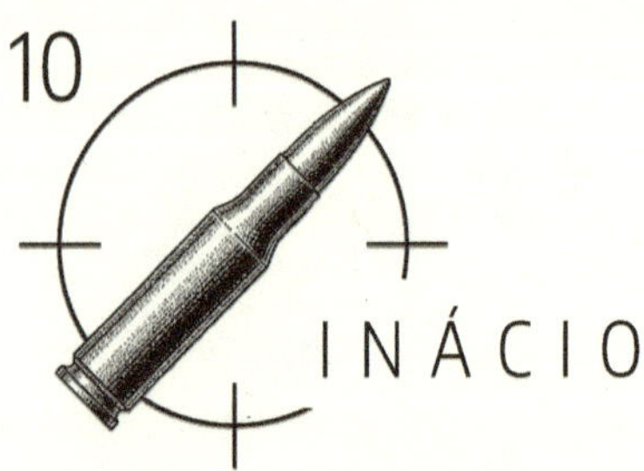

On the exhale, Inácio cleared his body of his soul. A shiver danced from his neck and down the ridges of his spine. The bullet raced in the direction of the woman and there was no time to see if his aim was true. He moved to his target, who was no longer out in the open. Geerman's driver was behind the wheel and the tires inched forward. Inácio locked his sight on the car's roof and took his best guess, moving his crosshairs in Geerman's direction.

The driver sprinted from behind the wheel, letting the car roll forward. On the other side of the car, blood and glass were painted across the ground. Witnesses scattered and ran into the hotel. It was safe to say Inácio had gotten Geerman. Inácio's heart seized as he scurried to find the woman. Her beautiful shape filled his lens, lying on the ground, still in one piece. Air returned to his lungs and he found his soul again.

His eyes feasted on the dead man nearby. The round had decimated the lookout and pierced the SUV he'd hidden behind. Inácio's lip curled as he panned over the rest of the lot. Her primary assailant vanished. *Kill him, kill him, kill him.* He was hungry for it, nothing more satisfying than to see the man's life snuffed with one flick of a trigger finger. Inácio's crosshairs slithered through the maze of vehicles, all while the mythical clock in his head counted down the minutes he had until the police locked down the area.

With no sign of the primary assailant, he had to let him go.

11

DELILAH

Moments Prior

Like a strike from the finger of God, a deafening sound detonated as loud as an explosive. Delilah clamped her eyes shut as if the darkness could protect her. An erratic squawking followed and the pressure that held her disappeared. She opened her eyes to see only the swirling sky. Head pain throbbed its way down to her belly, invoking the urge to vomit.

Hot acid reached her mouth before retreating back down. Delilah sat up, her brain rolling in her skull like a heavy ball. Her eyes worked to straighten out the shapes around her. Pebbles rolled off her dress the more she moved. She reached down to brush them off and got several nicks in return. She held her hand up and saw red.

Blood?

They weren't rocks, they were tiny pieces of glass, snagging her skin on the way to the ground. Yellow lights flashed only a few feet in front of her. Her awareness inched its way back and allowed her to decipher the strange, repeated pitch. The squeals of a car alarm shouted as it flashed its lights at her. With weary legs, she attempted to stand.

Behind the whistling SUV, an unusual shape was laid across the ground. Delilah squinted, ignoring the bright strobes. What she *thought* she saw made Delilah question her sanity. Red and other bodily shades were splattered at one end. A pair of legs, a torso, shoulders, then a head—or part of one. A crescent moon was cut out from one side of the skull. The person was a contorted mangled mess of blood, brain, glass, and bone.

Delilah gasped in horror and fell back onto the ground. With a thud, she became aware of screams from the direction of the hotel. They screeched through the air like a million wildcats. Her eyes were glued to the gruesome scene while she found her balance again. Nothing existed beyond her shock and confusion. Delilah didn't know if she was screaming, crying, both, or neither.

Where is everyone?

The panic was close, yet she stood in the lot alone. A sparkling form caught her eye, her suitcase still upright in the place where she'd been snatched. Delilah took it by the handle and stepped as far away from the dead man as she could. Weakness plagued her arms and legs. Delilah's head spun, but eventually she found the closest way out.

Anywhere but here.

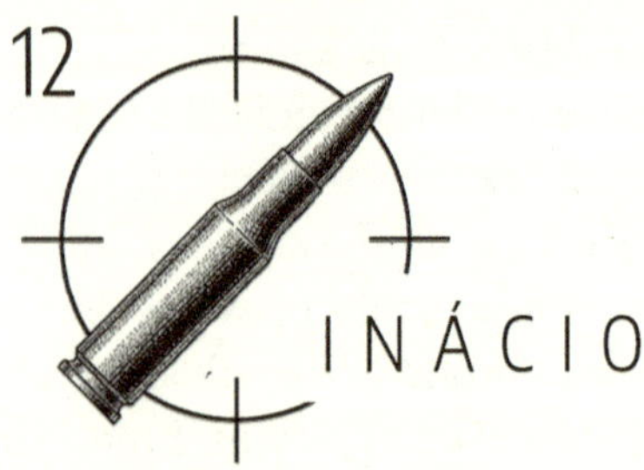

Inácio snapped the rifle's supporting rods back into place and untwisted the suppressor from the muzzle. A rapid police response was expected, but that wasn't what sent his heart rate battering out of control. A single shot of mercy was where his involvement ended. He'd spared a woman he didn't know from further brutality, a good deed that was enough to satisfy him for a lifetime. A smart man would leave it at that, yet his body rushed into action after seeing her wander away, wounded and confused.

The soft foam of the rifle case cradled his weapon. Every ejected shell was gathered, leaving behind no trace. With a solid arm, he supported the rifle's weight at his side with ease. Tan boots carried him well toward the exit at a brisk jog. In all his years as a soldier and assassin, he'd never gone down so many stairs so fast. The company car was parked where he'd left it, facing a hasty exit. Inácio popped open the trunk and dumped his illegal luggage inside. An army of sirens wailed across the sky from all directions.

As he got behind the wheel, he heard his panting breath and his heart urging him forward with loud thumps in his ears. In one smooth, fluid motion, the powerful coupe was kicked into gear and spun onto the road in the direction in which the girl took off. The RPM gauge rose quickly. He jerked and spun the wheel around corners, dodging motorbikes, taxis, and other bothersome objects in his way. He scanned everywhere for sparkling purple, aware how quickly a person on foot could evade a driver, even without trying.

Police cars blared their emergency sirens, their oscillating lights flashing on all sides. They were nothing to him but meaningless blurs. Inácio tightened his lips, refusing to deconstruct why he'd allowed a stranger to have so much power over him. The time on his dashboard accelerated, each number taking a bite out of his chances of locating her. Darkness stole the daylight, bringing out the city's nightlife and all the danger that came with it. If he allowed the shadows to swallow her up, then all of it would be for nothing.

13 DELILAH

It wasn't right for anyone to see things like that. She wondered if any of it was even real. Delilah didn't understand how her life could spiral faster in a single moment in a parking lot than all her years of descension into delinquency. Dad had taught her a lot of things, one of which was that people got what they put out into the world. Another, was to always be prepared for anything. Delilah had failed to heed his advice in every way.

Now look at you. He was right about everything. She was the reason for Carson's hatred. It was her fault that she'd *let* that man take control of her. Delilah was alone, not even wanted by her own father.

The world isn't all puppies and unicorns, Del. His voice echoed through her memory. As a detective, he was acquainted with the darker side of humans, but she'd never taken him seriously. Delilah reached out for the wall that bordered the sidewalk. She used to compare her headaches to being whacked on concrete. Now she knew what that really felt like. Blurred vision made it hard to see in the night. She tried holding back her vomit, but the dizzy spell refused to let up. Her empty stomach spat up hot acid at her feet.

Spitting, she tried to get the sour taste out of her mouth. Delilah groaned in misery.

It wasn't like at home where she could drive back to the house or call her mom for consolation. Her hand ran across the walls and gates to several properties in search of anyone who could help. Loud motorcycles and cars zoomed by like she was invisible. A nagging itch at her wrist drew in Delilah's nails for relief.

"Agh!" She winced.

Her nails lifted the tiny slits of sliced skin, catching on the bits of glass inside. With a slight jitter in her jaw, she carried on through the streets. Pedestrian faces were fuzzy and lacked any discerning details. The hilly pavement under her slowly began to break down into broken stones and fractured cement corners. Delilah stumbled over the jagged edges, the tiny wheels of her suitcase catching with a swift jerk to her arm.

No matter how difficult it became, she continued to yank and tug on the expanded handle. It was all she had from home and it was going with her no matter what. Mopeds, motorbikes, and clutter replaced the line of cars and trucks that lined the curb. The steep road twisted and winded into another neighborhood. The buildings around her closed in on a much more narrow street.

"H-hospital," she said to the strangers who passed by.

She tried to target the female figures and avoid the shirtless men smoking along the curb. Fear crawled across her skin whenever human shapes shifted in her periphery. The creeping terror collected in her throat, choking out her voice. With gaping mouths and shameless stares, some spat words into her ear as they went by, comments she didn't understand. Finally, a pointed finger offered direction.

"Hospital," a woman said. She pointed up and over the homes lining the sidewalk as if it was just around the corner.

"Hospital?"

"Yes, hospital. Doctor."

Delilah pushed forward, the sidewalk turning up a steep incline. White Shores, with its manicured landscape and affluent area, disappeared quicker than a blink. Gated drives were replaced by towering structures, smashed together like one enormous mass. Loud booms of fireworks erupted through the valley. Their sound skipped across brick buildings and cliff walls. She grabbed the wet spot bleeding into her hair with every explosion overhead.

Where am I? Where am I going? Everything slanted at a forty-five-degree angle.

Between the yellow streetlights was a tangle of power lines resembling giant black cobwebs. They draped over the crowded road in an overlapping bundle. As if on cue, the fireworks stopped, and the residents shut the metal doors of what looked to be shops in a hurry. Several men, seated around their card table, jumped up and slammed their overhead door down. Delilah turned to another shop.

A man shooed her away and locked himself behind a rolling security gate. Everyone else on foot scattered and disappeared into darker corners. The active street suddenly became eerily silent. A single shop light was left in sight. Another man in a Hawaiian shirt and flip-flops clutched the door, but seemed to pause after seeing Delilah. A cigarette hung from his lips and behind him were two small children who stared at her with big twinkling eyes.

"Excuse me, I need help sir." She reached out with a cut-up arm.

He judged her in a second before closing the door just as coldly as everyone else. Delilah spun around, using her suitcase for balance. Intense heat glowed at the back of her neck, followed by the roar of an engine. Death tickled her with its bony finger as the motorcycle dodged her in the nick of time. The driver never looked back and darted up the curvature of the street. Delilah's feet spun beneath her. Her hands propped themselves against her knees as she breathed in deep, the air still stained with exhaust gas.

The world was stuck on an eternal spin. Delilah stumbled down narrow walkways that broke off the main road. When she tried to find the way out, she just made it worse. The back of her hand wiped off the coating of sweat over her face, her tender cheek flinching at the touch. No building, no road, no alley was similar to any found in America. Little wheels ground over pebbles as she pressed on into another dimension. Delilah lit up at the voices around one of the dozens of corners.

Clumsy feet jogged toward the sound. The next road led to another incline, this one more gradual than the rest. Not fifty feet ahead were several men in police uniforms. Her shoulders dropped and her muscles relaxed.

"Excuse me." Her voice was slurred. She worked to steady herself. "I need help."

Delilah expected one of the officers to approach, but they just stood there and stared. They weren't alone. Several other men stood around them and they looked nothing like the police. The young men faced the police down with pistols stuffed in their waistbands and rifles weighing down their arms. Delilah's breath left her. The threat of danger straightened her spinning environment. Black masks concealed the identities of all the officers but one. These were not your typical friendly street patrol, ready to serve their community. More men, not in uniform, stood at the sides of the officers in defensive postures.

I'm not supposed to see this.

"Sorry!"

The unmasked officer yelled after her.

Delilah quickened her steps.

The sound of heavy boots closed in from behind.

A scream escaped her.

Two harsh hands seized her shoulders, spinning her around.

Delilah felt the thud of the nearest building against her back. A pitted, greasy face invaded the gap between them. She saw the piercing glint that hungered for evil. After her attack in the lot, Delilah was familiar with it. As she darted her attention away from his empty eyes, he shined a blinding light onto her face. Question after question he threw at her in Portuguese. She leaned away from him, trying to slip from his grasp. When she leaned too far, he yanked her upright.

"I'm sorry. Please, I don't understand… Let me go… Can you take me to the American embassy, please?"

He burst into laughter. "You're American, huh?"

"Yes, I'm lost."

"You sure are." The officer shook his head like he was dumbfounded at her stupidity. "You want me to take you to the embassy?"

"Yes, please?"

The man's voice switched to a growl. "You don't want to go anywhere with me. The embassy isn't where I would take you."

Both groups of men called out to him. A single shoulder of his rolled back as if to brush them off. A strong tug pulled on her purse strap until it was ripped from her hands. Her thin sandals slipped across the gravel, twisting her ankle. He went straight to her wallet and stole Carson's cash. After folding it into his uniform's pocket, he dug through one of the clear sleeves. His fingers pinched her driver's license. As he read the card, he looked at her, then back at the license.

Now he knows me.

Delilah turned into a sponge, absorbing all of him in return. Just in case there was a way out, just in case she survived. The officer was big, roughly six feet tall with curly black hair and insignia patches on his sleeves. He held rank but had removed his Velcroed name from the uniform. His cheeks were round, if not a little puffy. Eyelashes. The insignificant detail screamed at her to remember it. Delilah would have had to glue on a fake pair to match his. A finger lifted the end of her skirt and without hesitation, Delilah slapped his fingers down, giving him her most ferocious scorn.

Not again. This won't happen again.

"I can't let you go. You know this, right?" A unilateral smirk wrinkled the corner of his mouth.

"I won't tell anyone. I wouldn't even know what to say."

"You could say a lot more than you think." He tilted his head and scanned her like she was nothing but a pair of old shoes. Delilah imagined his thoughts.

Will I ever wear these again, or should I throw them away now?

One by one, his fingers tapped his holster. Her fate landed with each thud of consideration. The hood of his holster flipped down. His mind was made up. Delilah cowered as a pair of bright lights sped by. The beams illuminated the space beside them, barely missing them in the dark corner. Delilah stretched out her arm into its light just before it vanished. One last plea for mercy.

"Help me!"

"Move!" His hand wound through her hair like it was spaghetti, clenching its roots. Her body followed her hair as he yanked her toward the other men. Delilah clawed empty air after realizing she'd left her only possessions behind. The rocky road was ice beneath her feet with every attempt at resistance. She predicted her future ending with a bullet to the head in some forgotten alley. In seconds, she'd be nothing but a Jane Doe.

As they reached the group of officers at the center of the road, a startling squeal pierced her ears. The man in control wheeled around, bringing Delilah around with him. The car with the halogen lights spun its wheels in reverse on the intersecting street below. Under the poor lighting it was hard to tell if the car was black or gray. It skidded around until the blinding headlights spotlighted her and the rest of the men. It roared toward them, making his fingers hook deeper into her hair as he recoiled. They were so bright, a tint of blue burned out of the sharp white beams. Several men stepped up, their hands ready to pull their guns.

The stretch on her scalp suddenly loosened. Delilah pulled herself away into the direction of the mysterious vehicle. Her arms stretched out in front of her like they could get her closer to it. The sound of snapping strands of hair popped across her head when the officer regained control. He held her close and tight, forcing her to rise with his hand. He exchanged agitated words with several others.

The driver's side door opened and slammed. A robust masculine shape morphed into the blinding light. Delilah ignored the strain on her sensitive head and squinted to force a stare into the brightness. The edge of a square jaw was shadowed inside the glare. There was just enough light shining across his face to make out his brown skin. He was a silhouette of broad shoulders and a determined stance. His loose fingers tightened into balls. Delilah blinked away, unable to stare directly into the light any longer.

"Is this your friend?" The cop pulled back her head.

"No!" *I don't have any friends.*

14 INÁCIO

Ten Minutes Earlier

Inácio's engine rumbled at an idle. The determined handle he had on the steering wheel went slack under abrupt hesitancy. Rocinha, the neighborhood of his childhood, waited with open arms. A jitter rattled his jaw, the fear creating rare reluctance. Shame softened his intense eyes. The humble shops and homes stacked upon one another were the backdrop of every memory. He would have blindly fallen into its embrace if he hadn't been so afraid to face himself, the teenage boy who once roamed the streets and got into trouble.

The only other place she could be.

He was sure that if he let the car move forward, he'd suffocate. A chill swept over his skin as he imagined long tendrils of the past coiling around his waist and crippling him until his regret killed what life he had left. It would be the end of him—the end of a man who had nothing left but his own lethal strength. Inácio pulled on the gear shift and put it in reverse. He would not subject himself to his past, not tonight. By mistake, he took a final look ahead as he let the car roll backward.

Like one last plea for his return, the kindness that had defined his mother's spirit pulled him forward. Darkness was all he was, but not her. She was nothing but light. *My mother, the angel.* His mind's eye formed the image of the lost young woman wobbling Rocinha's twisting streets. She was no longer a stranger in need of help. She was a guide. Inácio switched his boot to the brake pedal. What if she'd walked into his crosshairs for a purpose? Inácio knew emotions clouded reason. Part of him felt stupid because of it, and the other half repeated two words:

Find her.

He propelled himself into Rocinha like both their lives depended on it. The surroundings changed in an instant, going from affluent to deprived. On the outside, not much changed. Basic square buildings on either side of the narrow street towered like stacked boxes in an attic. The only difference was the lively community he once remembered. There should have been a constant flow of traffic and people at every corner during Carnival, nothing but commotion.

He rolled his window down to listen to the silence. The only sound was the car and his thumb taps against the driver's side door. Empty. All the streets empty. Only danger could keep the people trapped in their homes. The smoky aftermath of fireworks blew through the window. Inácio recalled a twenty-five-year-old memory he'd forgotten all about. That deadly weekend one spring between gangs and police. Fireworks weren't used as a celebration that day, but instead as a community-wide signal. Something wasn't right. He went faster, weaving his way through the squiggling formation of roads.

Minutes slowed like they were hours, and the longer he searched, the more random his pattern became. There was no longer any thought that turned his wheels left or right. The woman he was sure would lead him to some kind of reconciliation had vanished. He slapped a fist onto the dash, unsure if he was more angry with his stupidity or losing her.

What did he think was going to happen when he found her?

Would he take her back to the safe house owned by an enterprise of killers?

Take her to the hospital where he'd put out more video evidence into the world of him cleaning up his mistakes?

Even through his crosshairs he could see she was someone who radiated the kind of femininity he craved. The corner of Inácio's mouth sunk into his cheek. He knew what he'd do. Protect her, care for her, and thus put her at further risk. Delicate features reeled him in, but a woman like her in his life wasn't a good idea. The flowers painted along Talia's thigh were as close to soft as he would ever get. Even then, those roses had thorns. Talia was beautiful but loving her was like ice to bare skin. Inácio was an idiot to think she could become more. Talia was a soulless killer, and that was never going to change.

Talia is as good as it's going to get for you.

A shrill scream startled him from his self-deprecation. A revitalized resolve stopped the coupe and threw it into reverse. He spun the car around in the direction of the sound. His headlights flashed across the sparkly suitcase his eyes were burning to see. When he finished his ninety-degree spin, a large group of men barricaded the road ahead.

Between their cruel figures was *her*, his missing purpose. Inácio's shoulders tensed after seeing her lavender hair under the strain of a man's fist, her slender neck cricked to the side. Her arms reached out to him, almost causing Inácio's heart to stop. She was so small and so helpless compared to those animals. *She needs me.*

Inácio evaluated the situation in seconds. Dirty cops and their henchmen with their motorbikes were on one side. Shiny pistols protruded from their clothes. The other males they met in darkness were Rocinha locals, and he knew the police were no friend of theirs. Inácio cracked his knuckles and pocketed his hesitation about confronting so many men. His own instinct to live warned him, but the terror across the woman's face fed his insanity. As far as he could tell, the only one she had to protect her that night was him. Inácio stepped out, walking around the hood until he was face-to-face with his new adversaries.

The officer manhandling her curled his top lip above a row of crooked teeth. His forearm swelled with his intense grip on her hair. He flexed his bicep on purpose as if he expected Inácio to be intimidated. Inácio's eyes fell from his threat to the terror in her doe eyes. He blinked away the distraction.

"Who the fuck are you?" the officer asked. The men around him tapped their pistol grips.

Inácio raised two open palms. "I am with the American embassy. She is the daughter of the ambassador," Inácio fibbed in Portuguese.

"*Embaixador?*" He relaxed his grip. Inácio was slow and careful with his response. If he could avoid a fight, he would.

"Yes, *Embaixador.* I do not know the identities of any officers here. It will stay that way if you release the girl and give her to me. We can forget about this." Inácio edged closer with every word, testing his boundaries. The gang behind them backed away to the cover of concrete buildings.

"Stop there! Place your hands on the top of your head!"

A flashlight blinded him out of nowhere. Inácio played along and obeyed the commands. The woman's whimpers made his fingers scratch at his scalp. Another officer, hidden behind a black balaclava, approached. He patted Inácio down, trying to find anything dangerous in his clothing. The flashlight left his eyes, giving his pupils only seconds to adjust. Inácio saw the men shift their positions before he was blinded again. All he could see beneath the beam was her feet twisting and curling in her sandals. They were dwarfed by the officer's chunky boots.

"He is unarmed, sergeant."

"No ID?"

"No, sir." The ugly captor waved them over. Inácio lowered his arms as he was shoved forward.

"Keep your hands up!" they ordered. Inácio took an exaggerated step and put himself only a foot away from the woman and the line of police. He stared down at her, restlessness clawing at his gut.

“What the fuck is this?” grumbled one of their accompanying thugs nearby. They paced in the corner of Inácio’s eye.

“Let me handle this,” the sergeant defended. “How can a man claim to represent the American embassy with no identification?”

“Look at his clothes. He looks military,” said one officer. With his free arm, the superior officer withdrew something rectangular from his pocket, spinning it until he could read it.

„You may not have an ID, but she does. If she is who you claim, then what’s her name?”

“You got me there.”

With a sudden and powerful force, Inácio struck the sergeant’s jaw with a firm fist. His forward explosion sent the cop toppling down, releasing the woman and landing like a fallen tree. The sergeant’s head rocked hard against the cement, putting him to sleep. The woman froze in place, crossing her arms over her head. Inácio reached for her until the other officers rushed him like a pack of wolves. Their strong bodies were reinforced with the weight of their armor and footwear, allowing for tougher strikes and solid traction against the slippery rocks. Inácio braced himself, taking in the heavy blows on all sides. His teeth ground and face scowled as he let out a guttural groan of resistance against the pain. Their fists drove into him without mercy.

“Get in the car!” Inácio screamed at her. There was no way he could see if she listened, let alone heard him over the virile sounds of the brawling men. Inácio’s skill outclassed each man, but that mattered less when the fight was four on one.

15

DELILAH

Colliding fists into flesh sent her swaying back on her heels. The impacts sounded wet, almost pulp-like. Delilah tripped over her own feet as a nasty cartilaginous crunch reached her ears. Rocks jabbed into her skin beneath her skirt, peppering down her thighs. Her eyes were sponges, taking in the violent scene spotlighted before her. Legs scuffled around one another, their bodies in a volatile collision. A man in uniform collapsed onto the cement, catching her toes beneath his back. Delilah crab-walked away from the crowd when a crack and a flash dropped another man's body beside her.

I have to get to the car. Gunfire sprayed across the road, humming overhead. Adrenaline puppeteered her limbs to flee for her life, bullets and men's screams chasing after her. Her legs led her to the passenger door, her safety only a pull away. Then she felt something. It felt like a touch, a simple brush of a hand across her arm. Delilah turned to see who was there.

No one but brawling men in the distance. A red stream captured her eye. Slapping an arm over her shoulder, Delilah's knees buckled, and her body slid down the side of the car. She opened her palm and saw her hand painted bright red.

Pop! Pop! Pop! Pop!

The shots grew so abundant, they were like a swarm, tracing lethal lines over the street. Delilah's nose crinkled at the acrid scent spreading through the air. She hadn't smelled gunpowder since she was a little girl. The association made her think of the first time her dad had brought her to the country to shoot at empty cans. Dad's eyes were serious as he explained the gun safety rules. His thick eyebrows curled across his brow like fuzzy caterpillars. Her tiny finger reached to touch them.

"You have to listen to me, Del. This isn't a game." He smacked away her hand. With hairy arms he helped her hold the pistol steady in front of her. His love stabilized her then. Delilah was safe from the world, safe from the weapon she held. A bullet flicked the soup can to the ground with a satisfying zing.

"I hit it!" She bounced in his arms.

"That's my girl!" His smile was all pride, no judgment. The recollection played out like the final images of a vintage film. The goodness fizzled into static as new images linked themselves to the reel.

Murder, torment, desperation, savageness.

Through the gun smoke she searched for the stranger. Men clashed and fell inside the haze. It was impossible to differentiate them among the disorder.

Is he alive?

Is he dead?

Too afraid to stand, she scooted herself around to the other side and hid behind the bumper of the car. Delilah squinted her eyes closed and curled into a ball. Her injury spilled its pain down her arm and soaked her skirt fabric. She should have been a better daughter and a better girlfriend. She should have been more attentive to Carson. Delilah recognized in that moment that she should have done a lot of things differently.

16 INÁCIO

Inácio struggled to one knee. Every part of his torso quivered from the onslaught of knuckles and elbows. One arm cradled his bruised ribs while the other blotted fresh blood dripping from his temple. On two feet he observed the carnage around him. Every officer was on the ground, unconscious or twisting in pain. A few young men from the favela leaned on each other and limped back toward their homes. Blood poured from their gunshot wounds in pints, their faces losing all pigmentation. Others lay so still, it was obvious they were dead. Inácio rolled his wrists until they cracked.

"*Cavalo dado não se olha os dentes!*" Inácio exclaimed. He let out a long, slow exhale. If the local gang hadn't opened fire on the police when they had, Inácio had his doubts he would've been able to overcome them. Weak Portuguese words mumbled from the pile of bodies. One of the police henchmen held up a small radio with crippled fingers. His sleeveless shirt was torn in several places from the bullets.

"We need… help. Backup, now!" The radio chirped.

"Vitor? Leo?"

Inácio defied his legs, heavy with exhaustion, and stomped toward the half-dead thug.

"Get away!" the thug said, squeezing the mic button. "Get... away from—"

Inácio swung his leg like a soccer goalie and kicked the radio from the man's hand. The device broke apart, cutting off the response on the other end. The man released a final groan before he laid his head back. Alarm gripped Inácio at the idea that more trouble could be on its way. Civilians opened their windows above the street and peered down. They showered him with expressions of shock and panic.

"Where are you?" Inácio called out. He stumbled to his car and yanked on the handle. The seats were empty. "Shit!"

He staggered to the end of the road, tossing his head every which way. A whimper sent him spinning around. There she was, bunched into a ball beneath the shadow of the rear bumper. In a few long strides, he reached her. She quivered like a scared rabbit. Inácio was unsure how to speak to her.

"I-I-It's okay." He squatted down.

The woman unfolded herself with a stranglehold over a gushing arm.

"You're hurt." Inácio reached out for the wound.

She pulled away.

He retracted his hand. "I won't hurt you. I'm here to help. My name is Inácio. What's yours?" His predator-trained ears picked up on the tension that shook her lungs.

She cleared her throat. "Delilah." Her voice was as small as the rest of her. Delilah.

"Don't be afraid. I've got you, Delilah." He reached out his arm again and leaned in. Inácio was unable to recognize if it was more his urgency or her blue eyes that pulled him forward. Their color matched the shallows of the ocean he remembered so vividly as a child. Their timid sparkle darkened with an immediate switch to pure terror.

The consoling smile on his face disappeared with the realization that she was seeing something he wasn't. Out of the corner of his eye, he saw the muzzle pointed at the back of his temple.

Click.

A lucky misfire.

"*Merda!*" the gunman cursed and barreled into Inácio. The force shoved him into the taillight, breaking the plastic to pieces. The sharp edges pressed into his neck, threatening to slice his neck open. Inácio flipped around and met the snarl of a surviving criminal shoving an eight-inch blade toward his torso. Grappling with the man's rigid grip on the handle, he looked down and watched the razor-sharp blade inch closer to his gut. Inácio's heels kicked at the ground, his feet slipping out from underneath him.

A wail split his eardrum as the woman bolted from his side. Inácio darted his eyes away from his attacker to see messy purple hair flutter away. Her brief distraction caused his strength to falter. The bowie knife's edge crept closer and closer. Its pointy steel cut through the threads on his shirt until a sharp pinch reached his skin. Inácio sucked in his stomach to buy milliseconds of time.

Orange teeth bared down, his enemy's hot breath suffocating the oxygen between them. Jerking forward, Inácio's forehead met the attacker's nose and split it in two. The man broke his hold over Inácio and collapsed to the side. A giant breath inflated Inácio's lungs, his chin reaching to the sky in relief at his newfound freedom. Without hesitation, Inácio grabbed the knife from the man's twitching hand and plunged it into his chest. He yanked it from his dead enemy and cleaned the steel on the man's clothes.

"I'll be taking this, asshole." The sound of skidding plastic wheels tore away his focus. The woman's adrenaline-propelled run took her at least fifty-meters from his reach. Her suitcase bounced and skipped behind her. "Delilah!" Inácio covered the ground behind her in shuffling strides.

He lurched forward and grabbed her around the waist. Delilah squirmed and kicked, trying to loosen herself from his bear hug. Inácio ran them both back to his vehicle, his hands full with her and the oversized suitcase. Her screams attracted more people peeking from behind their curtains. They'd become witnesses to a deadly street brawl, and now an apparent kidnapping. After reaching the car, Inácio covered her mouth and put his lips to her ears to quiet her panic.

"It's okay! It's me, it's just me." For a second, her stiff body relaxed. Setting her on her feet, her jaw rattled with her body tremors. He grabbed her suitcase and tossed it in the back seat. Inácio took her hand and led her to the passenger door.

"You're safe, Delilah." After opening the door, loud motorcycles thundered down the bluff above them. "Get in the car! Hurry!"

It was like the universe wanted to stomp his every effort to keep her alive. Instead of climbing into the open car door, Delilah fought his grasp and tried to make a break for it once again.

This had to be the end of his gentleness.

A firm elbow hugged her neck, flexing into the veins bringing blood to her brain. She pried at the lock around her throat and her head jolted back.

"Don't fight it," he said, guiding her into the blackness. Through his military training, he was familiar with the shower of tingles overcoming her consciousness. The tension in her legs dissipated, collapsing her, limp into his arms. Inácio swept her off her feet and placed her in the passenger seat. Delilah was a difficult capture, but there was no time to appreciate his achievement. The rumbling of the enemy bikes was close.

After shutting the passenger door, the unmistakable pop of a pistol sent shock waves down the winding valley. The bullet zipped past his head while another one skimmed the end of the vehicle's trunk. Inácio slid himself across the hood and made his way into the driver's seat. In one swift motion, he shifted into reverse, then into drive, stomping on the gas pedal, heading eastward. Inácio pulled Delilah's head into his lap to keep her secure. His fingers were gentle while running though her hair, as if he could undo the pain men had caused her.

Bright orbs filled his side mirrors. While holding her secure, he was forced to steer away from the danger one-handed. The motorcycles remained in hot pursuit, using their nimbleness to navigate through the narrow spaces. Inácio flew out of Rocinha at a solid eighty kph. Inácio smirked in his rear-view mirror, shifting his intolerance of the challenge to acceptance. As long as people stayed out of his way, he could easily outrun his pursuers.

He slammed on his breaks, letting the pedal rise just in time to swerve around a family walking up the oncoming traffic lane. Inácio spun around corners, watching several of the motorcyclists miss their turn. It sent their passengers on the backs tumbling off as they slammed the breaks. Those who remained took periodic pop shots at his car, putting two lucky rounds in his back windshield. The bullet-stopping glass put an end to their trajectory with thundering taps.

Keep it up, guys, and see what happens.

Inácio shook his head at the desperate abandon of the gang. Each turn and spin of his wheel was strategized. Inácio did not flee just anywhere, he kept in mind the crime scene left behind at the hotel and his mental waypoint of the safe house. As unknown as the girl was to him, he was not about to allow any more harm to come her way while she was in his presence. Another screech shocked his ear as Delilah awakened, sunken in her seat as if she found herself on a roller coaster.

"Put your seat belt on." His order was placid, failing to cut through the volume of her screaming. The bucolic scenery and buildings zipped past them like a darkened blur. She shielded her head as if she were bracing for impact. "Delilah, your seatbelt!" Inácio dove across her and secured the seat belt himself, flinging himself back behind the wheel.

The almost constant gravitational pulls threw Delilah into the door, then into his shoulder. Fixed and non-fixed objects closed in quickly, stopping just in time by Inácio's manipulation of the car's mechanics. After a few minutes, he spotted the perfect space between a line of cars. Inácio shut off his lights and cut the engine, blending into the others parked along the street. The woman slowly lifted her head and looked around with a slight wheeze in her breath.

"I thought you said I was safe."

"I said whatever I needed to so you would get in the car."

"What are we waiting for? Shouldn't we leave?"

"Shh..." A finger crossed over his lips. Inácio's focus returned to a motorcycle puttering closer to their vehicle. A single pursuer, broken away from what was left of his partners, was getting dangerously close. The biker peered through the shrubs and the many parked cars against their bumper. Inácio found the release button between the center console and his seat. With one press, a hidden chamber behind Delilah's seat unlocked. From it he pulled a fully loaded pistol with a long suppressor screwed to its barrel. The girl beside him watched him with worry and gripped onto the purse that somehow still hung across her body. Crossing the pistol over his chest, he rested the barrel at the edge of the cracked window.

He was ready to send a single silent shot to the biker's skull if necessary. One and done. Delilah's throbbing heartbeat shook their seats like low bass. The sharp contrast in their energies fed his fire for protection. His own biomechanics were calm, steady, and silent.

The motorcycle came parallel with the car's back wheel. All the driver had to do was look to his right and recognize the sleek gray car he had been chasing for the last three miles. His overheated engine stalled and caused the wheels to draw to a halt. The biker caught his balance with his foot and stared down his bike, ignorant that his head was in perfect alignment with a 9mm pistol. Inácio heard Delilah's breathing cease in anticipation.

Curses and agitation spat between failed sputters as the bike engine was kick-started again and again. Inácio held his gun still, preparing to fire if discovered. The biker looked behind him, responding to his friends who had already turned around. From their slouched postures, it was obvious they'd given up. After several seconds the motorbike was revived, and the driver continued to scan down the road.

"Are you coming or not?" another called from the intersection.

"Yeah, yeah," he hollered back. He cranked the accelerator and followed his friend back the way they came. Inácio filled his nostrils with relief. Too close. He holstered the weapon and turned to Delilah. Whimpers of pain escaped her throat.

"Now, it's over. I need to look at your arm." Inácio abruptly exited the car and retrieved a black bag from the trunk, digging around in it until he found a pen light. Getting a closer look on the passenger side, he placed his hand over hers, which was clamped down over the wound. "Let me see." Inácio kept his words soft. He could tell she was trying to figure him out, probably wondering if he was truly a friend or just another foe. The hole in her bicep continued to drip blood down her elbow. She was lucky to still have an arm. There was no exit wound and in the light, he could see the glint of the bullet. The wound was miraculously shallow. "Do you remember when this happened?"

"When I was running to the car, I think. Who knows." A vexed frown wrinkled her face.

"You're in far too good of shape for it to be a direct hit. It must have been a ricochet. I can't take the bullet out here. Your head is bleeding too." Inácio's fingertips barely danced over her scalp before wrapping gauze around her arm. He returned to the driver's seat and pushed the start button, bringing the velvety engine back to life. Before taking off, his swollen scuffed knuckles caught his eye. He felt her stare on them too.

"Are you taking me to the hospital, sir?" The words were tiny and polite. It only made him feel more guilty to deny her.

"I'm sorry, I can't take you there."

"Why not?" She stirred, unsettled.

"A bullet wound involves the police, especially after today."

"Can you at least drop me off?"

"No, I won't leave you there alone, not when I can do it myself."

"But I need a hospital, don't I?" He watched her panicked eyes fill with tears, a harsh reminder that what was normal for him was not for her.

"Delilah, listen to me." Inácio shifted to face her. "You're not going to die from a gunshot wound one inch deep into your muscle. I can't take you to the hospital because you know my face, the car I'm driving, and everything I did back there."

"I won't say anything, I promise."

"They will make you say it. You won't have a choice."

"But you helped me," she pleaded. "I don't know you. I wouldn't tell a soul."

"My beauty," he began in Portuguese, "you have no power in this decision."

Delilah dipped her head to her chest and cried.

"Where are you from?"

"Ohio." She refused to look at him.

"Here on vacation?"

"Yeah, an early spring break to catch Carnival." There was a tad bit of annoyance in her voice.

"Alone?"

"No, with my boyfriend. It's our senior year of college." She wiped away the tears with the back of her bloodied hand.

"He's probably already missing you."

She paused before responding. "Yes, he is. That's why I need to get back ASAP, and if I don't update my parents, they'll fly down here themselves."

"Of course."

"Do you think I could call them?"

"I don't have a phone you can use right now." Inácio twisted uncomfortably, feeling like a creep and kidnapper. It was an innocent request, but he had to protect himself.

"Why? They're all probably going insane already. Especially my boyfriend. You know, he's really into Muay Thai."

"I have no doubt you have a lot of people who care about you."

"And my dad is a detective so—Ahhh…" She winced sharply in pain and reached for her arm.

"Let me get that bullet out of you. Then, you can call whoever you want." His eyes looked over the attractive legs he'd enjoyed from his rifle's scope now pelted with injury and dirt. It was not her business to ever know he had rescued her twice that day. If his employers ever knew what he was up to, they'd make sure she could never utter a word.

"Where are we going?"

"My house."

Delilah gulped.

"I promise to get you help and to get you back to your boyfriend."

Inácio had sparked a chain of events in which there was no return. The evidence was all over his assigned vehicle. Never in his career did he have to talk his way out of anything before. He would give her first aid and let her be on her way. After all, he couldn't keep her long, even if he wanted to.

17

DELILAH

Delilah blinked her eyes open after hearing a low, almost grumbling voice.

"We're here, I said."

Neither the man's words nor her vision did anything to clarify where "here" was. Her environment pulsated to the beat of her pain. The only thing that was clear was a natural scent of sweat and exertion. The smell was pure masculinity. Delilah squinted to focus on the massive arm anchored to the wheel. The muscle fibers flexed and bulged like those of a man neck-deep in stress. Cupping her own head, Delilah sat up and forced her eyes to observe the bright white light beaming into the car.

"Where are we?"

"The garage," he said, like it was helpful information.

It didn't look like a garage. There were no tools, random storage bins, or shelves with miscellaneous items. There were a few steps leading to a platform just under the door. It was more like a government facility.

"Wait here a second."

"Where are you going?" A burst of nervous energy sprung her straight up in her seat.

"Going to make sure everything is ready for you, okay? I will be right back." Before she could question or protest, he disappeared from the car and through the door. The more minutes that passed, the more the silence radiated through her eardrums. Her nerves were too fried for even the quiet to be peaceful. A mythical clock compulsively ticked slowly at a snail's pace in her imagination.

Any normal person might describe the wait as five minutes long, but to her it was like an hour. Delilah couldn't stand it any longer, she had to get out of the car and rest her body. She fell out, knees first, into the brightest fluorescent-lit room she'd ever been in. Her eyes slammed shut and every joint competed with her head wound for intensity. In microsecond intervals, Delilah opened her eyes, using the open door to help herself stand.

A sound of godlike volume shouted from somewhere in the bright rays.

"Delilah!" An iron hold came around her waist and pulled her up. When her feet left the ground and she felt the firm embrace of his arms beneath her, she allowed the fight to leave her. Firm arms took hold of her and lifted her from the ground. In its place was instant relief. "What are you doing? Why didn't you stay in the car?"

"I can't be alone. Please, I need to lie down." Her head dropped to his shoulder.

"Let's get inside. It's going to be okay." It was the first time that night that she'd noticed his Brazilian accent. As she floated through his home, Delilah's hand reached up and around his neck. He was warm, and she wanted nothing more than to be pressed closer to him. Delilah stared up at the caramel-toned skin over his strong jaw. His thick neck formed into a pair of round shoulders. Never before had she felt so helpless. The only one who could make it all better was this stranger.

The moonlight moved through the windows and revealed the blood running down his temple. Delilah narrowed her eyes and studied every minute detail her blurred vision allowed. He looked older than her, maybe around ten years. Fine lines were beginning to crease around his eyes and between his brows. She soaked in as many details as possible to regain her bearings. To be with her boyfriend one moment and then carried by a stranger in an even stranger house the next was disorienting.

A soft bed replaced his arms, forcing her to adjust to another unknown environment. The blankets were cool and heartless in comparison to the man's cradle. His hands slithered out from under her while her fingers fiddled with the cloth underneath. It was coarse, like he'd put down bath towels over his sheets. Delilah's naked heels dug in, uncomfortable in her unrelenting pain.

Her host dropped a heavy duffle bag at the foot of the bed. Turning on the lamp at the bedside table, he rifled through its contents. A long steel tweezer-like tool appeared in his hand.

"What is that?" A hand concealed her pierced arm.

"What I need to help you." Beside it he set down a small glass bottle, thread, and a needle.

"Wait, let's just go to the hospital."

Without a hint of sympathy or acknowledgment, he continued to set up intimidating medical supplies. Delilah's weak eyes never left him. She tracked him past a large curtained window and into the master bath. His battered face reflected back at him in the mirror. The bathroom was dim, yet he never turned on a light. It made his eyes resemble black holes. As if he knew she was intruding, his dark irises stared beyond his reflection and at her. Before she caught herself turning away from her shyness, he darted his gaze away first.

Delilah couldn't help but look back again. He pulled at the ends of his shirt from his waistband and brought it over his head. It dropped to the tile in a wad. Bending over the sink, he rinsed himself off to the elbows. A distinct V shaped his back. A dark image, too far away to discern, was tattooed from scapula to waist.

He finally flipped the switch and lit up the line of bulbs about the mirror. The image came to life as a fearsome reaper. While he lifted his arm to examine his own wounds, his muscles shifted, giving the creature movement. Its ghoulish mouth pinched a cigarette between its teeth and a sniper rifle was clutched in its bony hand.

When he returned to his big bag on the bed, he withdrew some bandages and took them back to the bathroom. The judgment of Delilah's cynical father filled her head. If he saw where she was now, he'd go berserk. Delilah sighed. Maybe he was there in spirit, speaking to her because he was the last voice she'd heard before everything changed. She didn't need him after all because she had… whoever this guy was. Even her dad couldn't have done what this stranger performed. No regular person could handle that situation and survive.

Her savior returned with a white patch over his stomach. The edge of the bed sloped down under his weight as he sat down. Black strands fell out of what was probably once well-kept hair when he reached for the shiny pair of tweezers.

The tattoos covering his chest and shoulders made him even more beastly. It signaled for her that she had no choice, whatever he chose to do. His arms were a mural of uniformed soldiers depicted in scenes of battle. Some rappelled from a chopper and another over his shoulder kneeled at a grave. Across his left forearm a camouflaged face stared into a rifle scope, his finger on the trigger. It looked all very patriotic and… American. A large bald eagle artistically ripped the skin over his heart, revealing another layer. She recognized the green, yellow, and blue of the Brazil flag. An immigrant, maybe?

"*De Oppresso Liber?*" she asked, reading aloud some words across the inside of one of his arms.

"Mm-hmm." The man wrestled black latex gloves over his wide hands.

"What's it mean?"

"'To free the oppressed.'" The glove slapped over his palm and began unwinding the bandage from her arm. Delilah tensed her jaw and he seemed to notice. "I will be as gentle as possible."

Unable to fathom a long steel instrument in her skin, she pulled away.

"No, you cannot move." His hand reached across to her other elbow and brought her toward him.

"I'm not ready."

"I know what I'm doing. You have to trust me."

Trust a stranger. Right. With the bandage removed, she caught a glimpse of the bloody hole and turned away. Squinting her eyes, she breathed through her teeth. He brought himself to a kneeling position at her side.

"So, you're in your last year of college, you said?"

"Yep." She trembled, knowing the conversation was just a cute trick to keep her distracted so he could do his work.

"That makes you what, twenty-one?"

"Twenty-four." Two years behind where she should be.

"What are you studying?"

"Psychology." Her teeth ground as his thumb manipulated the shape of the wound.

"What do you plan on doing with that after graduation?"

"I want to be a—Mmm!" The cold metal touched her torn-up skin. "A psychiatrist, maybe."

"You want to help people."

"Yeah. My mom suffers from—Ahhh..."

"I've almost got it. Continue. Your mom suffers from what?"

"Psychotic depression. She's battled with it on and off for years. I've been taking care of her." Or at least, trying not to be the cause.

"So your reasons are very personal." A sharp pressure moved into her arm.

Delilah nodded, unable to speak from the pain.

"Here it comes."

A release of pressure.

"Oh, thank you." Warm blood trickled down.

"Where in Ohio are you from? Hold that towel there."

"Charm. Just farmers and Amish."

"Amish. I've seen them before."

"In Brazil?"

"America. I'm almost done."

"That feels a lot better."

"Here it is." In his palm was a little brown piece. "Full metal jacket."

"I guess that's better than hollow points."

"I didn't think you'd know what that is. You said your dad is a detective. Did he teach you about guns?"

"It was unsolicited, but yes. I got to shoot his duty weapon a few times."

"It's not over yet. I have to put in a few stitches," he warned. "What does he carry?"

"A Glock twenty-two, I'm pretty sure." A sharp needle prick followed.

"How did you do?" His hand channeled the thread through like a tailor. "Just a little more, I promise."

"I did okay, I guess. Nothing too impressive. When I miss though, I hit the head of the target instead of center mass."

"I'd say that's deadly accurate." He flashed a smile but quickly removed it. "Have you shot anything else?"

"Nope. He has a shotgun, but it's twelve gauge so he didn't trust me to handle that well."

"It's a pretty big kick for your size." The pressure from her arm dissipated along with her tension. "Can you see straight?" Huge hands cupped the sides of her small face.

"It's better, sort of. Was I that obvious?"

"A little." He searched her hair for the source of her other bleeding wound and found her shame. "This an old scar?" Delilah recoiled, reached up, and caught his hand over it. He pulled himself away at lightning speed. "Sorry."

"Yeah, it's an old scar."

"Well, there's a lump back there, but it's not too bad. I know you have a concussion." He moved on to her limbs, extracting the bits of glass from her skin. The room grew quiet while he picked out the pieces. She didn't feel like talking anymore. "Any more glass you're feeling?"

"Um, no. I think you got it." With all the sharp bits in his palm, he peeled off the glove, keeping them contained in the stretchy rubber, then retrieved a pill bottle from the duffle and handed it over.

"One a day should prevent infection."

"Can I ask you your name?"

"Inácio. There's a nice bath there. You should clean up, it'll help you feel better."

At nursing-home speed, she sat all the way up and placed her bare feet on the rug. The fibers tickled her tired soles. If she never set foot on the ground again, she wouldn't mind. Inácio offered his elbow. Taking it, Delilah made direct contact with his strength. Her fingers curled around him, getting smashed between the hard ridges of his bicep and radial. With ease, he lifted her and walked her pace to the bath.

Where did this man come from? What kind of person placed himself in mortal danger for a random stranger? She couldn't wrap her mind around his generosity or her luck. Did he have connections with those men? Her questions and bizarre theories perplexed her to the point that her achy brain begged her to stop. Discreetly, her eyes wandered to the tattoo under her fingers. She pressed into the artwork, bending the face of a soldier beneath. This man was a warrior and that was all she knew.

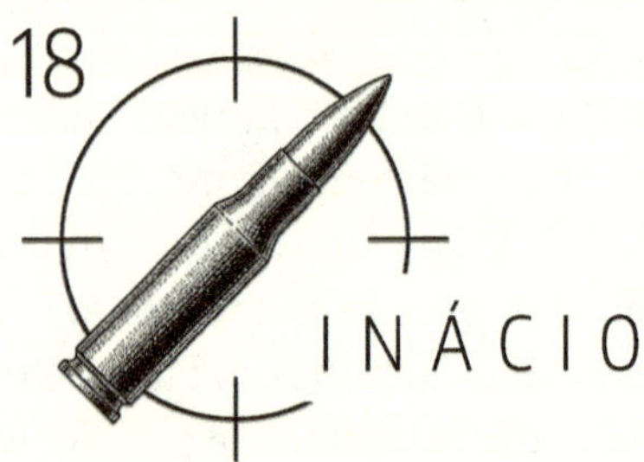

18 INÁCIO

You really fucked up this time.

Inácio leaned against the kitchen counter, arms locked. Running bathwater resounded from the master bedroom. He'd led her to the side of the Jacuzzi tub and got out of there before Delilah could affect him any further. Her need for him was a call to arms, but he had to hold it back. Closing his eyes didn't shut out the image of her looking at him through the mirror. Her white shirt soaked with her own blood. And those irises. Hazel. They were bright enough to see from the dim bathroom.

In a flash, Inácio's eyes burst wide open and he stomped over to the bedroom door, slamming it shut to muffle the sound of her presence. He returned to the edge of the sink and hung his head low. His next moves would either take care of this problem or magnify it. For the first time, it occurred to him how disturbing the control his employers had over his life was. Paranoia ruled at the thought of anyone finding out what he had done. Delilah was a walking billboard for the chain of events he'd started.

Change your mind. Take her to the hospital...

They would ask questions. Once she revealed that her injuries had happened at White Shores, the police would want a sketch of the man who'd taken on a mob of cops and thugs.

Let her go home. Drop her off at the airport first thing in the morning.

Not a bad plan, until he thought about her detective father that she'd subtly threatened him with. No option guaranteed anonymity. He'd made a big mistake, and there would be consequences. Then those scared eyes returned to his mind. Whether it was the way she looked at him or fear of discovery, the hair on his neck stood on end. *Why did you have to do it?* Now, two lives that were never meant to intersect had come into full collision.

The boss would kill her if he knew. Then she would be better off if Inácio left her with those men in the parking lot. Inácio himself may be killed because of it.

Or they don't kill anyone.

Inácio raised his chin with a twisted sense of hope. He could *take care of it.* Delilah wouldn't even know what happened. There didn't have to be any blood involved. Her neck was so tiny. It'd be over in a second. It was his most merciful option. Inácio imagined the entry point from an assassin's gunshot gushing down the front of her pretty face.

Yes, he would do it.

He had to be the one—when he was ready.

A sudden crash from the garage cut through his train of thought.

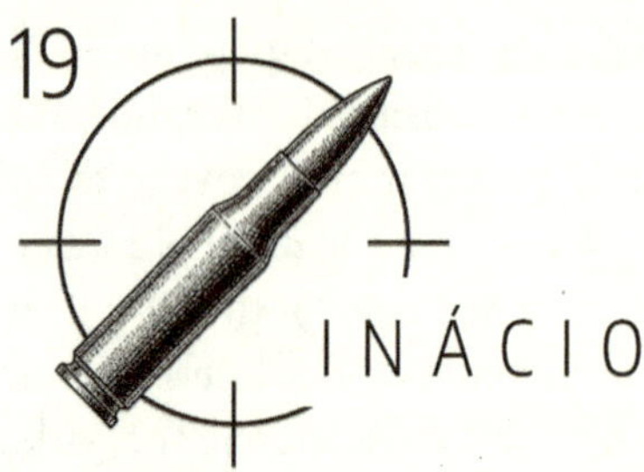

19 INÁCIO

What he saw in the garage made his stomach drop, his nerve endings chiming with alarm at the sight. Pouring out of an open car door, Delilah's belongings were strewn everywhere across the cement floor. An unzipped purple suitcase lay face down beside the back tire. Lacy bottoms, a bikini, shorts, dresses, and shoes were scattered.

They know.

The security panel beside the door blinked green, showing no signs of an illegal breach. The only sounds in the room were his own steps and the buzzing of a fluorescent bulb. Inácio clenched his jaw and made his approach. He half expected someone to be hiding in the back seat, but there was no one. A silky garment slipped under his foot, and out of some kind of secondhand embarrassment, Inácio crouched down and started picking it and the rest up.

His thumb caressed their softness before tossing them back in the suitcase. They weren't anything he should be looking at, let alone touching. As he piled them inside in no particular order, an ever so slight shuffle sent his hairs standing on end. Inácio spun around, and launched forward in a counterattack at whoever was behind him. The lurker collapsed beneath him. Inácio's hand was around their throat, until he recognized Talia in his grip.

"Of course." He released her and rose without helping her up.

Talia coughed and rubbed her neck. "Holy shit, Inácio."

"Do you want to die?"

"No. I wanted to see you. I thought you'd be expecting me."

"Really? Expecting you to sneak up behind me like that? You've never done that—unless..." Inácio walked forward, forcing Talia's back to the car behind her.

"Unless what?"

"Did they send you?"

"What? No one sends me anywhere. I go where I want. I'm not some mindless pawn like you." She pushed him away.

"That is *besteira*! What have you done?"

"It's not bullshit. I was investigating. What happened to you?" Talia held up one of Delilah's bras.

"These are not yours!" He snatched it and flung it toward the suitcase. "What right do you have to rummage through another woman's belongings?"

"Inácio, did you hit your head?"

He ignored her and continued to collect Delilah's clothes.

"Who is she to you?"

"Wouldn't you like to know."

"I already do." Talia pulled out something blue and square from her back pocket. It was Delilah's passport. "Delilah Johnson. Ohio, USA. Sex: female—" Inácio grabbed onto the little book and wrestled it away. Inácio noticed Talia's jaw drop in bewilderment as he bent it back into shape. "I could fucking kill you right now." Fire lit up her chocolate eyes.

"Try it, I dare you."

"You're not the first assassin to bring home a stray."

"No one would know better than you."

"You men act like you own this profession, but you guys have it all twisted. You're all the same: tragic and desperate for affection.

I've never met a hit woman who cared enough about anyone to make her so stupid."

"What do you want?"

"I told you over the phone: I want to see you. I wasn't expecting to find you drooling over some college snatch."

"You can fuck off, Talia." Inácio took a step back to allow her the space to leave.

"Wow, isn't it crazy how fast things change?" She circled him, arms crossed. "It wasn't too long ago that you were begging me to stay in bed with you." A rattle, similar to a chipper hyena, escaped her. "You were stumbling over your words then, trying to take back the L word."

"That was a mistake. I should have known you weren't capable of it."

"And I should have known what a sensitive guy you were. You work every day to make yourself a deadly giant, but inside you're just a sad little boy."

"Get the fuck out." The offense leaked through his voice.

"Hit a nerve? You can't fuck without falling in love and I can't fuck knowing you do. But you hate me now, don't you?"

"I don't hate you. You're nothing to me."

"Then fuck me like I'm nothing." Talia pulled him forward by the belt. "All I want to do is enjoy you."

"I don't think I could get hard if I tried with you."

"Are you sure? Do I need to be her?" Talia's long nails scratched down his chest as she wrapped her leg around his. "I was in the house, watching you two bond. What kinds of things did she say? Oh, I know. 'I don't want to be alone,'" she mocked. "'I'm majoring in psychology—'" Inácio's hand constricted hard around her wrist, twisting it around her back and shoving her away.

"Just leave!" He needed Talia to be far away from him. He couldn't smell her or feel her rubbing up against him. The wound was too fresh to think straight. A crooked smile came over her face while she rubbed her wrist.

"That's gonna bruise." The fact that she liked it made him even more angry.

"I hope it does." Talia puffed out her chest, forcing his gaze to her cleavage. Picking up a bikini top, she held it to her chest. Her shiny black nails flattened the fabric across her breast.

"It's a little small, don't you think?"

Inácio stormed toward her in fury. Talia turned her back to him and held Delilah's clothes close to her waist. He shoved himself behind her and reached around to take them away. Talia pushed herself back against his groin.

"What else did you take?" His hands patted her down and his fingers reached into her pockets. Inácio won back another piece of Delilah's clothing before a throbbing pressure startled him. He paused and looked down to see Talia's round ass grinding in all the right ways. A year of passion was hard to forget. Her hand reached behind her, grabbing the bulge, then stroking.

Talia was right: he was weak.

She turned to face him while long fingers undid his belt and popped the snap underneath, freeing his lust. Puffy lips kissed his chest, and she placed one hand over his bandage. She was gentle about it, offering the nurturing touch he always craved from her. It was all it took for his wide head to drip clear. Talia turned back around and leaned over the hood. Inácio missed her too much not to indulge.

In a jumbled mess of frustration, Inácio's hips pumped against her. He pulled down her pants harshly, just enough for him to reach inside. Inácio was aware of the trap, but he didn't know how to stop. The needs of his body drowned out the voice in his heart. It longed for the pleasure he hadn't had in months. Her warm hips in his hands made him believe he had everything he needed to relieve his stress. Inácio soaked two fingers and dabbed them inside her entrance just for a second. Talia was already soaking wet. Inácio spun his hand around her long black hair, making the strands wind around his wrist like a rope.

It took Inácio no time to find where he belonged.

He had her body memorized.

Unrelenting and without mercy, he shoved his entirety inside. An immediate heat and wetness surrounded him. The saturated sound spread across him with every thrust. Talia's body gave him instant gratification. Inácio moaned loudly through the relief she brought. He had been dry for too long. Staring down at her curvy shape, he established a hard and deep rhythm. Her ass shook and lifted to his pressure. Inácio couldn't decide if he loved seeing her beneath him or hated it.

"Take what you need!" she cried out. His thrusting grew faster, and he could feel her constricting around him with every other push. Inácio's hand smashed hers into the hood and he lowered his face until he felt her lush hair over his cheek. Talia smelled like jasmine and his teeth gently stroked her ear. Talia freely expressed the intensity of his rough handling, her favorite.

Inácio stared at her dark hair and her familiar gold piercings. He saw the bronze tone of her skin and felt her perfect ass against him. Even with all her details, he failed to see her. Another image replaced hers. Purple hair and narrower shoulders. Inácio admired her delicate jawline and creamy skin.

"What are you doing?" She twisted her neck around. Inácio's thrusts turned into strokes. He stopped pulling her hair and caressed her head like she was a kitten. "Stop touching me like that."

He paused inside her and opened his eyes. Talia's image returned to him. Still, he tried to finish, if only to settle his inner void. With every extra thrust, he wanted her less, each stroke letting her go. Talia's claws grabbed his ass and pushed him inside for encouragement. The pleasure promised him bliss. He shoved himself in as deep as he could, only growing softer.

Inácio's fist slammed onto the hood like a hammer, inflicting yet another blemish on the company car. Talia jumped and he pulled out like his life depended on it.

"What the hell was that? You look—"

"Exhausted?"

"I was going to say 'numb.'"

"I'm both." Inácio tucked himself inside his pants.

"Why? This is not the Inácio I know." She traced the vein popping out of his swollen arm. He slapped her hand away and braced himself against the hood to catch his breath. "The Inácio I know is passionate. The man I know adores female beauty. You look rough, and your poor Mercedes doesn't look much better."

No reply.

"What happened to the girl?"

"I don't want you talking about her. Do not speak her name or even think about her."

"Oh? Are you afraid they'll find out?"

"Keep it to yourself."

"Or what? What will you do if I mention that safe house number two is Code Pink?"

"I'll kill you." Inácio didn't want to be associated with the term. "Code Pink" was inside lingo for a hit man who brought back a woman to the safe house for a one-night stand. He had no idea what the term was called when a hit woman did this or anyone brought home a man. Code Blue maybe?

"What a joke." She laughed again. "What does she have that I don't?" There was a surprising jealous edge to her tone.

"This isn't about her. You need to leave," he said, standing up straight. Inácio didn't want Talia to be under the same roof as Delilah for another minute. He knew how dangerous she was.

"It's not? I've never seen anyone field-treat a gunshot wound as carefully as you did. She didn't feel a thing. Is that what you need?" Talia came closer. "You need a woman who will let you take care of her?"

"I need you to leave, for good."

"For good?" Her eyes narrowed. "You fuck me, do a really poor job at it, and then you want to kick me out? Something isn't right with you."

"I'm fed up with being used and I'm pretty tired. I'd like to get some sleep if possible."

"How can you kill humans for a living but get worked up over sex? That's all it is, just sex. Why do you need to catch feelings? So what? I want your body, not you. Get over it."

"Are you done?"

"Can I at least use your bathroom to clean up?"

"No. I'm not stupid." Inácio turned his body to block her way.

"We all know what happens to assassins who keep big secrets from the board."

"I know what happens to the ones who get in my way." He allowed the disgust to show across his face as he used his larger stature to push her back toward the garage door. Talia needed to understand it was over. Her pursed lips and tense shoulders made it obvious that it took everything within her not to fight back.

"I don't like complicated men."

"And I don't like being ignored. You better leave, or I'll have another secret to hide."

"Fucking gladly." Talia opened the garage door and pivoted to the other side. "Whatever game you're playing, you can't win. You're a hit man, Inácio. Your story doesn't have a happy ending."

"Neither does yours."

20 INÁCIO

He hovered over the bed, his hands ready to snap Delilah's neck.

Enough with the emotions.

There was only one way to get rid of the angst, and it was just to do it and get it over with. The longer she was there, the less capable he was of a good night's sleep. His hesitation welcomed the daylight, washing his innocent target in the morning light.

It's for her own good.

It's for your own good.

Talia knows. It's either they do it or you do it.

Delilah had been as restless as him and kicked the blankets off sometime in the night, leaving her skin exposed to the chilly air. Inácio drew close enough to see the chill spreading across her. It grew over her shoulder and down her arm to a pair of delicate wrists. Delilah turned away from him and curled into a ball.

Inácio gulped.

Her hair was a wild mess of purple shades across the pillow; a beautiful mess. The strands separated just enough to show off the scar she was so protective of. He frowned the worry off his face, taking her chin in one hand and the back of her head in the other. Inácio knew exactly how much force it would take. His fingers constricted tightly. Delilah turned on her side and readjusted her face into his palm as if his hold was adding comfort.

A loud mechanical rumble sent his creeping hands jolting back to his sides.

The garage door.

Inácio did a painful hop to the bedroom door, his bruises and cuts throbbing at his swiftness. He softly closed the door behind him and thumped his bare heels across the kitchen floor to the garage entrance. His heart sprung from his chest cavity as he opened the door and saw several men exit a large Suburban. They parked right beside a beaten-up coupe. There was no hiding the damage now.

The SUV rocked as one man after another stepped out like a carload of clowns. It didn't stop at four or five but continued until the seventh man slammed the door behind him. Inácio ran his fingers flat through his bedhead. Today, slight ease slowed his vitals when he noticed Schafer among the group. Woody trailed behind, looking like Schafer's nephew.

"Didn't expect you to be in your jammies. Sorry friend." Schafer smiled below a pair of striking split irises. His right eye was as deep brown as Inácio's and his left was a rich green. As usual, his dark blonde hair was kept short and neat. His dimples popped over a clean-shaven face. The two shook hands and greeted one another like old friends. "I brought someone for you to meet."

A dark-haired man with a thick mustache behind Schafer peeked out from over his shoulder. Four bodyguards encircled him, as if to create a wall between Inácio and who they were protecting. Inácio's shoulders raised with tension. The largest guard towered, forcefully spreading Inácio's limbs and patting down his drawstring shorts and plain T-shirt. A blade in its leather sheath slipped from his waistband.

Schafer laughed in amusement.

Inácio shot him a look.

"This is funny to you, huh?"

"Every time you're armed, and every time, they take it away."

"How did you fit this one in the car?" Inácio asked, catching the guard's eye.

"Can't you see there's no controlling this one?" Schafer held back a snort. There wasn't much that could rile him up. It was what made him a perfect handler. When Inácio was free, Schafer continued. "I would like you to meet Díaz, our newly promoted primary connection in South America. Díaz, we call this fine prodigy, Inácio."

A chubby hand shook his in a bone-crushing grip.

"They speak very well of you in high places, Inácio."

"That's nice."

Woody shifted behind Díaz, his eyes following the scrapes across Inácio's knuckles.

"I have always enjoyed the architecture of this house." Schafer strolled through the open floor plan, looking around. "This minimalist thing it's got going on, not so much. The style has no warmth, and no..." He snapped his fingers for the word as he looked through one of the enormous living room windows.

"Vibrance," Díaz filled in.

"Exactly! Where's the color? Oh well, I don't gotta stay here, but I think it fits Inácio's personality perfectly." He winked his green eye. "These windows though..." He knocked on the ceiling-high glass and nodded.

"They're ballistic, maybe." Inácio smiled, taking his seat on the sofa.

"Security gaps at a safe house? Never heard of such a thing."

"We might find out one day."

"True that!" Schafer whistled at Woody, walking two fingers in the air. Woody, who was just about to sit down, aborted the plan and retreated to the outdoor patio. The back of Inácio's neck tingled upon hearing the footsteps of the guards taking their stations around them.

Schafer slid his briefcase across the glass coffee table and plopped down. "Where shall we begin, Díaz? The next contract?"

"No, let us begin at the last contract first." His accent placed him from Peru, by Inácio's guess.

"Very well, you can start us off then." Schafer sat back in his chair. The natural light brought out the dimensions in his green iris.

"I will be truthful with you, Inácio. I received a very disturbing phone call last night," Díaz began.

"Sounds unfortunate."

Schafer grinned in silence.

"It is for you. Our client contacted us and is very unhappy. Normally, we never allow a client to contact us again without payment, but I made an exception."

"Sounds like great customer service. You realize we are a criminal enterprise?"

Díaz opened images on his phone and presented them. "This client wanted to know how our people could do such a sloppy job."

"Sloppy? Orders were to make it public and overly dramatic. I think I exceeded those standards." Inácio didn't pay much attention to the photos of the scene.

"Quite the opposite, actually." He swiped to different images. "By killing a man other than your target, you have directed the media attention away from the original target. Putting Geerman's death top in the headlines was also part of the deal. Did you not read the entire directive?"

"That other man was nothing compared to the target."

"The world begs to differ. That man was part of the protection detail for *the* Anita Reyes."

Inácio shrugged. "Who?"

"She's part of the US president's cabinet and the founder of an organization that rescues women from sex trafficking rings—"

Inácio choked on his spit, sending him into a coughing fit.

"Is there something funny about what I just said?"

"Erm, a little, but go on."

"As I was saying, because you brought her into this, the media is focusing more on her and her dead bodyguard than the client's target."

"The man's dead. What more does he want?" Inácio asked, pulling off a ball of lint from his pants.

"Your sloppiness has turned worldwide attention to the horrors of modern slavery instead of the corruption of a popular televised business investor. There are conspiracies flying all over the place that Reyes was the target, and it was all a secret plot to destroy her fight against trafficking."

"They got it all wrong. I did it for awareness."

"Schafer, when I was told about this man, I expected more. From what I have witnessed so far, he does not act or conduct himself with the professional nature that our organization demands of someone in his position."

"Alright. Díaz, I sincerely apologize for the impression you are getting from him right now. He is one of our best, and if something happened that was not in the agreement, I am positive he had a good reason. Right?"

"Is that reason splattered across the back of that Mercedes?" pressed Díaz.

Inácio began a staring contest in response.

"Señor Díaz, please," Schafer began. "It is my belief that we have to maintain a certain level of trust with our guns. Inácio has been operatin' under my supervision for years, and I have given him some wiggle room to work with. Now, he's used to that, and I don't think controlling a man's every move is good for him."

"And when a man takes advantage of that freedom, he needs to be reined in. Your wiggle room sounds like it was an absence of leadership."

"Something must have happened for things to go the way they did. That is all I'm saying. And as you can see, he handled whatever it was, and that is also his job."

"Tell us what happened. I would love to hear it." Díaz hunched forward.

"I want my next assignment, Schafer."

"You cannot ignore this, Inácio." Díaz sighed. "Okay. Let's play it your way. Nothing out of the ordinary happened. So, what then? You cannot hit a target from one-hundred meters?"

"I can see my targets just fine."

"I am not so sure about that. Maybe you hit the wrong guy first either out of inaccuracy or poor eyesight. Have you completed contracts from this distance before?"

"What kind of question is that?"

"Well, as someone who works behind a desk the majority of the time, can you describe to me the kind of detail you personally can see through the scope at that range?"

"I can see what a person is wearing, the way they style their hair, facial expressions." Images of wind-teased purple hair flashed through his memory. The way the man's large hand had wrapped around her neck. Inácio crunched the arm of the chair. That was who should have died.

"Are you listening? Can you distinguish between a male and a female, for example?"

"Yes."

"Can similar clothing and physical attributes throw you off? For instance, if your target is a man in a black suit and he is standing next to another man who is dressed the same with similar physical features, do you ever hesitate?"

"Are we talking twins or cousins?"

"We will see what the boss has to say about this." The new man locked his phone, making the pictures disappear.

Schafer's eyes bugged out. "He hasn't contacted me regarding this. Díaz, if the boss has a problem, he will reach out to us. That is how we know it's a real problem."

"Who do you think connected me with the unhappy client?"

"Well, in that case…" Schafer sat back in surrender.

"I haven't heard any concrete reason for this collateral damage, so I will be meeting with the Philosopher later this week. You can be sure there will be a *demotion*."

"Why should we wait? Let's call him now," Inácio suggested. Both men looked at him like he was crazy.

"How do you have his number? You must be bluffing!" Desperation exacerbated Díaz's voice. Inácio pulled his cell from his pocket and found a number he knew even Schafer was unaware of. Díaz shut his mouth and listened to the dial tone. He could imagine Schafer's ears would be bleeding if they could.

"I've got clout, as they say," Inácio informed.

No one called on the Philosopher. He always called on you.

A scrambled voice answered over speakerphone. A ghostly deep sound speaking from another dimension.

"Inácio, what can I do for you?"

"Thank you for accepting my call, sir. I have Schafer and your new man, Díaz, sitting across from me. We are discussing my contract at White Shores." Inácio couldn't help but glance over at the new associate's perplexed face. Díaz thought he knew how they operated, but Inácio was happy to educate him with the truth.

"How may I be of assistance?"

"I believe there is a misunderstanding in what I can and cannot do as your employee. I have always been led to believe collateral damage isn't an automatic demotion. As you know, I have had no other previous incidents like this come to light. Have I not earned a little trust that everything I do is for the success of the assignment?"

"You have. I only told Díaz to speak to the client, not discipline you. Why is there confusion?"

"You may want to ask Díaz, sir. He is adamant the hammer is coming down hard on this one."

"Let me speak to him." Díaz's eyes widened at the Philosopher's words. He reluctantly held out a sweaty palm, accepting the phone. After taking a breath, he answered. It was well known that the Philosopher had the final say in all matters of life and death, including for themselves. If "the man upstairs" wanted you dead, there was no escape.

With Díaz sweating in his chair, Inácio stood up.

"Want a drink?"

"Yes please," Schafer agreed. The two men fell back to the full-size bar near the kitchen. Schafer leaned over the counter while Inácio clinked around with the glasses from the other side. "Some psycho crap you pulled in there."

"I never claimed to be sane."

Schafer grabbed his glass of bourbon and sank it.

"Would you gentlemen like a drink as well?" Inácio sarcastically asked the guards, who were standing motionless around Schafer. No response, of course. Inácio threw his glass down once he finished it.

"It's alright Inácio, they're harmless."

"I know they are. I still don't like them here. Why punish the rest of us because of a few bad apples? It's been two years since one of us butchered their handler. Is this permanent now?"

"Why don't you make a complaint to the big man since you're so close?" Schafer finally took a seat in a stool.

"Not that close."

"I wonder if anyone is. Sometimes I wonder if he's American, or Italian, or Greek."

"Probably Russian."

"Heh, you know it. Coming to us live from the Russian Federation building in Moscow."

"Or Iranian."

"Mm, good point. Wait, don't stop there. How about North Korean?" There was a short pause of consideration but both men laughed at the absurdity.

"Another?" Inácio raised the bottle.

"You bet. We better be careful though. Who knows what will come out of our mouths after a few rounds. They probably bug every safe house with a bar."

A stick figure with four eyes appeared in the doorway.

"Sit down with us, Woody. Have a drink, my man." Schafer patted the stool beside him.

"Sir, when would you like me to go over the next contract?"

"Hand it to me, I'll do it. What would you like? Whisky? A dirty martini?"

"Uh, well I don't know. Still on the clock." His eyes darted around the room. He was the smallest creature there. Schafer patted him hard on the back.

"It's not a test, buddy. Don't worry. Go ahead and give him something girly. I can't imagine Woody here went to very many college parties while he was on campus, did ya?"

"If I did, I wouldn't have gotten a 4.0." His eyelids fluttered like he was above that kind of thing.

"Oh, that's true, ain't it? So maybe it's better you stayed in the library. You wouldn't be here otherwise." Schafer gave Inácio a discreet nod, its meaning only known between good friends. "Go ahead! It won't hurt you."

Woody drank it down like it was a glass of water, then returned it all over the bar top.

"Woo, I didn't realize how much I needed that today," the handler cackled.

"What was that?" Woody brushed his tongue with a towel.

"Here, drink some water." Inácio filled a new glass from the faucet and handed it to him.

Woody hesitated.

"It's water. You saw yourself where it came from," Schafer assured. Woody smelled it, carefully tasted it, then chugged it. "Damn. If that was whiskey, you'd be an alcoholic."

"That it?" Inácio pointed to the folder that had barely missed getting covered in tequila regurgitation.

"Yeah, it is, in fact." Schafer opened the folder and tossed the pictures over.

"He looks… flamboyant." Photos showed a colorful satin scarf over a tight-fitting shirt. The next target was dripping in bright jewelry and had a yellow streak in his swooped-back hairdo.

"Comes with the territory. He's a designer for Carnival floats or something like that."

"It's serious business." It wasn't sarcasm.

"Guess so. You should know better than any of us. The guy has a winning streak going."

"Success brings haters."

“This should be a Carnival to remember. The client wants no witnesses and no traces left behind.”

“It says here ‘during the performance.’ I’m supposed to kill this guy during the parade with millions of people watching?” Inácio couldn’t imagine it was possible.

“I’m leaving behind a lethal compound. My suggestion is, stick him somewhere hard for a medical examiner to notice. It will take only a minute or two for him to drop once you inject. The goal is to have people believe he died from a heart attack, doing what he loved. Client doesn’t want to make him into a martyr. Don’t tell me it’s too much for you after all you’ve done to that drug cartel.”

“I’ll get it done.” *Somehow.*

“The date for that is solid, and whenever is up to you. As long as it’s during the parade. You won’t be receiving any confirmation. Everything is all set and paid in full. Which reminds me, you might want to get your phone back.” Schafer looked back over his shoulder toward the living room.

“Ah, he looks a little busy with the boss. Afraid he’ll see my nudes?”

“I do need to be serious for a second.” The handler’s tone dropped.

“Go ahead.”

“Whatever happened at the hotel and to the car, it won’t blow back on us, right?”

“You know better than to ask that. It’s over.”

“Thank god.” Schafer slumped over in his seat. “Because right now the boss is giving that serious bastard the chewing out of his life—for you.”

“It’s not for me.”

“Either way, the boss is putting you in the clear. It would suck to lose you if anything happened.” They both knew he was talking about the Philosopher’s power to eliminate anyone.

“You would miss me?” Inácio forced a smile, trying to keep it lighthearted.

“A little. My workload wouldn’t be so heavy, so that’s a plus.” He shrugged. His finger rubbed his brown eye.

"I have a feeling I wouldn't be the only one paying the price. They'd at least take one of your fingers. I wouldn't want to see you punished like that."

"Shut up. You don't have feelings." Schafer swallowed down another sip.

"True." Inácio gently swished his drink around over the bar top. If only it were true, for his sake. Saving that girl was an irreversible blunder. His eyes moved from the bottom of his liquor to his index finger, tapping away at the glass. He forced it to stop. In front of him Schafer joked away with his trainee, and in the other room, the Philosopher was defending him to Díaz. Inácio had betrayed each of them and it was all because he *did have* feelings.

He had to fix this before it got worse.

21

DELILAH

Feverish dreams trapped Delilah inside her own subconscious. Knuckles connecting with flesh and the violent howling of men repeated on a loop, making her squirm beneath the covers. A heaviness settled into her chest. She breathed deeply to push against the pressure. Fallen tears tickled the corners of her eyes as she saw Carson instead of a stranger holding her down in the parking lot. Hatred burned with every punch and choke of his fingers. She kicked off the covers. It felt too real to be a nightmare. The hate was so familiar. Nearby was her dad, who didn't seem to notice or care.

Delilah forced the image of her rescuer's bulging muscles into her mind. To her relief, strong tatted arms entered the frame to take control of her adversary. The veins in Carson's neck strained until his head exploded. Goopy blood covered the sky and her entire body. Her ears hummed and rang at the imaginary gunfire. Delilah's heart raced as she waited for the torment to end.

Don't fight it, his voice said.

She fell and jolted awake to pitch darkness. Blinking away the distorted memories, she realized it was all a dream and only half-real.

With a heavy head, Delilah distanced herself from the bed. Anything to stop herself from reliving her worst experiences. Her balance returned when the wood turned to cold tile beneath her bare soles, the light to the bathroom causing her to shield her eyes.

When her groggy pupils stopped rejecting the light, an alarming sight stared back at her in the mirror. Slowly, she took her first good look at her reflection. It was like she had been swept into a whirlwind of danger and trauma and spit out again. Dark circles had formed under her sunken eyes. Delilah pressed against the cut on her swollen bottom lip, one of her cheeks puffy from a cut. Her stomach sank, recalling the man's brutal backhand. The dark hole called for her return. Giving up seemed like the easier way out than the fight to hold on to her dignity. Freezing sink water on her face broke her free from the thought. She tamed her wild hair until it settled into its natural waves, then forced her stitched-up arm to move.

Changed and refreshed, Delilah pulled the door toward her, cautious about making a sound in the strange home. She stopped to listen but heard nothing. The halls and rooms reached high and wide. The living room was empty and surrounded by long draping curtains. Her fingers ran across an unused dining table. It was hard for her to picture someone like her rescuer eating a bowl of cereal like a normal person.

In the living room, Delilah admired the tall windows. Only her own figure reflected back at her through the dark glass while she tiptoed by, her hand running into the curtains as she did. There was something haunting about the fancy home. She caressed the white fabric of the cushioned chairs until she brushed over a dark shirt hung sloppily over a headrest. Its width spread almost completely across the back of the chair. A T-shirt made for size.

Bulky equipment at the far end caught the corner of her eye. Large round weights were stacked beside a bench press. A rack of barbells stood nearby and a treadmill faced a window. The equipment looked out of place resting on shiny marble. There was no feminine touch anywhere. It was plain, practical, and had "bachelor pad" written all over it. A humid draft whispered over her skin, drawing Delilah to the sliding door. Deep panting huffed through the open crack. Outside, the pool spread its blue glow all around a walled outdoor patio. At the edge of the water was a dark shape, moving rapidly in a prone position. It was him: Inácio. His naked back was slick with sweat and he was in the middle of a round of push-ups.

No guy she'd met before was even in the same cosmos as this man. The amount of skill it took to achieve what he had the previous night was unfathomable to her normie brain. Still, it fell second to the *why* behind his actions as what baffled her the most. The chime of a ringtone interrupted his muscle pump. Inácio raised a knee and walked over to the patio table to answer the glowing brick. As a voice mumbled through the speaker, he paced, his chest rising and falling with labored breaths.

Delilah's greedy eyes drew her from behind the curtain, inch by inch. Blue reflected water shimmered over the waves of strength bound to his torso. His pearlescent skin was a bright radiance to a hungry soul. When her secret admiration turned intrusive, Delilah retreated from the patio door and returned to her millions of thoughts.

After finding a quiet place on the couch away from the grunts of masculine prowess, Delilah recited an explanation for her absence, her breakup, all of it, to her dad. Her reflection stared back at her through the glass coffee table.

"Dad, I am sorry… I apologize if my actions caused any worry about… Regarding my absence and failing to contact you after…" *What if he's more angry than worried? When was the last time he was actually worried about you?* Delilah knew there would need to be at least two speeches prepared, depending on how deep his frown lines went.

"Do you think being nosy is more of a woman trait or just an American one?"

Delilah had hardly noticed Inácio out of the corner of her eye before he spoke. "Oh my god!" Her hand clutched the center of her chest and she found herself scooting to the other side of the sofa. His wide frame towered over the armchair. "Did I do something?"

"Next time you want to stare, at least announce your presence." Inácio sidestepped around the back of the couch.

Delilah twisted around fast. Something inside her told her to keep an eye on him. He walked with an eerie rigidity, rounding the corner to the bedroom she slept in. This wasn't the hero she remembered. Should she get up? Should she apologize? The blackness that peeked from behind the enormous curtains attracted her eyes in her confusion.

"Turn your arm toward me." His sharp words jolted her from the cushion again. Delilah's toes perched themselves on the rug, ready to send her sprinting at a moment's notice.

"If you don't mind me saying, you're really quiet for someone your size." She looked for a reply, even a smile, but nothing.

Inácio, with medical supplies in his hand, joined Delilah on the love seat, sending a tsunami of force across the upholstery.

Delilah hugged her arm close. "Why do you want to help me if you're so mad at me?"

"It's not you. Now please, I need to clean your wound." Inácio's frown relaxed, but barely.

In one slow motion, Delilah gave over her maimed limb.

"It's nothing personal," he said while unwrapping the bandage.

Delilah replied in a soft, dejected tone. "Could've fooled me."

"Remember, I don't know you and you don't know me. That's the way it will stay." The sting of the alcohol in swollen flesh followed.

"Is that it?" Delilah inspected her arm.

"That's it," he said, screwing the cap back onto the bottle.

"I don't need a new bandage?"

"Let it breathe. You heal fast anyway. It'll be even better tomorrow." A flicker of anger came over his face, so quick one would miss it if they blinked. Inácio's constriction around Delilah's wrist tightened when he should have already let go. A nerve was pinched under the pressure.

"Ouch!"

Inácio's fingers released her.

"That hurt a little." Again, Delilah waited for a response. A casual "I'm sorry" would have settled the wariness in her gut. The only thing she got in return was a pair of dark eyes that were far detached from the present moment. A whiny rumble from her stomach broke the rising tension. It was the type of sound most people would find embarrassing for anyone else to hear.

"You're hungry," he said in a plain manner.

She only nodded.

"I bet you're starving." Inácio sprung up. "Let me get you something to eat."

Delilah clawed at her belly, angry with its vocal demands. She didn't want to be around this man anymore.

"I haven't felt it at all until now." Her small talk was a cover for how she was really feeling about him. Delilah took her time joining Inácio in the kitchen. She slinked her butt across a stool and rested her good arm across the cold counter. The refrigerator door revealed a bright light over his face. It highlighted the bluish bruise around his cut eyebrow.

"We have…" He rummaged through the shelves. "I hope you're not a vegan."

"Nope. My dad would never allow that." *Dad.* Never again would she squirm at the idea of calling him. At least he would be there for her no matter how disappointed he was.

"Good, because I only have protein and carbs." He took out a container and tossed it in the microwave.

"Um, can I ask what time it is?" Delilah's nail scratched at a slight imperfection in the smooth granite.

"It's 23:55." He glanced at his watch. "So for you that's—"

"Wow, it's so late."

"You know military time?"

"My dad uses it for work. He refused to let me grow up without knowing about it."

"Right, your dad… the detective." It was hard to tell if he hated that her dad was a detective or if he couldn't care less.

While her food spun, Inácio stood by with his big arms crossed. The T-shirt's sleeves were stretched tight over his biceps. They had the "fresh from the gym" look. Delilah noticed the veins cutting across his swollen muscles. She ran her eyes up to his shoulders and bulging traps. She would be no match for him. His chin was down and it looked like he was staring at a floor tile. He didn't make eye contact with her once.

The microwave screeched, ending the silence between them. Inácio stabbed a fork at the center of the food and put it in front of her.

"Thanks." She moved her utensil around a hot mound of rice and chicken. She dove in without thought. Her eyes teared up and she slapped her hand over her mouth.

"Too hot?"

"Well…" She swallowed. "More like spicy."

"Sorry, I should have warned you. I like a lot of flavor." He grabbed a glass and began filling it with milk. "That should help."

Delilah took a drink, letting the milk settle her tingling tongue.

"Do you need me to make you something else?"

"Don't worry about it. I have to leave soon anyway." She took a smaller bite this time, drinking the milk along with it.

"Where do you plan on going? Back to the hotel?" Inácio's palm flattened across the counter in front of her. Afterward, he took a swig of a cold shake from the fridge and finally looked at her, giving her a side-eye.

"The hotel? Never. So I should probably mention that I got dumped. That's how you found me way out… wherever I was. My boyfriend kicked me out."

"I see."

She set her glass down harder than she intended. *That's it? That's all he has to say?* She didn't understand him. As a stranger, he'd rescued her and never wondered what had gotten her in trouble in the first place? His coldness was contributing to the construction of her inner wall. Delilah was going to make it as high and impenetrable as possible.

"Well, I'm full now." Leaving the food unfinished, Delilah held it up for him to take as if he were nothing more than a waiter.

Inácio reached for the plastic bowl, his fingers brushing over hers. Delilah seized her hand back so fast, she practically punched herself in the stomach. The bowl bounced off the edge of the kitchen counter and splattered its contents on the floor. As the bowl oscillated its way to stillness, Delilah saw Inácio strangle the fingers which had touched her as if he were grabbing a searing pan. It was difficult to tell, but if she was right, she swore she saw a flash of concern lighten his eyes.

Then, like a computer program being reset, he dropped his fingers and straightened. "No worries," he said. Inácio took the bowl and glass and put them in the sink. Delilah's stomach churned with spices and worry. The man whom she considered to be her hero was still a stranger and very possibly a dangerous one.

"I'd like to call my parents now." Delilah sat upright and put her shoulders back as a show of confidence.

"You can later." He stared at the mess on the floor, expressionless. Delilah's hand came over the tingle in her chest, anxiety brewing.

"No, I'd like to now. They need to know I'm okay and that I'm not doing any of this on purpose." She sat up, refilling her shaky lungs to continue the display of composure.

"You've run away before?" Inácio raised his head with a slight twinkle in his eyes.

Delilah gulped. "I just need to make one call, that's it."

"You can't do that."

"Then I want to leave, please." Delilah lurched from the stool, but Inácio stayed silent, his murky gaze glued to her. The door through which he'd carried her glowed with the promise of freedom. Delilah locked in on her exit at a pace hardly able to hide the attempt at an escape. Her eye tracked the man in her periphery. "Thank you so much for all you've done," she said as she trailed off.

Delilah felt him behind her but couldn't hear him.

She didn't dare look back.

22 INÁCIO

"You won't get out that way." Inácio crossed his arms and came to terms with his own emotions being more transparent than he'd thought. The woman picked up on his intentions like prey sniffing out a crouching wolf. Delilah's entire body rattled as she yanked on the doorknob.

"What's the code?" Her finger jabbed at the touch screen, typing in random numbers.

"You're not leaving. It locks from the inside."

"Just tell me the password!"

"Delilah, stop." Inácio closed in.

"Why won't you let me leave?" Delilah panted as if she were running a marathon.

"Will you come sit down, please?" Without a thought, he grabbed her wrist, determined to *make* her calm down.

"Don't touch me!" Her sharp scream of resistance caught Inácio off guard and he let go immediately. Delilah fell back and hit the marble, hard.

"I'm sorry!" Inácio reached down, but Delilah scooted away and ran across the house toward the door leading to the back patio. The sliding door opened for her with ease. She shut it behind her as if something so trivial could slow him down. His heart surged with doubt. Controlling the situation was easy. Controlling her emotions was not.

Delilah ran straight for the padlocked exit in the far corner behind the pool. Her bare heel kicked the dense wood and she leaped for the top edge of the walls surrounding the property.

"Let me out!" After kicking the door once more, Delilah grabbed her ankle and winced in pain.

"There's no way out unless I let you out. You think you can kick down that door? Or jump over ten-foot walls?" Inácio edged his way around the pool, the blue water creating a flickering glow between them.

"Please, Inácio, unlock the door."

"You must love putting yourself in danger. How far do you think you can get while barefoot, with no money, no ID, and no one to protect you?"

"Far enough away from you!"

"You want to run into the same situation I found you in? Have some common sense!"

"I'm already in danger with you." Delilah stormed back toward the house, keeping herself out of arm's reach of Inácio. The anxiety that had ruled her senses before was now an unconquerable rage. He didn't dare try to grab her out of fear of her screams attracting anyone who happened to be nearby.

"What are you doing?" Inácio was on her heels, imagining the woman throwing a weighted plate from the gym through one of the windows and escaping across the jagged boulders leading down to the ocean.

Delilah marched through the living room without so much as a hint of the injury she must've suffered from kicking the door. Her purple hair swished as she sprinted around the corner beside the master bedroom. Inácio jogged, catching up just in time to see her gritting her teeth before slamming the door in his face. The lock clicked before he got a grip on the handle. Delilah looked every bit as angry as a woman could be, but he wasn't buying her show. She was scared of him and he knew it.

"Delilah, open the door."

Of course, she didn't.

He put his ear up to it and heard skidding furniture. "What are you doing?"

A loud thump sounded from the other side.

"Please, let me explain," he said. *Just do what needs to be done.* "I'm not going to hurt you." Inácio shoved his fist against his lips. That was a lie, right? *They're going to kill me if I don't.* "I don't know if I can do it," he whispered so only he could hear. He leaned his arm against the door and buried his forehead in his elbow. In twenty-four hours, he'd gone from hero to enemy in her eyes.

"Leave me alone!"

"This is not how this works."

"What are you going to do to me?"

"Nothing." *Clean this up.*

"You're lying!" A bang followed her words.

"Are you breaking the window? Stop!" *Better you than what she would have faced on the streets. It's a mercy kill, dammit.* Another metallic crash sounded from the other side. "Just stop!"

"No!" Delilah's voice turned raspy.

With a solid kick to the bedroom door, Inácio's sole connected with the sweet spot just below the handle. It moved as much as the padlocked patio door had for Delilah. Inácio stormed into the home gym and stole the heaviest round plate that he could lift over his head.

"I've had enough of this," he grumbled. He returned to the door, raised it over his head, and dropped it onto the handle. It bent down and he brought it down again. The metal handle snapped like a twig. Inácio shoved his shoulder into it, bracing himself on the frame. The furniture stacked on the other side screeched across the floor.

Through the growing opening, he could see Delilah chucking trash cans, her suitcase, and whatever else she could find at the picture window. The glass held its own, but cracks began to spread like the roots of a tree. Fury raged through his veins. Inácio charged the door and sent her barricade of chairs and a dresser toppling.

"Put it down," Inácio ordered. Delilah only clutched the trash can harder, and with her good arm, swung the metal can toward the weakened window. Inácio lurched forward and smacked her weapon to the floor. "That's it!" Inácio stepped forward and caught Delilah, trapping her arms at her sides. The moment his skin touched hers, he knew he couldn't kill her. Her soft hair flew in his face, wafting the smell of his own shampoo's fragrance.

"Don't hurt me! Let me go!" She kicked and squirmed, making him feel like a monster. Inácio lifted her higher to avoid her strikes.

"I'm not going to hurt you!" What was meant to communicate his gentleness came out in a growl. Inácio eased her down to the bedside rug until he kneeled beside her. Delilah continued to push back, trying to gain leverage. He tried to sound calm. "I am not going to hurt you." Inácio's cheek rested beside her temple. Delilah's heart thumped under his arm as she paused to catch her breath.

"Then why won't you let me call my parents?!" she huffed.

"Because…" Inácio's eyes squinted shut.

"Why?" Delilah pulled away. "It doesn't make any sense!"

"I know."

"Then what? Are you just planning to hold me hostage forever?"

"No." Inácio searched for a half-reasonable excuse.

"Why did you even rescue me? Why?!"

Inácio couldn't answer without scaring her—without scaring himself.

"I want to be safe. I just want to be safe!" Delilah buried her head between her knees. The desperation tightening her muscles shook as it released its hold. Delilah's weight dropped and Inácio unwrapped himself from her. She took her stitched arm in one hand and scooted until her back was pressed against the edge of the bed. Her glare, driven by her need for answers, scorched into him.

Inácio sat back against a nearby wardrobe. "Do you remember when you asked me to take you to the hospital?"

She nodded.

"And I said I couldn't let you because you'd seen my face?"

"Yeah, you didn't want to get in trouble for anything. But going to a hospital and calling my parents are two different things. I don't get it."

"Why do you think I don't want you talking to your dad?"

"Ohh… the detective thing? He's in the US, he wouldn't—He *couldn't* do anything about it." Delilah's teeth scraped against her bottom lip, telling him otherwise.

"I can't say I know any detectives personally, but I think one would want to find the truth after seeing his daughter injured."

"And the truth is?"

Inácio rested his arms over his knees. There was nothing he could say.

"You put your life at risk to help me. Why would you get in trouble for that?" Genuine confusion was written all over her face.

"Delilah, I don't know much about you. You know even less about me. We're not in a place where I can trust you with certain parts of my life, and I bet you feel the same when it comes to personal things about you."

The corners of her lips tightened.

"You've only been in this country for a matter of hours. I don't expect you to understand the ins and outs of the criminal world. You saw how violent those men were. That in itself is reason enough that neither you nor I should be associated with what happened last night."

"Then I want to go home, where it's safe." Her assertiveness returned. The idea made him nervous. All he could think about was his mistake coming back to bite him. How could he trust a twenty-something girl not to spill the details? If he was in her shoes, he would.

"I know you do." Inácio bit down on his tongue. It was hard to say no to a girl who looked as exhausted as she did. Delilah's wavy hair was snarled into a mess, dark circles were painted just above her cheekbones, and her eyes were red with fear and grief.

"You gotta understand, I have to get back to my mom. My dad isn't—or hasn't been—the most supportive lately. I'm the only one she has. If I'm not there, she could spiral again. I can't go—"

"Alright. If you need to get to your family as soon as possible, I'll make it happen." Shit.

"Really?" Delilah perked up, pink rushing to her cheeks.

"First, listen to me."

"Okay," she said with enthusiasm.

"You were never here and I never rescued you." Inácio refused to blink as he explained.

"Then how do I explain all this?" Delilah's hand motioned over her whole body.

"Maybe you got mugged. Maybe you did go to the hospital. Whatever your story is, it will not include me or the men I found you with."

"Whatever, I get it, that's no problem."

"No you don't. You're just excited to get home."

"It's not just that—"

"Delilah, if what happened to you gets out, more people like those bad men are going to come to your home and hurt your family. Do you see what I'm saying now?"

She swallowed.

"They know your name, and they won't forget it."

"Sure, I lost my license out there, but I can't see anyone coming after me in America."

"They will know because you are connected to me. That's all I can tell you."

"I'll lie. I promise." Delilah nodded with a look of certainty. It was as good of a promise as he was going to get.

"We'll go to the airport first thing in the morning." Inácio studied her as he rose to his feet, unsure of his decision. It wasn't the smartest decision, just the right one. It was rare for him to do the right thing.

"Thank you."

"Sure." Inácio cleaned up the mess in the room, returning the furniture to its proper place. He slid one curtain across the damaged window, then the other. The busted door he returned to, he could do nothing about.

"Inácio?" she called out. He halted in the doorway. To hear his name leave her lips ran chills down his spine, even if the name was just an alias. A faint desire that they could have met in another way whispered to him.

"Yes?"

"You never told me why you rescued me." Delilah sat beside her spilled clothes, folding each one. For the first time since he first saw her, she looked hopeful.

"You were all alone. Who else was going to do it?" Inácio turned and left the bedroom.

Things would get better once she was out of his life.

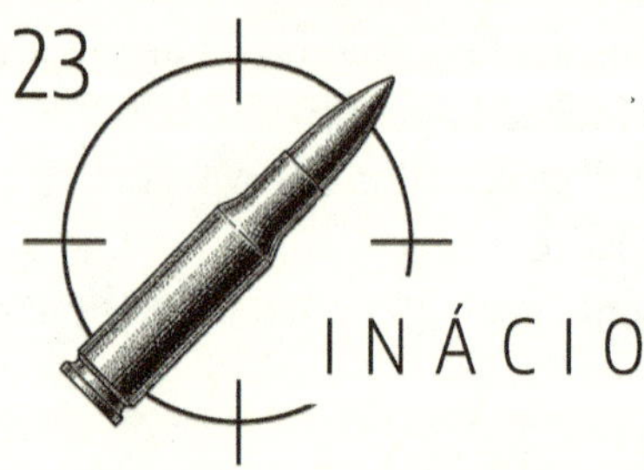

23 INÁCIO

Once Inácio squeezed into a space in the passenger drop-off zone, he habitually studied his surroundings. There was peak traffic at the airport, the wide automatic doors having little time to stay closed for more than a second. Their car was pinned between dozens of other vehicles, which forced them along the limited space of the curb. People were spilling out of taxis and vans, in an obvious hurry. Others took their time to savor group hugs before reluctantly walking away.

Right in front of his bumper, a young couple was intertwined, tears streaming down their faces. Drivers pounded on their horns and pedestrians hollered down the street, yet none of the noise broke the couple's concentration from each other. The man held her face and stared into her eyes like he was memorizing every detail. It was true love playing out right in front of him; something he could never have. Inácio finally broke his stare.

Other than the gushiness of the lovers, nothing else in his environment raised any hair on his body. Everything was normal and ordinary, just like the woman who stared out the passenger window toward the airport. Delilah's hair was brushed behind her back. The sunlight highlighted her clavicle running in front of her slender shoulder. In all his eagerness to get rid of her, he'd lost touch with his purpose for taking her in. His *real* purpose. Delilah's graceful features raised it to the surface. She dug around in her purse, locating her passport and other belongings.

"Do you have everything?"

"Everything but my driver's license." A cute dimple formed under a disappointed smirk.

"You've got your passport. It should be fine. Take this with you." Inácio handed over a burner. "You can text and make calls as long as you're connected to the Wi-Fi."

Delilah clicked the button on the side, waking up the screen. "Thanks. Kinda wish I had this sooner."

"Don't forget this." Scissored between two fingers was a wad of Brazilian bills.

She scoffed under her breath. "Keep your money."

Inácio grabbed the hand in her lap and slapped the money in her palm. While he cradled her hand between his own, she looked him in the eye. It was enough for him to snatch himself away and return to gripping the top of the steering wheel. The longer she lingered, the harder it was to get back to his proper numb self. Delilah sighed and shoved the cash into her empty wallet.

"Déjà vu. Chew her up and spit her out. It's okay as long as you give her money," Delilah muttered.

"And one more thing." Inácio twisted around to face her. "Do I need to remind you why you can't say a word about this?"

"No." Her eyes rolled. "They can hurt me or my family. I get it."

"Exactly."

"You really can't tell me who they are or who you are?"

"No."

"Figures."

"Give them anything but the truth."

"Don't worry, you never happened." It was everything and the last thing he wanted to hear all at once. Delilah flung the door open with her foot. Inácio watched her from his mirror. She stood beside the taillight, probably expecting him to get out and open the trunk for her. Inácio barely moved a centimeter before both hands clenched around the wheel. A force inside him refused to let him exit the car. Like a sadistic tease, the couple ahead of them were still glued to one another, the man unable to let the woman go. Back in the reflection of the rear-view mirror, Delilah crossed her arms and looked around. His ass still felt frozen in place.

Inácio hung his head low. The reality was, he was no different than the sappy boyfriend in front of him. Ever since he could remember, he'd been deprived of his innermost desires. The deprivation starved him like slow torture. It only took doing the right thing of saving a stranger for him to realize just how much.

His body allowed his arm to reach for the trunk lever. Inácio cringed, feeling the car barely jolt. *Just let her go.* Delilah dragged her enormous suitcase across the compartment and dropped it with a sloppy thud. Inácio's toes curled in his boots out of amazement and disappointment that he could let her struggle on her own. He could kill men for her, but acting like a gentleman was too far?

With a tug, she jumped the wheels to the curb and rolled it behind her. Inácio watched her disappear into the crowd. The back of her was the last he would ever see of Delilah. He had to forget about the beauty that had driven him to pull the trigger and ignore how buttery her skin had felt in his hands.

24

DELILAH

Delilah looked back over her shoulder. Between the rush of people, she could see his tinted windows, too dark for her to see his shape in the driver's seat. Behind his ice-cold personality, she sensed something warm. Although there were only glimpses of it between his rigidity, Delilah was sure of what she felt. She paused, a moment of gratitude enticing her to say one last thank you. Then Inácio and his dinged-up car sped off.

Never mind, all men are assholes—even the heroes, apparently.

A hard shove sent her new cell phone flying to the ground.

"*Desculpe-me*," said a man. Delilah gasped and squatted down to pick it up, teeth grinding as if in preparation for an attack.

The stranger jogged toward the airport doors with several bulky bags, hardly taking notice of her. Delilah wiped the screen, seeing only a few superficial scratches. With her protector gone, her surroundings became that much more potent. More future passengers brushed past, and the air stunk with the smell of idling engines.

A newfound sense of paranoia struck her.

Could she spot evil?

More importantly, could she spot good when she saw it?

Was the security guard who stood in the entrance a good man?

Would that other stranger with a briefcase hurt her if he had the chance?

An inner jolt rocked her each time a person entered out of the corner of her vision. Delilah studied their faces, trying to determine what was safe. She took her first step inside and saw the booking desks up ahead. Delilah blended into the shortest line which still snaked around with at least thirty people. Maybe if she called home, her sense of normalcy could return.

"Hello?" Her mom sounded tired.

"Mom?"

"Delilah! Where are you?"

"I'm still in Rio. I'm okay."

"I heard about the shooting at your hotel."

"I don't want you worrying about that. I wasn't there, I promise." Delilah left the line to find the nearest bench. She rested her head in her hand, wanting to confide in her mom just like any daughter would want to do. Delilah would give over every detail if it wouldn't break her already fragile mind.

"Are you coming home?"

"Yes, I'm getting a flight now."

Her dad's voice interrupted them in the background. "Let me see the phone, I need to talk to her."

Delilah anxiously sat up straight.

"Del?"

"It's me."

"I don't recognize this number."

"Something happened, Dad."

"Where have you been?"

"It doesn't matter. I want to come home now."

"One second." He consoled her mom and shut a door behind him. It was creaky like the front door. "Alright, I'm outside. I paid for your ticket and you disappeared. What happened?"

"I was attacked." Saying it out loud made her want to cry.

"You were there at the shooting? It's all over the news in the US."

"Sort of..."

"Stop being dodgy. Was this before or after you decided to run off with some guy?"

"What? What are you talking about?" Delilah stood up and began to pace.

"Carson told me everything."

"You talked to him?"

"I had to. You disappeared from the tracking app and I couldn't get ahold of you. He said you met a guy out there, some local from the beach. We came to the conclusion you probably ran off with him."

We?

"He said that's why you two broke up. Poor kid still sounded upset. Pretty selfish thing to do considering he basically gifted you a tropical vacation."

"And you believe I would do something like that?"

"You haven't given me much reason to think otherwise." His distrust in her made her want to rip her hair out. It was getting old.

"I've done everything I can to earn your trust back. I've been the one taking care of Mom for four years."

"It has hardly been four, and I take care of her too."

"Not as much as me. You're always at work."

"And you're away at school for nine months out of the year."

"And I still make sure she takes her meds every night."

"And who is the reason she's on all those medications, huh?"

"Whatever." Delilah couldn't argue with him on that one. "I was just calling to tell Mom I'm coming home."

"I don't think that's the best idea."

"Why not? This is not the spring break I signed up for. I'd rather be there for Mom."

"You can't keep putting her on this roller coaster and be there for her only when it's not working out for you. You need to give her space."

"How is that going to help?"

"I'll tell you. You're going to ask Carson to forgive you. Even if you don't get back together, I want you with him and his friends on the trip."

"I don't ever want to see him again." Delilah marched out of the airport as if she had somewhere else to be.

"If you want your mother to stop worrying about you then you will go back to the group. I'll call him and make sure he will at least let you tag along. He's a good kid, Del."

"He's a good kid," she mocked.

"When you do get back, I want you focused on your studies. I will take care of your mom. I think we all need a little break from you. You will be paying me back for that fligh—"

Delilah pulled the phone down from her ear and stared down at the open call.

Muted and powerless. *You're not wanted.* Her thumb found the hang-up button with ease. Delilah sniffled, wiping her face dry with the back of her hand, and pulled her wallet from her purse. Cash burst from its leather bindings.

A defiance fueled by pain and abandonment spun her toward the direction of the pick-up area. Her impulsiveness led her toward a long line of taxis. If she wasn't wanted by anyone, she didn't want them either. It was nauseating to know that everyone who came into her life seemed to want to take something from her. It was always something. Happiness, dignity, self-respect, and most recently, her life. The world wanted her to be alone, so she'd make it alone. A driver toward the back of the line leaned against his yellow car, chewing on his nails. He promptly stood up straight after noticing her approach, greeting her in Portuguese.

"Can you take me to a hostel?" she asked.

"Hostel? Yes, yes!" The driver lunged for her suitcase and lifted it with a raspy grunt. The lid to the trunk opened and then closed with a slam. Inácio's palm lay flat on the lid. The cab driver jumped away and shoved her suitcase toward him. Delilah raised her voice in instant confrontation.

"What the hell are you doing here?"

Inácio reclaimed her suitcase and grabbed her arm. "You were supposed to buy a plane ticket," he said, dragging her back toward the drop-off zone. His face was scorned with intensity.

"You left!" Delilah resisted his forceful walk down the sidewalk.

"I decided to drive by to make sure you weren't getting yourself into trouble again."

"So all the bad things that happen to me are my fault?"

He said nothing.

"Wait!" Delilah snatched her arm away. "I don't want to go home."

"I don't understand. I thought that's where you wanted to be anyway." Inácio sidestepped. His hand landed around her waist and edged her forward. She knew he could make it easy and launch her right into the airport, but he didn't. The touch was so soft, she almost wanted to follow his direction.

"Stop touching me! You're messing with my head."

Inácio released her and she planted her feet.

"Where were you trying to go?" A deep frown was etched between his eyebrows.

"Anywhere but home or back to my ex-boyfriend. I was just going to figure it out as I went along."

"That's a horrible idea."

"I know and I don't care. I really wanna know why you care. I'm nobody to you."

Tense eyebrows lifted into worry as the corners of his lips drooped.

"Tell me, or I am getting on the first taxi to nowhere."

Inácio clamped down on her wrist again. "It doesn't matter. After what happened to you before, I'm surprised by you." He pulled her farther along.

"Not that surprised, since you came back." Delilah dropped her weight and dug in her heels. "Ow!"

"Be quiet! You'll make people think that—"

"That you're hurting me? You are." Inácio let her go and she rubbed her wrist. Color slowly returned to it.

"I don't want to hurt you. I want you to be in America where you belong."

"Belong." Outrage. "Didn't you hear me? I can't go back."

"That's too bad, but you have to."

"You don't get it. I talked to my parents with the phone you gave me. My dad doesn't want me there. He'd rather me stay in Brazil, and that's what I'm going to do, without meeting his stupid conditions."

"I don't have time for this." He reached for her again and was slapped away.

"Then leave!"

"I'm trying to help you, Delilah." Inácio leaned in close, his frame blocking the sun.

"No you're not. You're trying to help yourself. You want me gone because you think I'm going to spill all your secrets or something." Delilah made a U-turn around Inácio and reached for her bag. It swung out of reach.

"What are you doing?"

"I am going to make a personal decision as an adult and run away from my problems."

"This is not adult behavior." The way he dangled her suitcase made her look and feel like a child.

Delilah cleared her throat. "I still don't know why it matters to you."

"It just does."

"You know what? Just keep it. All my clothes are yours. I have my purse and passport. That's all I need." Delilah spun on her heels and started back toward the taxis.

"Stop right there, Delilah." His hand covered her entire shoulder and whirled her around.

"If you don't want me either, why can't you just let me go?"

"I don't know." He shrugged.

"You're crazy. Now let me go!"

"I mean…" Inácio wiped the sweat forming on his forehead. "We've been through a lot together. You're not nothing. I can't help but feel responsible for you."

"So, I'm like some noble cause of yours? I am seriously grateful for everything you've done. I'm just over letting others make decisions for me. Only I can create my own happiness." Delilah drew in a breath and walked away, determined to leave with her dignity intact.

"Leave then, and take your suitcase with you."

With a turned-up nose, Delilah returned for her belongings as if it were an inconvenience. Not far in the distance, the same cabdriver watched on and tapped his leg like he hoped for another passenger other than Delilah to use his services. She tossed herself forward and he seized her bag's gold-chain strap. The unzipped purse slung over her shoulder deviated from her hip, showing off its contents. Inácio wasn't about to give up. With two fingers, he pinched her little blue passport book. It lifted from her bag with ease.

"Finally come to your senses?" she said patronizingly before noticing something familiar in his hand. "Give that back! It's the only identification I have!" Delilah grabbed at the air.

Now she'll follow me inside.

"I guess the only choice I have now is to sit right here on the sidewalk." Her butt flumped down onto the concrete, her legs crossed.

"Seriously?" Inácio tensed up.

Delilah propped herself up with one arm in a model pose.

"C'mon, I know concrete can't be comfortable on your bony butt."

"Aw, you noticed something about me," she said with a yawn. More than just the single cabdriver was interested in the drama unfolding before them. Several pulled down their sunglasses to take in the full colors. "Careful, people are starting to stare. Wouldn't want someone to tell security or something."

"This isn't what we agreed on. Why can't you just get up?"

"Why? I have nowhere to go without my passport, unless..."

Inácio was afraid to ask. "Unless what?"

"Unless I can come back to your house." Her puppy eyes made him recoil within himself.

"No. That's not possible."

She leaped to her feet. "Then just give me back what's mine and stop playing games with me."

"This isn't a game."

"It really feels like it. So unless you're going to travel with me all the way to campus to make sure I leave, just let me go. Either way, I'll be out of your life and you won't have to worry about me. Isn't that what you want?" Her lips were stretched thin in frustration. If it were feasible, he wouldn't be opposed to escorting her all the way to her dorm room. Delilah held out her palm, waiting for him to give in. "If you don't want me, just go. Turn around and let me leave."

"I can't." The response was an accident. Inácio thought he saw her eyes light up with the hope that she had somewhere to go. "I'm sorry, I know all I've done is make you upset. It's hard for me to express myself, especially when I feel like... I care deeply for someone." He fidgeted with the pages of her passport. Stress directed his focus to the sidewalk, but he couldn't stop looking at the woman he wanted. Delilah's fair skin resembled the velvety texture of new snow in a Colombian winter. Pink undertones flushed her lips to a warm rosy color. Her small jaw curved finely above her neck. Inácio wanted to slip his hand under her hair and embrace her elegant frame.

Delilah's lashes fluttered. "I really need to know what you mean by 'deeply.'"

Inácio was drawn to every motion of her lips. "What I mean is, I didn't want our time to end."

Delilah didn't advance, nor did she back away. "Why didn't you say that before?"

"Like I said, it's not easy." Inácio handed back her passport. "And it's not possible."

She flinched with disgust. "So, what now?"

"Now I leave you alone to make your own decisions. I can see that there's nothing I can do to make you go home. I can give you more money, that should help."

"No. I don't want it."

"If you're going to go your own way, you do. I really wish you'd go home. It's the safest option." *I will just stay awake all night, wondering if you're okay.* He turned from her and power-walked back down the walkway.

"Inácio, stop. You didn't even let me respond."

"It doesn't matter. I'd rather you not anyway."

"Are you scared I could feel the same way?"

Yes! I'm terrified.

"Just take the rest of my cash, Delilah." Inácio shoved another wad in her face. "Take it."

Delilah yelled after him.

"No! Just go." He couldn't handle it. Inácio stepped up his pace. Delilah needed to be out of eyesight, out of arm's reach. Zeroing in on his car, he took giant steps toward it. Her voice followed him.

"No, Inácio! Stop!" The sound of rubber wheels closed in so he went even faster.

Inácio raised his hand and motioned her away.

"This is not fair! You can't say that and just run away!"

Inácio's heart raced. He took deep breaths, trying to control the nerves that sent tremors down his legs. *Why are my legs shaking?* In a hop, he bounded off the curb and onto street level. As he reached for the car door, he saw her purple hair bounce along at the edge of his vision. Delilah's steps were choppy while she struggled to haul her suitcase and keep up with him.

It was too tempting not to flick his eyes in her direction for a second.

One second.

That was all he allowed himself.

Delilah's face was tormented with distress. Her blonde eyebrows were raised and her mouth was wide with fear. Pure fear of abandonment.

Inácio looked away.

He heard her suitcase fall from the curb and he threw himself in the driver's seat, his finger landing hard on the lock button. One hand went to the gear shift and the other wrapped tight around the steering wheel. Delilah pounded on his window and pulled the handle multiple times.

Don't look.

Inácio's foot left the brake but slammed back down after noticing the giant gaudy example of a suitcase blocking his exit. "Damnit." In the rear-view mirror another car rolled up and parked too close for him to reverse.

"Hey! Don't leave!"

Inácio rested his head in his hand, simultaneously shielding his eyes. A hollow drumming on the hood broke him from his avoidance.

"Oh my god." He peeked between his fingers and saw Delilah crawling up the hood to his windshield.

She knocked on the glass. "I can see you, kinda. Please talk to me!"

Inácio dropped his hand and took her in, all of her. Delilah was on her knees and staring right at him. He looked around and saw people pointing and gawking. It was only a matter of seconds before the authorities would get involved.

"Get off my hood and come over here," he said, punching the window down part way. Delilah jumped down, ending his impending heart attack. Sunlight and purple beauty flooded in, her fingers curling over the window's top edge. She didn't hold back.

"What I wanted to say before you walked away was that I felt it too. I could go home and be safe, but I wouldn't be happy. To hell with safe! I don't even know what that feels like. I've been living to please other people for like four freaking years. Look where it's gotten me! Why aren't we allowed to choose for ourselves? Please don't leave me, Inácio." Delilah leaned in close enough for him to smell his shampoo on her hair again.

A dryness he never knew before made it hard to swallow. A constriction settled in behind it, magnifying the discomfort. What was it? Sadness? Yearning? Inácio forced himself to stay rigid and unflinching, but his judgment faded.

"Did you hear me?" she asked, out of breath.

"Yeah, but—"

"No buts." She opened her hands as if to say, *What's the deal?* "Do you have a family or something?"

"No." Should've said yes.

"Then why are you running from me?"

"You don't know me, Delilah."

"I know you're the kind of man who would put his life on the line for a complete stranger."

"It's not safe for you to be with me. Please believe me."

"Are you some kind of career criminal or something?" Delilah's eyes narrowed.

Inácio leaned a tad closer. "What if I am? What if I'm nothing like the good person you believe me to be?"

"What if I'm not either? What if you were too quick to judge me because you think I'm my father's daughter?"

"That's completely different." Inácio started to roll up the window. Her fingers clung to the moving glass, unwilling to budge even when her fingers were an inch away from being smashed. Inácio reluctantly let it back down.

"It's not different. I've ruined lives! That's why I'm not welcome home. I've acted like the good girl for so long to make up for it. I did everything to redeem myself and still no one sees me. People throw me away like trash, but no, it's okay, it's just Delilah. Then god forbid I speak up for myself because then they just look at me like I'm still an addict."

Inácio rolled the window down all the way. Delilah's hand lowered through the window and she continued. "You're the only one who actually *saw* me when I needed help the most." Her hand landed on his, her warmth spreading. Inácio turned his hand over and held hers. "If you can accept my flaws, I can accept yours." The idea of choosing her raised the hair on the back of his neck. Delilah deserved better.

"Being with me is dangerous." Inácio held on to her harder. He wanted it. He wanted it more than his life.

"What's the saying? I'd rather die for something than live for nothing? I'm not afraid of it anymore. At least, I don't want to be. I know I'm safe with you."

Delilah's other hand came over his jaw.

Inácio forgot how to breathe.

Her lips were so close. A wavy strand hung over one eye as she drew closer. Inácio pushed his head against the headrest and felt her inevitable touch. Delilah's lips were even softer. Inácio took her face in both hands and gave in, returning the affection. He forced their lips to separate and looked her straight in the eye. Inácio promised himself that no one, no matter how powerful, could ever hurt them.

"Fuck it."

26

DELILAH

It was hard to see the danger Inácio insisted was there when all she felt was his protection. In spite of knowing next to nothing about him, she felt strangely comfortable in his presence. Tropical scenery and elegant homes she'd never thought she'd see again blurred beyond the car window, playing out like a colorful film at two-times the speed. Meanwhile, Delilah caught Inácio checking the rearview mirror dozens of times. If he wasn't glancing behind them, he was scanning from side to side.

It made her wonder if she felt too at ease. "Everything okay?"

He turned dismissive. "Of course. Why?"

"You seem paranoid." Delilah peeked into the side mirror. Nothing but blacktop and green shrubs fading into the distance.

"I'm just careful." His hand reached over to her lap and rested over hers. "If we're going to do this, leave the worrying to me."

For now, she could accept that but she knew her patience wouldn't last, especially after he tried to scare her away by insisting she wouldn't be safe. "Maybe one day you could tell me what makes you so *careful*."

"Sure. One day." His response was less promising and more grateful that the discussion was over. Delilah had a feeling that he had no immediate plans to tell her anything.

After a sharp turn, they rounded the driveway which began at the bottom of a steep hill. Delilah rolled down her window and stuck out her arm.

"What are you doing?"

"The ocean. It looks so gorgeous in this light." Delilah caught the wind in her hand, pretending she was touching the water. It was so still and calm, just like her. She realized then that there hadn't been many moments of genuine calmness in her life for a long time. They rolled to a stop while the garage opened in front of them. Resting her cheek on the car door, she watched her view be replaced with plain white walls. Once they were enclosed, the car engine died.

Beside her, Inácio stared forward in silence. Something about him felt locked down tight.

"Don't shut down." She reached for his arm, wrapping her fingers around his bicep. The power made her blush red from the neck down. They were the arms that had beat down her enemies. Delilah had never been so close to so much strength before, especially when it didn't want to hurt her. Inácio's muscles were hard and smooth all at once. His mocha eyes looked down at her and whispered.

"I don't want to." Inácio's lips parted, drawing in deeper breaths.

"Then don't. It's okay to let your guard down… sometimes."

"Is that what you've found?" His large hand engulfed hers that rested over his arm.

"I'm learning to, right now." Like she was born to be his, Inácio planted his lips firmly on hers. At least in his kiss she revealed no hesitation, only commitment. From his breath came repressed passion. Delilah felt it flow into her own lungs, chasing away any fear that she would end up alone again for the time being.

Her hands didn't know where to go first. Every one of his muscle groups flexed under her touch. Across his broad chest, she felt a strong heart thump beneath his dense power. Delilah hugged her arms around his neck, pulling herself closer until her hip hit the center console. The closer she got, the more she felt herself fall into freedom. Inácio kept her steady in his firm yet careful embrace.

Delilah pulled her lips away to catch her breath, but he didn't give her a moment to rest. Inácio's mouth snuck around her cheek and landed on her neck. The short stubble on his chin and cheek tickled like bristles beneath the corner of her jaw. Weakening with arousal, she found her head bob with heaviness.

"I think I'm learning to let go too," he said between his affection. "Let me take you inside."

Inácio flung his door open, not bothering to close it behind him. He couldn't get around to the other side fast enough. After pulling open the other door, he scooped her right out of her seat. Cradled in his arms, Delilah looked up at him just as she had the night he saved her. As he walked them into the house, things were physically clearer, yet much more murky on the psychological level. She didn't want to think about what made up the unknowns, just the hard facts of what he did.

Inácio was there when no one else was.

In the master bedroom, he pulled open the curtains and let the blue horizon fill the entire long window. He laid her down on the bed like she was nobility, the soft sheets welcoming her back. The daylight backlit Inácio as he climbed above her, resembling the terrifying figure who'd faced down a crowd of bad men. Delilah squirmed with anticipation. A mysterious and deadly stranger handling her with the most unexpected tenderness. His fingers kneaded her lust, stimulating further desire. Her gunshot wound, scrapes, and bruises were the target of every healing kiss.

Delilah stared up at his stout jaw. The panties pinched between her vulva were soaking wet. She pinched at the silver buttons of her shorts, popping each one free from its place. She left it at that and allowed him to do the rest. Every inch of her wanted to drown in his vigor, the only thing that could block out the darkness. Excitement flourished in her chest once he began tugging on the denim.

He ventured high up her thighs, pulling down her shorts from the bottom seams. Inácio ran his tongue just above the pretty lace below, sparking a shiver. Quickly, his shirt had fallen to the ground and Delilah sat back on her elbows to watch his virile body come to life little by little as he became liberated from his clothes.

Oh, shit.

Made in God's perfect image.

De Oppresso Liber stood out among the bruising and scuffs imprinted into his skin. Traces of suffering he'd endured for *her.* Delilah was in awe of the broad formation of muscles working in impeccable unison with every movement. *Do I really deserve this?* The question repeated itself, worded differently every time.

Inácio's belt hung open, knocking its cold parts against her hot skin. Delilah sat up to help him, his face buried in her neck. With a little tug, everything fastening him inside gave way.

The bulge underneath shoved the button from its slot and engaged the zipper. It resembled another limb through his boxer briefs. Delilah held her breath. Her fingers traced the defined shape from the base of his pelvis. She pushed him back until he was standing upright at the foot of the bed. Inácio stroked her head as her full attention focused only on pleasuring him.

"Delilah." He kicked his head back.

Hearing her name melt from his lips gave Delilah a sense of supremacy over his anatomy. Now free, his cock twitched and bobbed, as if trying to find her pussy. Delilah stopped pulling on his clothes and sat back, staring at what was about to be inside her. The band stopped just below his swollen balls, and he kicked off the rest. She noticed him stare in admiration at the way she looked at it. The blood in his shaft shoved against the limits of his girth. Delilah's hand arrived at the satin texture, veins rippling under her palm.

In a second, his ruthless presence changed into something… softer. The cry that was released from his throat caught her off guard. Her fingers curled around him, circling over his foreskin, something a little extra that Carson didn't have. Clear fluid flooded the opening, pouring over and coating the rest of him.

The powerful perfection who battled men with his bare hands and pointed his gun without thought was absent. Inácio swayed with weakness. With his cock in her hands, she had all the authority. It rattled her, knowing someone like him could succumb to someone like her. What would she do with her power? She didn't know how to wield it.

Delilah stroked from the tip to the bottom. His thick thighs shook. Every stroke pulled him forward until he popped one knee on the bed. A crooked smile was painted on Delilah's face. Staring up at his helpless eyes, she shifted her position, pulling him along with her. Delilah directed him with just a stroke, and he followed her through the bedroom obediently.

27 INÁCIO

Delilah rewarded his compliance with her warm, wet mouth. She was in complete control of his body, something that was dangerous to give up. Her hand cupped his entire length and led him to complete one full lap around the bedroom. If it wasn't for her teasing hand and devious smile, Inácio would have been on his knees at her feet. Using her thumb and forefinger like a ring, she pulled down on the foreskin, exposing his head.

Returning to the foot of the bed, Delilah squatted before him. Her mouth tingled every nerve at his end. Each swipe of her tongue prompted him to run heavy strokes of his hand through her hair. Delilah's massage quickened, his foreskin working in unison with the motions. Unable to stand against the fierce pleasure, Inácio guided her to her feet and backed her up across the bed. Inácio's hips crash-landed onto her pelvis. He couldn't take it anymore. He had to have her.

Precum stuck to her leg, the bed, and everywhere else it could land. Inácio tugged her shirt up, pulling it all away. Now he was in complete pure contact. Grabbing the sides of her ribcage, he ran his hands up and down. In that moment, he had to stop and appreciate what she was about to give to him. At the airport, he was ready to give up on her and yet here she was, still willing to trust him. He was the luckiest and most privileged man in the world. After she'd opened up about her past, Inácio recognized Delilah's vulnerability as a gift. The universe was giving him everything he ever wanted and he almost pushed her away.

"Thank you." Inácio dipped his back and moaned, her fingers lightly swiping down his spine.

"For what?" she asked with a sugary kiss.

His composure was narrowly held together with a hard swallow. "For challenging my bullshit."

Kindness lifted the corners of her lips. Like a sucker, he read into it, giving her smile meaning where there was likely none. It spoke of acceptance—impossible. If she really knew him, she'd run for the hills.

Inácio tried to abandon his feelings and began worshiping her skin with his lips starting with her sternum. He extended this motion around her breasts, pushing into their soft walls. Delilah's whimpers fulfilled every part of him. Sounds of pain were familiar to him, but her delight was like soothing music. Her nipples were hard, making it easy for him to suck and flick them with his tongue. *Just enjoy her.* Inácio put his mistakes that morning out of his mind and focused on her body. No worries about danger or regret. She demanded his full attention, and it was futile to resist.

Delilah's legs opened and he accepted the invitation immediately. His thickness rested over her pubic bone, rubbing against her smooth mound. Inácio dripped down over her hip, creating slick lubrication while he rubbed. His head protruded from the fold, showing off its immense size. The drizzling head slid from pubic bone to vulva. With just enough pressure, he found the opening between her soft folds.

"God, you're wet," he whispered. His tip teasingly flirted with her entrance. Only a centimeter in and her body lavished him with pleasure.

"Be gentle, Inácio." Delilah's request made him slow down and hold himself back before diving in. He knew how large he was, but it hadn't been a problem with... *Err. Don't even think about her.*

"Let me hold you," he said, sitting her up from the bed. Inácio sat at the foot of it while he guided her to face forward in his lap. "Look into the ocean and feel me."

Tiny chills dappled Delilah's skin like a rapid current over her shoulder. A sharp breath expanded her lungs. The effect he had on her body turned him on even more. A hand covered her belly while the other supported her butt. Arching his hips forward, he brought himself into perfect alignment with her pussy. Soft truths drawled from his lips into her ear.

"You are wanted."

Delilah's body brought out all the moisture possible to prepare for the tight fit, as if her flesh knew what was coming.

Gently, he lowered her while grazing his teeth along her back. His stream of vows continued to flow. "There is no one here to hurt you."

As he pushed his cock inside, he met some resistance. From her shoulders to between her thighs, every muscle stiffened in unison. He moaned, speaking for his cock that was throbbing to be deeper. Inácio refused to make her suffer, refused to be part of all the men who had hurt her. If Delilah couldn't handle him, he wouldn't be selfish.

"You're afraid."

"I'm not." She shook her head. He detected a lie.

"Don't be ashamed. Tell me. What are you afraid of?"

Her stomach quivered beneath his hand. "I..."

"Do you know you don't have to fear me?" That was the last thing he wanted when he rescued her, but the violence she witnessed was unavoidable.

"I know that I *shouldn't*." Shouldn't. It wasn't enough to convince him. His fingers pulsated around her body, soothing her and keeping him hard for the moment he received a definitive 'yes.'

"What are you thinking about?" Inácio ran his lips against her hair, running them over and back behind her ear. The ocean and clear sky in front of them craved to be the center of attention, but it was the last thing on his mind. The connection to her physical body was his sole concern. Delilah's stiff limbs, heightened heart rate, shaky breathing, and the wet tension seated on the head of his cock. Every part of her, in tune with his senses.

"I'm thinking that I almost died the other day. I'm thinking that no one has ever held me the way you are now. What if I can't handle it? What if I can't handle your gentleness or your… girth?"

"I have a feeling more men have hurt you than just the night I found you." The truth screamed through her tension.

"You could say that."

"Those men, the ones in your past, have trained your nervous system to resist the masculine, even when it holds you. It's going to take a long time to fix that."

Delilah deflated.

"I can help you bring down those walls if you let me."

"Please. I want you."

"Lean back." Inácio assisted her back against his chest. Her spine sat curved and rigid over him, her body betraying her desires. "Breath. Inhale on my count. One, two, three, four."

Delilah's ribs expanded on command.

"Hold it there." He counted to four again. "Now, exhale."

Her shoulders dropped as the air left her.

"One, two, three, four."

A slight loosening in her spine.

"Again. Keep your eyes on the water." Leading her through each breath in and breath out, Inácio felt her melt into him. Bit by bit, her nervous system released the false alarm that dictated his touch as a threat. The hand around her ass squeezed, his lust anticipating her relaxation. A quiet moan escaped her next exhale and enticed his hips to grind against her. The tip of his cock rubbed from her opening and across her lips before returning to her entrance.

After four revolutions of the breathwork, Delilah's spine finally rested. The calmness that spread through her opened up her pelvic floor muscles, causing her pussy to slip just under an inch down his head. *So tight. So warm.*

"Breath in. One, two, three, four."

She held her breath without his prompting, learning the pattern.

"And out."

Her body sank into his lap, his hands guiding her down.

"One, two, three, ohhhhh." Inácio meant to brace himself for the bliss he knew her body would offer. Her tight walls parted and hugged him all the way down. Nothing but natural hot constriction. "*Puta merda!*" His eyes threatened to roll into the back of his head.

Delilah's spine bent into a U and leaned back against his chest. Her hands ran themselves wildly through his hair. Further and further down his shaft she fell, her growing ease opening the door for greater satisfaction.

Delilah cried out. "Oh, my go—I've... never been... so..."

"Filled?"

"Mmmm, yes!"

Inácio's chest expanded behind her, moving her with his breath. Soon, they were one body moving in unison. Flashes of blue water and purple hair sucked him into a portal of ecstasy. Inácio growled like an animal into her ear.

"No one will ever hurt you again." It was a promise.

Her heels rubbed down his shins until her feet hung above the floor, making his cock and hands solely responsible for keeping her secure. It was more than an undeniable attraction, it was like she was turning her entire self over to him. Inácio's face nosed through her hair and across her neck. Furry rug fibers below were pinched between his clenched toes. Every inch of him was squeezed by a satin narrowness. Their harmony intensified, her hips sweeping forward and back. His hands moved to her chest and sank into her breasts.

Every breath from Inácio was purposeful and broken with exhaustion. His lustful grinding defined the failure of his strength to resist her. She had him from the start, from the very moment his crosshairs panned over her alluring body. There was no going back from giving in, only a way forward from here. Delilah was a violation to his discipline, Schafer's trust, and the Philosopher's confidence in him.

His cock couldn't care less.

Now that he'd had a taste, he was addicted. Delilah's pussy had a surprising amount of strength in its grip. She constricted around him like she never wanted to let go. Inácio wrapped his arms around her in a shielding embrace. Even if the world put a stop to their bond, she was his right then. The taste of her femininity had only ever existed in his dreams.

"Delilah." Her name excited him among measured moans. With one hand he moved his fingers down to her clitoris and massaged.

"Mmm! Ohh!" Her outburst told him that he hit the spot.

He maintained a solid, steady, and pulsating pressure.

"Oh my go—"

Inácio strained to speak. "Do you like that?"

"Yes, yes!"

He could barely utter a response between his exertions. "You feel like heaven." Sweat dripped down his back, and his heart pounded like he was in the middle of a training session.

Another loud moan shook through Delilah's body.

Squinting, Inácio gathered all of his willpower to hold back the unleashing of his climax. He wanted her pleasure to build until she couldn't hold it in any longer than he could.

Before long, their rhythm was at a sprint, and the pressure inside his cock rose to inhuman levels. Inácio's muscles contracted again and again, his cock widening to its max width. His abs clenched, fighting the load, but there was no stopping it.

In a swoop, he flipped their position, laying Delilah over the bed on her belly. He was careful to maintain his hold over her clit as his weight dropped against her ass. With a last squeeze, Delilah screamed into the sheets and her body tensed, this time in all the right ways. Her loud release opened the floodgates, forcing Inácio to pull out. He pinned his cock at the ridge of her tailbone and came in several forceful spurts. .

The release of air hissed through his teeth, and his dick twitched as if he were still inside her. Inácio descended over her, shoving his cock between himself and one of her ass cheeks, the temperature of their bodies only an imitation of what it felt like to be inside her. His lungs labored as he held himself up above her, muscles rattling from his arms down through his legs.

Delilah did the same, her ribs protruding in and out. Once Inácio regained a sense of control, he retrieved a towel, wiping it over himself and Delilah. He put his head on a pillow and brought her to him. She snuggled up close, her eyes even with his. Delilah stared at him, as if trying to figure him out. He knew the question was coming before she asked it.

"Who are you?"

Inácio took a deep breath and let it out slowly. "You already know who I am. You're just looking for the wrong answers."

28

DELILAH

Through the humid steam of her morning shower, Delilah wiped the mirror's center clear of fog. Beside the sink was a pair of holey jeans and a simple snug tee, the type of outfit Inácio had said she would need that day for his "surprise." Her reflection returned a bed of tousled hair that dropped beads of water over her shoulders. Each droplet bled into one another, creating tiny rivers of water across her skin. The edge of the ugly surgical scar showed itself between the chaos of hair.

No control.

Blood.

Mangled metal.

They made up only a few of the memories living rent free in her brain. Delilah's fingertips touched the crooked line in remembrance of the trauma she'd put herself and her family through. So many tears and so many lies had led up to a fractured skull. Could her father ever forgive her?

"What's your story, Delilah?" She abandoned the scar and saw Inácio dressed in a snug cotton tee through her muggy portrait in the mirror.

"It's stupid." Delilah reached for her bath towel, wadded by the sink, and wrapped it around her.

Inácio stepped inside and with one hand on her shoulder and the other swiping across her hair, said, "Yesterday, when I told you that there was no one here to hurt you, I also meant there's no one here to judge you."

"I want to believe that." As the fog faded from the glass, she saw just how large Inácio was in comparison to her. Her head reached only as high as his sternum and his broad chest made her want to fall back into it and trust him with everything. She felt something similar with Carson too before he diminished her past as nothing more than a trite tall tale.

"Let's make a deal. You tell me how you got that scar and you can ask me anything you want."

"Will you tell me the truth if I do?"

He nodded. "I promise." Delilah took a deep breath and remained facing the mirror. She felt Inácio's eye contact through the reflection, but she couldn't look at him.

"It was six years ago, the summer after high school graduation, only a few days into it, if I'm remembering right. By then, I was already getting high almost every day." Delilah glanced up to gauge his reaction. Not a flinch. "It started with simple stuff like weed. The people I was around were kinda intense. Then the drugs got harder."

Can we talk about this tomorrow? I have a test today, Carson's voice interjected.

Inácio massaged her shoulders like he knew she needed it.

Delilah cleared her throat. "I can remember the argument with my dad. He was furious because I skipped out on walking the stage. My grandparents went to the school all dressed up with my mom and dad. They sat through the ceremony until they got through the J's and noticed I wasn't one of them." Flicking her eyes up, she checked in on Inácio. Delilah waited for the "get over it" expression, yet his eyes remained kind and open.

"I'm listening."

"So that day, I was high and getting a little buzzed. When my dad told me the only way I would learn my lesson was if he took me to jail, I ran out of the house with my booze. He didn't know I took the keys to his truck though. They said I hit the curve a half mile from my house at eighty miles an hour. I was upside down in a culvert for at least two hours. The roof caved in at an angle that just missed crushing me to death."

Inácio cupped her jaw and caressed the scar with his lips. "Does it still hurt?"

"I get a lot of headaches, a seizure here and there."

Inácio turned her around to face him. He gazed straight into her like he saw her soul and accepted her for what she was—cracked and ruined. "We all do things we're not proud of. It's not all of you, just a piece."

"I'm not that person anymore," she asserted. "I went to rehab and have been on the straight and narrow ever since."

"Why are you justifying yourself?"

Emotion suffocated her lungs. Delilah's breath shuddered. "Isn't that what you want to hear? It's the only way for an addict to get anyone to talk to them again." She held her breath, blocking the tears.

"Not everyone. Some of us understand."

"I hope that's true."

"We both have a lot of trust to build." Inácio clutched the towel curled around her ribs as if he was playing around with the idea of stripping it away. "Your turn. Ask me anything."

"What do you do for a living?"

A brief pause. "Military contractor."

"And what does that entail?" Delilah's focus burned into his chocolate eyes. Was it when the pupil retracted or expanded that indicated a lie?

"Security, protecting assets. It takes me to many different countries." Inácio's gaze was empty. He sounded almost bored speaking about it, like many people did when asked about their job duties.

"So, this is one of those dangerous realities of being with you?"

"Yes."

"I don't see how being with you in your home is so dangerous."

"It's not always like this."

"That explains…" Delilah eyed the ink traveling up his arm. "You're in the military, aren't you?"

"I was."

"Which military? The way you talk, sometimes you sound so foreign and other times it's like you're American. Even some of your tattoos look like you served in the US."

"I'm both. I was born in Rio and taken to live with my father in Indiana."

"Indiana? We're neighbors." The reality that they were connected in any sense breathed chills down her neck in the cooling bathroom. There was so much to ask. When and where in Indiana? Had he been to Ohio? Were they a few towns over at one time and didn't know it? Apparently, telling the most personal story of her life was only worth a few baseline questions.

"Well, that's enough dwelling on the past for now. Let's do something fun."

****

Delilah shouldn't have been shocked at the nature of Inácio's surprise. He was an ambiguous man who could take on an armed mob and make a girl feel special one moment, thrown away the next, and valued again like no one else could. The large prison-like gate shut behind them as Inácio cruised the car across a rough path. A spiral of continuous razor wire topped the connecting tall fence which ran through skinny trees and overgrown weeds on each side. Outside her window, grasses grew halfway up dilapidated buildings made of plywood, their walls pelted with holes and sagging with rot. Delilah bobbed along while the car inched its way over ruts, the unkept land scratching at the undercarriage.

It was still unclear what his idea of "fun" was, but Inácio appeared relaxed. His hand flopped over the bottom rim of the wheel while he leaned out his open window with an elbow. Short sleeves were stacked under his shoulder, too snug to fall naturally over his biceps. His tan shirt was tucked into olive green pants, tactical in design, like the kind her dad wore to work. Delilah felt the brakes contract.

Ahead was a steep hill that acted more like a wall than a landmark. The fence ran up its sides and passed several trees before connecting. At its base, a few dozen metal discs were set up in various positions and heights. A concrete slab in front of it was barely visible under the invasive weeds which grew through its cracks. It was only then that the scene looked familiar.

"You're taking me shooting." Delilah recognized the circular dents in the metal.

"What gave it away?" Inácio grinned and adjusted his blue reflective aviators at her.

"Is this like a police department range?" She was lighthearted with her question. It was much more secure than any police shooting range she had ever seen.

"It's *like* one." Inácio got out and opened her door. Delilah took his hand and followed him to the open trunk. He unsnapped the dark cases and revealed an arsenal. There were more guns in Inácio's trunk than there were in her dad's safe, and her dad liked guns. If it was anyone else, she would think Inácio was trying to impress her. She had a hunch that this was perfectly ordinary to him.

"Are you going to make me shoot all of those?" Delilah ran her fingers through her hair and nervously tied her hair into two stubby braids.

"How long's it been since your dad took you to the range?"

"I don't know, I think I was fifteen."

"That's a long time without any practice. He only let you shoot a pistol, you said?"

"Only for a few seconds, really."

"I have plenty of those," he said, as if it should be nothing to her. "You'll want these." Inácio handed over bulky ear protection. Delilah placed the muffs over her head while Inácio inserted a pair of green ear plugs. They were big, obviously made for someone like him. She felt like a tiny burger patty in between two large buns. "Definitely not your size."

"I'm used to it. Head is too small."

Inácio held her hard ears and kissed her on the forehead.

Delilah gulped down a nervous knot in her throat.

"You're not shooting anything without these." He handed her a pair of safety glasses, then grabbed a handgun. "Remember," he began while ramming in a loaded magazine, "it doesn't matter that you haven't done much with guns. You can still hit your target with accuracy. It's all in your body mechanics."

Her heart pounded in the muffs.

"Are you okay?"

"Just nervous."

"I'll walk you through everything, like it's your first time."

"I'm not going to be very good." She looked all around her like there had to be some way out of it.

"It doesn't matter. We'll start with something simple: the nine millimeter."

"I don't think these are going to block the sound."

"They will. You can hear me so well because they allow voices to go through, but prevent the loud stuff."

"Oh." *Damnit, worth a shot.* Delilah trailed behind Inácio, leaving a breadth of a few feet between them. To be around guns again was never in her plan. She'd wanted to stay away from them and most importantly, avoid being on the wrong side again. Inácio reserved a few boxes of ammunition on the hood. Delilah planted her feet to the side and guarded herself with crossed arms. He faced the weapon downrange and waved her over. Groaning to herself, she stood beside him. Inácio took her shoulders and shifted her in front of him, his body completely enveloping hers.

"Lean against me as much as you want."

Delilah recoiled into him and he remained steady as a rock.

With his free hand he unfolded her arm from her ribs and brought it to the pistol. Delilah expected the metallic surface to be cold, but it was warm from his meaty hands. Inácio's trigger finger lifted hers away and guided it to the frame.

"Remember, finger off the trigger until you're ready to fire."

Delilah nodded, having no plans whatsoever to pull the trigger.

Inácio moved her other hand into a supportive position. "Are you okay? I can feel your heart pounding through your back."

"No, not really." She tried squatting and pivoting out from his control.

"Whoa whoa, don't do that. You have a dangerous weapon in your hands."

"I know that! Please take it! I can't do this, I'm sorry."

Delilah hailed every ounce of composure she had left and eased the transfer of the gun over to him. When she got away from it, Delilah's hand clenched around her bicep. An acute pinching spread from the injury just when it was starting to feel much better. She tried to catch her shaky breath. She almost stumbled, feeling light-headed. Her fingers locked around the back of her head.

Inácio was quiet. He stood on the line and rested the side of the gun on his leg.

"I hope you can understand." Delilah wished he could just like he'd said he did that morning. There was no emotional capacity within her to be so close to a gun and that was all there was to it. "I know you drove all this way. I'm just not ready."

Inácio's shoe flattened some nearby weeds. "You know, none of us are ready."

"What do you mean?" Delilah clenched her fists repeatedly, trying to force the tension from her muscles.

"Shit happens whether we want it to or not. It doesn't care if we're ready. Were you ready to get yourself caught up in a gang war?"

"No." Delilah crossed her arms again and took a small step back in the direction of the car.

"Exactly. You made a wrong turn and that's all it took."

"*You* looked pretty ready to me," she challenged.

"I keep myself prepared. If you had asked me if I was ready to fight an entire group of armed men on my own, I would have said no. But I didn't have a choice, did I?"

Delilah looked away from his candid expression. Her thumb covered the stitches on her arm. Still, it was easier to walk away.

"Why can't you just let me sit this one out? I don't want to do it."

"I shouldn't have to explain the dangers of this world to you. And it's not fair to you if I don't share my knowledge."

"What if it just makes it worse and I get more scared of it?"

"What if you're stronger after?" *Strong* wasn't a word she'd ever used to describe herself. It was easy to imagine it on him, but her? Never. "I won't leave your side. Come over here."

One, two, three… She counted every forced step back to him, hoping counting them could prove as effective as counting her breaths. *Nine.* How could putting herself through this change anything? Their bodies met and her hands were guided back in place. Delilah's finger wasn't even on the trigger and she was already squinting, expecting a violent flash.

"What are you focused on?" Inácio's voice sent fine vibrations through her spine. Delilah wanted to be in touch with his calm energy, but her fear ran wild.

"I don't know," she whimpered, fidgeting.

"Stay present and look at the front sight." His voice was gentle, enough to be a whisper. "That front dot on the end of the muzzle. It should be clear in your vision." Delilah stared down the green circle until it was all she saw. "Now, line up the front sight between the rear brackets." Her trembling hands bobbed the dot in and out of the rear sight. Inácio firmed up his grip. "I've got it. You don't have to worry about keeping it steady. It's pointed right at the target."

"I don't know if I can."

"You don't have to know anything. All you gotta do is press the trigger."

Delilah's finger barely brushed the tiny lever before returning beneath his hand. His skin was much warmer and comforting in comparison. The gray disc target in front of her morphed into something else in her mind. She looked right at it, seeing it transform into a sneering bearded man. His black eyes smiled with an evil grin. The face made her feel weak and defenseless all over again. Dark thoughts took her back to the basest of emotions of when it all began outside the hotel. Degradation. Humiliation. Treated like an object. Delilah wondered how much fight was left in her.

"I know you've been hurt. Don't let them win. I've got your back." His chin nuzzled against her head, just above her scar, his torso nudging her slightly. Delilah's finger felt the trigger. She pulled it back until her arms jerked her grip before following through. Delilah tried again and lurched forward without a bullet leaving the gun.

"Why won't it do anything?"

"You're anticipating. Steady and smooth, like this." Inácio's finger covered hers above the trigger and pressed back. With his hold around her, the gun barely jostled in her hands. A brief flash popped in front of her face followed by a shrill ding from the target. Birds squawked and fled from their nests into the blue sky.

Delilah's eyes squinted shut as she remembered the flash of bullets flying in her direction. Her teeth rattled like they had when she hid behind his car—the moment she'd thought her rescuer was getting cut down in the street. Her body followed her memory, making her shrink against him. Inácio was the only thing that kept her standing. Delilah's eyes opened. As if expecting someone else to fire back, her eyelids wanted to re-shut.

But it was only Inácio and the metal disc before her.

"I can't do it," Delilah choked out. Tremors shook her from her jaw to her feet.

"You can. You just did. Give me one more try."

"No, please!" Inácio's finger took control of hers and forced it back on the trigger. Another muffled pop and bright flash. The gun slid in her sweaty palms as the slide went back and rocked forward again. Delilah's eyes slammed shut and her arm twitched. Fragments of glass spit at her in her mind. "I can't do it!" Delilah dropped her weight and sunk to the ground. Her hands pressed into the rough pavement. The rocks and cracks embedded into her skin. Hard, skull-cracking concrete.

Inácio kneeled behind her, wrapping her up. "I'm here, Delilah." Bulging forearms flexed around her ribs like a shield. "We can stop." He pulled her onto his lap and moved one of her braids over the back of her shoulder, stroking her cheek. "Breathe, just like I showed you."

Delilah raised her chin to the sky and tried to slow her rapid breaths.

Inácio's hand rested on her chest. "Your heart is racing."

She worked to catch her breath enough to answer. "I just… keep thinking… about…"

"The night you were attacked," he finished.

She nodded.

Inácio pulled her upright. Hooking an arm around his neck, she was embraced by his soothing touch.

"That's it, in and out. Nice and slow." His presence cut through her downward spiral, fully orbited by his protection. He watched her with diligent concern. "The night everything happened," he began, touching her stitches, "is also the night we met." The touch of his breath warmed her temple.

Delilah almost smiled.

"I remember the look on your face," he continued. A soft caress tickled her jaw. "It wasn't much different than right now. Terrified." His fingers traced over her scar, dancing all the way down behind her ear. "Alone."

"Until you found me."

"You're not alone anymore, and neither am I. If I could, I'd go back to keep you from feeling any pain." Inácio pressed his lips against her own. The comfort from the kiss made her want to give it all over to him. *Just do it, just trust him.*

Delilah swallowed the fading jitters so she could speak. "You didn't see everything that happened to me."

"You can tell me."

"When you saw me, that wasn't the first time I was hurt by a man that day."

Inácio's body tightened.

"At the hotel, after the breakup…" Panic threatened to resurge in her lungs. Delilah took a deep breath. "A stranger assaulted me. That's how I actually got the bump on my head. He slammed me down and—" She cleared her throat. "I thought I was going to die."

Inácio squeezed her waist.

"He was really close to doing something horrible. When I talked to my mom on the phone, she said there was a shooting. I didn't understand what it was at the time. It's probably what saved me, as bad as it is to say. It scared the guy away. It happened right beside me. I don't know how I didn't get hit." Delilah's gaze dropped to the side. She felt herself falling back into the moment. Inácio held her cheek, bringing her back to the present.

"I'm here with you now. I won't let you feel helpless again, I promise."

"It's just my luck, I guess. I never used to believe in curses. Now, I think some people just are destined for bad things."

"It's the evil in this life that did this, not you. That's how this world works. There are predators and there are prey." Inácio planted his lips on hers again, wiping away the rest of her tears at the same time. She wanted to live surrounded by his power forever. He gave her hope and a sense of control. He made it sound so easy. "I know you're strong."

"I don't feel strong. I'm prey, just like you said."

"A weak woman wouldn't have chased me down and crawled on top of my car."

Delilah barely chuckled.

"I want you to feel as strong as I know you are. Do you want that?"

"I don't know how."

"Trust me and let me show you what it's like to push through the fear."

They returned to their position before the hanging disc. Its hinges squeaked like a mouse against the breeze. Behind the neon dot of her gun sight, the faces of her attackers twisted together into one distorted monstrosity. White Shores moved to the front of her thoughts. What Carson had done wasn't much better than the man in the lot. It was all part of degrading her worth as a human. Each of them had overcome her in seconds, but now the power was in her hands with reinforcement at her back. Despite how much Inácio wanted her to feel strong, she really didn't, but she could fake it. For Delilah, faking it was at least one step above fear.

She pretended Inácio's toughness bled into her. If she learned to rise above, what would it look like? The target, a meaningless thing that couldn't fight back, still managed to laugh at her. Her screw-ups, trauma, heartbreak, all a comedy skit in the shape of cruelty. The only difference in that moment was she wasn't going to be caught off guard. Not again. Out in the middle of a neglected range with oddly high security measures with an equally as obscure man, there was no better time to face it than right then.

Without any guidance, Delilah pressed the trigger to its threshold before the pin struck the primer and beyond. The disc buzzed with a high C note, and the first taste of courage was at the tip of her tongue. The birds who'd settled back on their branches fled away once more. One shot was a win, but two would be nothing less than a victory. Delilah brought the trigger all the way back and struck her target a second time.

Pop… Pop… Pop… Pop!

Her tempo was steady and she kept going, one after another, until the trigger locked back and the slide remained to the rear. A gritty scent of spent ammunition clouded the air. It wasn't until Delilah was out of bullets that she realized Inácio's hands had left hers completely. When, she did not know.

"Not cursed," he said. "This would be yours." Inácio traded the pistol for a warm empty bronze casing. "Your first shot without my help."

"Only 'cause I had you." Delilah watched herself shine in the ovals of his sunglasses.

Inácio stepped away and headed toward the trunk.

"Thank you," she reiterated, speed walking behind him, muffs and glasses in hand.

He set the gun back in its case. "You're welcome." Inácio's tone was as dull as the expression on his face.

"Everything okay?"

"We should be getting back." The items were snatched from her hands and thrown in, the trunk slammed closed.

"We just got here. You brought all those guns. You don't want to show me how you train with them for work?"

"No, I'd like to go." The rigidness in his body made her stomach drop.

"You have that look in your eye again."

"You can't see my eyes." Inácio pinched one of the hinges on his sunglasses.

"I don't need to. I feel it. I've developed a sixth sense for these kinds of things. You want to run from me again, don't you?"

"Did I say I wanted to run?" he asked, terse and unforgiving.

Delilah stepped forward, her new zing of confidence still ringing. "Just do it then. Leave me somewhere. I know you want to!"

Inácio cradled the back of her neck and pulled her toward him. He stared down at her with the same blank look, but with his hurried breath exposing his true nature. His lips met hers with force. Delilah returned the pressure and linked her good arm around the back of his shoulders. In a swift heave, Inácio picked her up and laid her horizontally across the hood. She was confused, even angry at his switch to a cool temperament. More than that, she was desperate to keep him. Her hands found his belt as he yanked her jeans down her thighs.

The snap of a thread could be heard as her panties followed her denim off her ankles. Once Inácio freed himself, Delilah's sore pussy clenched at the sight. So thick, so intimidating. Pulling her toward him, he wrapped her legs around his waist while his hips found the proper angle. With a crude spit into his palm, he wetted his cock and her. As his damp fingers swiped over her opening, Delilah bent her head back. The sky was a picture-perfect blue and birds swarmed back to green roosts. Inácio's massive power filled her completely in one thrust, her nails scratching at the car's sharp finish.

How long could their connection last?

She hoped, deep down, forever.

But she knew better.

29 DERRICK

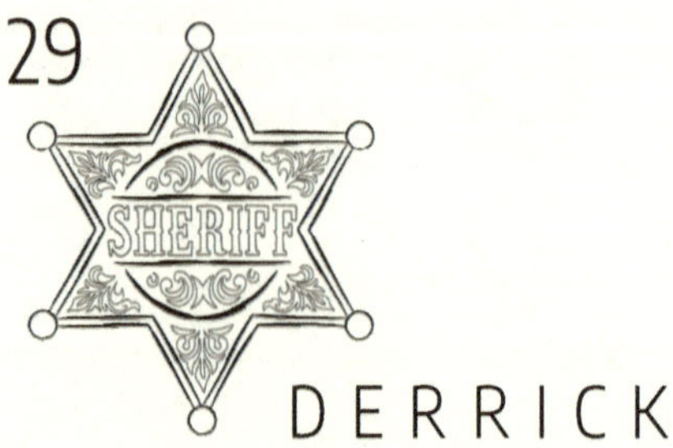

On the way to the sheriff's personal office, his fellow deputies threw over extra-polite nods. Rumors his daughter was missing spread fast, so pity was the only emotion he received all day. Derrick hated that word, *missing*. Delilah wasn't missing, he just hadn't had any contact with her in two days. Derrick power-walked all the way to the sheriff's desk. In his hand was a brown accordion folder containing everything he knew about Delilah's whereabouts. The hotel, the shooting, her timeline, and copies of her personal information.

"Take as much time as you need in Brazil. We support you, Johnson," said Sheriff Cox over a pair of reading glasses.

"Thank you, I really do appreciate it. Did you get in contact with Brazilian authorities?" Derrick sat up straight in his chair so Cox could see him over the tall paper stacks that lined his desk. He wasn't particularly tall, and the giant fortress of paperwork made it hard to have a conversation. Cox leaned back in his leather chair, making it that much harder to maintain eye contact. Derrick, too exhausted to care anymore, gave up and stood from the chair.

"As a matter of fact, yes. Here, I've written it down for you." Cox handed over a ripped-off corner of an envelope.

Derrick read *Captain Silva* with an office number and address.

"He said he would take your report and accept any information you got. He spoke English, so that's a plus. Got you and your trusty partner a hotel room right across the street from the station. No guarantee on the amenities, but I got you guys paid in full for five days. I want you to hit the ground running."

"I don't know how to thank you, Sheriff." Derrick spun around to leave. The small chaotic room was growing more claustrophobic every second.

"Make it known to Greg that if a big case opens out here, I expect him to fly back immediately."

"Yes, sir, of course."

"We will keep your family in our prayers, especially your daughter. If there's anything else we can do, you know where to ring us."

"Appreciate it."

Derrick jogged back to the Investigations Division and into the corner office. Greg was inside writing something down on a sticky note. Derrick's phone dinged with a message from his wife. Derrick typed away, updating her on the situation.

"Okay..." Derrick began, distracted.

"Okay what?"

"Everything is ready to go on my end." Derrick shoved his phone in his jacket pocket. "I have compiled all the information on Delilah we need to hand over to their local police."

"What did the sheriff say?"

"He said we're good to go. I got the impression I can stay in Rio as long as it takes to figure out where Delilah is. Can't say the same for you."

"You sure? Did you even see him?" Greg snickered, chewing on a toothpick.

"No, Greg," Derrick said, managing to grin. "I only heard him behind all that shit, but that's enough around here."

"You saw that new post Carson made on his Instagram, right?"

"No. Crap. I haven't had a minute where I wasn't doing ten things at once."

Greg pointed to his computer monitor until his finger hit the screen.

Derrick wove around the desk and got a good look at the group photo. He recognized Carson at the center, holding up his university's flag beside the ocean, surrounded by several others his age. They must have been the friends Delilah left the country with.

The air in Derrick's chest deflated. No sign of Delilah.

"No one seems worried, that's for sure." He felt Greg watching him.

"They're just kids. They really have no reason to worry."

"You seem a little worried."

"I am cautiously optimistic. There is a difference," Derrick said, holding up a finger.

"Optimistic enough to ask me to delay my cases and help search for your daughter in South America."

"Greg, it's just a precaution. Two heads are better than one."

"Whatever you say."

"You know what? This is mostly for the wife. Maggie was about to fly out herself if I didn't and we all know that's a bad idea. And just maybe her concern might be rubbing off on me."

"So, what's the plan when we get there?"

"Well besides finding a hotel, I am thinking we call this Sergeant Silva first, then catch up with Carson."

"You still think her boyfriend is going to give us any more info than we already know?"

"Correction, ex-boyfriend. In-person communication is always better. I think he'll be happy to help if he can. He's a good kid."

"I think your douche-dar is a little off."

"No, just you wait and see. Carson's family are huge supporters of law enforcement. His dad has donated somewhere around a hundred grand to first-responder charities. At least that's what Carson told me when we first met."

"Mmm."

"Really. I just don't understand why she never even tried going back to the hotel with Carson. Where else is she supposed to go?" Derrick checked his watch. "Damn, time has flown." A knock on the doorframe interrupted their conversation, revealing a young uniformed deputy.

"Hey, Johnson, the front office has that lady from the storage theft on the other line."

"Wow, she really listens when we tell her to call your phone and not the main office," Greg commented.

"Tell her I don't give a crap about her stolen Beanie Baby collection right now." Derrick's voice carried through the office halls.

"Sure, I'll tell her you're dealing with a family emergency." The deputy walked away.

"It's not an emergency, and thanks, peanut!" Derrick said.

"We're not supposed to call him that anymore, remember? Makes him feel bad."

Derrick's shoulders exaggeratedly shrugged. "I'm going to head home, grab my bag, and say goodbye to Maggie one more time."

"Surprised you convinced her to stay home."

"I want to be able to think clearly. I promised her I would come back with Delilah."

"Like I said, I'm surprised she's not coming."

"Are you headed to the airport soon?" Derrick asked, attempting to deflect from the subject of his marital life.

"Right behind you."

****

Derrick accelerated his work truck up the curved driveway. He'd lived in the same house for twenty years and during that time the only characteristics that had changed were the color of the flowers and the seasonal garden flag. Everything was perfect on the outside, and that was how he liked it. It was almost time to treat the manicured lawn and lay down fresh mulch, but household duties disappeared from his mind.

Black boots beat across the grass, something he only did when he was too lazy to follow the sidewalk. Maggie was waiting on the other side as soon as he stepped in. She was up and dressed—a good sign, all things considered.

"I thought you'd be here an hour ago, at least." Her voice was impatient and testy.

"Me too, but I had several cases I had to turn over. It takes a while." He slapped the briefcase on the kitchen counter, double-checking its contents. If he forgot anything, he'd have a meltdown.

"Don't forget to leave your work truck keys here."

"Oh yeah, there you go." Derrick tossed up the key fobs. Maggie caught them by their handcuff key attached to the ring. Her blonde hair hung uncurled at her shoulders and dark circles had formed under her once-bright blue eyes.

"I can't sit here in silence, Derrick. My heart is racing just thinking about being stuck here."

"Maggie, Maggie, please. There is nothing we can do about it now. I am sure she's fine." He took hold of his pacing wife. "Give me a few days to figure this out, just a few. If for some reason I have no answers by then, get a ticket. I need space to do my job." A minimal amount of understanding was present in her flustered nod, but he wouldn't be surprised if she showed up anyway. Derrick resumed collecting his things.

"I'm so glad they let Greg go with you."

"And you shouldn't be here alone either. Is there a friend you can spend some time with?"

"I made plans with Jennifer. She's bringing dinner here tonight. I can talk to her."

"Good. Keep doing that or you'll drive yourself crazy."

"I'm worried about you too. Jen sent me these podcasts that talked about the law enforcement in those countries—"

"Okay, and?" Derrick patted his pockets, his mind halfway to Brazil already.

"Well, she said the police in Latin America are very corrupt." Maggie emphasized her words close to his ear, pinching her fingers together.

"Latin America is a big place, Maggie. There's corrupt police here in the US!"

"I realize that, de-tectiiivvve! Jen said it's all over down there. They get money for doing things—"

"I know how corruption works, Maggie. I don't have time to discuss your true-crime mumbo jumbo at the moment. I wish you'd stop taking everything at face value." He lifted his luggage to leave. "Where are Delilah's car keys?"

"On the key hook where she left them."

"The only thing these podcasts do is make you paranoid about burglars and kidnappers—"

"Isn't that what you said though? Delilah could have been kidnapped." The pessimism made Derrick pause.

"I never said that."

"You implied it." Maggie scratched at a thin part of her scalp. She had been tearing her hair out again. Derrick put his arms around his wife.

"I said because of her refusal to listen to me, she could be putting herself in harm's way." He hoped he was wrong. "It's going to be okay."

"What if we never see her again?" She cried into his shoulder.

"That won't happen, I promise. She might be on her way here by now, who knows." *Or maybe she's been kidnapped.*

"I should go with you. I'm a terrible mother if I stay here."

"No, that's another reason why you need to stay, just for a little bit. If she does come home, she needs her mom to be here. Let Greg and I do what we were trained for."

"I want any and all updates."

"You got it, Mags. I love you."

"I love you." Derrick leaped down the stairs. "Your gun!" Maggie yelled.

"Oh, crap." Derrick yanked his holster from his belt and handed it to his wife. He ran to Delilah's blue Carolla parked in the street. "If anyone from work needs my truck, I told them to call you first!" He fumbled Delilah's heavy collection of keys in his hands. A leopard-print lanyard was connected to all sorts of plastic nonsense. Inside the car, school papers left behind on her passenger seat were crushed under his three bags, and the tires practically squealed as he left the curb.

****

At the airport, Delilah's car was added to the sea of long-term parking. They could be back in three days or three months, he was so unsure. He hustled down the space between himself and the entrance. The drag of his luggage slowed his steps, his duffle bag swinging from his elbow. The people and their noise flashed by in a blur. He paid no attention to their faces or what they were doing. Derrick responded quickly to instructions given to him by airport employees, but his mind was only half-present. The one thing going for him was the short lines. Navigating breathlessly through the busy terminals was the perfect symbol of how his mind was functioning. Greg might've been right. Maybe he was worried.

"Just in time, sir," said the woman at the desk. Derrick slapped his ticket on the scanner and bounced down the gangway.

At the center of the plane, a familiar dopey voice got his attention. "About time. Looks like I care more about your daughter than you." Greg was seat-belted in below where Derrick shoved his bags into the overhead.

"Phew, tell me about it. Shit." Derrick took his seat beside him in a sloppy mess.

"What happened? Accidently took off with your gun?"

"No, well yeah, but I caught that problem pretty quick. I had to park at the far end of the parking lot. It was ridiculous." Derrick pinched his uniform polo, utilizing it as a fan. He caught his breath before speaking again. "I should have brought my bags to work instead of going home. Didn't think one pit stop would suck up so much time."

"My wife could have swung by and got you too. Shoulda done that."

"If mine wasn't scared of driving in the city it wouldn't have been an issue. Too late now anyway."

"How was Maggie doing?"

"Eh, she was dressed, so that was surprising. Hanging on for now."

"Is she more of a true-crime junkie now, or less?"

"Oh, way more," he panted. "You wouldn't believe the number of South American murder cases I've been forced to hear about since Delilah agreed to go on that trip."

"That must be where all your patience is used up."

"It's like she applies the conclusion of every case she listens to to Delilah. Glad to be out of that house." Derrick patted a sweat bead dripping from his head.

"Careful, Derrick. Don't let that stuff get into your head too much. Gotta have an open mind."

"I know. I have been doing a decent job of that so far. It's just a little different when it's your only child."

"Yeah, I'd be the same if something happened to one of my kids. This is like the second big scare for you guys, too."

"Hopefully this is all it turns out to be. I mean, that's the most likely scenario."

"Of course." Greg patted him on the shoulder. Derrick unlocked his phone. He tried the number Delilah had called him from one more time.

"Any luck?" Greg asked.

"No, it's like some internet number." He sighed.

"Do you think they'll give us snacks?"

Derrick knew he was just trying to distract him. "Don't bet on it. It's just a short connecting flight."

"I'll settle for ice chips."

"You always have to have something in your mouth. Let's just hope they get this plane in the air already." Derrick kicked the briefcase under his seat. His sausage fingers grabbed the safety pamphlets in the seat pocket and upgraded his fan.

"I am too big for this plane."

"You're not at that point yet, Greg."

"My wife thinks so."

"You're tall. It evens out." Derrick laid his head back to rest his eyes. He could hear Greg clicking away on a last-minute text. The only thing standing between Derrick and Delilah for now was distance.

30

DERRICK

It was all a blur from Charm to Rio de Janeiro. Ushered into a tiny office at the end of a dim corridor of the police department, Derrick and Greg squished together like sardines to sit side by side before a cheap metal desk. He and his partner stared back at the police sergeant known as Silva. Derrick watched him closely, swearing he saw tears of pain swell up beneath a giant black eye. Silva creaked back in his peeling pleather chair and unwrapped the third lemon drop since the start of their meeting. The officer rubbed a bruised jaw, then picked at what was left of the material along the arm of his seat. Derrick caught Greg biting his lip, which happened during any awkward moment.

"So uh," Derrick said, clearing his throat, "I'm not saying it has anything to do with the shooting at the hotel, but it's a strange—"

Silva interrupted. "The shooter used a sniper rifle for what looks to be a hired kill. I hope your daughter was not involved in something like that."

"I didn't mean to imply—"

"Dee-lilah…" Silva tipped forward and read his notes. "John-son. That name…"

"Is it familiar to you?" Derrick sat up straight.

Opening the bottom desk drawer, Silva pulled out a small white card and flicked it to Derrick.

"Greg, look! It's her driver's license." Derrick pinched the card between his fingers, flashing back to the day he drove her to the DMV for that exact photo. "Did something happen to my daughter I don't know about?"

"I can't say. Someone gave it to lost and found." Silva shrugged.

"When?"

"I don't remember. It was a few days ago, maybe?"

"Did they say where they found it?"

Silva sighed. "Ack, where's my memory today?"

"Probably left wherever you got that beating," Greg said.

"Greg, c'mon now," Derrick said with a nudge. "Probably found it at White Shores, right?"

"Sure."

"Whoever brought her license in, was it some Brazilian or an American?"

"It was a Brazilian. No one suspicious. I hate to say that I didn't get their name."

"I see." Derrick's shoulders dropped. It was one less lead he could work with. The corner of her license tapped against his palm as he fidgeted. "You know, Greg, we gotta get over there and talk to Carson."

"If this is all the information you have on your missing daughter then I think my report is finished." Silva took the form and pages of notes Derrick had provided and shoved them into a folder.

"Where is my report going to go? In that folder and never seen again?" Derrick sensed there was no rush for answers from the man distracted by that much pain. Silva wouldn't stop dabbing his fingers across his injuries.

"Don't worry, Detective. It will show up in the system."

"And then what?"

"And then any officer can see her information in the list of missing people. Of course, it will be very difficult to locate her because you couldn't tell me what she was last wearing or where she was last seen. This is not a small city." Silva crinkled the wrapper to a fourth piece of candy.

"You can't even make some sort of announcement? This is my child!" Derrick's heart began thumping in his chest. He wanted to be cordial to a fellow police officer, but after seeing how busy the city was, it was overwhelming to comprehend locating one individual.

"Yes, your child, who is an adult. I can tell my team, if that's what you want."

"Yes! That's what I want!" Derrick was on the edge of his seat, his fist hammering Silva's desk like it was a hollow drum.

Greg's hand hooked over Derrick's shoulder and he spoke up in a much calmer voice. "Derrick, how about you give him all those missing-persons posters you printed back at home? He could hand them out to his officers."

"Sure, some of them, but not *all* of them," Derrick said. Around a dozen copies were forced from the thick stack. When they landed on the desk, the sting of reality made itself at home. The portrait photo of Delilah bounced off the page. It was a cropped, zoomed in version of the original photo taken during her last week in rehab. At that time, her hair wasn't even purple yet, and it sickened him to know he possessed no recent picture. "Sorry if the uh, Portuguese isn't exact. I googled it."

Silva dragged the posters toward him and stuck them in the same folder with the report.

Derrick gulped.

"It's time to go," Greg reminded.

All Derrick could do was hope Carson had any answer they could work with.

****

"This is where it all started." Derrick looked at White Shores, then at the construction site, and back again at the hotel. He recognized it all from the news footage. The front lot was almost empty and a fragment of police tape blew like a tumbleweed across the blacktop.

"Now you're thinking the shooting *did* have something to do with it?" Greg asked.

"Last time I spoke to her she said she was attacked, and I can't stop thinking about that. Based on the time she left and the time those people were killed, she would have been here."

"She never elaborated?"

"I never asked."

"Regardless, I'm not sure how many more tips your guy Carson can give us."

"Speaking to a witness in person is much different than just over the phone. You know that." Derrick rolled his shoulder and switched his briefcase to the other hand.

"If he ever shows. We've been out here waiting for thirty minutes."

"I'll cut the guy a little slack. My daughter broke his heart, but in the end I'm sure he'll be happy to help." Turning away from his skeptical partner, Derrick held on to his positivity; the alternative was an acknowledgment of a darker possibility. If they were lucky, what had happened with Delilah was all a dramatic act for attention.

In the next few minutes, a revolving door of exuberant students filled the lot with their noise.

"Hey! Carson! Over here!" Derrick waved. "You'll see, Greg. He's a young man with a bright future."

Carson broke off from his group at the driveway and headed their way.

"Hey there. I was afraid you wouldn't recognize me." Derrick reached out for a shake that prompted Carson's hand out of his pocket.

"No, I recognized you, same polo and cargo pants."

"This is my partner Greg Weaver over at the sheriff's department."

They had a friendly handshake.

"I'm not in trouble, am I?" Carson said under a brief chuckle.

"Uber's here!" one of his friends called out. According to Derrick's social media research, his name was Devan.

"Hey, uh, you think your friends know something you don't?" asked Greg.

"Go on without me, I'll catch up later!" Carson waved his friends on and faced them again. "Nah, they know even less than me." He pulled out his phone and began swiping at the screen.

"I don't want to worry you or interrupt your vacation," Derrick started, "but I want you to know she may have still been at the hotel during the shooting."

"Oh yeah? How do you know?" Carson asked, not looking up from his phone.

"Family tracking app. Her location disconnected about the time it happened in this parking lot, according to the news and the police. We just filed a missing-persons report."

"I wouldn't know. None of us were here when it happened." Carson put his phone away. "You did say you talked to her on the phone though later, sooo she's fine, right?"

"Well, I don't know. She told me she was attacked and I didn't take it too seriously. Father of the Year award."

"I wouldn't beat yourself up about it, man. You never know with addicts." An annoyed laugh escaped Carson. He straightened his expression like it was an accident.

"Erm, I guess that's what I was thinking too, at the time," Derrick replied in a quiet voice.

"So how long are you guys in the country?"

"I don't know. As long as it takes, at least for me," Derrick said.

"Wonderful. Well, you gotta do what you gotta do for family members. Despite their bad history."

"I wouldn't say—"

"Oh hey!" Carson raised his phone like a glass. "My ride is already here, I have to get going." Carson began backing away to the car pulling up to the front. "It's nice seeing you again, good luck! I'm sure she's fine. Like I said over the phone, she was hanging out with some guy on the beach, I'd start there."

"Carson, wait." Derrick opened his briefcase and handed him a pile of papers.

Carson stared down at the blown-up colorized photo of Delilah.

"Do you mind if you and your friends hand out these fliers while you're out? It's just a precaution really, but they could help."

"Oh."

"That bottom sheet there is the phone number she called me from. I haven't had any luck so far. Maybe you could call it every so often? She might pick up for you."

"Sure thing. Talk to you later, Mr. Johnson." Carson jogged off.

"You gave him most of our stack," Greg said with a bite of accusation.

"I don't know why I did that," Derrick said, watching Carson hustle away.

"Now that I've seen that guy in person, I am even more confident that he is a grade-A-douche-wad. You picked up on that, right?"

"Just a little." Derrick rubbed his short hair vigorously. "He kinda makes me wonder if I was right about Delilah. Maybe she did run off. And if that's the case, can I blame her?"

"She went incognito in Brazil because of her boyfriend?" Greg asked.

"Yeah, him… and because of me." Derrick jerked on the briefcase handle. "Damn! I've been such an ass!"

"Hey, shh!" Greg held up his hand. "What'd he just do over there?"

"What do you mean?" Derrick followed Greg's gaze.

"I swear he ducked behind that planter for a second."

Derrick followed Greg, who made a brisk beeline toward the entrance as the car with Carson zipped off. A trash can came into view behind the large plant. Greg pulled the top off and reached in. Derrick saw his partner retrieve the copies of Delilah's face.

"Shit." He sighed with a face-palm.

"I think you've been batting for the wrong team there, buddy." Greg dug through the trash to get the rest.

"I'm done wasting our time here. There's no way she'd ever come near here again." Derrick stormed toward the street. Terror rattled his confidence. The damage to their relationship was done, and now he was afraid it was too late for a second chance.

31

DELILAH

Drained and reduced to a limp corpse on the ground, Delilah dropped her legs flat against the wrestling mat and her heart thumped in a plea to give her body rest. Inácio's silhouette blocked the sunlight above her. While she felt she could vomit at any second, there was very little, if any, physical strain on his face. Ground-fighting instruction was obviously light work for Inácio.

"I'm sorry," she said after failing to meet his expectations for the dozenth time. Ever since her little victory on the range, she was in the never-ending role of pupil.

"Don't be sorry. I might be pushing you too hard."

"I suck at this. I mean, I appreciate you trying to show me how to protect myself, but I hate it."

"I don't like it either, trust me. I'd rather be on two feet."

"Let's do that instead! Show me how to punch someone or something. We've been at this for an hour."

"Thirty minutes, actually."

"Potato potahto. It's not like I could ever overpower you in a million years, let's face it." Delilah stared up at his torso. Inácio was stacked with blocks of strength. His muscles puffed out the fabric of his T-shirt. What was the point of even trying?

"That really bothers me."

"What bothers you?"

"Your attitude."

"Attitude? Um, sorry I'm not as fit and skillful as you." Delilah sat up and threw her arms over her knees.

"As in the belief that you've already lost. You think you can't get the upper hand with me, but you're wrong."

Delilah almost laughed. "Am I though? I told you about what happened at the hotel. When that guy attacked me, it was the most powerless I've ever felt. I tried to fight back then and I'm trying now. It's pointless."

"You know first hand about the dangers of being pinned on your back."

"Honestly, doing this is just bringing it all back. Every time is like taking my tragedy and throwing it back in my face, reminding me how I failed to protect myself." Underneath her self-doubt was more frustration with him than with herself. Didn't he understand? To be physically overcome over and over again was nothing more than a reminder that she was a victim. Weak, subpar.

"When all you know is defeat, you start believing in it. It's all a lie, Delilah."

She responded with a silent look.

"Think about what you did on the range. You overcame debilitating fear. There is no hidden bodily strength I'm trying to make you unlock. You're right, you will never overpower me, physically. But everything you need to know is up here." Inácio tapped his temple. "Strategy and technique can prevent a man from using his body weight against you."

"That's hard to picture going up against someone like you." She rested her chin in her palm.

"Let's try it again with the heat turned up a bit."

Delilah groaned. "How is making it harder supposed to help?"

"It's only me. Better here than out there again."

"What are you trying to say, Inácio? I am just destined for this kind of thing to happen to me again?"

"Stop it. You know that's not what I'm saying." He kneeled down in front of her and took her hand. "Trust me like you trusted me on the range." Delilah noticed the hope in his eyes. It was obvious he really wanted to help. After all he'd done for her, it was hard to say no. That's why she'd been putting up with his mentorship in the first place. A similar feeling pulled her away from wanting to please, an impulse whispering in her ear to walk away just as it had behind the gun. Delilah wanted to avoid failure and stay away from her worst memories. Yet, Inácio was still by her side despite her weaknesses. He hadn't given up on her like everyone else.

She tipped over on her back again and waited for him to cover her like the last dozen times. How he did it came as a surprise, if not a shock. He didn't climb over her and get into the perfect position like all the rounds before. Instead, he practically leaped over her and sank his weight in a dramatic attack.

Betrayal.

How could he?

Delilah yelped out of fear and tried kicking her legs. "Inácio, wait!"

"C'mon, Delilah, stop me!"

"I can't! Stop! Please!" Delilah knew she wasn't in real danger, but there was a part of her that believed that just maybe she was. Her mind resorted to panic instead of strategic thinking. Why was he doing this? How could he treat her like this after she'd confided in him about the assault? His grip was callous and his face was void of sympathy. All she could feel was the brunt of his strength taking over. Inácio's size trapped her to the mat.

"Are you going to let me do this to you? Look, my hands are around your neck. All I have to do is squeeze."

Terror wetted her eyes.

"C'mon, Delilah!" Inácio jerked his hands around her neck.

"Please, stop."

His grip expanded, showing the vast discrepancy between attacker and victim. "Remember what to do. You know!"

Delilah growled through her tears, inviting in her fury with Inácio's aggravating persistence. Her senses took in the cruel pinning of her body. If Inácio had really chosen to hurt her, she would have been dead by now. Still, the simulation gave off an eerie realism. With a scowl, Delilah stopped squirming.

Her foot wrapped around the flexed calf he used to prop himself onto her. She trapped his leg exactly as she was shown. Delilah's hand found his shirt collar and pulled him toward her, knocking Inácio off-balance with her hips. After his control over her slipped, Delilah used the small window of opportunity to roll on top and escape. A fighter's grunt rumbled through clenched teeth as she shadow-boxed Inácio's face as an imitation to what she would do in a real scenario. She backed away with her hands over her mouth in surprise. Once she committed, everything passed in a flash.

"I did it. It happened so fast!"

"*Fast*. That's how quick you have to be. Do you understand?"

Delilah agreed.

"Good job. That's all I wanted to see."

"That's good enough progress for me. I'm done."

"Only one way to make it second nature." Inácio winked.

Delilah rubbed her front teeth with her tongue, not surprised he wouldn't let her enjoy her little victory. Satisfaction came with tossing Inácio onto his back over and over. Each repetition happened faster and faster until there was little to no thought behind her hooking his foot and bucking him off. Shuffling and exasperated grunts repeated in one long monotonous cycle. Sooner than she'd imagined, his aggressive pouncing became less stressful. His shirt had come off and flawless fluidity followed the more she drilled.

When Inácio was down and stayed down, she knew their exercises were finally over. His chest pulsated with fatigue and if her eyes didn't deceive her, she saw sweat gloss his forehead. Her rising body temperature brought heat rushing to her cheeks. Delilah joined Inácio on the mat, their breaths syncing.

"I'd say you exceeded my expectations." He reached out and brought her against his shoulder. Resting her cheek across his chest, her hand felt his racing heart. Shade from passing clouds darkened his face in slow, strobed shadows.

"Was I too hard on you?" Delilah knew her dimples had to be showing.

"It's good for me to lose a little." He stroked the back of her sweaty neck.

"Do you want to know a secret?"

"I can keep secrets."

"I could stay here forever with you." Delilah waited for Inácio to push her away. When he didn't, a flutter of hope set in.

"That sounds amazing."

"You know, maybe I don't have to go back." She went onto her belly until they were face-to-face.

Inácio swallowed. "What about school?" *There it is.*

"What about it?" she grumbled.

Inácio turned away from the sky to her. His brown irises were glazed over with a grown-up sense of maturity.

Delilah revised what she was trying to communicate. "What if I finished it and then came back afterward?"

Inácio switched back to the sky, an elbow resting beneath his head. The heartbeat under her palm had slowed but now picked up the pace.

"Have you thought about it?" Delilah's fingertips played imaginary keys over his sternum. His response required patience.

"I do think about it."

She waited.

Strict logic faded from his expression. "When I do, it feels like peace." A smile crept over him. "And a little fun."

"Well, then? Could I come back after graduation?"

"Unfortunately for us, it's impossible with my job. I will probably be nowhere close to Rio when you finish school."

"Do we have any kind of future?" If it was possible, her heart would have ceased to beat right then.

"Hate to change the subject, but it's way too late in the day to be this serious." Inácio stood up and left her on the mat.

"You sure love dodging me, don't you?" She sat up on her elbows, her lips thin with disappointment.

"Hey, come here." Inácio pulled her up to her feet, then turned and offered his back to her. He opened his hands up behind him.

Delilah fought a grin with all her might. "Stop distracting me."

"Get on."

She laughed, getting sucked into whatever illusion he wanted her to believe.

"Hop on, Midwest girl."

"What are you going to do if I do?"

"Haven't I earned a little bit of trust?"

Yes… and no. Ignoring her heart, Delilah leaped up and wrapped her thighs around him. The second her thigh reached around his hip, Inácio propped her up.

"There. Not so bad, right?"

"Where is my steed taking me?" She rolled her eyes, secretly enjoying it.

Inácio paced and stretched his back. "You made me a little sore."

"Yeah right."

"It's true."

"You're a brick wall."

"I'm just an ordinary man."

"A machine, more like."

"A machine that needs to relax in the pool."

"No! Inácio!" Delilah squeezed around him hard with all four of her limbs as they caught air. Beneath the water, the echoes of her giggles cemented her mind into his temporary delusion of a life centered on love. Inácio chased her kicking legs through the blue until she made it to safety to the pool's edge. Flipping to face the water, the sun-heated pavement drank up the moisture from her shorts.

Inácio broke the surface and lifted his head between her knees. Sunlight glimmered off his slick face. Delilah reached for his wet hair, letting the water tickle off his ends. He floated upward as his hands crawled their way over her hips. The whiskers growing across his jaw pricked at the insides of her thighs. Brown eyes narrowed with intent. His fingers slithered up her legs and over her waistband, pulling on saturated fabric. They tickled their way around the seam until they reached the button and zipper in the front.

Delilah's hands tangled up his hair in anticipation. She was heading down the road of obsession, fast. The fixation of disappearing into the divine, a state of true bliss where she was valued as treasure. Her place in the past was nothing but fragmented memories of a life that no longer existed. She lost herself in the idea that she deserved happiness, a future where no one could hurt her again without feeling the wrath of Inácio.

Her shorts were dragged down her hips, the hold on the denim so tight. A pink evening hue took over the surrounding atmosphere. Delilah leaned back on her palms, giving in to her fantasies—pretending this man would never leave her. The beautiful view was unable to compete with Inácio's devilish smile. He was a puzzle, a challenge, and a deity of pleasure all in one. His sly hands made a move toward her panties. He swam his face further between her legs until his lips were so close she could feel his breath tickle the bud of her clit. Delilah was in his clutches and there was no place she would rather be than under his command.

Scheming eyes preceded a painful tease of the tongue. She watched in aching anticipation as the tip lingered barely beyond the reach of her pleasure, only to be withdrawn and planted on her thigh with a sloppy kiss. Up and down his lips explored, sucking, wetting, and nipping over her skin. When he returned to her pussy, more titillating touches hovered, testing her patience.

With a sharp bite, Delilah pinched her bottom lip and tipped back her chin. Only a millimeter separated her from his mouth. She pulled at his hair in desperation to bring his face closer. He didn't budge. A thirsty rock sent her hips swaying in his direction. *Please.* Inácio jutted his head out of the way, leaving Delilah to suffer.

A wicked chuckle purred between her legs. "You're a greedy little one."

"I want you. Right now." Her feet swam through the water like hungry sharks until she found his shoulders, rubbing, trying to persuade him to act.

"I'll have you when *I* am ready." He pressed his fingers in her hips, indenting her body wherever he touched.

Delilah tried to draw him in and protested with another lusty buck of her pelvis.

Inácio pinned her butt back to the tiles with a firm jolt and eyed her with a deadly sternness. "You shouldn't act that way in front of a man who wants to torture you with his tongue. You might just get a little more than that."

She grabbed his hands holding her. "Do it, I dare you."

Pulling away, Inácio seized her by the knees and split them apart.

Delilah gasped.

His mouth dive-bombed between her thighs.

She squealed.

He came to a swift halt and stopped again just before making contact. Delilah's pussy cried with unfulfilled fervor. Then a sensation, light and tender. It stirred its way up her puffy lips until touching the exposed head of her clit. Around the swelling bud it circled, giving just enough satisfaction while withholding all heavenly potential. Looking down, she caught Inácio studying her every reaction. Big hands run up her legs, thumbs settling at the top crests of her thighs.

Heat diverged from the point of his tongue, taking crude control over her body. Her back bowed and her knees spread wider, inviting him to torture her however he wished. Carson *never* went down on her, justifying his reasoning that it was a submissive position for a man. Inácio didn't feel beneath her at this moment; instead, he was a ruler over her experience. It took trust and surrender, two things she was unaware were lacking in her life before *him*.

In an abrupt shift, Inácio plunged into her. The shock took her breath away, her knees rising, feet ripping from the water. He was everywhere. Inside, under one pussy lip then the other, over her clit, and back inside her. Delilah tossed and squirmed in his grip. She tugged his hair and flung water across the pool with her toe. His mouth consumed every drop of her arousal, digging in like he needed her womanly essence to live. The intensity made each draw of breath a struggle until she could no longer repress her bliss.

Wails of pleasure cut through the quietness of the evening, which only seemed to embolden him, working her with more vigor. Layers of sensation were stacked on top of pleasures that were foreign to her before. The fountain of female pleasure and all its possibilities were nothing but legends and ambitions of women of mystical arts; everything out of reach for a girl like her. She was not spectacular. His tongue said otherwise. Delilah sought a moment of relief, just a second to catch her breath, but there was none.

Out of pure instinct. she escaped him just enough to be out of licking range. A rush of air restored some clarity.

Inácio pulled her back. "Where do you think you're going?" In one menacing leap, he escaped the pool and anchored one foot over the tiles, completely naked and entirely hard. Delilah fell back, watching the water drip from him as he crawled over her like a lion on the prowl. His body rained down onto hers while he gathered her up. "I warned you."

She was pulled upright and thrust onto his lap with ease. Inácio scooted to the edge of the pool and stripped her top off, making her as bare as he was. Delilah faced him and saw his admiration staring back. When would she ever experience a connection like this one again? If only he didn't pull away, he'd be absolutely perfect.

A bit of honesty snuck through. "Am I enough for you?"

His eyes narrowed before lifting her by the ass and lining up her pussy with his cock.

Delilah waited for an answer. She listened for words of commitment and searched for the safety that her heart needed in the darkness of his pupils. Nothing came except a thick force stretching out her pussy, filling her until the question fell to the priority of his cock. He was still a bombshell to her system even after a good warm up. And she wasn't the only one.

Inácio's eyes squinted shut and his jaw gaped from the acute pleasure. He fought for a complete breath and his struggle reminded Delilah of her own just seconds before. Wrapping him up with her arms and legs, she rocked herself back and forth, up and down. The more she moved, the more he let go of control.

Every broad inch of him became hers to influence. Since the night they met, it was always Inácio calling the shots and deciding when to draw close and when to retreat. Nothing made her feel more frightened than the idea he could drop her at any moment. How was it possible to be so afraid and yet so safe at the same time? If what they shared wasn't enough for him, she'd at least make sure he lived to regret it.

Delilah's abs burned as she tried so hard to tether herself to him with sensual rolls. His deep moans were marks of successes in her view. Inácio tilted his head back and leaned against locked arms. Her own scent on his breath wafted in her face. Something else that was brand new to her. The authority over his pleasure ignited both hope and determination.

Words huffed out of him like it was all he had left. "Oh god, Delilah."

Almost there.

Delilah threw herself over his torso and made Inácio look at her, her hips never quitting. "Is this not enough for you?"

"Yes, yes," he gasped. "You are… mmm-more than enough." His face twisted with the oncoming climax. "It's, it's me, not you."

From a nearby table, a phone call rattled the glass surface..

Inácio sat up straight and his breathless demeanor disappeared.

"Don't." Delilah grinded faster.

"I have to." He frowned as if the pleasure was more of a nuisance than a gift.

"Please?"

Inácio pulled her off and abandoned her at the pool.

Delilah remained by the edge and watched him out of the corner of her eye. Distance and responsibility made it all go away like magic. Inácio returned to the same man who rescued her from danger—all business and no play. Wet footprints followed while he stepped several paces away from her, tempering his volume.

Delilah lowered herself into the water in defeat and rolled onto her back, bending her body so she floated. A sequence from her childhood swim lessons directed her flow. *Chicken, airplane, jet.* She turned and did the same movements back to the other end, feeling completely silly and rejected. The water passed through her fingers like her flowery dream of keeping Inácio in her life. Tears sprinkled down, trailing her sadness behind her. It was nothing that he would notice. After a few laps, she gave up swimming and stilled herself at the surface. Delilah took it all in so she could take in every detail before it was all gone and a gut feeling said that was going to be sooner than she realized.

Warm water, glossy blue tiles, pink sunset, a happy heart—

"I have to go." Inácio stood above her, his form resembling an ancient Greek stature.

"Holy crap!" Delilah rolled over and grabbed the side.

"Did I startle you?"

"You're deadly when barefoot."

"I'll be gone a few hours."

"May I ask what for?" Delilah hopped and lifted herself out.

"It's work."

"Will you be doing something dangerous?"

"No, no. Nothing like that. It's not that interesting."

"You don't owe me an explanation. It's okay." Delilah crossed her arms.

"It would bore you to death, I promise," he said while pulling her waist close to his. Delilah analyzed what was behind his gaze. His eyes were blank. Inácio was working hard to conceal certain parts of himself.

She followed him into the master bedroom and watched as he dressed. If she was quicker on her feet, she would think of a clever question to trip him up. Inácio cracked open the closet door and reached in, the hangers swinging and knocking together.

"So, boring as in office work?" she asked, teetering forward and back on her soles.

"Yep." Inácio was miles away.

Delilah scanned the room, reminiscing on their week. Clothes and sheets were strewn in every other place than where they were meant to be. It was a good kind of mess. That was the Inácio she wanted. She took one of his wadded up T-shirts and slipped it on.

"Still got that phone?" he asked.

"Yeah, it's in the dresser, top drawer."

He retrieved it and began typing, then handed it to her after several seconds. "You are connected to Wi-Fi and I put my number on speed dial. Keep that with you at all times."

"I thought you said you'd only be gone a few hours."

"In case there's an emergency while I'm away."

"I don't know what kind of emergency could happen here, this place seems pretty locked down."

"Of course there won't be one. I just like to be prepared."

"I won't run off. I know how worried you get when I do." She forced a smile. Delilah waited for him to return the gesture, but he maintained his seriousness.

"While you're with me, I'm going to protect you. I can't leave you alone without giving you a way to call me." Inácio stepped closer and embraced her. Delilah wrapped her arms around him and clamped down hard with one terrifying thought: she could love this man.

He's going to break your heart.

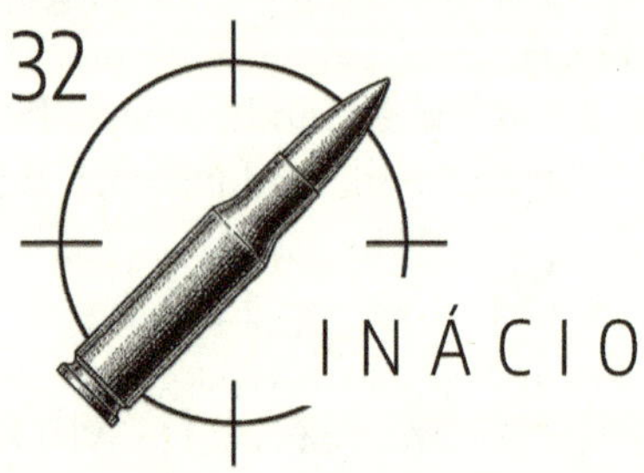

Samba City, the cradle of the world's largest and most extravagant parade floats. Team members scrambled everywhere to move their creations to the street where they would make their one and only debut at the parade grounds of the Sambadrome the following night. A stolen staff ID and a clipboard was all he needed to look official. Shiny outfits hung limp over his arm while he made his discrete exit from the designer's wardrobe. He made it outside and to the trunk of his car where he spun the costumes around like a cinnamon roll before stuffing them inside. The night was all about gathering information on the next target, finding out how in the world he would assassinate a man before millions. During the scheduled hit, nothing would look the same.

Inácio prowled down the narrow street, stopping against a young tree along the sidewalk. He leaned his shoulder against the trunk and observed the enormous structures inch their way down the road. To be back in the heart of the city was to be in his ultimate comfort zone. Across the road, samba music and a raging argument were emanating from the unadorned apartments. Small crowds of locals gathered under a streetlight to watch the famous enormous floats of Carnival pass by. Inácio remembered the time in his life when he was so fascinated by the floats, each an imaginative kingdom in itself.

Their creators were so careful to dodge low-hanging branches and estimate how exactly to make the next turn. Inácio jammed the clicker on his stolen pen up and down while waiting for a glimpse of the target. Time passed slower with someone pretty to live for. An hour turned to two before parents and children gathered around, all arguing about which float might win.

"It doesn't matter, son, they won't win with the famous Afonso on their side."

The name tickled Inácio's ears.

"If only our neighborhood could afford to hire him," said another.

"Isn't that him over there?"

Inácio traced a line from the child's finger to an approaching float, comparing the man with the image in his mind. Storming back and forth alongside the structure, his arms and heavy explosive steps expressed the tension within. His bald head and satin jacket shining under a streetlight gave him away. He was Edgar Afonso, the man standing between Inácio and Delilah's soothing presence. Studying every detail, Inácio memorized the way he paced, stomped, and screamed at his crew.

"This way! Turn it this way! If that branch so much as touches the horse's head, so help me!" Afonso's form was a distinct straight and rigid style. It was the kind of upright arrogance only earned after a six-year winning streak at the world's largest party. "Stop right there!"

Inácio saw his chance and approached the float.

"And watch the tarp! Are we trying to give away the whole show before we even start?" Afonso continued, climbing up a ladder attached to the back.

"Why does it matter? The horse's head is sticking out anyway. Everyone knows what it is," argued a staff member on the ground.

Afonso yelled from his thirty-foot perch. "It matters! Every detail matters! If it didn't, I wouldn't be on my way to making your loser of a neighborhood win their first Carnival in thirteen years!" He pulled on a corner of the tarp, securing it down.

Another member of the staff vented to Inácio, who happened to be closest. "He must think the Beija-Flor school is going to take their float back and redesign a year's worth of work just to copy him. Ha!"

When the designer was finished, he leaped from the ladder and landed athletically onto the street.

"Hello, Mr. Afonso," Inácio greeted.

"What do you want?" he asked irritably.

"My name is Antonio Lopes, and I am the assistant director of security for this year's Carnival."

"Uh-huh. Does that mean you work for João Costa?"

"I think you mean Francisco Costa." Inácio had done his homework.

"Just checking if you were some sort of spy." Afonso's eyes squinted as he tried to read the ID hanging from the lanyard.

"No spy."

"Good. I'm sick of the underhanded competition lately." His fists were glued to his hips.

"We are doing pre-performance structural checks of the floats. I have examined two other floats and now I need to inspect yours."

"*Que?*" Afonso laughed, turning back toward his micromanaging duties. "This is absurd. They have never done this before. Why now?"

"It's a new safety measure after the tragic collapse last year."

"Oh yes, what a tragedy."

"Yes, sir, it was. Innocent people were killed."

"And if you think you find something wrong with my float, what are you going to do? Disqualify us? Send us back to fix it?" The target waved him off. "This should have been done weeks ago if they really cared about our 'structural integrity.'"

"I think you've got them figured out, Mr. Afonso. It's more about liability than disqualifying anyone. Unless I find something extremely obvious."

"Hah! You will find no flaws here, Mr...."

"Lopes."

"Whatever. Feel free to do any inspections you'd like with that little clipboard of yours, but you're not touching my float without me."

"Sounds perfect." Inácio smiled.

Afonso gestured for him to follow.

"Do we need to stop, Mr. Afonso?" asked a member of the team.

"Nope! Not a chance. He won't be here long." Afonso climbed the float and showed Inácio a behind-the-curtain look into the build of his enormous creation.

Inácio's eyes were fixed on the man's bald head, taking note of every blemish and mole to identify him later.

"The float is meant to represent the city of Troy and this giant is the Trojan horse! It will be controlled with levers by a few strong guys down below. A lot of the men will be spilling out of it on these ramps that will be opened as if they are laying siege to the city! It's very structurally sound, see?" Afonso grabbed the horse's leg and shook. "It's perfect. It symbolizes what humans are willing to do for love. Ah, so beautiful."

"Is this where you will be during your performance?"

"Of course! Where else? I will be at the top!" Afonso looked up and saw a tree branch miss the Trojan horse by a centimeter. He sighed in relief and grabbed his chest. "This job is going to give me a heart attack."

33

DELILAH

Silence.

It only made things worse. No longer could she get lost in whimsical fantasies. An impulse, greater than any longing to be desired, took its place at the helm. It led her to search every drawer, cabinet, shelf, and forgotten corner of the house. Delilah expected to find something, yet not even one piece of mail with a full name and address was tossed at the backside of a counter or in a junk drawer. Junk drawers didn't exist in his home, either. In the master bedroom, his belongings were as simple as those of any single man, and in some sense less so. What she didn't understand was how he could take up so little space in a home so large. If it wasn't for the gym, it would be as if no one lived there at all.

After sliding the final closet closed, Delilah stumbled into the bedroom they both shared and tossed herself across the mattress. She zeroed in on the lack of sound. It continued to torment her with its trickery, making her believe she could hear white noise. Flipping the pillow beside her over her face, it was thrown to the floor just as quick. Inácio's scent was entwined in the fabric, traces of his cologne all over the bed. Delilah went limp and melted off of it.

To her left, the closet door was left cracked open just enough to catch a glimpse of one of his few button-up shirts. On all fours she crawled over and slammed it closed. Finding something else to look at was impossible. The cracked window reminded her of the night she'd tried escaping him. The broken door was an exhibit of Inácio's strength. On the bed, Delilah saw him treating her wounds and making love to her—or at least what she felt was love.

There was nowhere in the house where she didn't see him. Her mind refused to let go of the compulsive need to know more about him. When Inácio kissed her, she wanted to believe the intention behind it, but it was difficult to know how honest he was without understanding *who* he was. Inácio's noble deeds were not enough to make up for secrecy. In the back pocket of her shorts was the only way out of her self-induced torment that she had. With a Wi-Fi connection, she could search anything to help pass the time.

Delilah thought *entertainment*, but her fingers typed: *White Shores shooting.*

The screen was filled with news articles with shocking titles containing words like "*killed*" and "*murdered.*" However, the word that each title had in common was "*assassination.*" At times, the titles ended with a question mark, and at others, an explanation point. Her thumb found the most flashy one in English and clicked. Delilah gulped as the article loaded in. An accompanying video loaded at the top. She watched the loading ring spin until it was replaced with the elegant white walls of the hotel. Yellow police tape cut into the sublime resort image, switching between aerial images of the crime scene and the faces of the men who had been killed. An English voice-over drowned out the Portuguese police officer.

"It is this construction site that we believe the shooter was utilizing. Based on firearm forensics, we know that the gun used in the attack was this model." He opened his hand to an impressive rifle propped horizontally across the ground with a long scope. Another man lay flat on his belly to demonstrate. "The public should be able to enjoy the Carnival celebrations without fear. We believe at least one of these men to be the target of a professional. This crime was conducted by an assassin who is still at large."

Subdued under the sound of the video was a subtle noise from across the house.

Delilah pressed pause.

The sound was quick and simple like that of a door latching.

Through the following silence she listened, trying to work out fact from imagination.

If someone was there, there were no footsteps treading across the marble.

Delilah sat up in a crouching position and tiptoed toward the door. Inácio was quiet, but she wasn't sure if he had reason to be *that* quiet. All of his talk about mysterious "dangers" and the reporting on a rogue assassin intensified her already guarded state. Logically, it was ridiculous to assume the worst. But that was logic pre-Brazil. Life could turn into the worst-case scenario in a split second. Her fingers ran up the edge of the door to open it, stopping just before the crooked hinges ground together. With bare feet, she creeped to the kitchen doorway.

Finally, a glass-like rattle confirmed there was someone here. Relaxation quieted the alarm bells. Despite her restlessness surrounding Inácio, she was glad he was home. Delilah entered the kitchen and took a peek toward the bar. A threatening form was behind the bar top, but it was not Inácio's. Her knees buckled before she was seen, trying to process who she saw.

Tall.

Lean muscle.

Long black ponytail.

Blood-red fingernails.

Silver knife.

Delilah scrambled for somewhere to hide.

Don't do it.

Inácio looked back to Afonso's departing float. He palmed the case holding the lethal syringe in his pocket. It was a bad idea to bring it. To use it before the agreed time would be to break serious protocol. The assassination was meant to take place the following night. Sweat slicked the metal container. If there was a window to eliminate Afonso before an enormous crowd watched on, he planned to take it. It was a reasonable argument of self-preservation. However, he would be lying to himself if he said that was the only purpose. Inácio wanted nothing more than to make sure his time with Delilah was maximized, and that meant getting his job out of the way.

With slight pressure, he flipped open the case with his thumb. Afonso entered alone through a bottom flap into the heart of the imaginary city of Troy. The closest float was at least fifty feet behind. One slight prick of the needle and the job was done. Witnesses would only remember a stranger with a clipboard and badge. Determination sprung his legs into action. He could talk his way out of Schafer's disappointment and his employer's wrath. *Do they really expect me to risk the entire organization to fulfill some unreasonable request from the client?* Inácio had caught up to the float in seconds. His arm was moving the tarp when his phone rang.

He stumbled back, almost falling down. *What the hell am I doing?* Inácio turned back and jogged toward the sidewalk. Heart pounding out of his chest, he came face-to-face with how much Delilah kept his head out of the game. The mental interrogation began. Was he really willing to trade his life for an extra day with a woman? Did he actually believe there would be no consequences? Inácio fumbled with his cell and answered it, still continuing on to his car.

"*Pronto*."

"Inácio!" greeted a frantic whisper.

A pit grew in his stomach. "Delilah? What's wrong?"

"Someone is here!"

Inácio threw down the clipboard and badge.

"She has a knife and she's going through everything."

Fucking Talia. "Where are you?" He stood still for a moment to listen to any background noise.

"Under the sink in the bathroom." A crash was audible in the distance. "I think she's breaking things, too."

"You can't stay where you are or she'll find you."

"I don't get it. Who is she? Why is she trying to find me?" Terror rattled Delilah's voice.

"I will explain everything. Right now, you need to do exactly as I say or she will hurt you."

35

DELILAH

Delilah's toes pushed open the cabinet door. On her belly she backed out slowly from the cramped quarters. Her elbows dug into the stacks of towels, guiding her body out. Her bangs edged her nose as her hair smashed its way across the top of the shelf. Every second, she was afraid the intruder was going to pull her out by the ankles.

"Do you hear me?" Inácio asked, his voice like that of an archangel speaking to her from heaven. It gave her courage.

"Yes, I'm trying to get out," she groaned.

"Whatever you do, stay quiet. Once you make it to the panic room, everything will be fine." His order came from a guttural place in his throat.

Delilah fished the rest of her body out and closed the door silently. Disregarding the tangled hair hanging in her eyes, she crawled on her knees until she could see into the bedroom. It was empty. She tiptoed from the bathroom. Even with no shoes, her footsteps seemed to shake the floor beneath her.

"Where are you?"

"In the bedroom."

"Please, watch your corners."

Delilah stared into the hallway while she walked around the bed. The lamp on the nightstand enlarged her shadow across the wall. She skipped forward quickly until she was in darkness again. Delilah hugged the wall low into the hallway. The spare bedroom across the hall was open and ransacked worse than the master bedroom. A lamp lay broken on the floor and the drawers were pulled out from the table beside it. A sound of another bottle smashing came from the bar area.

"What was that?"

"She's at the bar, I think."

"And you?"

"I'm going to go for the stairs."

Delilah slid back down and army-crawled across the floor. She used the kitchen counter to the left to hide herself. Inácio's breath rushed loudly over the phone. Her hand stretched out, bringing her out into the open. The sight of the woman's ponytail made her recoil. Delilah didn't know what she was doing. She only heard loud scratching noises.

"You can do this," he said.

Delilah rushed along on her knees and elbows until she reached the stairs. The metal railing sung under her hand. Her feet ate up two stairs at a time until she was in the loft.

"Opening the door to the patio just like you said."

"Good, close it behind you. The balcony will lead you to the bedroom above the pool." Delilah looked down and saw the woman begin to walk out the back door leading to the pool area.

"She's coming outside." Delilah could barely maintain a whisper.

"Don't look back, just run." His instructions sent her flying. The blue glow of the pool below dimly lit her path. Her heart thumped hard enough to shake her teeth.

"I'm here!" Delilah skidded to a stop.

"Go to the closet."

Delilah pulled the mirrored sliding door to the right, revealing a hole of blackness.

"Get inside."

She obeyed.

"Make sure the door is closed behind you."

"Do I hide here?"

"In a way. Feel the back wall. You should come across a touch screen. It's at my eye level."

"I can't find anything. I can't see!"

"Keep your voice down! Breathe slowly and swipe your arm across the left end of the closet."

She waited for the closet door to slide open and see a pair of claws reaching in. Her death grip on her phone made her knuckles sore. Delilah felt her coolness spiral. The possibility that her future could be ripped away was very real and very close. It wasn't possible to hide her fear from Inácio, even over the phone.

"Come back to me, Delilah. I won't let anything happen. We don't react to what happens to us. We respond."

"I—I f-found a screen lit up." The smooth glass was flush with the wall.

"Great. Click it and enter into the keyboard four-three-one-zero-eight-four."

"Zero-eight-four?"

"Yes."

"Okay, I did. Nothing happened."

"Now type in '*de oppresso liber*.'"

"Can you spell that?"

Delilah listened to every letter. After she entered the last character, she heard the quiet sound of a latch shifting. The handle glowed beneath the keypad, and she slid it open with ease. The hidden door was thick, but swung over the floor like melted butter. Lights turned on inside the panic room and revealed all the information about him she'd ever wanted to know.

"It will shut behind you. Are you in?"

An arsenal covered the walls. The weapons, strictly organized by type, were flattered by backlights on their racks. Pistols hung with pistols and rifles with rifles. There were also bulletproof vests, ammunition, and other gear ready to be put into action. It was enough firepower to bring the city of Rio to its knees. Delilah stepped over to a stack of metal green canisters. One sat slightly ajar. Beneath the lid was a collection of enormous bullets, reaching a foot in depth.

Delilah's hand ran across the cold barrels and ridges of the weapons. Some were black while others were patterned with jungle camouflage. Her fingers barely tickled the belly of a grenade, an object she'd never expected to see in real life. Once again, she felt the safest and in the most danger she ever had all at once.

"Delilah, do you hear me? Hey!"

She grew quiet. "Sorry, I'm right here. Safe."

"I'm on my way. I'll get there soon as I can." His engine roared through the phone. "And one more thing. Don't touch anything."

"Sure, whatever." Delilah ended the call. Inside the hidden room was the part of Inácio she knew he'd never wanted her to see.

36 INÁCIO

"Delilah, it's me." Inside the armory, Delilah rested on the floor, her back to the gun rack. To see her surrounded by his violent world was a living nightmare. She whipped her head up and slid something behind her. There was no sign of relief in her at seeing him or even a hint of perplexity about what just happened. It was hard to tell if Delilah thought much of anything about her surroundings. Her sunken eyes showed only one thing: mental exhaustion. Inácio kneeled to her level. "Are you okay?" His hand covered her knee. Her slight frame drowned in his T-shirt. The bottom end fell down her thighs from the anxious sway of her legs and exposed her thong underneath.

She flinched away. "I'm fine."

"Sorry you had to go through that alone. I wish I was here when it happened."

"Yeah, me too." Delilah looked past him.

Inácio glanced over her shoulder to the open door. "I went through the entire house. She's gone."

Delilah didn't respond. She only picked at her nail polish.

Turning to his left, he noticed the gun case to his sniper rifle sitting wide open. Beside it was the backpack he traveled with everywhere, the front pocket left unzipped. "I thought I told you not to touch anything." He was direct, yet careful not to expose any frustration.

"It was like that when I got here." Delilah made a single shoulder shrug.

Now that was a lie. "What are you hiding?"

She squinted. "What are *you* hiding?"

"Behind your back. I saw you put something there."

Delilah restored eye contact. "I'm glad you're so happy I'm still alive."

"Don't try to distract me. Show me what you have." Inácio opened his palm flat.

"I don't have anything," she snapped.

His lungs filled with air, preparing himself for a confrontation he did not want. "Please, if you don't give it to me, I'm going to take it, and I don't want to do that to you."

Her legs acted like jacks and pressed her back against the wall harder. Inácio shoved his hand around her, the side of his finger sliced open by something smooth and fibrous. *My notebook.* He grabbed her shoulders and pulled her forward. Delilah tried to wrangle herself away and pounded her fists against his chest.

"Stop, that hurts!"

"Then stop fighting me. I don't want to hurt you!" They rolled to their sides. Inácio pinned her with his leg, wrapped her in a bear hug, and took back his notebook. "So, you went through my personal belongings too then?" He moved over to his bag and jammed it in its proper place. Delilah remained on the floor and stayed quiet. Red and white lines from his rough handling tattooed her arms. "Are you going to come out or stay here forever?"

"I don't know yet." Cute naked toes tapped in front of her.

"I realize we need to talk. Can we do it inside?" Inácio was willing to say anything to get her out of the armory. She was too close, literally encircled by the truth. It was unsettling.

"So you can do disaster control on what just happened? I can't trust what you tell me."

"What happened tonight… I didn't want that." Inácio scratched his growing whiskers.

"But it did. I try to ignore it, but at times you act so dodgy that nothing feels safe." A ray of sincerity shone from tired eyes.

"All I want is for you to be safe. I failed."

"You can protect me physically. I'm just not sure I can say the same for my heart. Will you tell me who the crazy woman with the knife was?"

"Some things aren't worth your time or mine."

"That figures." The corner of her mouth dimpled her cheek in disappointment.

"You don't understand. I don't want her to come between all that we have."

"And what do we have? You said yourself she would hurt me. I think she's already involved. Let me guess, a bat-shit ex-girlfriend."

"Talia means nothing to me." He slammed his lips shut. Emotion loosened his tongue. Never had he slipped a colleague's name to anyone who shouldn't know.

"So she does have a name." Delilah sat up straight. "Talia. That's pretty. She was beautiful, from what I could tell."

Inácio turned toward the entrance. "Can we do this somewhere else?" The small space had become hot and claustrophobic.

"No." Her soft nature was exchanged for a side that was foreign to him. It was rough, defensive, and untrusting. Delilah brought herself to her two feet. "I want to talk here in your closet of secrets."

Inácio shut his eyes and took a deep breath.

"Who is Talia?" One of Delilah's fingers slid across the wall, just below the pistols.

She wouldn't.

Delilah paused with a thoughtful look towards a .45 caliber.

"Talia is a colleague."

"And why would a coworker of yours want to hurt me?"

"To hurt me. I took away something she wanted and now she wants revenge."

"And that something is you?"

Inácio swallowed. "Yes."

"Did you have any idea she could be a threat to me?" Delilah hugged her healing arm. All Inácio wanted to do was earn back her trust and regain control of his unraveling life.

"I thought you'd be safe here, but I was wrong."

"Well, that wasn't a no."

"I'm sorry."

"Me too. It's not the thing that I'm most worried about."

Inácio's eyes fixated on the pocket storing the notebook.

The scorn of betrayal distorted her fair features. "*T home alone at 2000 hours. T walks dog every day at 1500 hours. T keeps key card in car overnight. T jogs alone in park 1940 to 2021 hours.*"

As she recounted the notes word for word, Inácio swayed. His hands shook like those of an old man. The more she recounted the contents of his notebook, the more his soul lifted from his body, giving him a bird's-eye view of the worst possible situation. Any assassin who found themselves there would be a fool not to protect themselves. Delilah had committed so many of his scribblings to heart that she was just asking for it.

"*Dark area in northeast corner of park is ideal location*," she went on, refusing to let up on how much she knew.

"Stop talking!"

"Then just a check mark, a list of other dates, and the letter T written to represent a different person each time."

"I'm warning you, Delilah. Stop it."

"And let's not forget about the numbers and tally marks on the last pages. What was it?" She put her finger to her lips. "Twenty-one last year, thirty-two the year before that? It looks like you were on number three so far for this year. A good start. T stands for 'target,' doesn't it? I was afraid you were a liar. A liar and a killer."

"I see you have it all figured out. I'm going to give you this one chance to leave before—"

"Before what? Before I become another check mark in your notebook? We never had a future together. Someone like you isn't capable."

"You don't think I'm capable of love?"

Delilah shook her head.

Heartbreak swelled in his throat. "I cared for you from the moment you walked out of White Shores."

His honesty made her pause. "What do you mean?"

"You haven't figured that part out, have you?"

Delilah flicked away a runaway tear, like it showed too much of her weakness.

"You were so upset. I could tell someone had hurt your heart."

She recoiled.

"I saw that monster attack you. I have his face burned into my memory."

Delilah's jaw relaxed until her lips separated.

"You're right about me. I kill people for money. And I was there to kill one man, but I shot two to save you." Inácio moved closer until their eyes were just inches apart.

"You're lying," she whispered. "You're using what I told you against me."

"How do you think I found you right in the nick of time? I have been lying to you, Delilah. But I'm not lying about what I feel for you." Inácio cupped her cheeks, fighting the urge to force his love on her lips.

"Don't confuse me."

"I'm not being deceptive. You are the greatest thing that has ever happened to me." It was then clear that to be discovered wouldn't be the worst situation—losing her would be.

"I care about you too." Gentleness returned to her face. "I don't know what to do from here."

"I have a… *job* tonight. Come with me."

Delilah desperately scanned the room.

"You'll be safe by my side. You can make up your mind about who I am after."

"I'm not sure if I trust my judgment right now. When you touch me, I feel blinded."

"Then I will open your eyes."

37

DERRICK

Derrick shook the flier to get his attention. "Can you please call me if you see her? Please, *desapare-ceeedo*," he encouraged, trying to use one of the only words in Brazilian Portuguese he'd learned: missing.

"I understand this. *Desaparecido*." The restaurant manager pulled the business card and poster toward him at the counter. It wasn't clear if the barista would look out for his daughter or not. He might even throw it in the trash like Carson had.

Derrick turned away toward the door. The sunshine from the most perfect weather he'd ever experienced beamed inside. It was the perfect contrast. Life flourished around him, but on the inside he was doing his best to control the turmoil. After finding that he was completely out of business cards and posters, it hit him how many hours he had been out canvassing for Delilah. And it was still not enough. Half of the people he encountered seemed too drunk or happy to pay attention to something so grim. He scanned the tables just in case a girl with purple hair popped into view. Of course, she wasn't there either.

Derrick stepped through the wall of heat, his throat becoming a bit irritated from the constant desperate chattering. Another wave of sweat took over and he sensed a hint of heat exhaustion within himself. He was wearing short sleeves, but his legs were trapped in a denim sauna. Down the street about a hundred feet were Greg's sunburned cheeks and ears heading toward him to regroup. Behind him was a street filled with bustling traffic and pedestrians.

"You look a little red," Greg said.

"So do you."

"The back of my neck is on fire. I think we'd be fried without our ball caps."

"Where did you go?" asked Derrick.

"All of those businesses for two blocks and the rest through the street. You?"

"Pretty much the same, but on the other side. How many people actually paid attention?"

"Quite a few actually. I said the hotel shooter kidnapped her. They were really interested after that. I'm out of fliers though."

"Yeah, me too, and business cards." Derrick put his hands on his hips and looked around. There was so much more to be done.

"We can't keep this up without flyers. It had Portuguese on it. Most people didn't understand me too well and if it wasn't for those—"

"I know. Not a whole lot of people seem to speak English around here." Derrick walked along the road bordering the long beach Delilah had enjoyed at one time. A wild block party moved down the street, their songs and music still plenty loud. "We need to get to the police station and see if they'll print more for us."

"Derrick, we've been at this for"—Greg checked his watch—"six hours straight. That's on top of the five hours we did yesterday."

"That's nothing. We need to keep going." Derrick hailed for a taxi once traffic began to flow again.

"We need a break. Let's sit down in some air-conditioning and talk about it, figure out our next steps."

"I really think we need to keep going. Someone has seen her, somewhere."

"Derrick, look at the beach, look at the sidewalks. There's gotta be a hundred thousand just in eyesight." A taxicab pulled up to the curb and Derrick waved Greg to join him in the back seat. He leaned close to the driver's ear.

"*Polícia Civil do Estado, da Relação Street.*" His basic Portuguese was rough, not coming out as he pictured it in his head. It was slow moving through the packed street. Pedestrians and cyclists littered the road behind the party. Derrick stared out the smudged window at the heavy police presence posted periodically through the most congested parts of the city. They all got a flier too.

"You don't really look too good."

"Thanks, Greg."

"When's the last time you drank any water?"

"I'm fine," Derrick brushed off. He didn't want to admit he was feeling sick, and dehydration was the obvious culprit. Taking a peek at his reflection in the driver's rear-view mirror showed a hot tamale. Only Derrick's inner drive held him together. If it wasn't for Delilah, he would already be a melted pile of mush cooking on the cement.

"I don't think you are, but besides that, I need to sit down. I'm hungry, tired, overheated, and I can't think straight anymore."

"I feel like there's someone out here who has seen her. If I give up, what if I miss the one person who remembers?"

"It's not really about who has already seen her though, you know? When she was on the beach, it was before she disappeared. Her last location was at the hotel. We're really getting people to recognize her in case they see her in the future. We already know she's been here."

Derrick wanted to rip the rest of his thinning hair out like Maggie. One parent needed to hold it together. "I don't know what to do. We have no leads. She's vanished, Greg."

"No, people don't vanish. We're missing a couple pieces of the puzzle is all."

"A couple?" Derrick spat.

"Committing suicide by canvassing isn't getting us anywhere. We can't help her if we get heat stroke."

After a slow commute, the cab screeched to a stop in front of the police station. Derrick handed their driver a wad of cash. It wasn't exactly cool in the taxi, but when he stepped outside again, he felt nauseated and dizzy. Objects meant to be stationary moved in ways they shouldn't.

"Okay Greg, you might be right. Let's order some food, get hydrated, and figure out where to go from here."

"Thank god." They survived one more busy street crossing before experiencing the frigid relief of their hotel. The desk agent stared at their appearances with obvious concern. Derrick smashed his palm down onto the button to summon the elevator, finally feeling his inner desperation give in to his fatigue.

"Do you think they got Mexican here?" Greg's stomach rumbled like an earthquake.

"I imagine they have everything here."

"Detectives!" a voice shouted from behind. They turned and saw Officer Silva walking eagerly toward them from the other end of the lobby.

"What's he doing here? He didn't seem interested in helping last time," Derrick muttered. A young officer with similar purple-yellow facial bruising was with him.

"Can I help you?" asked Derrick.

"You guys look very tired. No luck, huh?"

"No." Derrick frowned. *Why does he care, anyway?*

"Then I'm glad I found you. I might have information that could help you find your daughter. I came by earlier and called the number on your card. I didn't get an answer. I think you were busy."

"Oh." He glanced at the missed call on his phone, the words onscreen waving like water. "Sorry, didn't even hear it ring."

"That's alright, we are neighbors," Silva said. Derrick was unsure if he was really happy or if it was his poor condition that made Silva seem so energized. Either way, the man was hurting his ears. "I have good news."

"Go on."

"My officer here took a witness statement who said they remembered seeing a girl with purple hair."

"Okay? What does that mean? What's this about?" Derrick questioned.

"Get ready. There has been an investigation into a man for over a year now for murder. Very bad criminal. He is the very, what you call, *elusive* type. Anyway, this witness knows where he is now. This is great!"

"What does this have to do with my daughter?"

"The witness said he was seen with a girl with purple hair. This could be your daughter, no?"

"Are you going to arrest him then?"

"I wish we could, but the investigation isn't done yet. Just like in the United States, we are a country of laws. We still need more evidence, but I came to offer you a way to find your daughter—if it's her, of course."

"Do you want us to follow him?"

"No, not you." Silva chuckled. "We will do it together. You guys have a name for it. It's—"

"A stakeout," Greg said.

"Yes! We can help stake out the suspect. If your daughter is with this man, we can get help and rescue her."

"You can't get more help to rescue her now? Are you sure this is the best way?"

"Please understand, the Carnival and this shooting has made everyone very busy. Officer Belo here is the only man on my team I can spare. We both want to help you, and it can help us too, with our own investigation. So, what do you say?"

"One second," Greg said, taking his partner aside. "What do you think? Could this be anything?"

"We have nothing to go on. I can't nap in our hotel room knowing I passed this up, can you?"

"Guess not."

"Where are we going?" Derrick asked Silva.

The sergeant smiled and slapped an arm around his shoulder.

38

DERRICK

The excitement for a new lead wore off hours ago. Humidity, mosquitoes, and other creepy crawlies made every hour a fight to get to the next. Derrick, trapped on his stomach, was squished between Greg and Silva in the tree line beside the suspect's property. The late hour made Greg nod off. His nose dipped into the leaves of a viny plant. When it tickled too much, he popped his head back up, flipping his eyelids open for a second, only to repeat the sequence again. To Derrick's right, Silva and Belo didn't seem bothered or itchy from bug bites like he was.

If the lead panned out, the discomfort was worth it. If it wasn't—a complete waste of time. A decision that may cost him real answers. Derrick viewed the dream home like it was that of any other crook who made more money than him: with disdain. Crime always paid until they were captured. Since the stakeout had begun, the only sound was the ocean's tide.

Derrick should have expected it. It happened to him all the time in quiet public spaces. First, it was the erratic vibration, then the obnoxious old-timey ringtone rattling on full sound. Derrick's heart leaped from his chest. All three men snapped their heads toward the sound and Derrick shared in their mortification. His hand couldn't seem to keep a grip on the little brick and away it went, sliding down the steep slope behind them.

Derrick leaped from his hiding spot and dove after it. The ground was a dirty slide with the base of it being a concrete road. Hushes hissed after him, and to make matters worse, the phone's flashlight strobed as if he wasn't able to tell it was screaming at him. Derrick reached for it, sliding on his full stomach to where it settled under the lip of the curb. His thumb slid over the red button, ending the call from Maggie. Brushing off the streaks of dirt on his face, he wormed his way back to the top, returning to a prone position between Greg and Silva.

"Great job, *Detective*." Greg smirked.

"That could have been very bad."

"Important call?" Silva whispered.

"Eh, my wife."

"Ah, so very important."

"She's worried. I apologize, I should have had that thing on silent."

"Doesn't look like anyone noticed." Silva shrugged.

"Are you sure what's-his-name is even home?"

"He goes by the name Inácio, and not really."

"How long are you planning to wait here, you think?"

"I say we give him another hour, then we will decide what to do next. Unless you are willing to wait here all night?"

"Sounds agonizing, but I don't know what else to do."

"She will turn up." Silva nodded.

"How do you know?"

"Mmm, I think it's important to stay positive."

"I don't know how positive I can stay thinking about my daughter in the hands of a murderer. If it ends up being her in there."

"Not many fathers would."

"Do you have children?" Derrick asked.

"No. I don't have a lot of time for children."

"You're lucky. You've been spared a few heart attacks," he moaned.

Silva chuckled quietly. "Is your daughter that disobedient?"

"Well, ever since high school she's had a knack for getting in trouble. I guess that's most teens though."

"A knack?"

"Yeah, like, she's a gifted troublemaker."

"That's what I hear about American girls."

"I hope you don't mind me asking but, what happened to your face?" Derrick made a circling motion with a finger toward his own.

"I do a lot of work in the favelas. They are like the slums of the city, run by gangs. Dealing with the people there can be tense at times."

"Yeesh, glad you made it out of that. Whoever did that to you in jail now?"

"His time will come."

"Hey!" Greg alerted. "We got movement. Lights are turning off."

Derrick looked over to the upstairs windows just in time to see a glimpse of what he thought could be a female-shaped silhouette before it went black. After a few minutes, the garage door lifted, shedding its light across the driveway. The intense fluorescent lights looked like the opening gates of heaven to Derrick, who was over nesting with the bugs. A sleek car befitting the house spun around toward the road and swept its headlights over the watchers. Derrick and the others dropped their faces into the dirt until they were in the clear.

"Shit, we got to move," Derrick said.

Dirt and roots flew into the air as they slid. Their target car rounded the corner from the driveway and drove onto the street below. Derrick felt Silva's arm pinning him back to prevent him from giving away their location. They threw their awkward bodies back against the incline, then headed into full gear again when the suspect passed. Derrick was on Greg's tail as they sprinted to their vehicle and jumped in the back seat. The unmarked Fiat trampled the grassy trail again and whipped around to keep up.

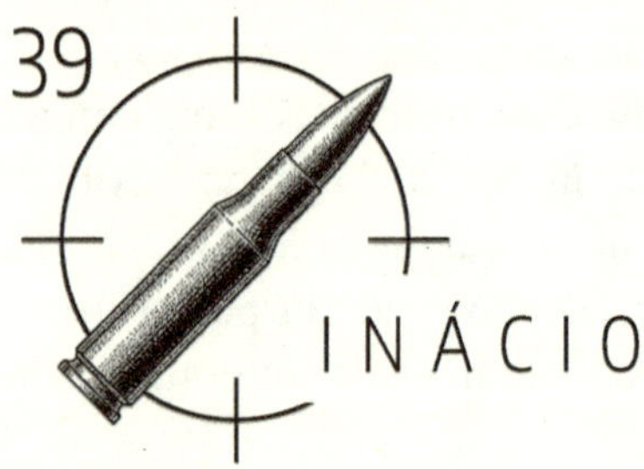

39 INÁCIO

Inácio hit the accelerator until he heard the satisfying purr he loved so much. As the winding road straightened, he accepted their drive would likely be their last moment together. He should have expected someone her age to bend to her curiosity, a mistake he was willing to take responsibility for. Inácio had selfishly opened the door for her to enter his world, then he'd expected her to be content with his vagueness. Delilah's allure backed him into a corner and made it difficult to formulate a plan out of the mess.

But none of it mattered anymore. At the next assassination, she could see firsthand the monster he was. There was no doubt in his mind she was going to choose to leave him forever. In a perfect world, he could have her, but nothing about his life was ideal. Talia was only one example. She'd left behind a kind note carved into a once-flawless bar top. *Matar ou ser morto.* Kill or be killed. Inácio had thrown a towel over the message before Delilah could see. At least he knew she was acting on her own—the Philosopher didn't send messages.

Searching for relief from his thoughts, his eyes drifted to the pair of legs beside him. There was a little color to them now. The golden dress was short, even on her. The stolen outfit was meant to be his gift to her. Now, it was part of her disguise as well. Large jewels dangled from the bottom end of it. They bounced and rattled with every bump in the road. The middle section was a cage-style design and covered in glistening sparkles. The plunging neckline flattered her small chest. When Delilah caught him staring, he immediately moved his focus back to the road.

He cleared his throat. "You're distracting in that dress."

"You're distracting in that sparkling bodysuit." Inácio caught her smile. He was happy she'd started to talk. She had been so quiet since their confrontation.

"Not the most comfortable." He pulled on the itchy fabric at his legs. Inácio rested his hand on the car's shifter and stared down the dark road. Up ahead, city lights grew closer. A shiver ran down his arm when Delilah put her hand over his. A little sadness hit him. Soon, she wasn't going to want to touch him. *Maybe it's for the best.* Taking a deep breath, he decided to enjoy her while he still had the chance.

40

DERRICK

Tucked away behind the corner and across the street from the suspect's vehicle, Derrick popped forward from the back seat for a better view. The doors of the supposed murderer hung open in the small parking lot. It was impossible to see who the passenger was from their secret vantage point.

"What are they doing?" Derrick squinted.

"Patience," shushed Silva from the passenger seat.

The man walked to the passenger side and stood in front of the open door.

"What is that man wearing? That's your murderer?" asked Derrick. The shiny outfit hugged tightly around their target's body. "What's he like, a gigolo or something?"

"This Inácio guy doesn't look too threatening to me," Greg said.

Silva stopped speaking to his officer and leaned back over the armrest. "You see all these people running toward those gates? They're all dressed like this because of *Carnaval.* See these guys in pretty colors? They're running late to their groups."

"Groups?" Derrick was far out of his element.

"Yes, dance groups. Every neighborhood in Rio designs their own float and dance."

"I think I saw some pictures online of this. It's like Mardi Gras, right?" asked Greg.

"Mardi Gras? Is that what they call it in America?"

"Yes. They dress up like this too and ride on floats."

"Let me look this up. Mar-dee Graw."

"It ends with an S," Derrick muttered after he saw the butchered spelling on the phone. Silva swiped through a few images on Google before he burst into laughter. He showed the phone to Belo and said something in their language. Belo cackled along with him.

"No, sir, this is not like your country's little Mar-deee Graaww." Silva tapped the ashes from his cigarette out of the cracked window.

Derrick ignored the insult and tried to see past those walking across their view. He burned to know the truth. Had his daughter really hooked up with a scumbag? Silva's phone did a vibrational dance across the dashboard and he snatched it up.

"*Alô?*" Derrick tried to listen as if he could understand. After Silva hung up, he said something else to his officer, who nodded with enthusiasm. It was hard not to feel out of the loop. At the office back home, he made it his job to be involved in every decision.

"Important call?" Derrick asked.

Silva did a double take before responding. "Yes, Detective. Backup is on the way here."

"That sure makes me feel a lot better." Derrick covered his heart like he'd been spared a heart attack.

"He's moving," Greg alerted.

No one sprung up as high as Derrick, his head whacking against the roof. On the other side of the fancily dressed man was a small female who climbed out of her seat. Silva handed Derrick the binoculars, but the crowd made it hard to see anything. Sparkly people were everywhere. The female herself was covered in a pattern of gems and feathers. At least from a distance, the female matched Delilah's height and stature.

"Derrick, is that her?" Greg's tone was serious.

"We have to get closer, I can't see from here." Without permission, Derrick jumped out of the vehicle and stormed toward the pair who walked hastily away in the direction of the large stadium. Derrick weaved through the crowd and sped up to a jog, Greg not far behind.

"Boys! Hey, come here a moment!" Silva called after them.

Derrick ignored him. He stayed hot on their tail while Greg stopped at the suspect's car, peeking through the dark windows. There was something eerie about the couple walking arm in arm. The girl had short purple hair and Derrick could hear the familiar laugh. In his gut, he knew it was her.

Why is she laughing so much? It hit him all at once. He'd never thought he'd find her in high spirits or with someone that could be a killer. In all his time searching, he'd prepared himself for the worst. And yet there she could be, giggling away. Confusion choked out the power from his words. He called her name, but she didn't turn. Derrick yelled again, but there was no way he could be heard over the thousands of voices that polluted the air. The girl mounted the suspect's back and he carried her through the crowd with her legs around his waist.

Derrick saw her figure with more clarity over the crowd. She looked around, giving Derrick a good glimpse of her features. Her smile, the way her eyes squinted when she was happy. He hadn't seen that look for a long time, but he instantly recognized it when he did.

A sense of panic rattled every limb. Derrick had to get to her, he had to take her home. The man who carried Delilah immersed himself in the thick of the crowd. Derrick tried shoving his way through too, keeping eye contact with the back of her head bouncing just above the other people. Costumed and non-costumed people danced into Derrick until he almost face-planted. Delilah dipped out of sight. Derrick jammed his way through anyone in between.

"Delilah!"

Everyone began to resemble a sparkling wave of colors and Derrick stopped being able to blend in so well. Delilah came into view for a brief second, her head facing his direction. *Did she hear me?* Derrick waved, but his daughter was pulled through to the other side of the gate and then disappeared into a denser crowd.

He grabbed the bars and shoved anyone around away from him. He screamed Delilah's name over and over again, but she never looked back again. Security guards forced Derrick away from the gate, shooing him away in their language.

"Please! My daughter! My daughter! Do you understand me? I need to get to her. Look, I am a police officer—" He raised his badge.

"Derrick!" A hand pulled him backward. It was Silva.

"He is a police officer. *Policia Civil*!" Derrick pointed at Silva.

"Derrick, Derrick, you need to come with me," Silva insisted.

"I saw her! She's with that guy! That Inácio guy!"

"Okay, okay! But she is gone!"

"No, not gone! We need to go inside!"

"We cannot. This is the Sambadrome. We will never find them in there! We will wait for them in the car!"

Derrick opened his palms. It was as if someone had stolen everything. "She was ten feet from me! Ten feet!"

"This is good! She is alive! We must wait for them to leave. You will see her again, I promise." Derrick let Silva lead him away from the stadium gates. Greg was there too, waiting in an open part of the street.

"I saw her, Greg. I was so close."

"She's alive and well. That's what matters." Greg hugged him. Derrick looked back and began to accept he had to wait a little longer. He took out his phone and thought about calling his wife. "Are you calling Maggie?"

"I should, but I think I'll wait. I will call when Delilah's in my arms and safe again."

"It's all going to be okay. We will get her back," Silva said. His hand made short strokes over Derrick's shoulder. "We have to be careful not to alert him."

"Yeah, Derrick," Greg agreed. "If he figures out we're following him, things could go south."

"You're right, you're right. That was stupid." At the car, Derrick stopped and shook Silva's hand. "When I made the report with you, I thought you couldn't care less. I was wrong. Thank you for everything."

"Anything for a fellow police officer."

41 DELILAH

Loud music and the screams of excited people wove into a thick blanket of sound. Inácio parted through elaborately dressed dancers. She had never been surrounded by this many people in her life. Beautiful faces passed by, each one with extravagant makeup designs. Usual barriers guarding personal space were surrendered. People brushed against them and brushed against each other, and no one seemed to mind. Inácio gripped her tightly under her thighs as they melted further into the chaos. The thought of being separated indulged her anxiety.

"Our group is at sector two by the *Cadae Correios* building!" Inácio hollered over his shoulder. "We're late, but not too late." Wading among the ocean of people, Delilah didn't even know what to look at. Her eyes were overwhelmed with the rush of incoming stimuli.

Behind the first section of towering bleachers was a man dressed almost identically to Inácio, waving his arms around and shouting at the top of his lungs. Delilah looked around to see they were surrounded by others just like them. Dozens of girls spun around in the same glimmering red-and-gold dress as her. "Spartan Princess" was the name of her costume, he had told her. Inácio finally put her down. Her legs quivered like Jell-O.

Inácio put his lips directly to her ear. "This is the wing president. He's leading the warm-up."

Even with the explanations, it was hard to know what was going on or how *he* knew. *Who is he going to kill?* The question caused a wave of blushing sweat to wash over her.

The wing president clapped his hands rhythmically and counted. Almost simultaneously, the dancers created a psychedelic glittering ball of gold, blue, and red. They went from zero to one hundred in a second. Inácio pushed her away and pulled her in again, spinning her, twirling around her. The contrast of this sudden finesse of his personality further scrambled her beliefs about him, his majestic costume warping her judgment. *There's no way, is there?* It had to be a joke. Inácio moved her body like a puppet and she tried to be as graceful as possible.

There was no choice but to imitate the women around her. This was what she was meant to be watching from the stands with Carson. Delilah felt pretty in her flashy costume, but the other matching women had the hips and rhythm to look even better. She was out of place among the dancers and out of sync with Inácio's intentions. When he stopped spinning her, she put her hand over her face in embarrassment. She couldn't hide her dizzy confusion.

"Delilah, look at me." Inácio cradled her sparkly face. "I will lead you and all you have to do is do your best to move like you know the pattern."

"How do you know the pattern?"

"I don't. I just know how to dance samba and I copy the other men. You know how to shake your booty?"

Delilah's brows furrowed. "Do I even have a booty?"

"Oh yes. I've seen it shaking plenty of times." He smiled.

It was hard to look at him. She didn't want to be there. Inácio was like a ticking time bomb. When would he strike?

"Just relax and have fun. I'll worry about everything else, okay?"

Delilah bounced and twirled on command, her curls springing before the blurry spread of colors. As blaring as the noise was, she could still hear her heart pounding in her ears. Inácio's face came in and out of view—the face she'd fallen for, and now the face she wondered if she should fear. Savior and killer. Delilah followed the forces of her body and hoped she could twirl her way into a normal reality. After a few messy practice sessions, the team began to shift their position around a massive float that crept in a steady motion forward. Men and women scrambled to get into position on, around, and inside the giant.

Inácio pointed toward a ladder and supported Delilah while she climbed the float in her high heels. The floor beneath her eased around the final corner to an open stage lined with bleachers full of screaming spectators on each side. In front and behind were the other dancers, all with completely different themes and colors. Delilah took in the enormous horse fixed at the center, so tall and wide she couldn't see the top from the bottom, built to match textbook images of the Trojan horse she'd learned about as a girl and adorned with vibrant colors and pulsating lights. The floor beneath her jerked, sending her tipping backward.

"I got you." His hand came against her lower back and caught her. The music and attention of the crowd invigorated those around her. Feet moved and booties shook. Without the rail and Inácio's steady hand, it would have been impossible to stay upright. The trembling refused to settle down. She slowed her breathing, but her mind was glued to their purpose.

Who was his next "T"?

When would it go down?

Had he somehow done it already without her knowledge?

What intensified her nerves even more was how well Inácio could read her. What would he do if he saw how scared she was? There was no doubt he felt her heart beating through her spine. He spun Delilah, making her hair wind around her face before winding her the other way. In between, she noticed his lack of expression. They were surrounded by smiles and laughter, yet Inácio was unmoved, his focus directed beyond them. The energy of Carnival begged to sweep her away in its intoxicating glamour. Delilah wanted to follow it into the utopia it created, but she was trapped right there with Inácio and his cold, heartless world.

She whipped back into him, his chest as hard as any stone wall.

"Stay here and keep dancing. I'll be right back." The warmth of his breath on her ear electrified down her neck. Delilah stiffened. There was no smile of assurance or tender fingers combing through her hair. Inácio just left her alone. The musical theater defined his departing steps. Only Delilah detected the sinister pep in his walk. Her body did as he said and swayed with the music until her steps began following her curious eyes.

Trailing behind him, she threaded her way around sparkling archaic pillars and barriers. Spying from around the corner, she saw Inácio travel at a cool pace. A man in a gold soldier's helmet climbed into an opening in the horse's front left leg. Inácio slipped in behind him. An urgency to stop him took over and she leaped forward in her heels. Before she could chase after him, Inácio dropped from the hidden door. Delilah halted. He danced away, around the opposite side of the float, falling out of view.

She waited.

And nothing happened.

Maybe it's all a lie.

Reality fell from the sky and landed with a heavy thud that shook the floor. A Greek-costumed commander lay lifeless as if he had fallen in a real battle. She joined a dozen or more people who stopped dancing and rushed to the body. The shattered helmet released a pool of blood under his head. Men from atop the Trojan horse screamed for help. Delilah leaned forward over those crouching at his side. The man's eyes were stuck open and his mouth gaped at a horridly skewed angle. A haunting emptiness drained the light from his eyes. His form was man, but he was nothing except a soulless vessel. There was no essence, no lifeforce, despite her seeing him alive only seconds before.

A large hand gripped her shoulder and squeezed.

Delilah shuddered and spun around to meet Inácio's icy bearing.

Two hundred thousand. That was the number of eyes in his direction, not including those at their televisions, yet the only ones that mattered to him were *hers*. Delilah's horror scared his heart. It marked the end of their bond. The float came to a standstill. People in the stands nearby grew quiet. Medics and volunteers lifted the rescue stretcher up the float to Afonso's body.

"You murdered him." Fear widened her eyes.

"Keep your voice down." Inácio took her hand and pulled her behind part of the float's fake city wall. "Come, this way." Hidden from view, he waited for the fallout. Delilah paced before him. The back of her hand rested on her forehead as if she were running a fever. A red blush ran from her clavicle to her neckline. She whistled out on the exhale, trying to control her panic. "You look sick."

"I feel sick," she said, fanning her face.

"You should sit down."

"I can't sit still. I need a minute."

"You're pale." He wanted to be sympathetic, yet her shock only felt like rejection. As much as Inácio was prepared for it, he didn't expect it to feel that bad.

"I'm always pale," she sneered.

"C'mon, Delilah, let's get this over with already." Inácio crossed his arms and leaned against one of the false pillars. Delilah spun toward him while keeping her distance.

"Why did you tell me to wait while you went and… did your thing?"

"To spare you an up-close view of what you just saw. It would have been just as apparent what I did if you had listened to me and stayed put."

"You had to have known I'd follow you."

"I was aware it was a possibility, but I hoped for better. Maybe you wouldn't be so upset right now if—"

"A man just died right in front of me."

"A stranger died right in front of you."

"Was he good or bad?" Inácio noticed her hands rubbing together. It was obvious Delilah wanted him to say "bad."

Inácio shrugged. "I don't know."

"Don't you care?"

"It's not my job to care." He growled under his breath. What was the point of a discussion on morality when they'd never come to a consensus? What was the point if she was just going to leave him?

"Who would want that guy to die?"

"Someone with money." *Someone likely in this very crowd.*

Delilah peered out from their hidden corner. Thoughtfulness brightened her blue eyes and her breathing slowed. As she watched the crowd, she said, "I was supposed to be one of them. I'm guessing Carson, Josh, Devan, and the rest of them are out there somewhere. They're all lucky, you know? Normal people, living normal lives. Things are predictable and *safe*."

"And I should have never taken you from it. Our worlds were never meant to touch."

A chuckle cracked a smile across Delilah's lips.

Inácio frowned. "What's so funny?"

"I was just thinking…" Delilah faced him again, this time getting closer. "This whole time I've been in Brazil, I have been struggling to feel normal again. It's been so hard to come to terms with everything that's happened to me."

He stepped back. "You don't need to explain. I want you to go back to it, back to normal."

"I'm not done yet." A sudden confidence sharpened her tone.

Inácio straightened up and listened.

"Then I find out you're somebody else entirely. It's been making my world spin. Everything I thought I knew about life, gone, just like that."

He lowered his head, almost in shame.

"I'm over here believing that it's only you who is different. That this is somehow me plus everyone versus you. Like over here is good and where you stand is wrong and evil."

Inácio took another step back. "Delilah—"

"What I'm saying is, as much as I've been trying to cling to a sense of normalcy, I actually don't know what that is. The first fourteen years or so of my life were relatively normal I guess, but some of it I don't even remember. I was too young. The peer pressure, the alcohol, the drugs, the pain, the despair, the betrayal, and the fear. My understanding of normal was stolen because of these things a long time ago."

Tension made it hard for him to swallow. "This is different. Don't get it confused."

"I'm not confused. No matter how hard I try, I don't fit in. They don't accept me. And forcing myself to be one of *them* has only set me back time and time again. You're right, I'm not cursed. I was just never meant to live a quiet life." Delilah reached forward and took his hand that was hanging at his side. Inácio grimaced.

"Why can't you make this easy on me? Why can't you just go? You don't want this. You don't want me!" Snatching his hand back, he put a finger to his bottom lid, the tip becoming wet from a rogue tear. What the fuck?

"Inácio, you're the only one who's ever made me know my value. It goes beyond the day you saved my life."

"Shut up," he groaned. He swayed off-balance and caught himself with his foot. The alternative to being alone was much worse. If he wanted love, he had to turn his back on everything he'd ever known. It would mean being in a constant state of extreme diligence to survive. The dark enemy would always lurk in the background, taking bites out of their happiness. *Enemy.* He'd never thought about his employers as enemies before, but if he was going to hold on to her, they would be.

Delilah caught his hand once more. "You accepted me and I want to accept you."

"Let go of my hand, please." Inácio pulled back, but Delilah refused to let go. She used his resistance to pull herself to his body. Inácio raised his chin and tried not to look at her. Another tear fell. Angrily, he wiped it away. Reaching up as high as she could, he felt her fingers run across his neck.

"I love you, Inácio." Words he'd never thought he'd hear in his entire life. Containing his weakness was futile. Everything he wanted was right in front of him, and not without its heavy price. Surrender washed over him and he suddenly dropped to his knees in front of her. Inácio held on to her hips, fingers kneading them, and buried his head in her stomach. Delilah's nurturing embrace wrapped around him. Love was dangerous, but with her, *he* was safe.

"I love you too, Delilah. I just don't know what to do with it. There's no life with me that doesn't put you in danger." Inácio looked up at Delilah, her profile encircled with the bright aura of Carnival. He needed her permission.

"I think you proved you can keep me safe. Let it happen, Inácio, and stop pushing me away." Delilah kneeled down and crawled in his direction.

Inácio was forced back into an even more private corner of Troy. There was no one to see them and no one to hear them. When he couldn't go any further, his costume zipper was already down. Delilah dug inside and pulled out his cock.

"You have no idea what you're signing up for," he whispered.

Her warm mouth engulfed him, making him completely wet and smooth all around. Saliva dripped down his stiffening ball sack where her hands gently massaged their hanging position. The roar of the crowd turned into nothing but white noise. Inácio tried to prop himself up, but his strength left him. Resistance dissipated with every dip of her head. Delilah's mouth expanded around his girth as it grew wider and longer. Red lips followed him as he melted into a puddle of steaming desire.

"Fuck it," he blurted. "Fuck them and fuck this whole world." Inácio was going to let it happen. He was going to send his life careening off the mountain of stability all to land in her soft bed of sweetness.

Inácio felt his cock dip to the back of her throat. As she sucked, her tongue tickled the bottom of his shaft. His veins protruded with blood and Inácio fell back, becoming completely incapacitated. The more he gave in, the more she tried to swallow him up whole. There was nothing he could do. Delilah had complete control.

Wet slurping sent him reaching for the walls around him. The float began to move again. Its historical energy shaking the floor under him only intensified his pleasure. Inácio watched her small mouth in awe. The way she was able to handle him defied the laws of physics. The air popping over his shaft tickled. Delilah's eyes watered. Energy reinvigorated his body, driving his hips up to a gentle bob.

"You're mine," he cried.

Delilah moved perfectly with him like they were meant to come together only like this. His fingers ran through his stiff hair, then hers. There was no better view than this, no greater sensation than her mouth around him. When devious eyes flickered at him, he shot his head back in agonizing satisfaction. To be powerless was freedom.

The base of his scrotum pulled tight with pressure, sharing it with the rest of his cock until it reached the tip. Inácio messied her hair even more, winding and unwinding through her hair until his hands could do nothing but stiffen with the rest of his body. Inácio's eyes were closed, and he knew that if he saw her face bouncing off his cock one more time, he would unleash his load. Just a little longer. He peeked, just enough to see her colorful hair and makeup running down her cheeks, Delilah's teary eyes and mouth overflowing with him and saliva. Cum shot down her throat in several sharp gobs. Delilah held still until the last drop.

His eyes rolled forward again as he woke up to a dreamlike ease. Delilah wiped her mouth, taking a few swallows before resting across his chest. For the duration of the god-size parade, they rested together in their secret corner. If Delilah was an assassin, she would be the most lethal kind.

43

DERRICK

Derrick stuffed a second sandwich into his mouth without looking at it. He was too busy staring out the windshield at Silva to pay attention to the taste or worry about the mystery meat inside. The sergeant lit a cigarette as he leaned into the driver's side window of a jeep. Two of them had parked just up ahead only minutes before. Their dark spot on the intersecting road had almost cleared itself of all pedestrian traffic. There was nothing interesting to look at besides Silva. Officer Belo stayed behind with him and Greg. Derrick tapped him on the shoulder.

"Undercover police, right?"

Belo returned his gaze with a blank stare.

"I don't think he speaks English," Greg said between sips of soda.

A rumble drummed in Derrick's throat. "I want to know what's going on. I need to be included in their plan. This is my daughter we're talking about."

"And this is their investigation and country." Greg opened his hands as if to say, *what are we supposed to do about it?*

"I'm glad you're so relaxed about it, Greg." Derrick crumpled up the sandwich wrapper and shoved it in the plastic bag with the rest of the trash. Finally, he took a moment to check out his food. Tuna? With a shrug, Derrick consumed the last corner of his sandwich.

"That is one tall glass of water." Greg watched out the windshield and scooped potato chips into his mouth like it was popcorn at a movie theater. Derrick saw the "tall glass of water" approach Silva in black heels and a tight pencil skirt. Aside from the obvious invitation to stare at her legs, she was smart with a feminine suit and tie.

"You know what? I'm just going to go ask." Derrick flung open his door, took a deep breath, and straightened the collar of his polo.

About twenty feet ahead, the woman opened her hand and a large stack of green bills landed in her palm, then in Silva's. Derrick paused. He wasn't sure what he just saw, but continued nonetheless. Clearing his throat, they stopped speaking and turned without a word. Silva took another puff of his cigarette and blew the smoke into the air. With her high ponytail and heels, the woman stood taller than the rest. It was the first time Derrick had ever seen her, but she looked at him with no question in her eyes of who he was. He felt judged most by the man in the driver's seat. Derrick was only far enough down the street to see the left profile of his face and his single visible eye shot him a bone-chilling glare.

"Excuse me," Derrick began, feeling himself want to stutter. "I was just looking for an update on the plan, if you guys had one?"

"A plan is in the works," Silva said without inviting him in on it.

Derrick glanced at the woman, who smiled in silence.

"Wait for me in the car, Detective. I'll explain it all to you later." Silva dropped his cigarette and squashed it with his toe. The driver of the jeep didn't blink. Stiff legs carried Derrick back to his place in the back seat. Relief to be away from the situation ran out his nostrils.

"So, did you find out anything?" Greg seemed oblivious. Derrick opened his mouth to tell him he didn't know what the hell was going on, but thought twice about it with Officer Belo behind the wheel. It was only assumed that Belo knew no English.

"They're still working on it, they said."

"Cool."

Derrick pulled his phone off the charger to start a private texting conversation with Greg. Once the backup had arrived, something felt off for the first time. Maybe it was his ignorance of the country or Maggie's tall tales or his absurd itch to micromanage. Either way, secrecy and bricks of cash didn't sit right.

Halfway through typing out his concerns, Derrick's door swung wide open. With a grin, the woman slid in, pushing him to the middle seat beside Greg. He locked his phone. Silva joined them from the front seat and introduced their new companion.

"Detectives, meet one of our detectives, Miss Alves. Alves, this is Greg and Derrick."

"Pleased to meet you." She held out her hand.

Derrick took it, feeling like a floppy fish within her strong grip. "Hi."

"I hope you don't mind that I join you."

"Greg, can you roll down the window?" Derrick asked.

"Sure." A breeze moved through the stuffy car. Derrick abandoned his idea of a private text exchange and sat up straight, stiff as a board.

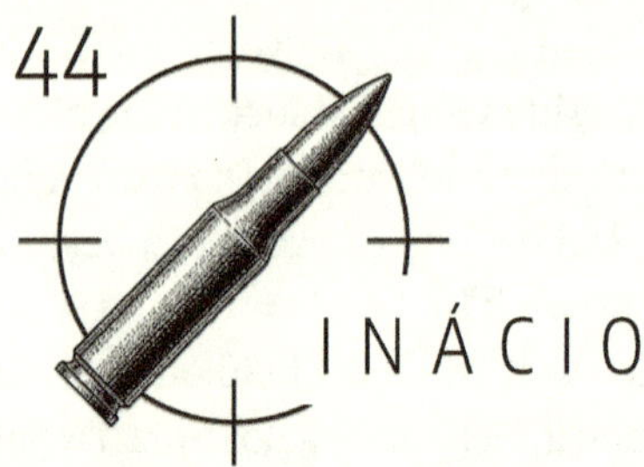

44 INÁCIO

Reaching out his hands, he helped Delilah down the long ladder. When she was low enough, he pulled her off the rails and set her on solid ground. For Afonso and his float, it was all over. For them, everything was different. Even the way she felt in his hands changed. Delilah was no longer a tangible representation of his fantasies, she… was his reality. The thought freed him and shackled him all at once. The road he'd chosen required greater diligence and responsibility.

"That wasn't exactly the Carnival experience my ex-boyfriend promised," Delilah said, hanging on to Inácio's arm. They broke through the tired crowd. Exhausted dancers held each other as they dispersed. To their right, medics were busy treating the dehydrated and taking the most severe cases to the nearest hospital. Inácio absorbed every detail of his surroundings. "Is something wrong?" She tugged on his elbow. He looked down at her messy, beautiful hair. Knowing the reason for the smudged makeup around her eyes brought him back to his inner bliss.

"Everything is perfect."

Delilah leaned into him more.

"Are you tired?" he asked.

"'Drained' is a better word for it. My nerves are shot. What time is it?"

"Very early. Let me carry you." Inácio lifted her across his arms.

Delilah rested her head on his shoulder and closed her eyes. That was what trust looked like; he hoped he could keep it. Inácio walked down the street, the length of the stadium, back toward the company car. Carrying her gave him a taste of independence he hadn't known since he was a boy. Delilah was his decision and no one else's. At the center of the road, Inácio scanned beyond emergency lights and the disbursing crowd.

Delilah nestled further against him. "Take me home."

He wished it was their home. At the car, he set the sleepy Delilah inside. Inácio took a brief look over his shoulder before getting in. It was more of a mindless habit than a diligent assessment. He checked their surroundings as he made it to the driver's side. Inácio was occupied with plans of how to abandon his profession. Asking for help from trusted friends and connections in other countries may be the only way. Plotting and analyzing cemented his eyes to the road in front of him. They were freed only by a message from Schafer reminding him of their meet-up at a discreet location. Returning to reality, he turned the car around and followed another route.

****

There was a tinge of daylight across the horizon by the time he reached the rural place of their meet. Inácio pulled the car into the drive of a small, abandoned house in the middle of the countryside. Dry gravel dust fluffed into a cloud from beneath the tires. Schafer had said he'd be waiting out back, so Inácio shifted to park before turning the corner.

"Delilah." His fingers ran up and down her arm.

"Yeah?" She woke up and looked around. "Where are we?"

"I have to meet with a coworker. I won't be long, but I need you to stay in the car. Do you understand?"

"You don't have to do that anymore." She yawned.

"Do what?"

"Make everything seem normal, like nothing's happening."

"I'm meeting the man in charge of me. I don't want him to see you. That's why I need you to stay put."

"Thank you for the honesty. I can do that." A confident nod reassured him that she really did understand.

Inácio cut the lights. He walked up the rocky drive and saw Schafer waiting in a plastic patio chair. His handler stood up and shook his hand when he noticed him.

"Look at you," Schafer said with amusement. "You're very pretty."

"It's done." Inácio handed over the empty syringe.

"Wow, he got the whole dose. Good for him." Amusement brightened Schafer's face in the darkness. "Did anyone notice?"

"When he fell from thirty-five meters, sure."

"Dang, wonder if they got that on camera. I'd like to see that."

"I'm sure it's there." Inácio swiped back a rogue strand that was in his face. "I need to report some—"

"I have something I need to tell— Sorry, you first." Schafer took a wider stance as if to become stronger for whatever bad news was about to come his way.

"It's Talia."

Schafer's lips fluttered. "Please spare me this one. I know you two are an item. Just keep the drama to yourself so I don't gotta make sure y'all on jobs in opposite corners of the continent."

"You'll want to hear this one." Inácio rolled his eyes in embarrassment for himself.

"Fine. Make it quick. I have something much more important to tell you." Schafer raked his fingers across his scalp as if he were scrubbing out dirt.

"She got into the safe house while I was away yesterday."

"*And?*"

"And… she vandalized the place."

"Aw, c'mon!"

"Smashed some liquor bottles, tipped over a lot of furniture, and ruined the bar top."

Schafer shook his head in disbelief. "What did you do to her?"

"Me? Does it even matter? She's crazy and she's always been crazy. Talia gets away, no pun unintended, with murder. Will there ever be a time where she will face any sort of consequences?"

"Well, you're right, she does get away with a lot."

"That's an understatement."

"*Aannnd* I will do my best to communicate how unacceptable that kind of behavior is. Something like that should not happen among professionals. But don't be surprised if the damages still come out of your paycheck."

"Now that is bullshit," Inácio pointed out.

Schafer raised his hands. "It's out of my control. Not to hurt your feelings, but she must be sleeping with somebody at the top or be related to somebody powerful because that's the only explanation I can think of for how she gets away with so much."

"Whatever." *Soon it won't matter.*

"Hey, hey, forget about that." Schafer got close and started to whisper even though no one was around to hear. "Someone has put a price on your head."

Inácio shrank back. "Where did you hear this?"

"From a member on the board, one of the executives. Looks like you made a mistake in Colombia."

Avoiding Schafer's gaze, Inácio clenched his teeth and tightened his lips.

"You know what I'm talking about, don't you?"

"By the time I saw the camera, it was too late."

The handler exhaled pure disappointment. "That sucks, brother. The Colombians you targeted have your face and they're on the hunt for your identity."

"Do you happen to know if anyone gave me up?"

"Nope. Last time I heard, one of their leaders is asking around and offering a lot of money for answers."

"And the Philosopher? What does he think?"

"I think he will be happy to use a tool until he can't use it anymore."

"Like my dad always said, when it rains it pours."

"Why? Are you dealing with something else?"

"Nah, I'm just…" Inácio placed his hands over his hips and backed away. "I need to get going."

"If it makes you feel any better, it doesn't mean they'll get what they want. They are much weaker now because of your skill set."

"Not for long." He turned his back and walked away.

"Inácio!" Schafer called. "Watch your back."

Inácio returned to his car and whipped out of the driveway. A slight shakiness took over his arms. Change was coming and enemies were multiplying. He began to feel an emotion he was only used to seeing in others: *fear.*

45 DELILAH

The open-air bedroom welcomed a cool breeze that swept across her hair, stirring her from her dreams. Lightweight curtains hanging from the bed's canopy shifted with a strong wind, awakening the rest of her sleepy senses. Clouds shaded the property from broad daylight. Delilah was draped over Inácio, their bare skin in direct contact. They were in a different bed because she wanted to be near the panic room in case the woman, Talia, returned. He was sitting up against the pillows and his legs were stretched out, poking out from the sheets. His eyes were distant, but not empty. A million things at once stirred behind his pupils. Delilah pinched his chin.

"Why aren't you sleeping?"

"I am. I do it with my eyes open."

"Right. Are you more comfortable inside the house? We can move."

"It's late in the afternoon, there's no point. I don't mind the change. I can see everything from here." Inácio didn't break his gaze from the horizon. She watched his pupils contract and expand with the varied rays of light.

"Are we okay after last night?" Delilah feared his cold feet.

"I got a call when you were asleep. There's an incoming job and I will have to leave soon." She zeroed in on his use of "I" instead of "we."

"So you leave for a little while and then you come back here."

"I could, or... I could in five years."

"You don't get to stay here?"

"This isn't my house, Delilah. It belongs to the people I work for. I stay where they tell me to stay. In other words, I have no home."

"Is the job close?"

"Chile. I don't know what my living arrangements will be. It might be as nice as this, or it could be in a tent in the middle of nowhere."

"Oh." Delilah's nose began to ache with the rise in her emotion, a sign she was about to cry. Everything she had pictured in her mind about being with him had been ruined. "I guess I was thinking..." Embarrassment flushed her cheeks. She thought last night had solidified their potential future.

"Thinking what?"

"It's stupid."

"I know it's not. Tell me." Inácio sunk into the blankets and cuddled up to her side. Delilah interlocked her fingers with his and studied how his bronze grip engulfed hers. A future without his touch sounded sad and lonely.

"For some reason I imagined us living here together. This was our home and you did your hitman thing and I finished school and came back to live with you. I thought I'd learn Portuguese and get a job here or something. Maybe even work from home. I don't know why I thought that." Delilah pinched the comforter. Inácio reached out for her cheek.

"That's what I'd rather have more than anything else in this world."

"But it's not possible."

"No, it never will be." His honesty sent Delilah's heart sinking into her gut. Of course the one thing in her life that made her happy was never meant to work out.

"We go our separate ways and be thankful for the time we had." Numbness overtook her nerves, a deep-seated indifference settling in. This was the way of her world, and if she was going to lose him, she'd grit her teeth and be sour about it. Anything was better than heartbreak.

"It will never work *here*, that is."

Delilah sprung up from the sheets. "You better explain to me what you mean by that."

He shot her a serious expression. "We would have to leave. Not just this house or Brazil, but all of it. Everything I know and everything you know." Inácio's finger stabbed her chest. "You couldn't talk to your friends or family for a long time. Don't ask me how long, because I don't know."

"Wait, wait—"

"We'd have to stay in one place for as little time as possible. I want to believe sharing a permanent home together is in our future, but that is very far away."

"Do you really mean it's all or nothing?"

"Choosing each other means being on the run."

"Kill or be killed. That's what Talia carved into the wood, right?"

"You saw that? How do you know what that said?"

"I'm a Johnson. Really good at investigating." She smiled, but it wasn't out of happiness. "I looked it up with the phone you gave me. Was that because of me? Do your people, whoever they are, want you dead?"

"What Talia said was a warning and for her own selfish reasons. It had nothing to do with those in power. It was her twisted way of trying to save me from myself—because I want you."

"And if those in power knew about us..."

"Then they wouldn't waste time leaving a message."

"I don't get it! Why can't you be with someone you love?"

"Nothing exists outside of my profession. I signed my life over to them. Snuffing out love is the only way my employers can be this successful. No attachments, no emotions, no leaked secrets. It's all about money, just like everything in life." Inácio massaged her thigh, the affection now feeling completely illegal.

"You're backing me into a corner." Delilah almost wished he'd never brought up a solution, if this could even be considered one. The stakes sounded too high. Before Brazil, her degree was her only hope for a brighter future. Would running away with him make her a hero to the hopeless romantic archetype or a fool?

"I'm not expecting you to do this. Even after all we've been through, you still don't know the whole me."

Delilah sat up against the leather headboard. He was right. Despite knowing the truth of his profession, he was still a stranger in the end. What other sides of him had she not seen?

"I understand if it's a no. And there's no time to figure it out. If I only get to love you once, it's better than never loving you at all."

"Then tell me." Delilah swung her leg over and straddled him. "Tell me who I will be giving up my whole life for." She squeezed his forearms. They were so thick, her fingers didn't even reach halfway around them.

"It's better if I just show you. But I still can't promise it will be enough for you."

46 DERRICK

Another unfortunate stick snapped between Derrick's hands. He tossed it onto the heaping pile while hidden once again in the suspect's bushes. Every twig took the brunt of his regret. Derrick grew impatient with Silva and his constant insistence that they "wait" for the right moment. There was never a solid plan, or at least, if there was, no one was telling him. Squashed mosquitoes created a mural over sweat-soaked arms. Over time, the unrelenting afternoon sun was swallowed up by gray clouds. A downpour wouldn't be *unwelcome*, if only to alleviate the suffocating humidity. Leaves rustled behind him. It was Greg, crawling through the bushes with a load of snacks in his hand.

"Protein bar?"

"Where'd you get all that?" Derrick took it and split open the foil.

"Gas station."

"When was that?"

"Just got back with Silva. Got some energy drinks in the car if you want some." Greg took a chunk out of a granola bar.

"You mean you left me here alone? That was smart. What if something happened?"

"There's us and two jeeps full of Silva's guys lined up the road. They would have tailed 'em."

"Yeah, *they* would have. For me, I'd be stuck up here alone while some murderer takes my daughter somewhere and I can't do anything about it!"

"I wasn't thinking."

"Just thinking about your stomach."

"Let me make it up to you. Here's another protein bar."

"I don't need it. I just need Delilah."

"Uh, yes you do. Have you seen yourself?"

"Here we go again. I look terrible, I get it."

"Never in my life have I seen circles under someone's eyes that deep."

"Jesus."

"You've skipped out on three opportunities to take a break. Make Silva and his crew do it for once today. At this point, they're taking advantage of you."

"I don't care. Honestly, I'm avoiding that woman who teamed up with us."

"Are you intimidated?" Greg grinned. "That's cute."

"Hardly. She just looks like a vampire. Never says much, just stares."

"I guarantee if you crawl into the back seat, anyone sitting in the AC will jump right out. You smell like death."

"You know what, Greg? I'll do that. Only because you are such bad company." Derrick backed out of his home in the weeds.

"I bought a stick of deodorant too. It's next to the drinks," Greg had to add.

Flicking off dirt and leaves from his undershirt, Derrick dabbed his face with the polo in his hand. He raised an arm and took a big whiff. It could be worse. Tight tendons and sore bones creaked across the road to the nearby tree line. Their spot in the foliage began to feel like home base. Officer Belo was kicked back against the rear bumper of the Fiat, phone in hand. Belo didn't break his gaze from his screen, even as Derrick opened the back seat. It was empty, no vampire woman in sight. With a long sigh of relief, he dove forward, the leather a perfect cool surface for his sweaty body.

"Phew! You are ripe, my friend!"

Derrick jumped up to see Silva and Vampire Lady in the front. "Sorry, didn't see you there. I can leave." He went for the door handle.

"No, Detective Johnson. You cool down whatever is cooking under those pits and we'll stretch our legs." Greg's premonition had been right, and both of them hustled out of the car. He heard their muffled speech as they grouped up with Belo.

Derrick swung his arms across his head, letting himself air out, and closed his eyes. Handling how others thought of him wasn't a big deal when his mind was all over his past, present, and future. He wanted to piece together all the events that had led himself and Delilah to Brazil. Was it a lack of love that drove her to drugs and then into the arms of a killer? Derrick didn't feel like he'd deprived her of the TLC she deserved as a child.

The fondest memories of his daughter were all around when she was elementary age. Almost every day he picked her up from school. When he pulled in, she was always off on her own entertaining herself with chalk or ladybugs. He'd honk his low-toned police horn that made everyone jump except for her. Delilah never walked but ran to the sheriff's logo on his squad car, her backpack bouncing side to side. Derrick's badge used to be a symbol of safety for her, not oppression, as it became later. Even as she grew up, the backpack always looked too big and of course, it was always purple. His work vehicles changed from cars to trucks, yet one thing that always remained the same was her smile when she saw him.

On the way home, he learned the art of tuning out her endless yapping. Most of what she said bore no relevance to his preoccupied thoughts of work. He could now only think that maybe something could have changed if he'd engaged with her more. Then one day, Delilah had tuned *him* out. The maturing girl stopped smiling at him and grinned at her phone instead. She replaced her run with a walk and quit carrying her backpack altogether. Soon, she didn't bring any books home and those days made for long, argumentative rides back home over mediocre grades.

The rabbit hole of Delilah's descent into darkness held him captive in a dreamy state. Derrick stirred after recalling the day he'd caught a glimpse of a liquor bottle in her purse. The little red cap had protruded from the open zipper before he snatched it away, screaming louder than he ever had. Her attitude, her clothes, and her habits became comparable to those of druggies on the streets. It didn't seem real that she began to resemble the same people he arrested on a regular basis.

It was the last time she accepted a ride home. He never figured out who she went with after that. Delilah came home later and later until it became normal for her to skip dinner. Maggie fought tooth and nail with Delilah to keep her grades at a B average and succeeded only because his wife did Delilah's homework. Derrick ripped through Delilah's room weekly in search for drugs or alcohol. The cocaine was hidden in her pillowcase. Tossing and turning, images of sparks from the fire department's saw cutting into his wrecked truck to rescue his daughter pulled him in and out of rest. Blood streaking down her face and her fading consciousness—it was all still there in vivid color.

****

"Wake up, buttercup!" A hard smack abused Derrick awake. Greg shoved his resting legs off the seat and joined him in the back. The door Derrick rested his head against opened to the female detective he was so off put by. Derrick sat up and blinked away his sleep.

"Is he on the move?"

"You missed it! He opened the garage door before getting in the car and I saw her get in. Delilah's in there alright," said Greg with excitement.

"Are you serious?" Derrick shook his head. "Every opportunity to get to her is taken away from me."

Silva skidded the tires at takeoff. "Don't be angry, Detective. Tonight is your night."

"You're finally making a move?"

"The men above me wanted to wait until we were sure we could get him without his escape or a fight. Sorry, I had no other choice but to hold you back."

"But we got the go-ahead tonight, right? Wait, what time is it?"

"Dinner time," Silva replied. "The first chance we get, we make our move."

"I wish we could be armed like you, sergeant." Derrick patted his empty hip.

"We've dealt with plenty of criminals and none of those times ended with a shoot-out." Silva flipped his hand like *no big deal.*

"Neither one of us has shot our guns at anyone, ever," Greg clarified.

"Don't worry boys, we got your back." Silva smiled, twisting around to the back seat.

47 DELILAH

To leave everything behind for love. It was hard to imagine. No mother, no father, no more rushing to an 8:00 AM class, no heading home for the holidays—only love. Delilah took him in as he held out his hand to help her from the car. A gray T-shirt showed off his tattooed arms. It was up to her if he was her forever or her nothing. Resting her palm in his, he assisted her over the curb. Gated households surrounded them. The rough sputter of a motorbike zipped by. Startled, Delilah arched her back and fell into him. He didn't say anything, just held her against him with an unspoken understanding.

"Is this what you wanted to show me?" she asked, nervously tugging on the ends of her tank top. It looked like somewhere he would take her. It was a wealthy area set high into the mountainous topography.

"Not here. Up ahead." Inácio nodded toward beautiful green cliffs not a hundred yards ahead, wrapped in civilization. While they moved ahead, the heavy moisture in the air was hard to miss. Clouds began to take over the sunlight beaming through the branches. Birds glided from trees to homes, freely singing away. Right up the road, an entirely different environment existed. Towering shoddy buildings lined the busy sidewalks packed with people and pop-up stands.

"We're going in there?" She didn't mean to make it sound as insensitive as it came out. There was just something about it, even at a distance, that made her feel uneasy.

"We are. It's one of the slums in the city. This one is called Rocinha."

"Is it… safe?"

"No less safe than anywhere else you've ever been in Brazil so far." Inácio gave her a slow wink.

She followed his casual pace westward into the disorder, his arm wrapped around her waist, pulling her securely to him. Inácio's hold was all she needed to know she was safe. Wealth quickly shifted into poverty. Sheet metal awnings appeared overhead. They shaded only about half the sidewalk. Below were open shops selling everything from native foods to clothes. Vendor merchandise spilled out into the walkway, forcing them to walk around the racks and mannequins.

Delilah leaned her weight into him while they walked, feeling out of place in her purple hair and fair skin. A continual flow of people passed by, clicking away in their flip-flops. They were mothers with their children, bare-chested men carrying heavy loads over one shoulder, and groups of skinny teenagers chatting away. Some of them overtly stared at her while others were drawn to Inácio's tattoos.

"What I'd like to show you is up the street a little more," he said.

Some locals lay back in white plastic chairs, finding coverage under the sheet metal. Delilah cleared her throat as an old man carelessly blew out his smoke right in front of them. She looked up at Inácio, who seemed too dreamy in his observations to think twice. Delilah wasn't sure what he had planned, but it was strange to think of him being from a place like Rocinha, as he called it. Sometimes the sidewalk narrowed so much, they were forced to cut into the street.

A slightly steep slope was scooped out along the gutters for drainage. Motorcycles were lined wheel to wheel down the streets, intermittently making space for a delivery truck. They walked around one

Sprinter van unloading massive cases of bottled water. On the other side, garbage and other scrap were piled beside the street just before the sidewalk widened again. He led her past more shops selling pizza, sweets, and colorful plastic toys, stopping at a building adjacent to a hilly intersection.

"Are we here?" Delilah clung to his arm.

"Good enough place as any to start." Inácio looked up at a green building jutting out of the steep incline. What's left of the sunlight highlighted his clean-shaven face. Delilah saw him swallow, then loose a sigh. "I was born in that hospital right there."

"May I ask when?" Delilah almost couldn't believe she was asking his age now. In a perfect world, she would have known those basic facts *before* learning he was an assassin.

"February eighteenth, thirty-four years ago." Graffiti-covered walls bordered a ramp leading all the way to the front door. Every window in the two-story structure was wide open. She imagined a tiny screaming Inácio breathing life for the first time. The thought made him seem almost mortal.

"Happy belated birthday, then. What about siblings?"

"I do… Or did." His eyebrows pinched together for a second. "Haven't seen any of them since I was a teenager. My mom went and had other kids with another guy a few years after me."

"What's your mom like?"

Inácio took a deep breath and leaned one shoulder against the defaced wall. The corner of his mouth wrinkled and drooped a bit. "She was sort of like you. Gentle, caring, and accepting."

"Does she still live here?"

He just shook his head. Inácio put his arm around Delilah's back and began leading her away from the hospital. "She died when I was fifteen."

"Forgive me, I'm sorry."

They walked up another winding road enclosed by more unembellished homes stacked above tiny shops. The further he took her into the tightly packed neighborhoods, the hotter it felt. Even on a cloudy evening in February, the humidity hid in the lost corners like a stagnant vapor. It only took another fifty feet before she felt him break contact. Delilah turned and noticed him hesitating to go any further.

"Inácio?"

He stood up straight and squinted his eyes closed, his fingers pinching the top of his nose. Delilah at least knew enough to tell he was holding back a flood of emotions.

"You know, you're not the only one who thought it could be fate that we were brought together. Before the night you were attacked, I had been working in Rio off and on for ten years. I had so many chances to come back here but never did. After moving away, I was like an outsider."

"Why did you have to leave?"

"My mom wanted to give me a chance at another life. I was skipping school and getting into the wrong crowd. The only future I had was in a gang. So she sent me to live with my dad. He's an American and was a soldier at the time he met her. Probably looked like Rambo to a poor girl like her. I didn't have much contact with him until he took me back with him to nowhere Indiana. I can respect him as a soldier, but as a father, not as much. He tried, but we didn't understand each other. He wanted an American son, not some foreign kid from the slums. I learned a year later, it only took a few months for my mother's boyfriend to beat her to death. Apparently, I was the only one standing in the way of his escalating abuse. I failed her by leaving. I should have pushed back more."

Delilah put her hand over her mouth and felt a deeper connection with him than she ever had. He wasn't an invincible god sent from Heaven. Inácio was human. To witness his weakness was both heartbreaking and a gift. Despite the heat, she embraced him with all her might. Emotion jolted his lungs. Eventually, he cleared his throat and his torso grew rigid and strong.

"So, anyway, that's why I wasn't able to face it until you."

"Until me?"

"You don't recognize any of this?"

"I don't think so."

"This is where I found you after you wandered off from the hotel."

Delilah opened her eyes wide. Her head had been so foggy that night. The thick mess of power lines criss-crossing above Inácio's head brought back a vague flash. The memory was dark and jumbled.

"This alley here, does it feel familiar?" To the left was an empty space lined with nothing but more homes.

"Well, maybe?" Delilah stepped onto the street and felt the small slippery rocks beneath her sandals. She looked to the wall and imagined a terrifying police officer shoving her against it, then Inácio's fast car flying to fill the space. The blur of clashing men played out in her mind's eye. In the daylight, it didn't look like anything violent had ever happened until she spotted a spent shell casing tucked against the side of the curb.

"This is where I found you. It was like the universe was leading me somewhere. The home I grew up in is right over there." He pointed to a nearby door that would have been right beside the action. "Of course, I didn't have much time to think about it when your life was in danger."

Delilah was lost for words. Could it be fate? The odds of her, just a regular girl from the Midwest, walking in front of the crosshairs of an assassin, had to be next to zero. Even more slim were the chances that the assassin cared enough to save her. "Empathy" and "contract killer" weren't two words she'd ever put together. Yet there he was, affected by the sight of his childhood home, the man tormented by his past and questioning everything he knew because of *her.*

Out of nowhere, Inácio pulled her against him and rested his cheek on her head.

"I love you, no matter what," he whispered. "I accept whatever you decide."

"Your heart is racing."

"I just want what's best for you."

"Were you feeling just as lost as I was when you saved me?"

He gently rocked her back and forth in his arms. "'Asleep' is more accurate. I could have fought more for what I cared about. I let my dad take me because it's what my mom thought was best, and our family paid the price. I don't want to keep letting things happen to me while others suffer. If the right thing to do is let you go, I will. If it means I'm supposed to upend the world to be with you, I will."

"I don't want to give up, Inácio. And I don't want these other people to decide whether we're happy or not. I know I've been pouring my energy into the wrong places just for a hint of joy that never came."

"I get that more than you know."

"Then why can't we have it like anyone else?"

"Are you saying you want to do this?" Inácio's heart pounded harder in her ear.

"Yes," she said with a nod.

He grabbed her arms and looked her in the eyes. "Then tell me you trust me."

"I trust you."

"Do you mean it?"

"I mean it."

"I am going to give us the best life I can. I promise."

"I know you will. I just need to know one more thing. What is your full name? Is 'Inácio' even real?"

"No, it's not my real name." His breath became labored.

"Tell me you trust me." Delilah was willing to change her mind if she didn't know this one essential detail.

"I trust you." Inácio brushed her hair behind her ear and drew in close. He whispered the name so quietly, it was as if it was never meant to be uttered out loud again.

48

DELILAH

Through the world Inácio had shown her, everything was brand new. There was hope and there was fear. Both emotions were equal to one another, neither dominating for too long before the other chimed in with its thoughts. A sprinkle of rain dotted Delilah's window as Inácio drove them through the hilly curves of Rio's streets. The sky darkened and with it came the guilt that she could be doing true harm to her family with her decision to leave. She was at peace with her short disappearance stint, but long-term? Time would tell. Inácio spoke low and calm over the phone.

"I appreciate it. I will let you know when we're on our way… I look forward to meeting him too." When he was done, he stashed the phone in the center console.

"Who was that?"

"A friend who promised to help us."

"So soon? Huh."

"We don't have much time."

"It really is happening then." A sudden dip in the road tickled her belly with butterflies.

"It is. Everything is about to change."

"For the better though, right?"

"That's the goal. It's going to get worse before it gets better, but you let me worry about that part." Inácio picked up her hand and kissed it.

"You seem so calm. Everything feels so weird to me now."

"I can handle the pressure, for both of us."

"Does this mean we're leaving now?"

"Tonight and very late. First, I want to take you somewhere nice. It's going to be tough for a while." He cracked the window to let in the breeze on his face.

"Who is the friend?"

"We call him Don Joaquín. He's an old guy who escaped from my organization—just like we are doing—a long time ago."

"And he gets to live the life that he wants to now, right?"

"Um, I'm not sure about that." Inácio scratched his temple.

"So, we really could be on the run forever." Delilah sank in her seat as low as she could go.

Inácio scooted forward. "It's different with him. He was one of the founders, and rumor has it we're not the only ones he's helped escape. He's a taboo topic. The only man to fight for our autonomy. His work would put him in the crosshairs indefinitely."

"We're different." Delilah sat up and flopped her arm just under the car door window with courage she didn't feel. How could she know anything about being different from the rest when she knew absolutely nothing about how it all worked? Just a plea for reassurance.

"Yes, Delilah. We are different." A crooked smile and a twinkle of confidence in his eye shoved away any negativity for the time being.

"I guess this is where trust comes in."

"We trust each other and I'll handle everyone else. Right now though, I want to enjoy a nice evening with you."

Delilah observed a Hollywood-esque street. "I can't wait to see what you have waiting for me."

"We're going right here." Inácio pulled the car up to a restaurant as the words left his mouth. Decoratively arranged bricks made up the U-shaped drive. Black lampposts illuminated the corners of the building. Healthy grape vines lushly covered lattices beside the front door. Inside, a relaxing glow lit up the sidewalk from the entrance. Two young valets in red vests approached the car.

One of the young men opened her door, the other speaking to Inácio through his cracked window in Portuguese.

"Reservation for Johnson," he replied. Somehow Delilah wasn't surprised that he'd pre-planned everything. She assumed this is how he would be in their new life together. Inácio always strategizing his next move, always one step ahead of danger.

"Is that a real valet?" she asked.

"Your first time?"

"Yeah, just a little."

"He's going to park the car. Let's go." Inácio grabbed his suit jacket from the back seat.

"I feel a little underdressed," she said. Her outfit was just like the one she'd worn while walking into White Shores; casual and ordinary.

"You'd look fuckable in a trashbag," Inácio said with one of his sly winks.

A blush heated her cheeks. How was a reference to garbage somehow the best compliment she ever had?

They entered through the vine-coated archway into a busy but calming atmosphere. The hostess led the way through tables filled with couples on romantic dates and small family gatherings. Just about everyone had a bottle of wine opened, served by well-dressed staff. Women darted their eyes in Inácio's direction, but only seconds at a time, as if they wanted to keep their wandering gaze a secret. He was a man who was hard to miss, especially when the other males around him were more fragile in appearance.

They sat politely behind framed glasses and well-combed hair. The fingers twirling around their pinks and reds were free from calluses. Male patrons rested their muscle-free arms around the backs of their women's chairs like they were able enough to keep them safe. Delilah noticed they couldn't help but peek a glance over Inácio's way either. Money likely always made up the difference for their shortcomings, until Inácio reminded them otherwise. Their jealous eyes made her forget all about her jean shorts and sandals.

The hostess left behind leather-bound menus on a patio table and swept up the *Reserved: Johnson* label.

"We're the Johnson family, huh?"

"Tonight we are." Inácio pulled out a chair for her beside him.

The energy outside was far more exciting than it was indoors. Over the patio rail sat a racetrack that had every look of a Kentucky horse park. The only thing giving it away were the exotic grass-covered cliffs in the background. A herd of sprinting horses with their jockeys breezed by with breathtaking speed and power. Once the thunder of hooves was out of reach, sprinkles of rain drops tapped across their overhang.

"Wow this is amazing!" She grinned, looking back at the horses.

"I'm glad you like it. I *assumed* you'd appreciate horses, being from where you are."

"I love horses," she exclaimed. "Especially seeing them run like that. The power."

"Strength attracts you."

"Mm, maybe." Delilah shrugged flirtingly. Their host approached the table, spewing out quick Portuguese.

"Huh?" Delilah asked innocently.

"He is asking if we want wine," Inácio informed. She listened to their foreign banter.

"Did you just order wine?" she asked.

"I did."

"Sounded fancy. Everything here looks expensive." Silverware shined and the plates on other tables were presented with colorful, dainty foods.

"Are you concerned about money?" His hand pulled her shoulders toward him.

"Habit."

"You worry, Delilah." One of his fingers brushed her hair back, exposing her neck.

"It's been passed down from generation to generation on my mom's side. In high school I never thought for a second I'd become her, but here I am!" Her voice was raised slightly with humor while picking at the bread bowl, a bread bowl that resembled real crystal.

"I can't wait to know everything about you. And now we have forever to do it."

A frenzy of excitement and anxiousness zipped through her fingers like electricity. "In a few hours, you'll be with a hunted man. How does that make you feel?"

"Like I want to hang on to every moment we have for dear life."

"They're going to do everything they can to find us. It won't be like Talia, who left a message behind. They will be there to kill, and they won't blink when they pull the trigger."

"I know." Delilah broke out in chills. The host returned with a full bottle of wine and opened it in front of them. He gracefully poured the deep color into their glasses. Inácio thanked the server, who promptly departed.

"You don't really know until you've lived it," he said. He picked up his glass and tasted it. "Pretty good. Are you going to try it?"

"Pretty sure I already know what it's like to have guns fired in my direction. Can we be a little more positive?"

"You're not ignorant, I'm sorry. It's not negativity, it's only my realism coming through."

Delilah sipped on the wine's rich flavor, putting the glass to her lips like she was doing something wrong. The extravagance made everything taste sacred.

Inácio laughed at her.

"What? I think it's good!" Delilah went after him with an elbow to the ribs. His eyes squinted with joy.

"I'm so glad I was there when you walked out of that hotel." Inácio sat back in his chair, arm wrapped around her. It gave her a wider view of his lap and Delilah noticed he was fishing around in his pocket. Inácio began to withdraw something, then stopped. He left whatever it was inside and reached for the bread.

“What’s that?”

“It can wait.” He smiled with flushed cheeks.

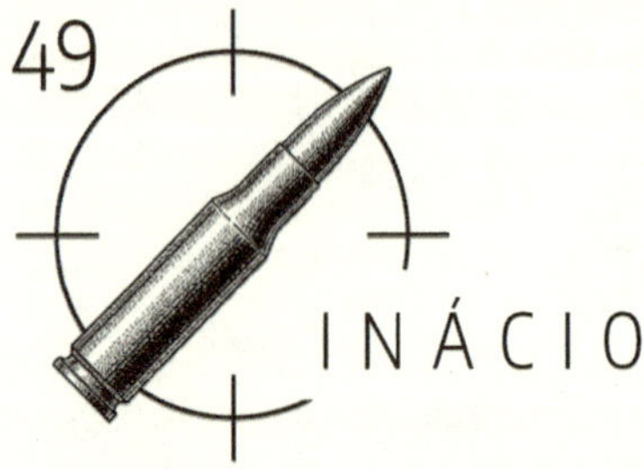

Delilah's skin. As smooth as silk and sweet like vanilla chocolate, her body, a manifestation of his fantasies turned reality. Feminine. Delicate. The slight breeze moved through her purple waves as it would through wind chimes. The energy Delilah carried with her was neither brash nor commanding. There was a gentleness to it, a need for him in her life. Inácio knew the challenge ahead. He felt its immense weight on his shoulders. Yet through all the stress, Delilah possessed a quiet strength only known to those who were willing to truly know her. Inácio needed that strength. He needed her.

With the road of forever ahead of them, it was impossible to keep his hands or his mouth away from her. Delilah was a temptation that overrode the social norms of a public setting. Inácio tasted the slight ridge along her clavicle, letting her melt into his mouth. No professionally crafted dessert they waited on could ever match her flavor. He let it all fade away for just a moment. There was no restaurant or strangers. It was just them and the rain. Every now and again, a sprinkle would catch her arm and Inácio would thin it with his massaging thumb.

"Delilah!"

A scream from nearby ripped him from his loving trance. The low, guttural sound of her name, blasting from another man, ignited a blaze within. Who in the fuck?

Blood rushed to Inácio's muscles and rage inflated his chest. Quick like a queen's bodyguard, he jumped up and knocked his chair to the floor. It landed with a bang loud enough to cut through the noise of the entire patio. Coming toward their table was a chubby, short man with a taller, sturdier man at his heels. Both were half-soaked from the rain and the short one burned with a fury as hot as Inácio's. His teeth snarled like those of a rottweiler and his frown was so deep, his eyebrows made it hard to see his eyes. Inácio postured himself against him, blocking his access.

"Get out of my way!" His order rasped from his throat with little self-control. Their surprise visitor craned his neck back and his eyes shot Inácio with death lasers. It was then that Inácio could see his irises—and they were familiar. Deep and rich in color as the ocean view he'd admired since childhood. It was the same shade that brightened Delilah's face.

"Dad?!" Her squeal was like nails on a chalkboard. Delilah's family. The only ones who could mess up everything. How her dad had found them was another question.

Her dad tried to step around Inácio and failed. "You're coming with me and Greg. We're here to take you home now." He didn't take his eyes off Inácio once.

"This is really your dad?" Inácio looked her dad's pudgy body up and down, judging every part of him.

"Yesssss," Delilah whimpered.

"Derrick Johnson, in the flesh," her dad growled.

"And who are you?" Inácio asked, pointing to the second man holding back her father.

"I'm her dad's partner, Greg."

"Work partner," her dad added.

"Yeah, work partner. She has a mom."

"Thanks for the clarification," Inácio said. "A fight here would be ugly, don't you think?"

"You must be the douchebag keeping my daughter from her family," Derrick said.

"You need to control yourself," Inácio warned. There was nothing else for him to lose, no cover to maintain or reputation with his employers to nurture. A scuffle in public didn't matter to him anymore. At least it would be quick.

A managerial-looking employee accompanied by another large man approached the table, ready to throw out Inácio's two new problems. Inácio addressed them in their native tongue.

"What are you telling them?" her dad demanded to know.

"Do you want to sit down and talk like a civilized human or should they put you out on the street?" Inácio asked. He had to know how they'd tracked them down. Delilah wouldn't have called him behind his back, would she?

"Derrick, let's sit down. C'mon man," Greg encouraged. Derrick's eyes switched from Delilah to Inácio as if he were weighing what was most important to him: his ego or his daughter.

"Okay, okay fine." Derrick brushed off his partner's hand and took his seat across from Inácio. Greg sat across from Delilah. Her father scooted in, the metal legs of the chair screeching over the brick among a dead-silent restaurant.

"Everyone is staring at us. Thanks, man," whispered Greg. Derrick remained stiff.

"Everything is fine, gentlemen. It was just a misunderstanding. They will not disrupt the other guests again," Inácio said to the lingering staff. Reluctantly, they backed away, not straying too far. Inácio took note of the number of eyes on them and gritted his teeth. The discomfort was not for himself, but for Delilah.

"Are you okay?" Inácio held Delilah close, making it clear they were not free to snatch her away. She buried her face in his shoulder and covered her face with her hand. Delilah's cheeks were warm with embarrassment and shock. Her father's approach was anything but acceptable to Inácio. He didn't appreciate it. "This is how you choose to act in front of your daughter?"

Derrick clawed at the tablecloth, then glanced at the nearby staff who were clearly the only ones keeping him from doing something stupid. He cleared his throat and blinked away whatever dark thought lurked in his mind.

"Look at this wine." Derrick unballed his fists, poured their bottle into Delilah's glass, then stole it from her. "You don't need any of this." The wine disappeared in one swig. "Wow, that's expensive."

Inácio heard her dad's inner rumblings before the man belched in his direction. Delilah shook like a leaf under his arm.

"Excuse me, that was rude." Derrick slapped his chest. "I guess crime pays, huh?"

"I'm not sure what you're getting at," Inácio said.

"It makes me wonder what sort of things you do on the side."

"On the side?"

"You know, outside of murdering someone."

"What are you talking about?"

"They said you're a killer." Derrick spun the wine glass between his fingers in the most nonchalant manner.

"Who is *they*?" Inácio leaned forward, closing in until they were just inches apart.

"Who do you think? The police. They're on to you, genius." Her dad shook his head as if he were disappointed and stole more wine. "You criminals are all the same. You never think you're going to get caught, no matter how many stupid mistakes you make."

"What do you think you know about me?" Inácio felt his upper lip twitch. He worked desperately to control himself. He didn't want to give her dad the satisfaction of getting under his skin.

"Pff! Nothing. All I know is that you killed someone and the cops want you bad. That's enough information for me to know what kind of person you really are. You know, you should really be more aware of your surroundings."

"You've been following us?" A sinking feeling dropped in Inácio's stomach.

"For a couple of days, actually. You have a lovely home. Right on the water."

"Derrick!" Greg scolded. "Why are you saying all these things to him?" He turned toward Inácio. "Ignore him. He's pretending to know more than he does."

"How did you get hooked up with these cops?" Inácio tried to ignore the fact that Delilah's dad could have been creeping outside the safe house the entire time. There was no way Derrick could know its location on his own.

"I'm not telling you anything! I'm here to bring my daughter home. Looks like I was right to think she was in trouble."

"What's wrong with you?" Delilah lifted her head from Inácio's shoulder. Tears that he had once erased were back, streaming down her cheeks. Her visible pain made the entire situation more fucked up. "He's not a bad man. Why did you even come here? I don't want anything to do with you, especially now."

Derrick leaned forward and pointed an accusatory finger. "You have no right to tell me how to be right now. Do you realize what you've put us through? Your mom is at home having an emotional breakdown. Don't cover for him just because he's supplying your alcohol habit and who knows what else. I thought you were in mortal danger, but I see you're just down here having a good time with this scumbag."

Inácio squeezed her waist and looked Derrick straight in the eye. "You need to revise the way you're speaking to her, or she won't be going anywhere with you, Mr. Johnson." To his surprise, Derrick listened. His face relaxed and his voice softened when he addressed Delilah again.

"Greg, who's been there for our family through thick and thin, came all the way out here with me just to look for you. For you, Delilah! We've been running around with our heads cut off trying to find you in this crazy place."

Delilah glanced up at her dad before returning her eyes to the table.

"You know, Del, I've tried so hard to teach you to see through guys like this. People like him will say anything to manipulate you."

"You mean like Carson? The guy you idolized over me? If you want to blame anyone for everything that's happened, blame him. He used me for years. And you didn't even believe me when I told you he hurt me. Or maybe you just didn't care."

"Listen to me, Del—"

"He abandoned me. I was stupid to think he was ever loyal. Carson doesn't give a crap that he hurt me. So, I am applying the 'moral values' you taught me. I found the quality of man you always wanted for me, but I'm sorry he's not what you pictured."

"I know what kind of a douche Carson is now. But jumping from one jerk-off to another is not the way you gain back your dignity."

Fortunately or unfortunately, Inácio could see the love this asshole had for his daughter, even if Delilah couldn't. It was the kind of love that couldn't let go. Inácio was well acquainted with the different modes of masculinity. Her dad was afraid of losing her, afraid she wanted to lose him, and afraid what his life would mean without her. Inácio could relate to that.

"Your dad means well," her dad's partner interrupted. "As much as it feels like he doesn't." Greg cleared his throat loud enough to force Delilah to look at him again.

"See, we both want to make sure you're safe." Derrick's tone shifted closer to desperation.

"I am safe," she defended. Inácio pecked her temple as a reminder that he was still there to be her strength. Her dad scoffed and rubbed his face as if to wipe the memory of it away.

"We are really happy to see that you're okay," Greg said.

"Can you be honest and tell me if you were ever in any trouble?" her dad asked. "This wasn't some sort of attempt to fake your death and run away, was it? When you called, I had my doubts. Then when we got here, I thought maybe I was wrong. Now seeing you here with *him,* I don't know what to think anymore."

"Of course she was in danger," Inácio asserted.

"She can speak for herself, thank you, Escobar."

"Yes, Dad, I was in danger. He saved me, or I wouldn't be sitting here right now. I'd be *dead.*"

"Are you talking about the shooting at your hotel?" Derrick asked.

"Yes, and I really don't want to talk about it. Not with you. Ever."

"That's okay, we understand," said her dad's partner. Inácio knew what he was doing: trying to play the nice guy.

"I don't know about that, Greg," Derrick said. The rain intensified and dropped like black water from the evening sky.

"I'm sorry about Mom. I can't believe you guys came all the way here," Delilah said. "I've been just fine since that day, honest."

"I can see that," her dad muttered.

"Delilah," Greg interrupted again, "I know your dad is coming off like a jerk, but he's not actually mad at you. You're not in trouble, I promise. Your mom and everyone at the sheriff's department are really concerned for your safety." He maintained steady eye contact with Delilah. "Everyone at home is praying for you. Even the sheriff has been helping us try to find you. He's called like, what, five times at least for updates?"

"Yep, five, at least."

"And your mom is a mess, from what I hear. I haven't talked to her myself, but I overheard her talking on the phone with your dad. That lady has called your dad a thousand times. I'm sure you can imagine her heartache, right?"

"Of course," Delilah whispered. She stirred in her chair.

"I don't think she could survive without you, to be honest."

"No, she wouldn't make it," Derrick reflected, folding his hands together.

"I get it though. You're an adult and can make your own decisions. We can't make you do anything." His partner shrugged.

"Hey, slow down there, Greg," Derrick said, but his partner kept going.

"I mean, if I were in your position, I'd want to stay in this place too. Your hometown can't compete with a tropical city like this. This is where we dream of going on vacation. You found a guy who is obviously more than capable of providing for you. You've been through a lot back home, and here I'm sure. I can only imagine how good it feels to be living this new life, away from it all."

Greg leaned in.

"It's just that all those things that you think you've escaped from are still there. Your college degree is weeks away from being completed. I wish I could have finished college. That's something I regret to this day. Most importantly, your parents are still going to be there in Charm wishing you were with them. Their feelings don't just go away because you've decided to do a one-eighty and live another life. And do you smell that?"

Greg pinched the air.

"This guy next to me is a dirty dehydrated mess. He's almost killed himself three times because he refused to take a break from searching for you. He apologizes for acting like a mad man, but that's just because he is one. He's crazy about you and your well-being, and that's something he will never apologize for."

Although Greg spoke to Delilah, Inácio felt that the message was for him.

This man is good.

"I think the greatest gift your mom could ever have in her life is a call from us telling her that all three of us are on our way home."

"She'd feel so much better, Delilah. You'd fix her," her dad argued.

"It's up to you though. You're twenty-four. We can't force you to go back to her."

"I know what you're saying," Delilah said. "I love Mom too, and I feel really lucky that you came all this way to find me, but I'm sorry.

I can't go back with you. I know what's waiting for me if I do. No matter what I do, I'm the one who will always be striving to earn trust I'll never get back. If it's between love and emptiness, I choose love. We're about to leave here and find a place where we can make a new life together. I love him. I love him, Dad." Delilah looked up at Inácio and put her hand over his cheek, massaging the prickly heads barely protruding from his shaven face.

Inácio sighed, took her hand, and kissed it. He held himself there.

Delilah glared back, surprised at his silence. "Right? We're leaving, together."

"Delilah..." Grief broke his voice. Inácio's heart burned. He stared back at the face he had been falling for more and more each day. There wasn't a life without her, but this wasn't about him. Inácio had backtracked on his opinion of her father. If Inácio wanted her that badly after just days, he could only imagine how much her family wanted her after knowing Delilah her entire life. "You will never be who you were meant to be with me. I can't take you away from your family. It's not fair for me to expect that."

"Inácio?"

"Please..." He didn't know how much more of her tears he could take before breaking down himself.

"I don't want that. I want you. I was meant to be with you. Wha-What?"

Delilah's despair was agonizing. The entranced side of him wanted to believe that she could run away with no regrets. But there was a stronger reality behind both of them which would always find a way to spoil their happiness. Neither of their pasts would let them go without a fight.

"You're not seeing things clearly. I guess I didn't realize how much your mom needed you." Inácio strained through his words.

"That's not what—I thought you loved me. That's what you said! Why are you backing out? It was your idea!" Her small fist hammered against his chest. The pain of his betrayal was delivered through the impact. Inácio didn't stop her. She did it a second time, then a third. She could claw and slap at him and he would take it. He deserved the punishment.

"I do, Delilah. I do love you. If I could go back, I'd give anything to care for my mother. It's the kind of regret you never get over. You don't want to leave your mom broken, do you?"

"What's wrong with you?" A shakiness seemed to seize her chest, making it hard to speak or take a full breath. Delilah peeled Inácio's arm from around her waist. "W-what happened to choosing love over everything?"

"Please stop crying." His plea made her that much louder. The more he listened to it, the more he wanted to carry her off. "It's over, Delilah. It's better this way," he choked out. "You need to leave with your dad now. Go home."

He hoped she could get over him because he never would get over her. Delilah was meant to marry a man and have kids. Children were something he couldn't give her. His employers made sure of that. She could watch her children play in their white-picket-fenced yard. One day she would appreciate her life and know she'd literally dodged a bullet.

"It's time to go, Delilah." Derrick rose and held out his hand.

"Wait, I can't think!" Delilah grabbed her head.

"There's nothing to think about," Greg said. The empty dishware clinked under her shaking hands. As she stood, Inácio reached out to touch her one last time.

"Don't touch me!" Delilah twisted around and looked at him like she wished she'd never met him. "Here I go, just another man's trash." Her dad's arms came around her as she cried in his chest, walking away.

"God fucking dammit," Inácio cursed to himself. He felt like he'd stuffed his heart in the shredder. It wasn't like the pain of being used by Talia and it was worse than losing his mother. He picked up the wine bottle and splashed it in his glass. The bottle vibrated in his hand and he grabbed it with his other for support. Like a tsunami, she had swept away everything he thought he was, and then she was gone. Nosy customers stared at him from behind their dessert menus, relishing their privilege at having witnessed the entire fiasco. Inácio drank his wine and stared back until the patrons were too uncomfortable to look again.

"Do you want to talk to your mom now?"

Delilah nodded while she wiped away tears from her puffy eyes. There was no one else she'd rather speak to than her mom, even if Delilah was the one who had to comfort her most of the time.

"Like they say, there are more fish in the sea," Greg commented.

"There sure are, but I think you could take a break from the ocean, if you ask me," said her dad. Following close behind was the manager, who shooed them away in pretty, foreign words. "Yeah, yeah we get it. We won't be back. That's a promise."

"Food looks good though," Greg said.

"Even airport food sounds good to me at this point."

"Dad, how am I supposed to travel anywhere without my passport?" asked Delilah. They met the wall of rain outside. It soaked her like a shower.

"Where is your passport?"

"At the house."

"Oh, 'the house.'" Her dad smirked. "I'm glad you've made yourself at home here, Del."

"That's going to be an awkward conversation," said Greg.

"No, Greg, we are not going back to talk to that crook again."

Delilah didn't argue. Abandoning her belongings was the least of her worries. She couldn't imagine returning and enduring the torture of looking at Inácio's face once more.

"We will make a pit stop at the US embassy. They gotta be able to do something."

"*Or* while we're here, let's take the easy road and ask him to give us her stuff," Greg suggested.

"Do you see Silva?" Delilah's father scanned the street in both directions as water cascaded from the bill of his hat.

"Derrick! Did you hear me?" It was the first time Delilah had ever heard Greg raise his voice.

"I don't wanna go back there, Greg!" Derrick snapped.

"I'll do it then! They won't let you back in, but they might let me."

"Let's see what Silva thinks. They might be planning a raid."

"A what?" Delilah scrunched her nose. "Who are you talking about?"

"Ah, there's his headlights coming this way, I think. I'll let him know." Her dad waved his hand out on the street.

"What's going on?" she demanded. Delilah stood wet and cold at the curb with her arms crossed.

"Relax, they're the police. They helped us find you." His tone was short.

"Fuck the police," she mumbled.

Derrick jerked her arm. "What did you just say?"

"Don't worry about it." Delilah spun away from him.

"You need a jacket and a damn attitude check."

"My jacket is with my passport," she reiterated. "You're not telling me what's going on."

"Don't worry about it, okay?"

"Here they are," Greg announced. An SUV pulled to the curb, splashing a wave of water at their feet. Two jeeps followed. A driver got out from behind the wheel and walked around to the back door of the first jeep. Its brake lights glowed a bright red. Someone hollered from the SUV.

"Wow, this is so good to see. The gang's back together again, huh?"

"His voice..." Delilah began. She bent down to see inside.

"What are you doing?" her dad asked.

"Need your input on something, sarge," Greg said.

"What about?" the passenger asked. The man leaned over the center console, letting the streetlamps highlight his face. It was him, the officer who'd assaulted her and stolen her license. Inácio's handiwork still marked his face. Delilah jerked back, slipping out of her sandals. Her dad moved to catch her.

"Delilah, stop! My daughter here forgot to get her belongings from the target. It's at the house evidently."

"I-I-I know that guy, Dad!" Drenched grass shifted under her bare feet, letting her sink into the soil. She wanted to run, but her dad's hold on her arm was firm and he wasn't listening.

"You guys get out of the rain. My officers in the jeeps will take her to the police station. We're arresting him tonight anyway. We will do our best, but we can't go back right now."

"I understand. Silva, do you mind if I ride with her?" Derrick requested.

"Not at all."

"Delilah!" Derrick struggled to keep her still. "What's the matter with you?"

"Inácio!" she screamed.

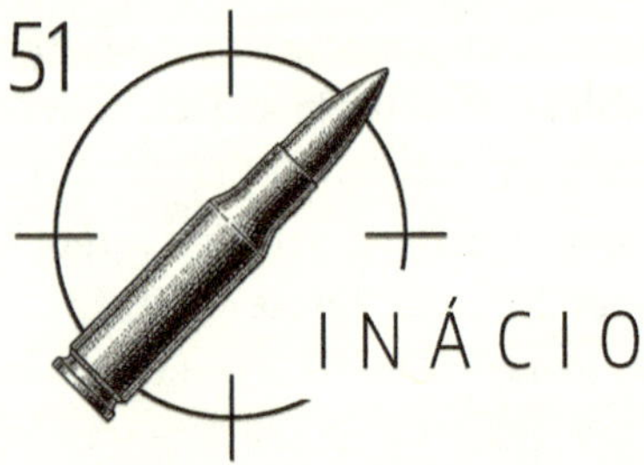

51 INÁCIO

The fog of heartbreak glued him to his table. Inácio could sit there all night and stew in his own despair. The seat beside him was still warm. It was the last time he would ever be given the privilege to feel her closeness. Pink lip gloss stained her napkin and her fingerprint marked the glass tabletop. The thoroughbreds on the track broke through the rain like Moses, splitting the water in half. The waiter returned to the table and asked something. Inácio looked up with dead eyes. He felt dead.

"No." Throwing down some bills, he tipped him generously and left the table. "Keep the change." Inácio walked through the restaurant. A sliver of a tear lingered around the bottom rim of his eyelid, blurring his periphery. Tonight, he was determined to care very little about anything. Maybe he'd go back to the safe house and get blackout drunk.

As he stepped outside, the heavy rain collided with his face, sticking in his eyes. It struck his numb skin with no effect. The valet jogged to the back lot to retrieve his car. He felt his body decay under the buckets of water. The rain could drown him for all he cared. The weather would be chilly for Delilah. She wasn't dressed for it. Inácio's heart sank as he remembered he'd never returned her suitcase. The jacket she needed was a good drive away. *You're pathetic. You gave up that privilege of caring for her.*

Through the weather, Inácio swore he heard a scream. It was easily a figment of his lonely imagination. A memory of Delilah in need.

Then it happened again.

Inácio's protective drive kicked in.

Jogging away from the restaurant, he brushed beyond the large ferns blocking the view of the street just in time. An eruption of men's screams were added to hers. At the curb, Derrick and Greg were blindsided by two attackers. Another man carried Delilah away to a green jeep about ten feet away. Her wet hair flung around aimlessly, her feet kicking the air.

Delilah screamed *his* name over and over.

Inácio took off at a sprint.

Then she was sucked into the darkness of the vehicle.

Inácio's arms were reaching out to grab her when the back seat slammed shut, the last image he saw a grown man wrapped completely around her, his legs trapping her own. Inácio slammed his body against the locked door but it took off, throwing him off-balance.

A scream of godlike frequency escaped his mouth. The second jeep behind it screeched away from the curb, barely missing him in the street. Inácio took note of its slightly darker shade of green.

"Nice to see you again, assassin!" Inácio whipped his head toward a familiar face. The corrupt police officer took off in the opposite direction of the jeeps. Behind him, the back window rolled down. Plump red lips grinned and long fingernails taunted him with a wave.

Talia.

Left behind in the mud were Delilah's father and partner, and next to them, Delilah's shoes.

52

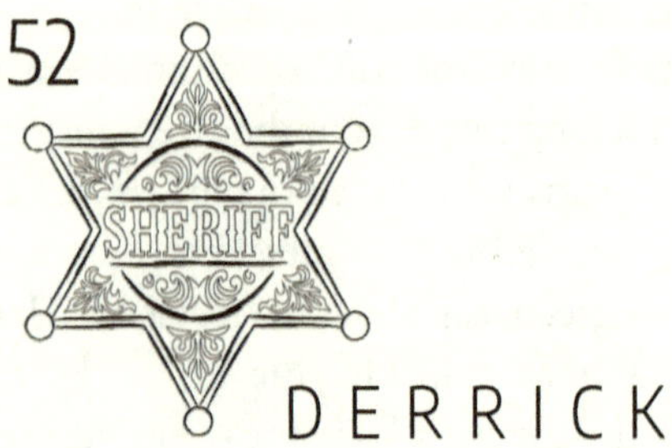

DERRICK

He was smashed into the mud so hard, it took a forceful suction to pop his face from the ground. It had happened so fast, and just like that, Delilah was gone. Derrick's vision spun from shock. Greg lay nearby, holding his jaw. Derrick's ears rang and he struggled to catch his breath.

"W-what the fuck just happened? What just happened?" Derrick choked out.

Two fists suddenly twisted the collar of his polo. He faced the fierceness of Inácio. Barely intelligible through Inácio's accented rage, his spit splashed onto Derrick's face in unison with the rain.

"What have you done?! You killed her! I hope you know you fucking killed your daughter!" He let go of his shirt collar and ran off. Derrick's head smacked back against the ground. Greg stood over him next and held out his hand.

"Are you okay?" Greg snapped his fingers. "Earth to Derrick!" He shook away the stars and watched Inácio sprinting back toward the restaurant. His anger could be heard from the roadside.

"What are you looking at?! Where's my fucking car?" he shouted at the valet.

Derrick took Greg's help and got to his feet. "Shit, Greg, what have I done?" Grief stirred in his chest. "I can't breathe."

"They went this way!" Greg ran to the edge of the drive and pointed down the street. Derrick joined him. An uncontrollable helplessness threatened to weaken his mind and body. Alone and in a foreign country, he didn't know what to do.

Headlights and a roaring engine barreled down the drive, making an unnecessary swerve toward himself and Greg before straightening again. The wheels came to an abrupt halt and the passenger door flung open. Behind the wheel was Inácio the murderer, or whoever the hell he was.

"Get in!"

"Let's go, Derrick!" Greg leaped in the front while Derrick threw himself in the back. He was barely inside before the car accelerated, scooping him up in the process. The momentum slammed Derrick's door closed. Flung across to one side, he hastily took hold of the grab handle. They reached racing speeds in mere seconds.

"Is that the jeep with Delilah up there?" Derrick asked.

"No," Inácio curtly replied.

"Why did they take her?" Greg asked, sounding just as panicked as Derrick. "Those were police officers, right?"

"I don't know, Greg, I don't fucking know!" Derrick said frantically. "I'm about to have a damn heart attack." The city lights flashed by in streaks. Their driver disobeyed every stoplight and dodged every vehicle about to T-bone them.

"Is that it?" Greg pointed at a jeep. "It's turning. Same color."

"No, that's the other jeep," Inácio said. "They're trying to throw us off. It's a lighter green."

Derrick clutched the driver's seat, feeling the tail end wanting to spin out across the standing water. The rain coated all the windows in a glossy blur.

"Damn, how can you see?" Greg whipped his seat belt on.

"I can't," Inácio groaned. The Mercedes accelerated within easy reach of a bumper. Derrick recognized the jeep.

"There they fucking are!"

"Yep." Inácio got closer.

"There they go!" Derrick alerted again. The jeep took a sudden sharp turn, almost sliding into the wall of an exit ramp. Inácio spun the wheel and hydroplaned passed it. They spun back around and made their way up the wrong lane until they joined the kidnappers on the ramp.

"This has something to do with *you*, doesn't it?" Derrick said, pointing at Inácio and losing his center of gravity for a second. He popped back up and held onto the front seats for balance, moving with the abrupt angles of the car. "Hey, I'm talking to you, Inácio!"

"I will ask you later where you got my name."

"What kind of shit did you get my daughter into?"

No reply.

"What kind of name is that? Your first name? A street name?"

"Shut up! We don't have time for this!"

"They're cops! Why would they take her? They want you that bad, huh? This country is corrupt!"

"Derrick, can we like, not argue right now?" Greg asked, his voice shaking a bit.

"Was this a drug deal gone wrong? How typical! Or is this how the police do their business? Either way—"

"Are you going to get that?" Inácio interrupted.

"What?"

"Pick-up-your-phone!" he enunciated.

"I don't have time for a call! Are you kidding me?" What did a phone call have to do with his kidnapped daughter? Inácio pounded his fist so hard on the dash, it was a surprise the airbags didn't deploy.

"Dammit, answer your damn phone, now!" Every vein and muscle popped from Inácio's neck. If only to appease the man who was in control of all their lives, Derrick took the phone from his pocket. The number across the screen was unknown.

"The number's blocked."

"Answer it, Derrick! Jesus!" Greg cried. He finally obeyed and as he did so, the jeep suddenly slowed to a more manageable speed down the highway.

"Hello?"

"Put me on speakerphone, Detective," ordered the strange voice.

"Okay, you're on speaker."

"Can you hear me, Inácio?"

"I can hear you," he replied irritably.

"Step one: back off."

Inácio twisted his grip around the steering wheel.

"Your English must be a little rusty. Let me help you. Stop following or I throw your girl out of the car at sixty-two kilometers per hour. Do you understand me now?"

"What's step two?" Inácio asked, falling back and pulling off onto an exit. Delilah faded into the distance.

"What are you doing?!" Derrick yelled in horror.

"Shut your mouth," Inácio demanded.

"I am sending Dad an address. Leave your two new American friends and whoever else you'll be tempted to bring at home. Come alone, unarmed, if you want to spare her. Your life for hers. I don't have to explain what will happen if you try to resist, do I?"

"No."

"Good. We'll be waiting for you."

"Who sent you?"

"You did," the voice replied before hanging up. Inácio made a U-turn and sped up in the opposite direction.

"We need to call the police," Derrick announced, fumbling with his phone. He'd never had a problem operating the device before, but right now his thumb opened every random app other than the call button.

"You guys did a great job of doing that before," Inácio said.

"What's the emergency number here?"

"You're not calling anyone," Inácio said.

"She was taken because of you! I didn't kill her, you did! You're the scum of the earth and now my daughter may never get to see home again!" Derrick leaned closer and closer to Inácio with every word. He ended his blame with a scream only a grieving parent could make.

"You better control your partner," Inácio told Greg.

"Stop it, stop it, Derrick!" Greg completely turned around in his seat. Derrick practically felt the flames shooting from his ears. All he could do was lean back, pray, and get his heart rate down before he dropped dead.

"Come on in." The invitation came out as annoyed as Inácio meant it. He held open the door and watched the detectives tramp into the safe house. Water and dirt tracked across the white floor. The filth which dirtied the house was secondary to the mess he'd made for himself and Delilah. They wandered into the living room, taking in every detail. Inácio would be lying if he said he didn't feel like he'd just invited the enemy home. Greg at least held himself together, but her father was a different story. The pressure of guilt and blame was about to burst from Derrick's red eyeballs. It wasn't anything Inácio didn't feel. "Stay here, I'll be right back." Inácio jogged away and up the stairs.

Putting his phone to his ear, he called the only person who might help him.

"Hey bud, what's up?" Schafer answered.

"I need your help with something."

"Shoot. I'm about to board my plane for home. First leave in five years."

"Shit, that's right."

"Something in your voice, it sounds off. Tell me what you need."

"I've gotten myself into a little situation."

"Is this an emergency?"

"The worst. I don't know how I'm going to get through this."

"Fudge this vacation then. I've never heard you sound like this before. I'm comin'!"

"Thank you, Schafer. Thank you so much."

"Where am I headed?"

"The safe house. Come alone and tell no one."

As Inácio made his way to the weapons safe, all he could see was Delilah's heartbreak. He reached for the railings, trying to stay upright. *I did this.* He was responsible for everything. Talia had warned him what she was prepared to do, but he didn't listen. Inácio was forced to rethink everything he once assumed about her jealousy and the police sergeant he had beaten down and put out of his mind. The man wasn't meant to be a problem beyond the night Inácio had saved Delilah from his clutches. *I should have killed him.*

Guilt and hopelessness dug their claws into his gut. The bed they'd lain in together hours before was only feet away. Delilah's Carnival dress was still crumpled on the floor. They should have left then, before her dad and Inácio's enemies caught up to them. Talia's evil smile smearing across her face poisoned his mind.

Inácio white-knuckled the railing overlooking the pool, succumbing to his own self-fulfilling prophecy. Falling to a greater foe was always meant to be, yet this was much worse than getting popped in the head or sliced across the throat. This was a stab to the heart.

Except he didn't die.

The voice over the phone…

The mistake in Colombia had caught up with him.

Tonight was it. Tonight, he was to meet his maker.

A mix of wine and mush erupted from his mouth, splashing into the pool below. The puke gurgled through his esophagus, burning on its way out. Inácio's stomach clenched and spasmed uncontrollably. After a few heaves, there was nothing left but spits of acid.

"Oh, forgive me, Delilah."

54 DERRICK

What was almost as surreal as his daughter's abduction was being in the home which he'd spent tireless hours surveilling. Derrick steadied himself against the back of the sofa chair. The ultimate betrayal from Officer Silva built up in his mind. They'd shaken his hand, eaten with him, thanked him, and opened up to him. Derrick itched for justice. If it wasn't for Greg by his side, he wasn't sure what he would do. To imagine being alone in Brazil with a kidnapped daughter was unbearable. It wasn't only Delilah's life he was worried about, it was Greg's too. If he lost either of them, Derrick doubted he could live with himself.

Derrick took a knee. Greg was beside him, trying to console him. Nothing but his daughter's safety could bring him out of his inner frenzy. He squeezed his fists as tightly as possible. The threat of hopelessness crept in, but Derrick had to stay determined. There was no choice but to keep going, somehow.

"We fucked up."

"That's one way to put it," replied Greg.

"If we couldn't see the shit these guys were about to pull, we deserve to lose our jobs."

"Well—"

"No, we should be flipping burgers. That's all we're good for."

"Blaming yourself isn't going to help. Stand up. We've got to figure out a way to get your daughter back." Greg brushed off Derrick's shirt. "She needs us to be strong."

"This dude she fell for must be worse than we thought. He must be some kind of big-time drug lord. Look at this place." Derrick looked around at a home he could never dream of owning on his hourly pay. Black and white shades of marble were found on the floor and tables. The ceiling rose taller than his own roof in Charm. He could *almost* see how a girl Delilah's age could be attracted to a man who lived like this. To her, it probably seemed romantic. It was what was represented in the media women consumed. Handsome men with money always appeared more attractive than they should.

"It's not like any drug house we've ever been in."

"Nope, this is fed-level stuff we're in." Derrick shook his head.

"Delilah got herself into some dark stuff. They said he murdered someone, but they didn't say anything about drugs."

"Who knows what was a lie and what was the truth. I don't want to be here. I feel like I'm wasting time."

"He's the only help we got right now," Greg said.

"I don't know about that. I trust him as much as I trust those phony cops."

"We're fish out of water. These people obviously know him. If he's all they want, maybe that's how we get her back. I'm not comfortable going to the police station again, are you?"

"Okay, so let's get answers first, then we'll see how dependent we are on this thug." Derrick began exploring the house.

"What do you think you're going to find?"

"I don't know, Greg. Maybe there's some evidence here in plain view. How's the charge on your phone?"

"It's uh, seventy-two percent now."

"Mine is on thirty. Our damn chargers are still in that sissy Fiat. Since you got more charge, take some pictures of this place."

"Anywhere specific?" Greg asked, pulling up his camera.

"Everywhere. We'll show them to who we need to when this is all over."

"You got a plan for how you're gonna solve this problem? Because I don't."

"I'll figure it out. I'll call the American embassy for starters. Then we need to tell the sheriff. People need to know what's going on." Derrick located the impressive, fully equipped bar beside the kitchen. "Look at this Greg. This guy is loaded." Leather panels lined the front face of the bar. Wild prints covered the stools, feeling too soft to be fake. It was genuine tiger fur. A golden compass design overlooked the space from the ceiling above. Derrick searched for and dialed the embassy's number.

"Derrick," Greg said.

"One second, it's ringing."

"Derrick, put the phone down."

"What?"

"Stop calling the embassy." Greg's voice was more on edge.

A woman answered on the other line. "H-hello?" Derrick said. "Yes, I need to speak to someone about a security matter… Yes, I'm an American citizen… Well—" Before Derrick could tell any authorities about their situation, Greg snatched away his phone. "What the fuck? What are you doing?"

"I don't think this is a good idea," Greg said, shaking his head, putting the phone in his own pocket.

"What do you mean? My daughter has been abducted by really dangerous people! We need all—"

"Exactly. You just said it. Dangerous." Greg stepped closer to Derrick and lowered his voice. "Use your cop brain for one second. What do you think this guy is going to do to us if he knows we called for help?"

"I don't really care. I'm not here for him. Now give me my phone back."

"Derrick! We're already cops, aka the enemy. We're gonna be lucky to get out of this in one piece as it is."

"C'mon."

"I just think if we want to find Delilah, we need to wait and see what we find out before panicking and telling everyone we know what's happened."

"You should listen to your friend," Inácio interrupted, somehow teleporting right beside them. His shoulders were covered in a criss-cross pattern of nylon straps. One by one, he pulled the duffle bags over his head and dropped them on the bar counter. One bore the soft outline of a long rifle. "I hope you two have been keeping up on your aim. We're probably going to need it." Inácio laid out boxes of ammunition and piles of magazines, some loaded, others empty. His jacket was off and tattoos covered almost every inch of his arms.

".45 hollow points, .338s, and slugs?" Greg asked.

"The slugs are for these bad boys. I only have two of them, so one for each of you." Inácio placed the shotguns beside the shells.

Greg's curiosity continued. "Are those Benellis?"

"Yes. They're semi-automatic, so you won't need to pump the forearm between shots."

"So, who are we using these on?"

"Anyone that won't die."

"Ohhh-kay." Greg took a step back from the counter, holding his stomach like he was nauseated. Inácio didn't stop lining up the weapons. M-4s, pistols, and something else. The object had weight and rattled the glasses behind the bar. A roll of wire was tossed on top, capped with two little boxes with the word *inert* printed on the side.

"What's that?" Derrick pointed. Inácio gave him a look like he should already know.

"I hope you want Delilah back as much as I do," Inácio said.

"I'm her father. Who the hell are you?" Derrick stepped forward.

Inácio ignored him and began thumbing the rifle rounds into a magazine. "Anyone going to help me? I'd like to get this show on the road ASAP."

Derrick reached for another empty M-4 magazine and pulled a few rounds from the open box. "C'mon Greg, let's do it," he encouraged.

"I'd like to know what we're doing with all this first."

"Me too, but you heard the man," he said, topping off the last of his rounds.

"I think it's obvious what we're about to do," Inácio commented. Derrick waited only a few more seconds before making sure Inácio had looked away. In one quick maneuver, Derrick took his fully loaded magazine and reached for the rifle. M-4s were a familiar weapon from training.

"Derrick!" Greg yelled. Before anyone could stop him, Derrick loaded the rifle and pointed it toward Inácio's face.

"You're going to tell us what's going on, asshole! Enough of this bullshit! I am her family! You're just a scumbag like the rest of them, so tell us who took her and why!" Sweat trickled down his brow.

"Sounds like you've got it all figured out."

"I want fucking answers! Besides Delilah, my friend and I look to be putting ourselves in danger. You did that. For our families' sake, you're going to tell us what the hell we're about to walk into."

"Sure, why not," Inácio began. "I just can't talk with a weapon in my face."

Derrick wasn't sure what came first, the crack to his nose or the gun disappearing from his hands. Blood spewed from his flattened wound. He fell to his knees and held on to his face.

Greg moved at record speed and ambushed Inácio from the side. Collapsing onto Delilah's boyfriend, Greg's elbow pinned him to the ground. Derrick only had to blink before he saw blood leaking from Greg's gums and Inácio standing on two feet.

"Aww crap! Is my jaw broken?" Greg felt around it. "Is your nose broken?"

"Oh yeah," Derrick said through his gooey blood.

"Well, that was a bad idea."

"Mhm. I'm going to listen to you from now on."

"Good. You're a fucking idiot." Greg chuckled, stretching out his jaw. Another bag was thrown at their feet.

"That's a first aid kit. You can fix yourselves up on your own," Inácio directed.

"Uh-huh, thanks." Greg sluggishly reached for the bag and brought it toward them. Their host grabbed another magazine and began loading it.

"You can help me or be against me. That's your call. Delilah needs us and it's better if we're one team. I don't know you and you don't know me and that's how it's going to stay. If you guys insist on working against me or calling for help again, I won't be so nice next time."

55

DELILAH

A scream, louder than any she'd ever heard, clashed from wall to wall. The screech caused her own ears to deafen. When awareness returned to her own body, Delilah realized the scream had come from her. Closing in were heavily armed men who were dressed like soldiers, yet something malicious set them apart from the real thing. Still wet, Delilah shivered, her clothes doing nothing to keep her from freezing. A towering ceiling topped the enormous space she was in. The building looked dark, abandoned, and worst of all, forgotten. Sheets of rain pounded against the windows and sprinkled through broken panes.

Delilah squirmed away from her captors' hold, prompting their pursuit. They surrounded her as hunters would a fox. Behind her were large silver drums. She melted between them, using the structures as protection. Her hands squeaked across their metallic surfaces. Encircled within, she hoped they could keep her safe if only for a little longer. Delilah felt her palms coated with some type of soot from the dirty floor.

"She's just a woman!" echoed a voice.

"*Señor*, she's like a squirrel," another said.

Beams of flashlights spotlighted her position. No matter where she crawled, their lights always found her. The body armor worn by the captors multiplied the size of their shadows into monsters. Their arms extended between the silver drums as far as they could go, trying to snatch her up. Fear permeated down to her bones just like it had with the attacker at White Shores and the crooked cop. This time, however, something was different about her.

Delilah expected her composure to be completely shattered at any second. It was too much trauma in such a short span of time for one person to handle. There was no way her spirit could endure another round of tragedy. Yet somehow, she felt strength. It was nothing like the power wielded by the assassin who broke her heart, barely a spark compared to that, but it was there, nonetheless.

She crawled deeper between the fat barrels, zig-zagging her way through them, but Delilah didn't break then either. Her eyes saw every detail of her surroundings, everything crystal clear. Delilah noticed her dirty hands and the carbon smell of ash all around her. She dodged their grasps, whipping herself away from each one. Their boots kicked at the drums, making them bang and vibrate all around her. And still her inner strength was intact.

"Go away!" It was a pointless request, Delilah knew. She was familiar enough with evil to know better than to beg for mercy. A frustration greater than any fear boiled within.

Powerless. Always powerless.

Always on the receiving end of pain, and she was sick of it.

What would Inácio want me to do?

She knew what he wouldn't want: he wouldn't want her to panic.

Delilah was surprised to see that one of the men trying to get to her wasn't a man at all. Thick dark hair hung freely over the woman's camouflaged shoulders. Bullets graced her uniform like they were part of the boldest necklace. Her caramel skin was young and her teeth bright white. Their shared femininity offered no sympathy. Pointing her rifle in the crevice of Delilah's hiding place, the woman cussed and shouted something in rage.

"No!" The same voice from before, echoing again. Reluctantly, the woman backed off and pointed her muzzle to the ground. Delilah's lungs released the hold on her breath. If she stayed in one place, she was safe. Numerous intense eyes stared at her from between the spaces in the equipment. They surrounded her and it became impossible to sit still without at least one man attempting to squeeze through behind her. More yelling and pounding harassed her from every corner. Knives scraped their way in, jabbing at her with greater reach. They scratched and cut past the drums.

"Please come for me, please come," she whispered, hoping that in some spiritually telepathic way, Inácio could hear it. Delilah squinted her eyes shut and tried to summon his presence even if it wasn't actually possible.

When she opened them, a scarring image of the woman soldier tramping on all fours played out like a nightmare. She scurried toward Delilah like a lioness on the trail of her prey, invading Delilah's hiding spot. A flashlight silhouetted her shape, and long dark hair swinging over her face created a cinematic sight of horror. Delilah dove out from the machinery, preferring to face the giants outside. She didn't make it a foot until she was caught again and shoved back onto the chilly concrete.

A man propped himself between her legs and pushed his weight onto her chest. Her bare feet swiped at his legs. He yelled for his friends and he stared at her wide-eyed under the bill of his military-style cap. The man's words blew through his thick moustache, his spit misting onto her face.

Delilah's naked ankle fell over the thick leather of his combat boot, propping itself over his own ankle. She ignored the fact that her leg was tiny in comparison to his and the fact that his arms were stronger than her entire body. Delilah ignored the fact that he had a gun, ignored the pain that accompanied his backhanded strike across her lip.

The pain, the fear, the lack of control, happened all at once.

She couldn't internalize it all, so she disregarded them.

Delilah had been taught by the best, and this guy wasn't prepared.

Purple nails curled over his military collar and in one swift movement, Delilah was on top of him. The heels of her palms targeted his eyes and nose until he released her. A scream followed, not out of terror, but from the will to survive. Her bad luck streak was not going to take her down without a fight. Her bare feet slapped across the ground toward a dark corner of the room. Their flashlights highlighted a door and she booked it.

"Delilah!" hollered the mysterious voice in charge.

Delilah didn't look back. She pulled and yanked on the handle of the locked door. When it wouldn't budge, she spun around to face the dozen or more flashlights bearing down on her. Shielding her eyes, a single man approached. Delilah barely made out his handlebar mustache.

"Who are you?" she asked, backing into the door.

"You need to come to me, peacefully."

"I don't want to." Delilah slid away against the wall.

"You have no choice. At any moment, your boyfriend will be coming to save you, and he can't do that if you're dead." He took out a pistol, its shape backlit at his side. "If I have to shoot you, that means all he will see is your body. And then I will shoot him. His rescue will be in vain. What a waste. But if you come with me, you will see him again. I don't want to destroy your pretty face. Don't make me do that to you, Delilah. I can't imagine how your mother would feel if she got that in the mail. Just your face, nothing else."

Delilah held out her wrists and stepped forward. The plastic bracelets bound her with no give. She wanted to live long enough to see Inácio again.

"I can see you're pissed," said Inácio, who sat alone with his handler out of earshot of the American cops. Schafer forced down a gulp of tequila then stared at the weather pounding against the living room windows from his chair.

"And that's why you killed two men instead of one at White Shores." It wasn't a question. Schafer understood the whole story. "Out of everyone I supervise—"

"I know."

"Doesn't seem like you. None of this does, to be honest." The handler looked blankly into his empty glass. "I could use the whole bottle about now."

"We all have secrets in this game."

"Ha, apparently. I should have sensed something was off with you. I feel like I'm talkin' to a stranger." Schafer shook his head, clearly disappointed.

"I can't tell you not to bring upper management into this."

"You're right, you can't."

"But I'd appreciate it if you held off." Inácio rubbed his hands together, anxious. It wasn't because of Schafer's answer, but because of the time Delilah was spending in the clutches of her captors. Every second ticked by like a pounding hammer in his mind's eye.

"It's not only you who would be on the chopping block," Schafer said. "I'd be right there next to you. Everyone on my team is my responsibility. If they were to find out this mess was going on on my watch..." He ended his sentence with a laugh and not a happy one. "I agree with you on one thing: Talia definitely sold you out to the Colombians. Some of the local cops must be in some deep crap to be involved. You not only gave yourself up to one enemy but made a second one in the process, and they've managed to team up together. That's a new one."

"I get it."

"The way you've described this rescue operation makes me believe you won't be around for any official punishment. How am I going to explain that one?"

"I'm prepared to face death. I have been since my army days."

"Yeah, well I'm not. It's been forever since I was granted any time to get away. I wanted to see my brothers, the mountains, all of it. Now you got me staring down the barrel of a gun."

"I'm sorry, Schafe. I wasn't thinking about anyone except myself."

"You got that right. A woman, man's greatest weakness. You know this takes out more guys like you than the jobs themselves, right?"

"You never told me that."

"Yeah well, there's a lot of things I can't tell you. Guess I should've though. Maybe you could have spared both of us the trouble."

"Not sure if there was anything you could've said. I am in charge of my own actions."

"Just tell me one thing, and I need complete transparency. You weren't planning on running off with this chick, right? That is something I need to know. I would take that sort of betrayal personally."

"No, of course not. I was sending her home when all this went down." *We were going to be together forever.*

"Does she know what you are?"

"Absolutely not." *Absolutely.*

"She just might after this. So it's over?"

"Yes, it's over." *I wish it wasn't.*

"But you still love her enough to put us and those chunky monkeys out there at risk?" Schafer pointed with his thumb to the detectives who waited not so patiently outside under the awning of the back patio. The storm pelted them with diagonal rain and the wind threatened to rip off their worn-out ball caps.

"Only if you got my back. I'm not sure if we can pull it off without you—"

"Save it. Your flattery isn't going to sway me one way or another. What a dang mess. The nerve to bring a civilian to this place and play house..." Schafer almost slammed his empty glass onto the coffee table.

"We can go back and forth all night on this. What are you going to do?" Inácio sat on the edge of his seat, ready to go with or without Schafer.

"You've pinned me into a corner. I do not appreciate it. You know I have no other choice but to try to execute damage control. That's the only way we *might* have a chance out of this. It's not just our lives on the line, it's our reputations." His fingers pinched and pulled on the stitching of the chair's arm. "You messed up. You did. I ain't gonna lie about that. Just so ya know, I'm not gonna trust your butt ever again. I'll get my crap out of the car and meet you suckers at the bar."

****

The detectives panted like two wet dogs as Schafer settled in at the bar. Inácio stood nearby, running his eyes across the loaded weapons.

"You're the dad, right?" Schafer asked Derrick.

"Yes..."

"I can tell. Your eyes are red." Schafer flipped open the laptop in front of him. "I'm sorry about your daughter."

"I'm glad you're sorry, but are we leaving to rescue her anytime soon?"

"That's the goal, my friend." Keys clicked away.

"I'm not your friend."

"He's your friend tonight," Inácio reminded him. "We are all friends tonight. You can call him Joe."

"Really?" Schafer asked with a look.

Inácio shrugged.

"This is all very weird." Derrick sighed. Inácio stepped forward toward the bruised middle-aged man. Blood leaked through his nose bandage.

"Do we need to have another conversation about this?"

"No, he doesn't need it," his partner said. Greg's hand slapped down onto his shoulder. "Right, Derrick? We're all here to help Delilah."

"I've heard that one before." Derrick winced from the pain in his nose, hovering his hand over it.

Schafer snapped his fingers. "I need that address."

"I got it. They sent it to my phone over an hour ago." Derrick pulled it out of his pocket and handed it over. "I tried searching it on Google Maps. It's just a bunch of trees." Schafer punched in the address, using software and access the detectives didn't have.

"I see you got the C-4 out," the handler said to Inácio.

"You never know."

"And everything else," Schafer muttered.

"Better to have a tool you don't need."

"Here we are, my fine gents." Inácio and the detectives gathered behind Schafer. "The address is for a factory that was forced to close down last December due to a fire. You didn't see it on your online maps, Derrick, because it was fairly new before insurance claimed the building. I've got the blueprint right here."

"How'd you—" Derrick started.

"It's a pretty basic setup. Two floors and a warehouse."

"Suzanne Cosmetics?" Inácio raised a brow.

"Yep, they're holding up in a makeup factory."

"Zoom out on the entrances."

"Looks like a double-door entrance on the south end along with two shop doors on either side. We have no entrances on the east side, but we do have a lot of windows."

"Perfect," Inácio nodded.

"There is a door leading to the warehouse section at the north end. There are two semi-truck shipping doors, but those aren't really places of entry. One more door on the west side, closer to the front entrance."

"What's on the first floor on the other side of the front doors?" Inácio asked, his tactical plan formulating.

"The manufacturing room. Beware, there is a skywalk overlooking the entire area. It leads to office spaces, as you can see here. Below that is storage. The roofs look like a flat design, so we can expect some friends to be up there."

"Do you have any idea who these people are?" Derrick asked, directing his question to Schafer.

"Couldn't tell ya."

"Alright, listen up!" Inácio hollered. It was time to take action. "I am going to tell you all how this is going to work." Inácio expected an argument, but Derrick surprised him with his silence. "Our one and only goal is to rescue Delilah. We will leave together. However, I will go in first, alone. Expect roughly twenty to thirty guys. I hope this is a huge overestimation, but in my experience, this is what we're most likely looking at. On the other side of that grassy lot east of the factory are storage units. *Joe*, pick a roof and assess the situation with these thermals. I want you to do a count and try to locate where they're keeping her. These guys will be on alert after I show up. I need you all to hold back until it looks like they've let their guard down. Greg and Derrick will approach *carefully* from the east, and Joe, you will be covering them with a rifle."

"You're giving me too much credit here," Schafer said. "It's been a minute."

"You know what you're doing."

He scratched his head.

"If they got two guys on the roof, pop 'em both. Be quick about it. Each of you will be given a radio with an earpiece. Joe will be your extra set of eyes. All three of you need to communicate what's going on."

"We can do that." Greg nodded.

"Good. I want you two headed to the north door. It's up these stairs." Inácio pointed to the photo on the screen. "Here you will create a diversion and bring the majority of the men to this door. You guys will need to move fast and enter either through the front entrance or the west door."

"What if Delilah is over there? We don't know where they're holding her," Derrick questioned.

"If Joe can't determine where she is, he might direct you to create the diversion somewhere else. I'm assuming they favor the space with the skywalk, but you're right, Derrick, we need to be prepared for anything. When you enter, you'll be meeting some resistance, so be prepared to take lives. Locate Delilah and both of you get the hell out of there. I'm sure I don't need to explain how to be tactical about all this?"

"No, we understand what to do," Derrick said.

"So, that's it? They take her and leave?" Schafer asked.

"Yeah, that's it."

"I feel like you're leaving some details out."

"This is how it's got to be. If an opportunity presents itself, I'll be coming back too, but shit happens."

"I don't know if I share your philosophy," said Schafer.

"I know. Greg, you're a big guy. These two bags are yours." He sat the heavy sacks loaded with guns and ammunition beside him. "You will carry these at all times. Look through them, get to know what's where. Each of you have pistols with suppressors, otherwise everything else goes bang-bang. You probably won't need all that, but with so few of you, I want you overcompensating." Inácio turned to Delilah's father.

"Derrick, almost everything you need is in that duffle, and I have something else for you." Inácio handed him two unopened boxes of explosives. "This is your diversion. I want you to be in charge of the explosives, so don't get shot. What you're going to do is take this knife, cut one of the bricks in half, and stick it to where Joe tells you. These little boxes here hold your blasting caps." Inácio opened one and demonstrated. "You will hold it like this and in this manner exactly. You will not place your hand over the cap or you will create static electricity, and if God's on your side, you will only lose your hand."

"I insert that into the C-4?"

"Yes. At this wired end you will connect the command wire and trigger switch. Keep your distance."

"Why am I using only half?"

"Half is all you need at a place like this."

"Alright, I got it. Half."

"Want another pistol, Joe?" Inácio pulled out the gun from his waistband and held it out to Schafer.

"I'll hold it for you."

"Derrick, if everything goes right, you'll be on your way home with Delilah in no time."

"Four American rejects and dozens of potential enemies. What could go wrong?" Schafer smirked, putting away his laptop.

"You're American?" Greg asked Inácio.

"Don't judge a book by its cover," Schafer reminded.

57 INÁCIO

The night was dark, and with the heavy rain coming down, it made it even harder to see the entrance of the factory. Inácio glanced in his rear-view mirror, making sure Schafer turned early into the storage units. Inácio knew he could trust Schafer with just about anything. However, he could never know how much Delilah really knew. That worry ended the moment he broke away and drove into the overgrown factory lot. His palms were sweaty with a slight shake. Inácio swallowed hard and prayed she was still alive and that no one had touched her.

The coupe's engine barely shut down before a fist pounded on his window.

A twisting inside almost made him react violently. When he cracked the door open, two men in camouflage forcefully grabbed him from his seat and contorted his arms behind him. The smaller men were lucky he cared about someone more than himself. Inácio looked up to see several more armed men waiting to make their move.

"Walk!" they ordered, rushing him to the south double doors. They opened heavy and loud. Inácio entered a dark pit illuminated only by the sharp lumens of weapon lights. The blueprint ran through his mind as they forced him to the center of the room. His eyes darted around, trying to find his girl anywhere. He knew she was scared, and all he wanted to do was comfort her.

A fist came out of the darkness and rammed deep into his gut.

This is what I deserve.

Momentarily incapacitated, he was slammed onto a chair and felt the rings of a chain bruise his torso as the men pulled it tighter across his chest. Barely enough room was left for him to take a full breath. Inácio groaned, trying to recover from the blow. A feminine voice perked up his ears. He raised his head, disregarding his pain. *Where is she?* Only darkness and confusion were around him. His enemies stood so close, he could feel the heat from their lights on his face. The feminine cry sounded again.

"Delilah?" he called. Another blow to the jaw punished him for his curiosity. Being forced to remain still during the process let the pain linger and radiate across the skull. The punch didn't stop him from calling out her name again and again. He was penalized every time her name left his mouth.

"Light her up," said a voice from his right. It was the same voice from the phone call. The same man who'd threatened her life and demanded Inácio's. Per the man's command, someone shined their light onto Delilah. There she was, gagged, bound, and restrained to a metal beam supporting the skywalk in front of him. Inácio was right, they were holding her in the manufacturing room. In that way it was a relief. Her dad's job would be that much easier.

Tears soaked her eyes, and he noticed the same look within her as he had a week earlier. It was more painful to see her like that than to endure any amount of torture his enemies could bring to him. She was sitting on the cold, damp, dirty floor and he could only imagine the temptation of his enemies. Delilah's shorts were still buttoned and her thighs clear. Inácio hoped those were good signs.

"Delilah! I'm here! It's okay. It's going to be okay."

"Don't lie to her, Inácio." It was the same man speaking. "She put up a pretty good fight against my men. The only thing that kept her from escaping was threatening your life. She really does love you."

"Who are you?"

"A man who is tired of losing my leaders to you," he said. He stopped hiding in the dark and stepped into the bright beams. He was a tall but slightly pudgy man of around fifty. A well-groomed mustache draped over the corners of his lips. His dark hair had some white showing through. He wore a bulky golden watch and a thick rope chain hung across his shoulders. His clothing was simple, just a light green T-shirt tucked into cargo pants. Inácio didn't recognize him, but he knew the group he represented. The stranger punched him in his gut, then his mouth. Inácio growled and spat out blood on the floor.

He decided to play dumb, only to buy time. "Who the hell are you?"

"A really pissed-off boss." He punched him again, this time sending Inácio's head whipping back harshly.

"You're going to have to be more specific," Inácio said through gritted teeth.

"Spend much time in Colombia lately?"

"A bit. I like their coffee," he said, looking up as the man struck Inácio's shin with his boot. He squinted and hissed.

"You've done more than that, *assassin*. Five. That's how many officers of mine you've killed."

"Oh, I see what this is about. You're hurting now, aren't you?"

"Nothing will hurt us. No one will take us down."

"How about you take it up with whoever is paying for my services?"

"Their time will come too. Right now, it's about getting rid of their dog."

"Do you really think this will make a difference?"

"It will make me feel better." He drew in close.

"My English must be rusty. Say that again?"

"You should have been more careful with your mask after you killed her."

"After I killed who?"

"Paula! Paula Sánchez!"

"Ah, the Medusa. I barely remember."

"You may not, but I do."

Inácio thought back to the Medusa's last words. The name she called just before he invaded her private hut. "You're Rojas."

"How do you know that?" Rojas snapped.

"Your name was the last to leave her lips before I ended her wretched existence."

"You will pay, both of you." Rojas looked back at Delilah.

"She has nothing to do with anything I've done. Let her go now before it's too late for you."

"You think I'm not ready for your people to make a move? Who do you have coming? Operators or those dumb detectives?"

"You know, your English is really good for a backwater *paisa* playing soldier," Inácio taunted, using the man's own slang to aggravate him. His captor spit in his face.

"You underestimated us, and that is why you're tied to my chair."

"You brought all these men for one guy? Doesn't sound like I did." Inácio heard Delilah's muffled cry after he was struck again, his eyes always resetting back to her. They could strike him, they could make him bleed, they could insult him, but his sole concern was her. Only he had earned this destiny, not Delilah. When she was safe, he could die in peace. Until then, he'd fight for every breath.

"I want to show you something." The Colombian took a photo out of his uniform pocket. "Do you remember this? Tenth of January."

Inácio looked at the picture.

"That's your face on one of our many trail cameras. We should have put them up a long time ago, but we can all get a little comfortable sometimes, am I right?"

Inácio stayed quiet and kept his focus on Delilah.

"My contact was so eager to identify you. A few dollars and someone close to you was willing to give me everything I needed to know to find you. You know, I have been wondering about something." The man punched him again. "Do you remember any of the names of your targets? Is there anything in that soulless abyss of yours?" His finger jabbed into his chest.

Inácio grinned back with a bloody smile.

"Hang this son of a bitch by a chain!"

58 DELILAH

The soldiers descended on him like the predators they were, all aggression as they jerked him out of his chains. Four men held him down on the ground while a fifth threw up a bulky chain. Its clang pulsated across the building. Buttons sprung into the air while they tore his clothes from his body. The man who Delilah had only ever seen as invincible now squirmed and struggled against their body weight, pinned down under crushing forms. She made heart-wrenching eye contact with Inácio as his face was forced to the ground by a man's knee. He stared back at her with what could only be described as regret and love.

Delilah could do nothing but watch them abuse and break his body.

"I love you. I've made a terrible mistake." Blood spat from his lips.

I love you and I forgive you, she wanted to say. The cloth gag in her mouth made it impossible to communicate. Whatever happened that evening didn't matter to her anymore. Delilah's heartache about how things had ended was nothing compared to the bone-chilling torture happening before her. Any confusion or doubt that he loved her was wiped from her consciousness. Inácio was there, sacrificing himself for her. There was no love greater.

The stress sent tingling sensations across her scar and the dullness of a headache grew more intense. Delilah pulled against the restraints around her wrists, embedding bruises across her skin in the process. Panic overtook her seeing the chain wrapped around Inácio's wrists pull him higher and higher off the ground. The captors cheered and shot their guns in the air in celebration. Deafening blasts nurtured the illness growing in her gut. It made her sick. Nothing could be more evil or atrocious.

The strong, able body she'd once rested safely on now hung immobile three feet off the ground. Inácio's wrists took the strain of his entire weight under the constriction of the harsh links. The cruel man returned to Inácio again with another chain in his hands. This one was smaller and beginning to rust.

"To answer your question," Inácio antagonized, "I do remember something about my targets."

Delilah winced for him, wishing he would stop provoking them.

"What's that?"

"The way their life drains from their eyes." He laughed.

"Now it's your turn." The chain in the man's hands began to spin.

"Paula Sánchez," Inácio said. His captor lifted his shoulders and hunched near Inácio like an enraged Dracula. "I remember the shock on her face before I pulled the trigger. God, she looked pathetic lying there with a hole between her eyes. I hope she's burning in hell with the rest of them." He spit a wad of blood into the man's face.

Delilah dipped her head in despair for what she was about to witness.

"Tonight, you will pay, and your girl will watch every second while your life slips away."

The chain spun in a propeller fashion until the man achieved enough momentum to whip Inácio across the torso. Her love's stoic demeanor ended and his reaction to the pain flowed freely from his mouth. The outburst of pain aged him forty years. Rough, weak, and feeble was his voice. His stretched torso shook from the impact. Delilah wanted to die before she saw any more, but after each strike he lowered his chin and looked right at her. Looking away felt like abandonment. Delilah had to be there with him through every second of it. Sweat and blood ran down his face, his eyes growing red and glossy.

"Paula Sánchez!" *Whack.* "Diego Torres!" *Whack.* "Aaron Vargas!" *Whack.* "Rodrigo Valencia!" *Smack.* "Gilberto Romero!" *Smack.*

59

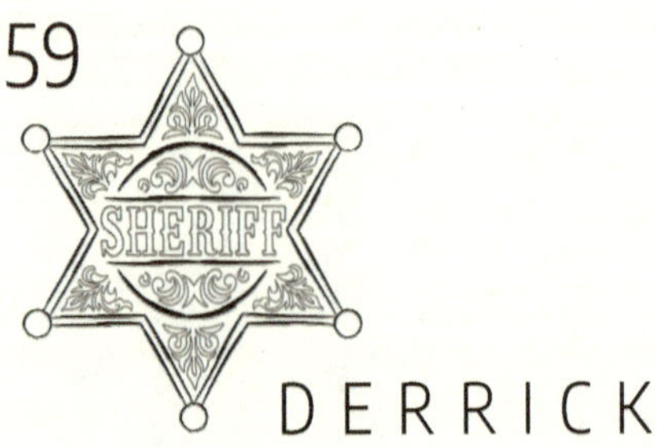

DERRICK

Scooting into position beside Joe, Derrick was able to achieve a decent vantage point on the roof of one of the many storage units. Below, Greg waited on solid ground, the rocks beneath his boots shuffling around like a bed of beads. The relentless rain clouds had soaked through his ball cap a long time ago, making it practically useless. The bill wicked away some of the water from his eyes, but he was no less wet.

"Here." Joe handed over a pair of binoculars. "So you can see what we're working with. Looks like the lookouts are finally letting down their guard."

Large windows along the ceiling of the eastern wall made it possible to see the glowing red human figures. A guard passed around the factory roof, staring down at his phone. Below him, guards around the outer perimeter joined the rest inside. Torture was apparently too good to miss. If Derrick listened close enough, shouts could faintly be heard through the rain. "I see someone tied up. Looks like they're encircling 'em."

"That would be Inácio I reckon." Joe opened his hand for his turn and put the binoculars to his eyes.

"I didn't see anyone that looked like my daughter." Derrick couldn't care less about her boyfriend, or whoever he was.

"Me neither, but I bet you she's in the same room somewhere. We just can't see her."

"How can you be so sure?" A brick of C-4 was something Derrick didn't want to detonate just anywhere.

"Well, why wouldn't she be? They'd want to use them against each other, would they not? Damn, these guys are really giving him hell. His hands are turning blue through the thermals. That's not good. We don't have much time. Let's get this show on the road."

Derrick and Joe hopped down from the roof and landed on the hood. Anger, determination, and a drive to right his wrongs filled Derrick's spirit. Greg, who was normally calm, shifted his weight from one foot to the other in an antsy fashion. Back home, there was always a chance a lethal situation could unfold. Here, death was unavoidable. No one to call, no one to rescue them.

"The only way out of this is through, boys," Joe announced before jumping into a puddle. "I count at least twenty of them in there. It's just like we planned. Distraction will be made at the back door beside the loading docks."

"I'm gonna kill 'em. Every last one of them if I can," Derrick hissed.

"Boys, listen to me. These guys are likely expecting to face a big retaliation. What they're not expecting is two seasoned cops like you to outwit them. Now they're probably in there wondering if they brought too many dudes, and we're going to prove them wrong. Avoid center-mass shots. This isn't white-picket-fence America. This is Brazil. Shoot to kill. I've got your back, fellas."

"Thank you, sir." Greg nodded.

"Stick them earpieces in. Can you hear me? Check check."

"Copy that," they replied.

"Clear on my end too."

Derrick joined Greg in strapping on the rifles.

"Picking the M-4s first, I see. Are your bags situated where you can get to them?" Joe asked.

"Yep," they confirmed.

"Are you confident with that C-4, chief?"

"10-4." Derrick danced in place.

"Alright, move out. I will get back on the roof to cover you two." Upon Joe's command, Derrick raised the rifle to his shoulder, Greg doing the same. They marched quickly and tactically forward.

"If either of you have an opening, do the right thing and give my friend in there a chance," said Joe's voice through the earpiece.

"Copy that," Greg replied. Derrick ignored him. The only ones that mattered in order of importance were Delilah, Greg, and then himself. No one else existed on his list.

Trekking through the tall grass, Derrick's heart was close to bursting from his chest. The vegetation and drenched air made it impossible to see more than a couple feet ahead. Anticipation manifested in his body as it always did before serious actions like executing search warrants, but he never allowed the anxiety to take over. The enormous difference was that they usually knew what was waiting for them, and the odds now weren't good. Still, if he could stay alive long enough to save Delilah, that was the only victory he could reasonably hope for.

"You're about a hundred and fifty yards from the fence," Joe alerted.

"Are we straight? It's kinda hard to see through this crap," said Greg.

"You're level with the northeast corner of the building. Right where you want to be. I know it's pretty thick down there. You're on it, boys."

"Remember, Greg," Derrick began, "we have another advantage. This is personal for us."

"Alright guys, you are fifty yards out. There's going to be a body dropping ahead, so don't be alarmed," Joe informed.

Derrick saw the break in the overgrown lot and took a giant step to escape it, his clothes covered in weeds and blades of grass. The muddy rainwater was high enough to reach his boot laces. On the other side of the fence lining the factory lot, they were greeted with the dead weight of a body dropping with a loud splash.

"Holy shit," said Greg.

"Got him," Joe said happily. "You're clear to proceed, my friends."

"Up and over, Greg." Derrick climbed the six-foot chain-link fence as silently as possible. The extra gear didn't make it easy. With a little effort, he made it over cleanly. The fence stretched back from the weight of Greg and his two full duffle bags of weapons.

"Aw shit, I don't know about this."

"C'mon Greg, you can do this."

"It's been a while since the PT test."

"One hundred plus pounds later, but you got this."

Greg hung on for a few seconds, then let go. "I can't, man, I'm sorry." He splashed back in the grass.

"What the fuck, Greg!" he yelled in a whisper. "You can't let me down now!"

"Y'all need to keep moving," Joe pushed.

"The fence is cut over here. I'll crawl."

"Don't do that, dammit." Derrick groaned. Greg bent back the flopping piece of chain-link, forcing his way into the opening. His rifle and vest snagged on their way through.

"Pull me though, Derrick."

"Good god, Greg." Derrick groaned, pulling on his vest.

"My foot's stuck on some vine. Grrr, almost there. Okay I'm good, I'm good."

"Let's go."

"Get that C-4 ready, Derrick," Joe said.

"10-4, I'm gettin' it."

He unzipped the bag and took out the cardboard box, throwing it to the ground. Derrick was too focused on his next task to worry about the horrific ambient sounds, from the broken windows to the loud voices of men screaming and cheering. It sounded like a party. A dreadful cry from Inácio sent chills down Derrick's spine.

They jogged right past the first kill. Blood poured from a mushy hole in his eye socket. The red was swept away by the rising rainwater. The image wouldn't haunt him now. Too much to think about. It was sure to stick in his mind in the future if they made it through.

Derrick ran up the short set of stairs to the south door and slapped on the explosive material, throwing the box containing the blasting cap to the soaked ground. Just like he had been instructed, he held it by the end and inserted it into the clay-like material. Derrick's mind told him he was ready, but his body said otherwise. An image of the explosive blasting into his face unexpectedly played through in his mind, causing his hands to jitter.

"Hey," alerted Greg through the earpiece. "You were supposed to cut that in half, right?"

Derrick shook his head.

"He said to use half of it."

"It's fine," Derrick brushed off. "They won't hear half, but they'll hear the whole thing if it explodes."

"How do you know?"

"Just shut up and trust me." Derrick unrolled the wire and stepped down the stairs.

"Hurry up, things are escalating in there. They don't have much more time," Joe said, his demanding voice piercing Derrick's ear. Derrick and Greg kneeled by the fence, backing against it as far as it could stretch.

"Bombs away," Derrick warned. He and Greg took out their earpieces.

"Wait." Greg grabbed his hand.

"What?"

"Are we back far enough? Do we even know what a whole block of C-4 is going to do?"

"There's only one way to find out." Derrick's thumb jammed the trigger button down anyway.

Deep cutting pain tore at Inácio under the burden of his shoulders. His dead weight created a painful stretch that cut into his sockets. Every tendon fiber frayed and snapped, one by one. It was both hollow agony and dull numbness. Hanging there dense and heavy, there was nothing to do but suffer. Inácio's numb hands felt like they were disconnecting from his body. They felt dead and motionless, crushed between the chains. Exhaustion drooped his head low. The pool of blood below grew a deeper red. As easy as it would be to give in and crumble, he was determined to hold it together, just a little longer.

A red film coated his injured right eye. With Rojas's increased violence, the sadistic crowd laughed and spat out insults. Broken shards of glass were thrown at him like shurikens. The sharp edges sliced him open. When they stuck to his flesh, they cheered even harder. All mutilation was welcome if it bought more time for Delilah's rescue, yet their clock was ticking. Inácio lost track of time, however, unaware if he had been hanging for twenty minutes or an hour. Tears escaped his eyes, mixing with the blood below his feet. His heart cried out for Delilah. Inácio would rather them chop him to pieces before letting anything happen to her.

"Water!" With one hand, Rojas caught the flying bottle and gulped it down until it was empty. He dropped the chain onto the concrete floor with a bang. His hands were blistered and he backed up, thoughtfully looking over Inácio like he was an art project. The other men settled down, the silence bringing out the searing stings from the lashes. Rojas's dirty fingers screwed on the white cap just enough to send it flying away with a pop after a good twist of the plastic. It caught air and landed at Delilah's toes. A sneaky grin stretched across their captor's face.

Rojas sat down beside her, his hips hugging her own. He reached his sweaty arm around the pole she was tied to and rested his hand over her shoulder. Territorial rage burned in Inácio's eyes, pumping life into his body.

"There he is!" Rojas snickered.

Delilah leaned as far away as possible.

"Hey girl, where do you think you're going? Our night's just started." His finger squeezed around her jaw. "What do you think I should do to him next?"

"Why don't you pick on someone your own size? Got a small dick or something?" Inácio interrupted.

"*¡Qué mierda!*" Rojas left Delilah's side.

"Let's go, stubby. If twirling around on a chain is all you've got, I'm not very impressed." Inácio ejected another glob of blood across his torturer's face. "Weak. You're nothing."

"You want to compare dick sizes?!" A knife was shoved against Inácio's groin. "I can guarantee I will win that one! I'll send your dick flapping to the ground like a dead worm! I wonder if she will still want you after. Will she cry for you when you're no longer a man?"

"I don't know, do the girls cry when they see you?"

"I can fix that tongue too!" Rojas twisted the blade sadistically in the air.

Boom!

Glass from the level above crashed to the ground, the entire factory shifting on its foundation. The ear-splitting blast lingered, lengthening the sudden disorientation. A flustered Rojas gathered most of his men, their rifle lights skipping everywhere like a light show. After a few quick orders, the captor and most of his men left the room and toward the sound. With Rojas gone, Inácio managed a smile.

"You're going to be safe soon, Delilah." Inácio promised to survive long enough to see that Delilah was safe, then he could let go.

A metal door behind him slammed open and an outbreak of machine guns blasted around them. Inácio could only see Delilah in the chaos of the muzzle flashes. The noise rumbled like thunder and chattered his teeth with an unrelenting clamor.

"Keep your head down!" he screamed to her. Inácio, helpless to protect Delilah or himself, hung in place, waiting to be torn up by the bullets.

61 DELILAH

The iron smell of Inácio's plasma and the savage burning of rapid fire washed over Delilah with perpetual nausea. The rancid air was reinforced by the strobe of weapon flashes over her head. She remained as low as possible, peeking up only to make out what was happening, but the blinding shutters made everything incoherent. Only Inácio's shape could be made out. In the havoc, the woman fighter came between Delilah and Inácio, using him to shield herself from the rounds that whizzed by. The female soldier bent at the waist, shooting her rifle in full auto.

Inácio wrapped one leg around her head, then the other.

The woman went limp and dropped.

Large blasts, deeper than those of the other bullets, shook the air until the shots faded altogether. A nasty gurgle echoed from across the room in the relief of silence.

"I got you covered! Get the guy up top!" Delilah heard a familiar voice yell.

Dad?

Shortly after his words, a man fell from the railing above and landed like a bag of potatoes. His skull split open dramatically beside Delilah and Inácio.

The ties around her wrists dug in deep as she strained to see the action on the other side of the metal drums. She could barely make out multiple figures moving in circles, taking pop shots at one another. The shots became increasingly sporadic until they stopped.

"Delilah!" Someone slid in like a ball player to her side. The gag was yanked from her mouth. Blue blobs painted her sight, her vision still mimicking the shooting. Delilah squinted and saw a face she'd never thought she'd be happy to see.

"Dad! Oh my god, Dad!"

"We gotta go!" He pulled out his knife and began slicing through her bonds like they were tough pieces of meat.

"You have to get Inácio! Please, get him down!"

"No, Delilah, just go," Inácio said, sounding exhausted. "There's no time."

Greg appeared at Inácio's side, his weapon light highlighting his form. He walked around him and cracked over a pile of broken glass. Inácio's fresh blood dripped from his body like sap. Greg pulled out a shard of glass poking from his side. It shattered to the ground with the rest. Inácio barely flinched. Greg looked him over with both disgust and pity.

"Are you okay?" her dad panted. Delilah fell over once the bindings were removed. Rough indents were stamped around her wrists.

"I don't feel well," she said.

"C'mon, I'll carry you if I have to."

"They're coming!" Greg alerted, angry shouts resounding from another part of the building.

"Can you walk?" Her dad helped her to her feet.

"Yeah, I can walk."

"Let's get outta here!" Delilah was yanked by one hand, her dad anchoring his rifle over his other shoulder. "Greg, c'mon!"

"Inácio!" Delilah pulled away, reaching out almost far enough to touch him.

"I'll get him down!" Greg announced.

"Forget him!"

"I'm cutting him loose, Derrick!" he yelled back.

"There's no time!"

Delilah swung around, holding back her dad from his forward movement.

"Dammit," he growled.

Greg raised his rifle toward the chain, aiming through his laser sights. The chain rattled and jerked until the third round broke a link. Inácio fell and cried out in agony. Greg swooped in and snatched the knife from her dad's waistband.

"Hey!" he protested, slapping a hand over the sheath.

His partner frantically cut away at the jerry-rigged cords around the chains. "You're free, you're free!"

Delilah worked on twisting her way out of her dad's death grip on her wrist.

"Give me one of those bags!" Inácio groaned.

Greg dropped the bag of weapons from one of his shoulders. Inácio's barely mobile arms raked at the strap.

"Put it over my shoulder."

Greg obeyed.

Delilah pulled herself free. She dove for Inácio, wrapping her arms over his shoulders.

"Delilah, no! We have to leave!" She heard her dad's storming steps draw closer.

"Come with us!" Delilah begged. "I love you! Please!"

"Derrick, get your daughter! Get her out of here!" Inácio bellowed.

"No, no!" Delilah clenched his battered body tighter. Her dad's grip pried her off little by little.

"You're everything to me, but you need to go." His puffy bloodied lip planted a sloppy kiss on her cheek before she was ripped away. Greg also tossed the dead woman's rifle into his lap and ran, helping to pull Delilah along. All breath left her lungs, making her chest seize in despair as she abandoned the only man who could bring her back to life again.

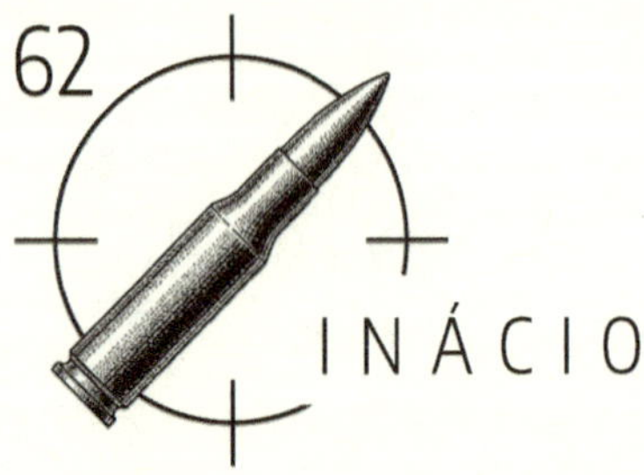

With all the strength Inácio had left, he slowly dragged himself on his elbows, finding cover behind more manufacturing equipment. Rojas and his men returned, shooting at the door closing behind Delilah, Derrick, and Greg. Inácio slapped his forearm across the rifle's light switch until it shut off, then he scooted between the group of towering tanks and into their darkest corner. A metal stairway leading to their control valves on top boxed him in well. Inácio grimaced, trying to wake up his stinging hands. He could fight through the rest of the pain. He just needed dexterity. Needles peppered the tips and his index finger made its first twitch.

"They're escaping! What do we do?" they asked.

Inácio watched them through the open sliver between the tanks.

"Wait!" Rojas held his hand up. His eyes followed Inácio's blood trail. "He's still here! Aye, fucker!"

Strong enough to point his weapon, Inácio held down the trigger, letting the rifle bounce erratically in his weak grip.

Rojas and the others dropped for cover and fired back.

Inácio clenched his hand above his knee, experiencing a burn worse than any beating from a chain. He'd been hit. A hole was gouged into his thigh, biting its damage to the bone. Blood and spit foamed around his gums. The mix ran down his chin in pure misery. *It's over, it's over, it's over. This is it.* When the drumming of the bullets stopped pelting his cover, wafting out the smells of chemicals, he heard just how loud his weakness was. Inácio cried out freely in pain.

"We have him!" yelled a voice.

From around the edge of a drum, he saw the Colombians perk up their heads from their hiding places. Like hunters, they carefully approached his location. Inácio used his one good eye to scan everywhere, unsure if he was looking for an escape or divine intervention. *More time. She just needs a little more time to escape.*

Nearby, the stairs to the skywalk were only twenty feet away. Only. Inácio reloaded and forced himself up. He didn't have to make it. He didn't expect to. It was all about buying as many seconds as possible for Delilah. Her life, her future free from danger, was at the front of his mind as he gave everything he had to limp away. Even the smallest amount of weight on his injured leg was excruciating.

Hopping toward the stairs, Inácio clicked back the trigger, sending away round after round. He pounced up each stair with the strength of a single leg. His pursuers leaped behind anything they could and fired back. Their rounds shook the metal below his feet. Inácio pressed the trigger back until the gun ran dry. He tossed the weapon away and used both railings to pull himself up the top few stairs. His blood-slicked hands edged up the rail with a sketchy grip. Torn shoulders threatened to give way under the drag of his weight.

At the top of the skywalk was a busted glass door, leading into what he assumed was the office space. Inácio staggered his way through, pulling out another gun and firing it blindly behind him. He turned into a room to the left and collapsed behind the first structure he saw.

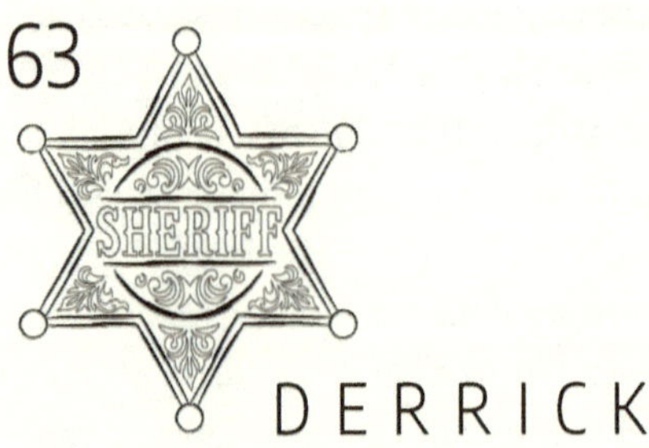

63 DERRICK

Nothing in the world could stop Derrick from getting his daughter home. She could fight him all she wanted, but he wasn't letting go. The frown that was already on his face grew deeper, her weight leaning in the complete opposite direction. They'd just found her tied to a pole and she was acting nothing like someone who was just *now* being kidnapped. Where was the gratitude? He yanked her around to his side.

"C'mon! What are you doing? Do you want us to die?!" The flooded lot was ankle-deep, making him feel like he was sprinting in slow motion in one of his own nightmares.

"Someone give me the status of Inácio!" Joe's voice rang loudly in their ears.

"I cut him loose! He's still inside. We're running to the south side now." Greg's information was met without a response. Their boots splashed in the water, exploding the pools of rain like dynamite in a lake.

"Geez, Del! You're barefoot. I gotta get you out of here. Work with me here!" Inácio's Mercedes was revealed as they rounded the first corner. It shined brilliantly under the streetlights. "Check the car! Can we use it?"

"I'm looking!" Greg entered through the driver's side, fumbling with the visor, seats, and floor mat for a key.

"Th-this is In-Inácio's c-car." Delilah shivered.

"We gotta get you out of here," Derrick insisted. He pulled her close, sensing her leaning back the way they came. "Anything, Greg?"

"He needs it th-though," Delilah argued. Her words slurred and meshed into one jumbled sound. Derrick shot her a worried expression. He began to wonder if her skewed speech was more to do with her seizures than the cold.

"Forget it, Greg. Let's get to the storage units."

"She's pretty pale," Greg observed.

"I think she's about to have a seiz—" More gunfire exploded from inside the factory. Derrick wrapped Delilah up with one arm and all three ducked and ran for the fence. Delilah was pushed through the break in the fence first, crawling through the muck on her hands and knees. Light from the gun battle inside flashed like white lightning.

"Delilah!" Derrick reached forward, missing his daughter as she dropped limply to the ground. "Dammit!"

"Is she okay?"

"She's having a seizure." Delilah was laid out in a grassy puddle, dead still. Derrick quickly snatched her up, slinging her over his shoulder.

"Don't people convulse when they have seizures?"

"It's not that kind of seizure, Greg. I don't have time to describe all the types to you right now."

As they sprinted back toward the storage units, a man emerged through the rain, and Derrick shuddered in surprise.

"Wait by the car!" It was Joe. He ran toward the factory without pausing.

"We're not waitin' for shit," Derrick replied. "Not for you, not for anyone!"

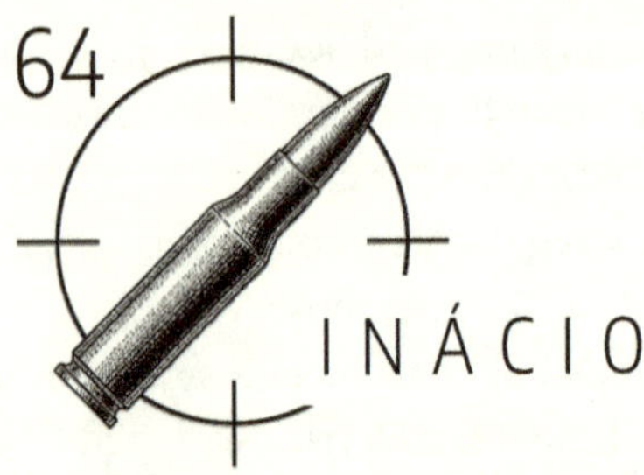

64 INÁCIO

The entire room, including the desk he hid behind, was charred black from the fire that had shut the factory down. Inácio blinked away the salt stinging his eyes. His hand fell down his leg, feeling the pant leg soaked in blood. He drew in a deep breath knowing he didn't have long until he would be unable to fight back. Boots clunked across the metal balcony. They were close. Quietly, he unzipped the duffle bag and felt for the shotgun. The boots crunched over broken glass, signaling they were just outside the door.

Inácio rested the barrel on the surface above him. He stayed low, his weapon and hair blending into the burned surroundings. His aim was fixed on the heads of the men, their tac lights giving away the positions of their most vulnerable body parts. Two rows of four moved methodically down the hallway.

Boom! Boom! Boom!

The butt of the shotgun jammed into his shoulder with a punch. Stuffing from a half-melted couch bounced in the air like popcorn and every chair in front of the desk was destroyed from the buckshot. What hearing he had left was deafened with a sharp ring.

Inácio saw the men fall back before he hobbled to the next room connected to the office. The door was so charred, he put his finger straight through the wood. Closing it behind him, Inácio huffed his way on top of the long meeting room table.

On the other side, Inácio heard the men enter the office he was just in. Kicked furniture and angry shouts were easy indicators of their location. Inácio switched back to a rifle. He blasted through the damaged door, taking a guess as to where their heads were. Based on the screams of terror and surprise, he knew he was right on target. When the magazine emptied, he rolled off the table and sprung for the cubicles across the hall.

He dove toward a far corner and reloaded, quietly locking the magazine into place. The carpet made it hard to listen for incoming threats. Using the wall to prop himself up higher, he peeked over half-melted computers and fragmented cubicle walls. Fragments of office debris cut his face open as one commando fired at his head. Inácio felt his face, questioning if he had been hit or not. Blood gushed down his temple. He felt for holes. Only a lucky graze.

Inácio shot through the office separators to get to the rest of the men, unaware of how many were left. He sent two full magazines in their direction anyway, making a point to fire from different positions, his good knee taking all the strain. Then a scream that signaled at least one of his rounds was successful.

There was no return fire, only silence.

"The hell?" Inácio muttered to himself. Easing his way up again, he scanned for signs of life. A flash, then a sharp sting in his shoulder, forced him to lose his balance, pushing his head back into a corner desk. Someone flanked him from the left, embedding a bullet inside him. Inácio threw himself back into the corner of the office where he could monitor the east and north walls. He put down his weapon and switched to the shotgun, feeling like a living pincushion. He forced his arm to support the Banelli and waited for their next move.

Death inched closer.

Can't give up, don't give up.

"You're done, assassin!" Rojas yelled from the breakroom. "I know I got you."

Inácio maintained his silence.

"That poor girl. She's going to be so sad when I tell her you're dead."

"Not dead yet."

"Let it go, man." He laughed. "Give yourself up and I'll make it quick."

"Come over here yourself. Finish the job."

"I'm not falling for your tricks."

"You're right, it's over for me. Get over here, I have something to tell you before you kill me."

"What other plans do you have up your sleeve?" Rojas popped into view as his two final men circled around to surprise him. Inácio tapped the trigger and dropped them. One landed flat on his face while the other fell straight back, AK-47 still in hand. Rojas ducked out of view before Inácio could shoot him.

"Hey! You alive?" a voice asked, surprising Inácio. He pointed his weapon around before realizing it was Schafer. His handler bent down and reached for his bloody torso as if he could heal him right there.

"No, Schafer, there!" Inácio whispered. "Their leader is over there!"

Schafer turned his head around toward the cubicles. "He's in the cubicles?"

"I think the room on the other side. It was the first room on the right when you entered from the skywalk. That's where I'd be."

"Alright, I'll get him. Don't move."

"Not going anywhere, trust me." Inácio sat up and gritted his teeth. He felt useless sitting there while Schafer went to face Rojas on his own. Schafer worked behind a desk. He wasn't used to utilizing skills he was taught years ago. Inácio watched the top of his friend's head round the corner followed by several bone-chilling pops.

"Schafer!" Inácio reached for a fresh pistol and abandoned the bag of weapons in the corner, unable to carry it anymore. Crashing and banging resounded from the room. Inácio half crawled, half limped toward the sounds. Schafer wasn't supposed to die, only him. “Schafer!” The abrasive carpet burned beneath his elbows as he scooted himself closer.

At the doorway, Inácio dropped himself completely to the floor. He turned on the pistol light and tried aiming toward the Colombian who was grappling with his handler. Inácio's aim wobbled and the men moved too fast, throwing themselves against the walls and kitchen appliances. Schafer made an enormous leap and sent his captor falling onto the ground. Inácio flinched, feeling the floor beneath him shift. He looked down, then up at his handler. The damaged floor sunk in and then completely gave way. The hole took the men and several objects along with it.

“Schafer!” he yelled. Inácio scooted to the edge of the hole and pointed his light down until more of the floor began to slowly sink. Schafer's painful echoes were heard below. Based on a blueprint burned into Inácio's memory, he knew they'd fallen into the warehouse. Inácio grabbed the doorway, bringing himself upright. His eyes watered from the intensity of his injuries. Not one part of him had been spared. He limped as fast as he could toward the stairs.

65

DELILAH

"Greg, it's this way! Go this way!" Her dad's screaming was the first thing Delilah heard when she was brought to consciousness a third time. Her atonic seizures had come conveniently in clusters during their escape. The first time she woke up, she was slung over her dad's shoulder. The second time she heard her dad arguing with Greg about whether they should stay or go. Delilah was conscious the longest that time. She listened to their heated fight from the back seat, feeling her strength returning. Delilah sat up and saw Greg was driving them. Her dad had obviously won the debate. "Lie down, Delilah!"

"The guy turned this way, I remember!" Greg circled through the maze of storage units. The place was as large as a compound. Roosting birds flew out of view of their headlights. The spinning car made her reach for the window for stability. The rain beat down on the glass, obscuring the view of where she'd left Inácio behind. She pulled on the car door handle, wanting to jump out and find him. Damn child lock!

"You're facing east, Greg! That's south! We need to go south before we turn east, dumb-dumb! Del, would you put your seat belt on already?"

"I can't! Stop yelling at each other, please!" The storage units passed by her window and the car spun over the thick gravel like a mouse in a maze.

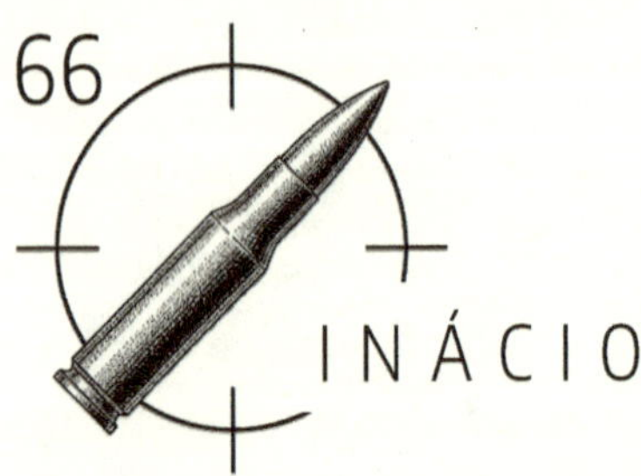

66 INÁCIO

Rivers of blood streamed down his body through the rain in crooked lines. Yelling and a gun's pop told him Schafer and Rojas made it out of the factory and into the tall grasses. The chain-link fence bowed and stretched, his fist clinging to it for balance after crawling through. Flattened paths of mangled grass and weeds traced through the empty lot. Inácio had no idea which one to follow.

The grey atmosphere obscured his impaired vision and a creeping weakness leaked its poison through his veins. Dizzy and lightheaded, Inácio followed Schafer's screams as they traveled across the area in fragments as though the sounds were coming from all directions. Inácio gambled and chose a path.

A guttural cry escaped him with every limp. Muddy water and thick leaves dragged his momentum back, making it that much harder. Inácio followed the sound, or at least where he thought the sound was coming from, until he could see the side profile of Rojas only a few feet ahead. On the ground was Schafer, who held his hands up in a blocking motion as Rojas stood, pointing a pistol at his head. Inácio rushed forward, pointing his own gun. A click signaled that the round had jammed, failing to fire. Rojas spotted Inácio and, using the only advantage he had left, Inácio leaped onto him, crushing him with his bodyweight.

Their skulls collided with a loud crack. With his good fist, he punched down onto Rojas's nose while his injured arm strained to keep Rojas's gun hand pinned to the boggy grass.

Crack!

Inácio felt the Colombian's boot crunch directly into his ball sack. Groaning at the sharp pain, Inácio rolled off his captor and onto his back in the grass. Rojas dove for the gun before Schafer could save it, taking off toward the road. Inácio rose to a knee, determined not to let him get away.

Schafer remained in pursuit.

Rojas made it fifty feet away before turning and firing two desperate shots in their direction. Inácio stopped and covered his lower abdomen. Blood pooled inside his palms. He felt his body slow and his ability to keep pushing fizzle. An intense urge to lie down and close his eyes took over.

"No, not yet." *Where's Delilah? Is she safe?*

"Inácio!" Schafer stopped dead in his tracks and stared at his wound. Inácio read the severity in his eyes. They both knew he wasn't going to make it.

"Go! We can't let him get away now. I'm right behind you."

"But, Inácio—"

"Go! I've got pressure on it." Inácio crawled forward and collapsed.

67

DELILAH

The car fishtailed onto the highway, sending Delilah knocking against the door. The water was like ice, sending them sliding into the opposite lane. Despite it, Greg abruptly accelerated, flopping her back in her seat. She clung to the strap of her seat belt, all while her dad shouted out a string of cuss words at him. His hands were braced against the dash as if he could stop the car with sheer willpower. Like a predator in the night, Inácio's torturer emerged through the hazy headlights, gun pointed toward someone.

Delilah screamed and watched him point the gun in their direction, his mustache drenched over his lips. Greg pressed forward, refusing to let up or swerve. Before a shot could be fired, the gunman dented the hood, his body cracking the windshield and bouncing off the roof.

"Holy shit, Greg!" her dad yelled. A pair of shoes fell from the sky, one bouncing off the hood and the other resting in the crevice under a windshield wiper. Greg slammed the brakes and spun around to a stop. His hands were stuck white-knuckling the steering wheel.

"Del, you okay?" her dad asked.

Delilah nodded, looking around.

"I get now why you turned west instead of east. You might have just saved all our asses."

"You're writing my reports for a year. I hope you know that," Greg said.

"That's fair," Derrick agreed.

"Let me out!" Delilah screamed, pounding on a back window.

"No, Del, you stay in the—"

Click.

Delilah pounced into the rainy water, hearing her dad scold Greg. She splashed toward the building, grey and blurry in the distance, until someone shouted her voice through the darkness. Delilah halted, seeing nothing but rain in her eyes.

"Are you *her*?" A man broke through the weather. The distant light of a streetlamp showed a streak of blood running down his brow and leaking over his teeth.

Delilah jumped back.

"It's okay, I'm a friend."

"Where is he?"

"Joe?" her dad called from the car.

The man pointed to the body behind the car. "Derrick, make sure he's dead. Greg, you come with me!" The stranger's face darkened and addressed her. "Wait here."

Greg rushed by, joining the stranger at his side into the marshy grass. They disappeared into the black as the clouds eased up in severity. Delilah whipped her head around, her cold hair slapping against her cheeks. Her dad stood above the body in the street and gave it a swift kick.

"No! Make sure he's dead! Shoot him!" Delilah stormed over, considering shooting him herself.

"Stop right there, Del!" He held his hand up like he was directing traffic.

"I'll do it!" she screamed. Her dad moved forward to stop her.

"Oh no you won't!"

Delilah wrestled with his blocking arms.

“Would you cut it out? He’s dead!”

“You have no idea what he’s done to me!” Delilah screamed.

“Someone open the car door, now!” the stranger said from behind her.

Her dad left her and ran to the car, parked crooked and halfway into the empty road. Braced between the stranger and Greg was a limp body, dragging at the feet.

“Inácio, oh my god.” She ran to him, putting his lax head between her hands. So much of his body was covered in lashes and more blood and more blood than she’d ever thought possible leaked from him.

“Make way! We gotta get him in the car.” The stranger’s frown was deadly serious.

“He’s alive,” Greg said under labored breath, his free arm stuck out to his side for stability.

“Barely,” the other man added. They shimmied Inácio into the front passenger seat, lowering the back of it all the way down. Delilah jumped in the back seat and folded her hands around his head and shoulders. He was pale, cold, and his shut eyes were sunken in. There were so many injuries, she didn’t know where to begin to help him. Greg flew in and put his jacket over Inácio’s abdomen.

“Hold that there,” he ordered. Delilah listened and wiped away her tears, which landed on Inácio’s face.

“Please don’t go, please.” She pressed down on the wet jacket as if she could force him to live. Her dad, Greg, and the stranger stood at the open door, talking.

“Let’s go!” she screamed. The third man eyed her before giving orders to her dad and Greg before they ran off. Delilah remained with Inácio, switching from crying to telling him how much she loved him. She held her lips to his cold forehead, imagining them never having gone to the restaurant, never running into her dad, just leaving everything behind. What if…

A small explosion awakened her from her fantasies. Flames roared from the building, bursting from every window.

"Hey, I'm riding with you. I'm not letting her out of my sight again," she heard her dad say outside. The door beside her opened, her dad stuffing himself in behind her.

"Is he going to die?" she whimpered.

"Just hold him still," said the stranger as he popped a cracked phone from his pocket. "I'm calling in a mobile medical unit to meet us at the house. They're our only hope." He took off like a rocket, tearing up the grassy median in the opposite direction.

68

DELILAH

"To the master bedroom right over there," the stranger ordered between breaths. Inácio was slumped in his arms, her dad walking backward, carrying his feet. Delilah paced to the side, keeping pressure on Inácio's abdomen with Greg's coat. She flipped over one of his hands and her palm became drenched in his blood. "Delilah, thank you, but you need to get back. Derrick, you're gonna need to move a little faster. We have to get him to the bed now!"

"I'm movin' as quick as I can." Inácio's head flopped to the side, his life force leaving a trail across the floor. He'd looked bad enough in the dark, but under the current lighting, the lacerations to his face and body were inhuman.

"Jesus," Greg said, holding the bedroom door open. Delilah eagerly followed them into the room, watching them lay his body onto the bed. Tears ran down Inácio's inflamed cheeks. Their bloody jagged trails spread down his neck and along his chest. Delilah backed up until her butt jostled the dresser. Her dad advanced toward her.

"Del, get out, you don't need to be here."

"You can't keep me out."

"Yes, I can." He shoved her to the side.

"No! This is our room!" Delilah pushed back as if she had real rights to it.

"*Our?* What is that supposed to mean?"

"Derrick!" the stranger yelled. "Do you have the tac med kit?"

"It's right here." Greg forcefully cleared the lamp and clock from the nightstand and slammed the bag down.

"Cut his pants off, Greg. I need to make a phone call." The stranger looked over at her dad again and pointed. "Stop worrying about her and help him."

Delilah watched her dad let her go with a scowl before helping. Greg cut the pant legs while her dad pulled them off. Inácio's bare legs revealed more wounds, more blood. She looked away, opting to tune in to the stranger's phone call. His worried voice wasn't as quiet as he probably thought it was.

"Location is safe house two… Can we get Doctor Gomez? Yeah? Well, tell him to hurry then." He ended the call and caught her listening.

Delilah snapped her head away.

Inácio's pants were in a torn pile on the floor. Bruising and patterned slicing were scattered across his thighs. Carefully, she scanned the corner of the room where the stranger was, finding him gone and at the bathroom sink. With clean hands, he returned with a handful of towels and threw them on the bed, directing Greg to maintain steady pressure wherever he could. Greg listened without question.

"The leg and shoulder will have to wait. Gotta start at his gut first." The stranger inspected the area. "Dang it. Not lucky enough for a through-'n-through. Derrick, hand me the pen light and the longest forceps you can find." He held out his hand until the items fell into his hand. "I am not the one who should be doing this."

"Shouldn't we go to the hospital? He doesn't look like he's going to make it if we stay here," Greg said.

"No!" the stranger snapped. "I got someone comin', but it's gonna be a while. Too long." He took a deep breath, blinking away his own blood from dripping in his eye. "It's going to take both of you to hold him."

"We got him," they said. The detectives pinned Inácio down by the elbows on either side.

Delilah put her fingers in her ears. She wasn't sure she could see him endure any more suffering.

"You're gonna feel this, buddy." The towel was removed from Inácio's side and the forceps dipped into his gut. Inácio grunted and fought the pain. The detectives flattened him to the mattress. Delilah stepped around the bed for a better view. She wanted to be there for him, but her legs wanted to run. He wailed and bayed in agony. The metal prongs protruded into the swollen walls of the wound, forcing their way down into the damaged skin.

"I got it, it's just a stubborn little…" The forceps hit something, making a metallic click. Inácio shook. "Hold him down, please!"

"We are!" said her dad.

"Do better then! I can't grab the bullet with him moving like this." The stranger wiped his forehead with the back of his hand and reentered the wound.

Delilah lurched forward, holding down his hip.

"I think he's gettin' a little stronger," Greg said through clenched teeth.

"At least he's got some fight in him." Using two hands to steady the bullet between the forceps, the stranger pulled it straight out. Inácio fell back with an exacerbated grunt. His healthy eye opened, then slowly closed, his expression still frozen in a scowl.

"For a dying guy, he's pretty alive," Greg commented.

"Ack, this dude ain't dyin', not yet."

"I don't know about that," Derrick muttered. The comment made Delilah wince. Her dad preferred him to be dead, she just knew it.

"We're not done yet though." The stranger moved to the hole above Inácio's knee. Its swelling had spread across his entire leg, making the wound resemble a crater. Blood pooled inside like a black soup. The veins protruding from Inácio's neck were settling down, but Delilah knew that was about to change. "Derrick, hold his shin. Greg, stay on his shoulder. Delilah—"

"I can't do it!" she admitted. Even if she was helping, she would feel complicit in his agony.

"Then maybe you should get out then!" he bellowed.

Delilah walked backward into the hallway, staring at their work.

"Alrighty, here we go again." The metal ends disappeared into the flooded hole.

Inácio's leg jerked back violently.

"Shit!" her dad spat.

"Be ready for the next one," the stranger warned. Like the living dead, Inácio rose up and groaned in pain. Delilah slammed the door shut, blocking her view. She retreated to the wall, her knees buckling.

"Hold him down!" The screams continued.

This was it. It was all coming to an end. She wondered if she'd ever see him alive again. Ever get to tell him she loved him. Ever get to feel his fingers caress her scar beneath her hair. Knowing her luck, she never would again.

69 DELILAH

When the door finally opened, Delilah saw her dad drenched in sweat. Greg was almost as bad and they shuffled to the kitchen. She took her hands from her ears and saw the other man sitting over him. The yelling finally ceased. Inácio's damaged body lay on the bed they once shared, the bed where he'd removed the bullet from her arm and soothed her fear. Their love was cultivated under those covers, and now they were stained with his blood. Even lying there while still and crippled, he was the strongest man she had ever met. Delilah got up to see him.

"No, not yet." The guy she didn't know waved her away. "The emergency surgeon is here." He bolted out of the bedroom and brought a doctor wearing the classic white coat and several male nurses in scrubs. They stomped by, brushing past.

Her dad walked in, between her and the bedroom.

"C'mon." He reached out his hand.

"No thanks." She pouted.

"Let the professionals handle it. You don't need to see him like that. You shouldn't be seeing any man like that."

"Heh," she chuckled, without feeling the humor of it. Her dad had no idea the kinds of things she'd seen.

"I will do what I can," she heard the doctor say.

On a perfect count, the nurses raised the board and carried Inácio away. The stranger followed quietly behind, arms crossed in front of him, looking like he was part of a funeral service. As they passed through the kitchen, Delilah reached out for him. Her fingers ran down the length of his arm.

Her dad grabbed her hand from her lap and pulled her away from the hall. In the kitchen they all quietly hydrated and stood around in an exhausted silence. After the most eventful day of their lives, no one had anything to talk about.

70

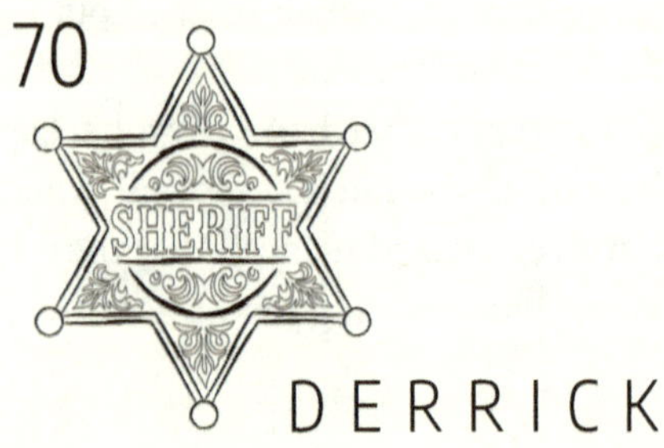

DERRICK

After wandering around the home gym for the tenth time, Derrick picked up a twenty-five kg plate, testing the weight out of either boredom or impatience. Greg was sprawled across the love seat, lost in dream land and breathing like a dragon. One hand rested over the bandage wrapped over his shoulder. Derrick's partner could nap anywhere, under any conditions. The bullet went clean through. Greg was lucky to be alive. They all were.

Joe cut into view, marching his bare feet across the living room. Stopping at one of the tall windows, he manipulated some type of lock and pulled. The glass turned into a door, the bottom half of the window seamlessly splitting from the top. Outside, Joe fell back into a padded wicker chair. Derrick, full of questions with no answers, stalked over to the open door. The yellowing sky and morning breeze were the only ones to greet him.

Derrick waited for Joe to acknowledge him, but Joe just reached into his dirty jacket and retrieved a flat black case. He opened it like a book and pulled out a cigar. Embers crackled from the end of it at the strike of a lighter. Joe stared across the ocean. Smoke escaped his mouth, making Derrick jealous of his apparent relaxation. Wincing, Joe petted his fat lip until finally speaking. Even still, he barely looked Derrick's way.

"How you doin', Dad?" It came out almost chipper.

"I don't know, to be honest."

"Well, you got whatcha came for. Your family is all in one piece. That's what matters. Right?" Joe refocused on the water. After a couple puffs, he did a double take as if he was surprised Derrick was still there. "Can I help you with something, Detective?"

"Possibly."

"Ah, you have questions. I would too, I guess. Probably wondering what the hell just happened."

"A little bit." Derrick clamped down on his shaking hand. Even after hours having passed, he still hadn't come down from the "excitement."

"I wouldn't overthink it too much right now. Closure will come in time. To be honest though, I feel like I'm preaching to the choir, you bein' a cop and all."

"How are *you* connected with these people?"

Joe scoffed. "You mean 'cause I'm a white American?"

"Mm-hmm, yeah." Derrick shrugged. "You don't seem like the typical Spanish speaker, or whatever they call it around here."

"Yep. People don't really see it comin' out of the typical Southern boy."

"So, are you a narco like those other guys or what?"

"A narco?" Joe wheezed out a laugh.

"Yes?"

"You expect me to answer willingly to a cop?"

"I guess not." Derrick groaned to himself. When arriving in Brazil, he'd internally prepared for a missing daughter, but what had come next was unimaginable. Besides the obvious, something else in the air didn't feel kosher. He could take Joe's advice and put it behind him… *or* he could follow his detective nose while he was here. There was a dishonest stench in the air and it wasn't coming from the cigar. "Hope you're not wrapped up in the cartel business. I want nothing to do with that."

"It's a little too late to wonder. I bet you're happy to be home soon." Joe's tone seemed too friendly for Derrick's taste. He preferred raw honesty, no matter how brutal.

"I don't think I can say the same thing about my daughter."

"Eh, don't take it too personal. She's just smitten."

"Smitten with who, that's the question." Derrick eyed Joe. It took a moment for him to reply.

"A hell of a guy, but probably a dead one. You won't need to worry about it for very long, I'm sure."

"A Green Beret, huh?"

"Pardon?"

"Inácio's ink. I noticed them when you were treating him in there. I'm pretty good at reading tattoos. All that suspect identification stuff."

"Like I said before, don't judge a book by its cover." Joe cleared his throat. "Anyways, if you don't mind, I think I will rest my eyes for a few minutes. Long night." Joe set his half-burned cigar in the ashtray next to him and leaned back.

Having no other choice, Derrick left him alone outside and stood at the center of the living room, not knowing what to do. He took in the open space. It was bothersome to think that this was where Delilah had been the entire time. They'd cooked in the sun passing out fliers while she was here with a pool and fluffy pillows. Despite everything working out in his favor, he felt no less played. Derrick needed time to figure out who had betrayed him the most, Silva or Delilah. Half-defeated, he rested in a cushioned chair beside Greg. His partner's throaty gear shifts weren't enough to keep him awake. Before he knew it, Derrick succumbed to a much-needed rest.

****

A thump startled Derrick awake. He lifted his head to see he'd knocked the first aid bag off the arm of his chair. He used the back of his calf to turn it right side up. Normally, he could sleep through any noise, especially when his body was experiencing a thousand pounds of lethargy. A crowd of footsteps awakened the whole house. Derrick cranked his head around to see Inácio's arm hanging limp over the side of a stretcher followed by a doctor looking almost as beaten down as Derrick himself. Greg looked their way, then flopped his head back down, drifting off to sleep while Joe charged in from the veranda. Derrick quickly reset his sleeping position, making Joe believe he was still out. Out of one eye, the detective tracked him until he disappeared into the bedroom behind the doctor. With the new distraction, this could be his only chance to find answers.

71 DELILAH

A jolt bounced Delilah, who wasn't sleeping anyway. Two male nurses in blue scrubs dumped Inácio onto the mattress beside her. Sprinkles of blood dotted their blue uniforms. They took their flat stretcher and carried it away, leaving behind the doctor. A face mask hung loose around his neck and his hands rustled around in his front coat pockets.

Delilah tossed away the pillow she was coiled around and rushed to Inácio's side. The aroma of chemicals mixed with iron from his body struck her nose. Two slashes under his swollen eye were stitched closed. The rest of his body was covered in large patches of wrapped gauze. He was warm to the touch but still appeared no closer to health. She thought he would look better after surgery, yet he was closer to Dr. Frankenstein's creations, still unconscious and more monstrous. The stranger she'd met in the rain hurried into the bedroom.

"So, is there good news? He was in there a while," he asked in his Southern accent.

"I might have good news if he hadn't destroyed my work," the doctor hissed. Anger tinted his cheeks and eyes red.

"Destroyed?"

"Your man here woke up twice, fought my staff, and ripped my surgical progress to shreds!" he sprayed.

Delilah lit up with hope.

"How's that possible? He's supposed to be sedated for that stuff." The stranger opened his hand, gesturing toward Inácio. The two argued like Delilah was invisible.

"Listen, I have no anesthesiologist. She was called away to Colombia." The doctor ripped off the mask hanging around his neck and shoved it in his pocket. "I took my best guess." Inácio's friend, or whoever he was, took the doctor by the arm and led him a couple feet away from the bed. They began to whisper in Portuguese. Delilah didn't need to know the language to understand there was nothing positive being said. Taking Inácio's face in her hands, she spoke to him softly.

"This was not how this was supposed to end. You can't die. Please don't."

He couldn't go, not like this.

Inácio was unbreakable.

Right?

"Thank you, doc," she heard the stranger say. The doctor then turned to leave. A drop of fluid drained from Inácio's mutilated eye. Delilah snagged a corner of the bed sheets to soak it up.

"His eye!" she cried. "Why didn't they do anything about his eye?" His iris and pupil were hidden beneath the goopy film.

The man approached the bed. "There isn't much they can do for him. So, I guess they figured—"

"They figured he wasn't worth it because he's going to die anyway?" Delilah clutched her chest. The anguish was twisting and churning her heart before ripping it from her body. Inácio was supposed to be her future, her everything. The corners of her mouth drooped in complete sadness.

"Soon, he won't feel any more pain."

"And that's supposed to make everything better? Am I supposed to forget how they tortured him right in front of me?"

"No and no."

"He can't die, he can't go out like this." Delilah hovered over Inácio. "I'm so sorry. If it wasn't for me—"

"It's not your fault," the man, Inácio's friend, corrected.

"Yes, it is," she insisted, almost offended.

"No," he almost shouted. "This is all him. He chose this."

"I don't even know who you are." *Who is he to say all this?*

"A close friend. The name's Joe." Joe pointed an aggressive finger toward Inácio. "There is nothin' you could have done different to keep him from his deathbed. He made his own decision without givin' a crap what it would do to others."

"Well, I'm sorry anyway." Delilah turned toward Inácio again, unable to keep her attention off him for long.

"I guess um, I shouldn't be surprised then." Joe crossed his arms and leaned his shoulder against the wall beside the headboard.

"About what?"

"About you two. About him risking his neck to help you. A couple of times, I've heard." Joe's leading comment made her head perk up. She was unsure of how to take it.

"When did you find out about us?"

"He told me after he asked for my help to rescue you."

She looked at Inácio with sympathy and regret.

"I mean, he didn't tell me everything. Makes me curious how much detail was left out."

"I'm not sure what you're getting at." Her voice shook, nervous for Inácio, nervous for herself.

"Darlin', I lie for a living, and so did Inácio. Not even he could fool me, though. I'm about ninety-nine percent positive you know more than you should."

"I don't," she said, shaking her head.

Joe gave a condescending smile. "Your face tells the truth when your words don't."

"I don't know anything and I don't care. I only care about him."

A chuckle broke Joe's seriousness. "Acckk, it's all good. There's nothing you gotta worry about, from me at least."

"I promise he didn't tell—"

Joe's voice grew dark again. "Don't make me do anything to make his sacrifice in vain. Inácio died for something he believed in. That's more than anyone else in the business can say, no matter how stupid the reason."

"What sacrifice? He's still breathing."

"According to the doc, he won't be for long. I don't have to tell you what happens if you take any of these secrets to America, do I?"

"No, sir."

"Good. I figured," he said, waving her off with a friendly grin. "If anyone here knows danger best, it's you." Joe paced toward the doorway. "Oh, I almost forgot." He backtracked and pulled something small from his pocket. "He asked me to give you this after you were safe. I don't think he was expecting to get out of this alive." Joe set a ring down on Inácio's slowly rising chest.

Delilah stared at it before reaching for the purple jewel. Its dozens of cut edges formed a perfectly round stone. Silver crowned the rock like it belonged to royalty. She choked on a new lump of emotion. Delilah took it and slipped it over her ring finger. It fit perfectly. Dreams of a dead future played through her mind. Delilah stopped and recoiled, catching Joe reading her before heading toward the door again.

"My dad won't tell either. Or Greg. I promise," Delilah said, concealing the fear that her dad was too ethical to lie.

"Time will tell. You know, Delilah, I don't know what it was about you that made him forget who he was, but whatever you've got is more dangerous than Inácio could ever be." He reached through the entrance and closed the mangled door behind him.

72

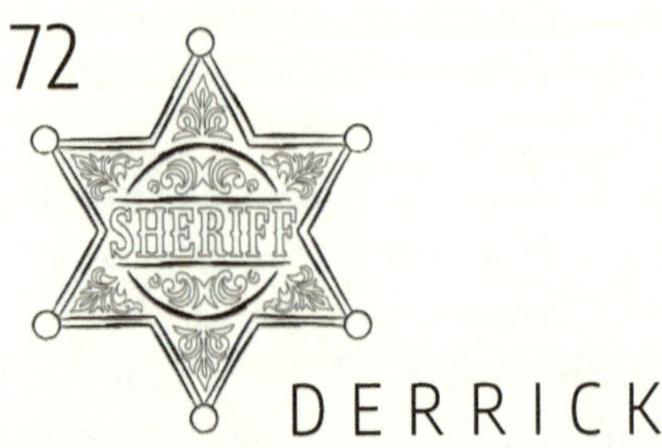

DERRICK

Derrick Johnson was known for his thoroughness in vehicle searches. His normally impatient personality made it a surprising skill to his coworkers. Unlike others, it wasn't attention to detail that drove his systematic process. Derrick was motivated to dig up as much incriminating evidence as possible. It was satisfying to show suspects they could not outwit the police. Any creative hiding place or jerry-rigged compartment was busted into, spilling its paraphernalia or illegal substances. He expected a challenge while searching Joe's car, but its answers were unexpectedly obvious.

Happy Greg was still asleep, Derrick located two concealed guns and a tablet he couldn't unlock. There was no way he could go home and be okay with the little information they had. Delilah had almost been killed and so had they. Men had died at their hands, and for what?

What's the bigger picture?

Whose enemies were they?

Who the hell is Joe?

If Derrick went back to America without seeking answers, he'd always regret it. The phony cops, the White Shores shootings, Delilah, and the militants were all connected—somehow.

Like opening a chest of gold being opened by a pirate, the trunk opened with a beep. His hand went for a leather briefcase that leaned against unzipped luggage. Derrick peeked around the car, seeing no one at the door. Quickly, he took the briefcase in his lap, dropping the trunk lid. With his back resting against the bumper, he scooted to the ground. A combination lock blocked his access.

"Damn." Still, he fruitlessly fiddled with the latches until the top suddenly cracked open. The briefcase wasn't quite latched. Derrick gasped at his luck. Heart racing, he peeked around the taillight, checking the door. It remained closed. Inside, there was another password-protected tablet and several folders. They were just like the ones he used at work to store case files.

Flipping over the first cover, he saw small and enlarged photos of the same man. Behind it was an array of times paired with activities, floor plans, and other data. A lot of it wasn't even in English. He moved on to the next one, discovering pictures of a woman. Satellite photos were beneath her with more foreign gibberish. Instead of skipping over it, he read closer. At the end of one page read: *Technique: Open.*

"Technique... Assigned to 431084...' Okay?" Derrick flipped back to the previous folder. "'Technique: Open, assigned to 33125.' What?" He opened another folder. "'Last confirmed location: Cali, Colombia. Service completed by 431084. Public? No... Required Parameters: lethal dose of—"

Derrick's adrenaline spiked with a paired sense of danger. He slapped the folder shut and looked around. His investigative mind screamed the answer, but he was a slave to his curiosity. Derrick opened another folder. A drop of sweat dripped to its pages, right beside a familiar face. He pinched the photo between his shaky fingers. "I know you, Benjamin Geerman." He read on. *Assigned to 431084. Service Completed. Public? Yes. Collateral? Yes.* Below it was an invitation to a global business conference and beneath that, a layout of the White Shores Hotel. It all began connecting in his mind. Without a doubt, this event had triggered Delilah's disappearance, and 431084 was, in all likelihood, Inácio. Derrick slammed it shut, trying to place things back where he'd found them.

"I was supposed to archive those." The upbeat voice practically shook Derrick out of his shoes. Rising to his feet, he let the briefcase drop from his lap. A brown folder slipped from under Derrick's shirt, its papers fanning across the ground. Joe's split-colored eyes stared at him with malice. His natural appearance made him resemble a villain from the movies. "You think it's okay to steal?" He took a step forward.

"Get back!" Derrick took slow steps back and Joe followed, his hands wringing themselves at his sides. Out of habit, Derrick reached for his hip, finding no service weapon to protect him.

"We helped get your daughter back and this is how you repay us? My friend gave his life for her."

"All I want is to get my daughter and my partner and we'll leave." Derrick's hands were raised, ready to defend himself.

"Then why are you making yourself at home?" Joe almost chuckled.

"Look, you guys are part of something I want nothing to do with." He continued to back around the car.

"I think you do."

"Please. Don't hurt my daughter or Greg. Let us leave." Derrick situated himself beside the driver's door where he'd know he'd find the first pistol.

"Seriously? You can't leave with this knowledge."

"I won't tell anyone, I—" Derrick cut himself off, flinging the door open and reaching for the discrete release button on the holster. Joe rushed Derrick, throwing him off-balance. He slammed the car door shut and reached down to slap Derrick repeatedly over the back of his head like a child. Derrick braced against him, ready to fight back when an unforgiving pistol muzzle pressed into his broken nose. "Awwww!"

"Shut up and listen, or I will shoot you right here. If you make me do this, I will have to kill Greg and your daughter. Do you understand?"

"Aw, yes! Yes!" Tears ran down his cheeks from the pain.

"I have your prints. I have your name. I know where you live. If you love your wife, if you love your child, if you care about your partner, you will keep everything that's happened to yourself. I don't care what you tell them, but it will be a lie. We can reach you anywhere. If you go back to Ohio and begin an investigation, everyone you love is dead. Do you want that, Johnson?" Joe raised his voice. "Do you want your wife and daughter to be murdered in their sleep?"

"No, please!" Blood drained into his mouth, leaking between his teeth.

"You will forget everything that happened here or I will kill Delilah myself."

"I understand! Just let us go, please." The gun pressed in harder.

"You got what you came for. Now leave before I take it away." Joe lifted the pressure from his face, leaving him to writhe in pain. Derrick ran inside the house, waking the sleeping giant with his fist. Greg grabbed at his chest and jumped awake.

"Ow!"

"We're leaving, Greg, now!"

"What the—" He rubbed his sleepy eyes.

"Ack, shit!" Derrick dunked his head under the faucet, letting the water wash the blood from his mouth.

"You're bleeding."

"Thanks, I kinda figured that out." Derrick practically leaped toward the bedroom door, the heat of a blazing Southern fire at his back.

"Delilah! Get up!" Her eyes startled awake and she clung to Inácio's side. Even while dying, Derrick saw the man's presence as a threat to his daughter. She was in love with an assassin.

"What are you doing? I can't leave yet! Let me be with him just a little longer!"

"Nope! We're not staying here a minute more." Derrick grabbed her arm. Delilah reached for the pillows, the nightstand, the headboard, but Derrick was in survival mode. He made a death grip around her wrist, ignoring her cry when it hurt.

Greg appeared in the doorway.

Derrick yanked her away from the bed but Delilah twisted her arm, forcing him to let go. She fell back on the bed, her hand slipping through his. Left behind in his palm was a silver ring with an impressive jewel. Derrick studied it.

"That's mine!" Delilah snatched it back like he was trying to steal it.

"You need to listen to me, goddammit!" His desperation was at a raging boil.

"Just let me say goodbye!" Delilah begged, gasping for air. "I'm not ready. It's too soon." She covered her chest.

"Uh, Derrick, why don't you let her say goodbye?" Greg suggested.

Derrick shook his head.

"I think that's a good idea, Johnson. Let her be," Joe said from behind Greg. His green eye peeked around the other side of Greg's shoulder.

Derrick backed away until his back hit the wall.

"Make it quick, Del," he snapped, refusing to take his eyes off Joe. He listened to her goodbye, his focus all on Joe.

"Inácio. If you can hear me, know that I love you so damn much. I wish we left when we had the chance. You gave me my life back. I'll never forget you. Thank you." Derrick heard a kiss. Seconds passed like hours, and after the period of silence, he looked at his daughter. She stared at the rise and fall of Inácio's chest, as if waiting for his last breath.

"That's enough," Derrick said with a sense of composure. He reached over, slowly pulling her away. Relief that she didn't fight him washed over him. A purple suitcase rested upright against the dresser. "It's a wild guess, but I think this is ours." He pulled it along with Delilah. Willingly, she followed his lead, looking back to the bed the whole way out.

"Who pissed in your Cheerios?" Greg asked as he shoved by. Joe prowled alongside.

"For once!" Derrick said.

"I'll get the garage door for you fellas," Joe said in a cordial manner. Derrick stormed on. Delilah hung her head to the side, her steps as coordinated as those of a zombie. The garage door rose, his escape to freedom and life.

"So, no lunch then, huh?"

"So help me, Greg!" The further down the drive Derrick got, the more he could breathe. Derrick turned his head to make sure they weren't being followed.

"What now? Do we call an Uber?" Greg held his sore shoulder. Joe stood as frozen as a statue in the opening of the garage. His stare was icy with the promise that if they told anyone anything, everyone was dead.

73

DELILAH

Delilah parked her suitcase by the door and stared at her dorm room. All of it, from the terror to the love, was over. Pens and textbooks were laid out exactly how she'd left them. It was like traveling back to the past. Her bed was unmade, the comforter hanging over the side. Delilah saw herself frazzled and in a rush to get out the door and head to the airport. The pajamas she'd stripped off were still wrinkled in a pile on the floor. She'd been so nervous to fly international. That girl had zero clue about the pain, the joy, and the anguish she was about to go through. If she wanted to, she could jump back into her old life, forgetting any of it ever happened. The only problem was, Inácio was not someone she could ever forget.

His face was stuck permanently in her mind. The way he'd touched her, kissed her, loved her, and the torture he'd put up with for her. She clung to an image of him smiling, but it always circled back to his excruciating end. Delilah couldn't stop thinking of him lingering, wondering if he was going to pass away in sixty seconds or thirty. Her new ring caught the light from her window and sent bright orbs spreading like stars over the ceiling. Never could she exactly know what the ring was meant for.

Looking around room 32B made her that much sicker to her stomach. The stupid books, the stupid mini fridge, the stupid… everything. Facing the monotony of going to class and surviving senior finals felt impossible. How could she be surrounded by students who knew nothing of the real world? She'd aged ten years in a week. Things that were once a big deal were completely unimportant. The academic struggles, Carson, maintaining her purple hair, all of it meant nothing to her.

With two fingers she slid her pen holder to the edge of her desk and let it fall to the floor. The glass jar broke in two and she stared down at it with numbness. She moved on to her textbooks and watched them flop to the floor. A visceral rise in grief drove her to target anything not anchored down. Delilah flung it all across the room. Outfits were ripped from their hangers, becoming trampled under her feet. Drawers were emptied and papers floated down through the air. A jewelry box gifted by Carson that was filled with pretty accessories paid for with his family wealth got it the worst. The mahogany wood was left splintered over the thin carpet, and she destroyed the cute shiny objects inside. Delilah fell to her knees.

The girl who'd left for Brazil was dead.

Delilah couldn't see herself going back to the person she was before.

Weak and unloved… *unloved.*

Was there anyone who could love her like he had?

"Here's the rest of the food your mom sent." Delilah heard her dad shuffle to a stop, the glass containers sliding over her now-empty desk. His sigh was loud and tense. Her dad took two steps and then he was at her side. Delilah felt him hovering. "What the heck happened in here? Why are you on the floor?"

Does he really need to ask?

"I know we haven't talked about what happened since we left. Can't believe it's only been a few days. Feels like an eternity ago and sometimes like just yesterday."

Weeping brewed in her chest. With every second it intensified in volume. It was pain she was forced to hide from her mother. The truth stopped with her, her dad, and his partner. Her dad sat down with her, and Delilah couldn't hold back the embrace. She needed to be held, to experience comfort by someone who'd witnessed the same horrors she had.

"I don't want to be here or at home," Delilah admitted. "I hate it. I hate all of it."

"I know. I wouldn't either, but you have to. At least you'll be away from your mom awhile. Pretending everything is fine with her is taking its toll on me too."

"It sucks she can never know. I just wish he—"

"Yeah, it does suck," he said. "Just remember, it's for her own good and ours."

"Ours? What do you mean?" She leaned her head away from his shoulder, her tears pausing for her to think.

"N-n-no, that's not what I meant. I mean it's easier on us to keep your mother out of this. She'd lose it if she knew what you got caught up in." He pulled Delilah back into him.

"I want to tell her everything."

"Me too, but it's the way it is. It'll be our secret we take to our graves. You, me, and Greg." Dad stroked her hair, a kind of affection that had been absent for much of her life.

"You know, Dad, you can't hide your broken nose from a building full of cops."

"Tell that to Greg, he's the one who got shot."

"He can hide his, unlike you."

"Eh, well I'll just tell 'em I opened a taxi door on my face again. It's happened before, so now I'm just getting better at it." He grinned as if the magnitude of the lie was no biggie.

Delilah made a crooked purse of her lips.

"Nah, we're sticking to our mugging story. My coworkers don't need to know anything either, as much as I'd like to tell them. A lot of evil, a lot of injustice took place. I wish I could fix it."

"At least you didn't lose anyone."

"I almost lost you. That was too close."

"I can't get Inácio out of my head." She sniffled. *Or out of my body.* The history left behind by his rigorous passion lived on in nipping throbs.

"It's going to take time."

"I feel so empty. The world around me feels even worse without him." Her dad fidgeted. Delilah knew him well enough to know it was an uncomfortable shiver.

"I didn't really know the guy. Uh, I guess he gave his life for you though." He paused before clearing his throat. "His sacrifice wasn't so you could keep living in depression. You've been through more than I have in my entire life. I wish none of it ever happened, but it's the past now. *He* is the past. You have to find a way to rise above it."

"I can't move on like that. I'm officially trapped in the past."

"I'm not telling you to forget him. I'm telling you to honor what he did for you, that's all. Think of it that way. From what I saw, he wanted you to be home. You're meant to be here because that's where he wanted you. Just a little longer and you can get out of this noisy dorm for good."

"Honor his memory, you're saying."

"Yes, or what was the point of it all?"

"I'll try. Thank you, Dad." Delilah squeezed him in the most sincere hug they'd shared in years.

74

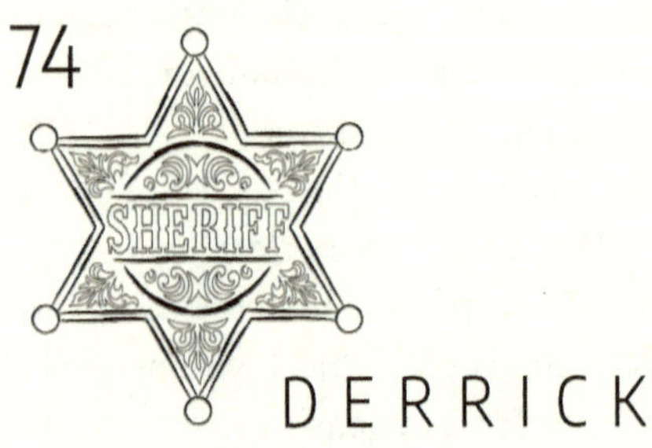

DERRICK

Three Months Later

"Hello?" Derrick dipped away from his stadium seat, catching Maggie giving him a cold stare before he pinched one ear closed to hear the caller better.

"I took a look. There's a lot of background noise. Should I call later?"

"No, no. I'm actually at my daughter's graduation right now." Derrick disappeared around the corner into the empty hallway. "Is that better?"

"Your daughter's graduation? This can wait."

"They're not to her yet. I have some time, I think."

"Where did you say you got these documents again?"

"I can't say, at least right now." Derrick returned to the moment Joe had seen one folder fall from under his clothes, but not the other. "What do you think?"

"If this is legit, it's far beyond you and me. I may hail from the city, but I'm just a detective, like you. This contains information on a real person who was killed. The dates, location data, everything lines up with what actually happened. I think you should hand this over to the FBI or something."

"No! I sent this to you so I could avoid that."

"I don't understand. Why wouldn't you want to report this? It's a big deal, Derrick. I'm also not sure why you're refusing to be honest with me on where and how you've obtained it. Did this put you in danger?"

"Yes. It's a matter of personal safety. Neither of us can speak a word of this to anyone, at least for now. I want to investigate it on my own before all that."

"Assuming this is authentic, which it looks to be, it implies that there's some global assassination network out there. Does this put me in danger as well?"

"Shit! They're in the J's already. I gotta go."

"That's it? That's all you wanted from me?"

"I'll call you back. And no, you don't have anything to worry about." Derrick looked behind him into the hallway. There was no one there, but it felt like eyes were everywhere.

He returned to the seat beside his wife, and she stood and began to whistle. Derrick took a deep breath and wiped away the sweat from his brow. Delilah waited to the side near the stage, next in line to be called. Greg bent forward on the other side of Maggie and squinted at him. Derrick knew he was getting suspicious. He would tell him about the stolen file in time. Who he wouldn't be honest with was his daughter.

75

DELILAH

"Delilah Johnson, Bachelor of Arts in Psychology."

Her fresh glossy black heels strutted over the varnished wood. Two female classmates had already lost their footing in their smooth-soled stilettos, but she felt confident in her walk. The cheering wasn't close to dying down from the last student when her name was announced over the loudspeakers. Friends and family in the audience blended into one large choir who moved their hands like a wave at a baseball game. The microphone was turned up to max in order to be heard over the audience.

The president of the university waited with fatigued, smiling cheeks. With a handshake, the president began the transfer of her degree. The cameraman's flash captured the moment and Delilah quickly moved on. The achievement resting in her grasp brought her more joy than she'd anticipated. She pulled straightened ends from behind her ears, revealing her blushing smile. Her mom's new fancy phone was without a doubt zoomed 100x onto her face. She clutched the diploma with the gold-inscribed cover across her chest and returned to her chair.

Delilah was one of hundreds who took peeks inside at what they'd earned. On the outside, it was nothing but pretty words behind plastic. Sitting through commencement in a hard chair holding that simple sheet of paper was Inácio's sacrifice. A dark cloud of heartbreak lingered, hovering its shadow across the gym. The sting from his touch between her legs evaporated months ago. The morning she woke up without the discomfort was devastating. She had bursted from her blankets in a cold sweat from another nightmare, and the proof he was ever there disappeared.

The only thing she could do was close her eyes again and haunt herself with his memory, freezing herself in time. If she allowed the clock to tick, would her love for him cease to exist? Life on day one in Ohio didn't care. The tedious schedules of routine charged the day and months ahead without regard for grief. The call to transfer back into the ordinary screamed as loud as her classmates. Joy around her rose and filled the space to the brim. It shook the floor, rattled her chair, and convulsed across her large graduating class.

Delilah forced a smile, wanting to share in the emotion. Only an imitation of happiness followed. Inácio's wails of misery rang and pierced through the cheery whoops and the booming microphone. She eyed the dense crowd. If Delilah listened close enough, she tuned in to his pain, the clash of chain with flesh, the blood splattering to the floor. Delilah smiled harder.

Forcing, forcing, forcing.

After a while, hundreds of graduation caps spun freely into the air, prompting Delilah to toss hers. The sparkling cap art disappeared into the muddle, and she let it get lost. She squeezed through the crowd until she found her family.

"You did it! I am so proud of you, darling!" Her mom squeezed her. "Are you alright?" Her fingers reached for her wet eyes.

"Yes, of course. Just happy." *Another lie.*

"Yeah, you really did it," her dad said, waiting for his hug.

"I proved you all wrong," she replied.

"What? We were rooting for you the whole time," he refuted.

"C's get degrees!" Greg laughed.

"Thanks for coming. You didn't have to."

"Now off to graduate school," her dad joked. His scarred nose was still hard not to notice.

"Derrick, stop that. I think she's had enough academics for a while," said her mom. "Maybe she wants to stay home."

"So, let's see it," her dad demanded. She handed it to him and everyone crowded around.

"That's uh, a nice piece of paper," Greg observed.

"It's wonderful!" her mom exclaimed. She brought her hands together in admiration.

"It will be if she uses it," Delilah heard her dad say.

"Derrick, why do you have to do that?" her mom snapped quietly.

Delilah tuned out her bickering family and looked over the gymnasium. Most graduated faces were strangers, and it didn't bother her that this was the last time she would see them. One face who was familiar was standing no more than two families away. Josh towered above everyone else and his laugh projected over the clamor. Delilah smiled a little until remembering that wherever Josh was, Carson wouldn't be far away. She watched as Josh practically twirled away to talk to someone else. His back blocked who he was speaking to, but she didn't need to see their whole form to know. The corner of Carson's sparkling grin flashed from behind Josh's arm. It was the glowing pride of success and endless potential. Their breakup hadn't slowed him down a beat.

"What are you looking at?" her dad asked. He gripped her arm as if he expected her to disappear again. She hesitated to answer.

"Uh, nothing." Josh stepped to the side, revealing all of Carson.

"Oh lord. You wanna get stuck in the past, that's it, right there."

"You used to love him, don't you remember? Because I do." Delilah didn't let her dad see her eye roll.

"Well, I changed my mind in Brazil." Her father snorted. "*He* changed my mind, more like. Why are you worrying about him, Del?"

"I don't know. I mean, I'm not."

"Don't forget, everything our family went through is because of him. He's the one who kicked you out of the hotel. He did that to us."

"He's alone," she said.

"He doesn't look alone."

"That's Josh's family. I'm surprised his dad's not even here."

"Okay, let's not get too carried away with the sympathy." Her dad led her away from her fixation. "C'mon, we got steakhouse reservations and I'm starving."

"Hold on," she brushed off. In clear view of Carson, Delilah waited for him to make some sort of acknowledgement of her. Carson unzipped his robe, revealing a slim-fitting suit. He popped his head up and looked directly at her. No polite smile or friendly wave. Carson turned away like he never saw her. "He sees me. I know he does."

"Of course he does, but he's a coward, and we don't waste our time with those anymore."

"He still has nothing to say?"

His eyes continued to fan over her like she was another faceless student in the crowd.

"You're not getting back together with that prick, are you?" The question disgusted her just as much as the sight of Carson disgusted her dad.

"Seriously, Dad? I'll be right back." Before he could stop her, she marched toward the towering family and their shorter addition.

"Oh, shit," Josh blurted. Carson twisted around, eyeing her irritatingly up and down. She stomped her heels to a stop.

"Carson, I just want to say, congratulations." Delilah snatched his hand from his side and shook it. One of his eyebrows raised.

"Uh, thanks?"

"I know you're going to work so hard to make so much money. Also, thank you for giving me a vacation I'll never forget."

"Wow!" Josh piped in. "That's a really nice thing to say considering—"

"Considering you were such an asshole," Delilah finished. She raised her hand and slapped Carson across the cheek. With the fleshy sound and the sting spreading over her palm, an unexpected sense of power returned. He froze and held his reddening cheek. Only a few months ago, she'd believed he was better than her. Delilah had thought she had to earn the right to be by his side. Not anymore. No one was ever going to treat her like a doormat again.

"Dang!" Josh clenched a fist and brought it to his lips. If everyone was staring, Delilah didn't notice. "Didn't see that comin' from her! I'm impressed."

"Thanks, Josh, for the support as always," Carson groaned, stretching out his jaw.

"Have fun being rich and alone," she said. With an about-face, she turned her back on Carson for the last time. She wasn't the world's punching bag anymore; she was a survivor who was going to honor her second chance at life.

76 INÁCIO

As he lay beneath the patio table soaked in aged whiskey, he'd never felt so worthless. Inácio pushed away what was left of the shattered bottle from his chest. Someone might as well have re-snapped his fractured leg. He groaned through the deep knee-jerk reaction to scream in pain, refusing to give in to the demands of his weakness.

"Hang in there, buddy!" Schafer was by his side before Inácio could glow red with embarrassment.

"It's fine," he said, pushing away his helpful hands.

"It's not fine. You just broke a $300 bottle of bourbon." Schafer cradled his back.

"No, I need to learn how to get up on my own." Inácio dropped his weight.

"Oh no you don't. I'm helping you. You can't even get out of a chair without hurting yourself. You think you're going to get up from the ground?" Schafer forced Inácio's arm around his shoulders. "On the count of three. One, two, heave!"

Inácio grunted his way onto his "healthy" leg, the one sprained from all the extra force placed on it. His ankle stung under pressure.

"Phew, good thing I've been doing my squats. Here's your crutches."

Inácio opened his hands but didn't see them.

"Over here."

"Shit," he muttered, turning his head to see them right beside him.

"Don't worry about it. You'll get used to the eyepatch. The doctor said it takes time."

Sticking the crutches under his armpits, he both loathed the metal sticks and felt grateful for them.

"To think, you are only a couple feet away from the pool. What if you fell in?" Schafer patted his shoulder and smiled. The last three months had been filled with the handler forcing humor into his pathetic situation.

"You'd finally get to fill out that accidental death report on me you've always wanted."

"Nonsense!"

"I've put you through hell this year. I deserve it." Inácio gazed at the open bedroom overlooking the patio and ocean view. The bed with its satin curtains sat with spooky stillness. It was a ghoulish object of a past life that had been over in the blink of an eye. His single brown eye absorbed all of the room's detail. It was only one of many extensions of the safe house that haunted him.

"Watching you, of all people, struggling to get around has been enough karma for me. I'm over it just as much as you are." Schafer's phone clamored from his front jean pocket. It was ringing in a tone Inácio had never heard come from his phone since Schafer had started to raise him back to health. The handler's mismatched eyes bulged from his face.

"Ex-girlfriend?" Inácio asked in an attempt to maintain the lightheartedness.

"I only had this number call me one other time in my career." Schafer's flat voice was rippled with little hints of anxiety.

When he answered, he turned away and directed his attention back into the safe house. After a few compliant yeses, Schafer stuffed the phone back in his pocket and flipped out a tiny comb. The plastic bristles tilled his golden hair into rows of finely planted fibers. He spun around, his attention unable to lock onto a single object. Beads of sweat dappled his top lip. "Get inside and wait for me. I'll try to clean this up so no one sees."

"So who doesn't see?"

"It's *him*." Schafer placed the table back on its legs and scooped the glass into a pile with his shoes with frantic energy.

"Him?" Inácio swallowed, already knowing.

"The Philosopher. He's here."

****

Death never held reign over Inácio's heart. It was a fact of life and a close companion for an assassin until it inevitably turned its scythe on them. That time had come, but the acceptance he'd expected to feel was absent. Inácio was scared, but not for himself. He was as still as a rock as he waited in one of the living room chairs, his cast leg resting on a footstool. It faced the garage door entrance, and his eye was glued to it.

"Here, take this, quick." Schafer stood over him with a fresh button-up free of the overwhelming smell of a bar.

"Too late."

Through the door, over a dozen mercenaries spread themselves throughout the safe house, covering each level. Doors opened and slammed while they searched for potential threats. Schafer sat on the edge of his seat beside Inácio, rubbing his palms together, wincing at every crash.

"You don't deserve this," Inácio said to him.

"I wish I could have visited home one last time. Could've used the peace and quiet out on the lake."

"This is my fault. I'm sorry." Inácio cleared his throat, feeling his heart race.

"Can't rewind time. We knew I couldn't hide you away forever. The boss was always gonna find out the full story."

"It's been a good ride, friend." Inácio knew he was seeing Schafer for the last time.

Several images of the Philosopher had been created in Inácio's imagination. Was he as large and imposing as his magnitude of power? Or was he a shadow of what a man should be? Inácio was about to find out who had owned his life for the past decade. Three brick-wall bodyguards approached. Their bear paws grabbed Inácio on all sides, forcing him out of his chair. The men patted him down with a heightened aggression as if he were just a pinball. Inácio stumbled and grabbed at the pain coursing through his femur.

"Hey, fellas!" Schafer jumped to his feet. "Can't you see the guy is injured? I swear to you, he has nothin' on him!"

A voice called out from across the room. "Schafer, be silent. Your lies have cost you all credibility." There was something familiar about the sound, the crisp masculine tone that could be faintly heard beneath the scramble on a voice call with the Philosopher. Inácio was thrown back in his chair, making the healing wounds in his torso sear. When the bulky guards departed, Inácio saw his full form.

The Philosopher towered over most of his men, but he was no stick figure like the lanky Woody. There was a pudgy round gut underneath his sharp dress shirt which melted over his belt like a scoop of ice cream. A balaclava covered every facial feature with the exception of a pair of dark eyes. The evil within dimmed the entire room.

Schafer dropped himself into his chair as if to kneel before the king.

"Oh Schafer, you will not be staying here anymore." With the mere direction of the Philosopher's gaze, two mercenaries held Schafer down in his chair while another one from behind wrapped duct tape several times around his head and over around his mouth. Inácio's handler kicked, his screams unable to escape his throat. His bulging brown eye found Inácio before a dark hood swallowed Schafer's face. Plastic zip ties pinned his ankles together and he was carried out the door and into the garage, struggling the whole way.

Inácio relaxed the fists he'd had no idea he clenched. The Philosopher walked to the love seat across from him, his gaze holding

Inácio like that of a cobra. He could tell his boss was white with peppery hair, according to his eyebrows. The man rested his elbows on his knees and interlocked his fingers.

"Why, look at you," he began.

"Why am I still alive?" *Just get it over with.*

"Because I haven't decided to kill you yet. And I won't have to as long as you remain my loyal dog." He sat back, comfortable while encircled with bodyguards.

"I've already committed a capital sin. How can you expect that from me?" Inácio would rather be dead than be used any longer.

"Oh, Inácio. You aren't the first to fall in love and you won't be the last. It happens here and there, but you took it too far and used my resources for your personal benefit. Your actions could topple everything I have created."

"You look like you're doing just fine."

"And so is your girlfriend, for now."

Inácio shuddered.

"Días has something to show you." Out from around a pillar separating the living room and bar was the hairy Colombian, and behind him, Talia. Red stilettos graced her catwalk in her approach. A tight black skirt and low-cut top hugged her taunting curves. Thick hair hung down the length of her back, but what Inácio noticed most were her white fangs glistening behind cherry lipstick. She'd dressed up for the occasion.

Días displayed video on a tablet. Talia disappeared in Inácio's periphery as he saw the camera zoom in. On a stage surrounded by an enormous crowd, Delilah's big smile dimpled her cheeks. A golden tassel jiggled over the edge of a graduation cap, her hand clutching a leatherbound bachelor's degree. Blackness framed his vision and created a tunnel to her face. As she walked away, the camera zoomed out and captured the backs of family members in a standing ovation in the row just ahead of the camera. The lens focused on the side profile of Derrick, who rushed to take his seat in front of the cameraman.

Días shut the video off.

Inácio had no words, only a helpless sense of dread.

"Días will be your new direct supervisor. As long as you obey, she will live. Your skills are far too valuable to me. I need you functioning, so fortunately for you, Talia volunteered to be your caretaker." The Philosopher rose. "Let's go."

"Don't do this to me," Inácio begged with a shaking voice. *Just kill me.*

"God bless you, son," the Philosopher said, so gentle and yet so cold. Every man in the room departed, leaving Talia behind. Inácio could barely look at her. Everything within him wanted to kill her, but he was a slave to his broken body. Talia stared at him with hunger and thirst.

"Planning to finish the job your cartel thugs couldn't?"

Talia stood from her chair. "You're right, I wanted them to kill you. But some failures are a blessing in disguise."

"Get away from me," he snarled.

"Don't look so worried, love. I will take excellent care of you." She clicked her heels over to the crutches resting at his feet.

Inácio grabbed for them.

"No, no. You need to learn how to walk on your own." They were stolen from reach. "You are *mine*."

Talia carried the crutches like a trophy through the patio door and threw them into the pool.

www.ingramcontent.com/pod-product-compliance
Lightning Source LLC
LaVergne TN
LVHW090547110826
845146LV00001B/50

* 9 7 9 8 2 3 4 0 8 5 3 1 3 *